Linkershim
Sovereign of the Seven Isles: Book Six

by

David A. Wells

LINKERSHIM

Copyright © 2013 by David A. Wells

Edited by Carol L. Wells

This is a work of fiction. Characters, events and organizations in this novel are creations of the author's imagination.

www.SovereignOfTheSevenIsles.com

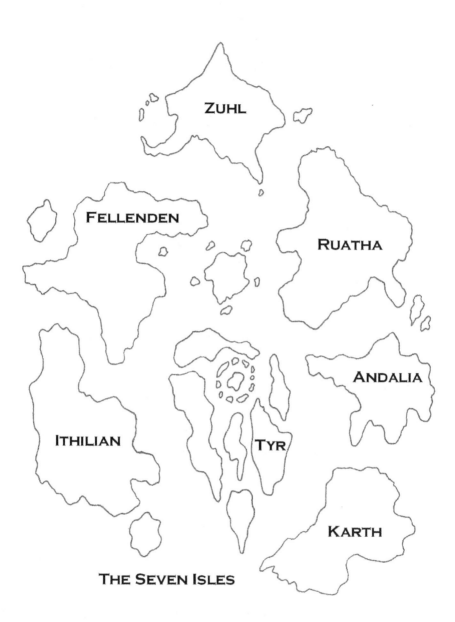

ZUHL

FELLENDEN

RUATHA

ANDALIA

ITHILIAN

TYR

KARTH

THE SEVEN ISLES

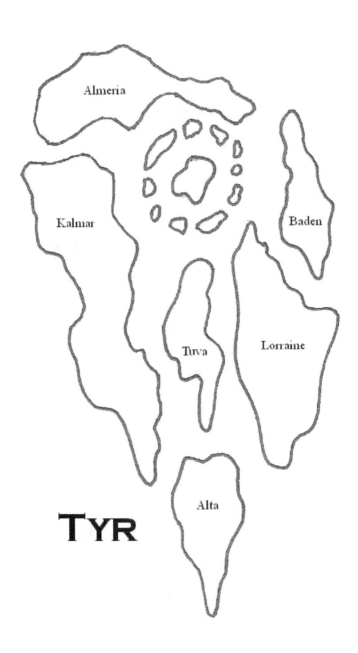

TYR

Linkershim

Chapter 1

"That was close," Jack said.

"A little too close," Alexander replied.

The ballista bolt had fallen several yards short, leaving nothing but a patch of white frothy bubbles where it had plunged into the ocean.

Captain Kalderson's hoarse voice carried his orders over the wind, pushing his crew to coax more speed out of the sails and oarsmen. And it was working ... the gap was widening.

Hours after Kalderson's ship had passed out of the protected waters within the ring of sharp stone peaks surrounding the dragons' home, the watchman in the crow's nest had called out in warning, pointing to the horizon. Alexander's all around sight didn't reach far enough for him to see the threat, but judging from the flare of fear and anxiety in Jack's and Kalderson's colors just moments after the alarm, he knew it was bad.

In the first few minutes after the small armada had been spotted, Alexander chided himself for failing to anticipate Phane's next move. He knew full well that the Reishi Arch Mage could see nearly as well as he could. It was naive to expect that Phane wouldn't be waiting for him. A few minutes of clairvoyant reconnaissance would have provided all the warning Alexander needed. And yet, it hadn't occurred to him. Too many weeks of lying in bed, he rationalized.

Over the course of the afternoon and early evening, the ships trailing behind them became strung out as each captain pushed his crew to the limit.

Shortly after the enemy had been spotted, Alexander went to his stateroom and spent a few minutes gathering information about his pursuers. Through his clairvoyance, he discovered that they flew the flag of Tyr, and the lead ship was commanded by the heir of the House of Tyr, the man Alexander had taken the Thinblade from. He suspected the man wanted it back.

Now, standing at the railing with Jack, blind to the enemy in the distance, Alexander could do nothing but wait while Kalderson's crew struggled to stay ahead of them.

He felt the sensation of imminent danger flood his mind just moments before another ballista bolt hit home, high on the hull of the ship. It wasn't a particularly damaging shot but it was proof positive that at least one of the enemy ships had closed to weapons' range.

Captain Kalderson came running up next to them, leaning over the gunnel to inspect the damage.

"It looks like that bolt has four tines," Jack said.

"It's a shredder. Pirates use them to tear up a ship's sails." Kalderson looked out at the enemy ship and shook his head. "Makes no sense. They shouldn't be gaining on us like that."

"They have a wizard on board," Alexander said.

Kalderson looked at him and swallowed. "Lord Reishi, I don't know how long we can keep this up. My rowers are getting tired."

"I know," Alexander said. "It's after dusk … maybe we can lose them in the dark."

Before Kalderson could respond, the watchman in the crow's nest cried out, pointing dead ahead.

"Dear Maker," Kalderson whispered.

"What do you see?" Alexander asked, frustration welling up in his belly at his blindness.

"A blockade," Kalderson said. "Looks like twenty ships or more stretched out between Baden and Almeria … they're still a long way off, just a string of lights on the horizon."

"Douse all your lanterns, wait for dark, and then turn due south," Alexander said.

"The wind isn't with us," Kalderson said. "We'll have to rely on the oars."

"As long as they can't see us, it won't matter," Alexander said.

"The strait between Baden and Lorraine is dangerous, shallow in places," Kalderson said. "Trying to navigate it in the dark is risky."

"Not as risky as trying to run a blockade," Alexander said.

Night fell, moonless and clear, countless stars casting a soft, eerie glow on the calm water. The ship turned in the dark and set a course along the western coast of Baden. The crew held their breath as the enemy ships slid past them in the night.

Alexander went to his stateroom and opened the door to his Wizard's Den. He sat cross-legged inside his magic circle and within seconds, he was floating against the ceiling in the captain's mess of the enemy ship.

Several men were seated around the worn and stained table bolted to the floor in the middle of the room. Tyr sat at the head of the table, lamplight shining off his bald head as he absentmindedly twisted his jet-black goatee. A wizard sat to his right and the ship's captain and first mate sat to his left. At the opposite end of the table, facing the captain across the length of it, sat a wraithkin.

"We know he can cast illusions," Tyr said, "so it stands to reason he's still nearby."

"Perhaps," the wizard said, "though he may have simply eluded us in the dark."

"So how do we find him?" Tyr asked.

"Patience," the wizard said. "All avenues of escape are being watched. You've worked tirelessly all winter to prepare for this day. It's only a matter of time before his ship is disabled and then we'll have him."

The wraithkin started laughing softly, drawing disconcerted and nervous looks from the other men at the table.

"What's so funny?" the first mate asked.

"You underestimate your quarry," the wraithkin said, vanishing a moment later, leaving faint wisps of black smoke in his wake.

"I don't like him," the first mate said.

"Neither do I, but he may be useful," Tyr said.

"And he may be right," the wizard said. "Phane has spent the past year trying to kill the pretender and yet he still lives. I would advise caution."

Tyr snorted, shaking his head. "I have almost fifty ships under my command. I've sold or bartered everything in my hold to make ready for this day. I will have my sword back if it costs me the lives of every single sailor in this fleet."

"I'm simply suggesting that you spend the lives of those aboard other ships rather than risk those of us aboard this ship," the wizard said.

"That goes without saying," Tyr said.

Alexander drifted up through the decks into the sky; then with a thought, he was floating over the blockade stretching between Almeria and Baden. More than twenty ships spanned the gap between the two sub-islands of Tyr. He moved south, the island of Baden passing by in a blur, and found another blockade stretching across the gap between Baden and Lorraine. A few more minutes of exploration told him that all of the channels leading from the interior of the Isles of Tyr to the open ocean were blocked by ships either flying the flag of Tyr or allied with him.

The only way out was through the enemy. He opened his eyes and sighed, shaking his head as he stepped out of his Wizard's Den.

"Anything you want to talk about?" Jack asked from his bunk.

"Looks like we're going to have to fight our way through."

"I was afraid of that."

***

Dawn brought clear skies and a shift in the wind, but most importantly, a clear horizon.

"Looks like your gambit worked, Lord Reishi," Kalderson said, smiling broadly.

"For now, Captain," Alexander said. "But I'm afraid we're headed for another blockade. Fortunately, the dozen or so ships in our way aren't carrying any wizards."

"What are we going to do?" Kalderson asked.

"Run the blockade," Alexander said with a shrug.

"You do remember what happened the last time we ran a blockade, yes?"

Alexander nodded. "Show me your maps, Captain."

A few minutes later in the captain's stateroom, Alexander tapped a spot in the channel between Baden and Lorraine.

"Here. I counted twelve ships, four flying the flag of Baden, seven flying the flag of Lorraine and one flying the flag of Tyr. I suspect that one's the command ship, since this whole thing has been orchestrated by Tyr.

"So how do we get through?"

"We'll slip through at night," Alexander said. "How long until we get close enough for them to see us?"

"Two days, depending on the winds."

"Time it so we arrive in the dark," Alexander said. "That should give your men time to rest. We'll need all their strength when we make our move."

"Understood, Lord Reishi."

***

They reached the blockade two days later, arriving well after dark. Throughout the night, Alexander scouted the waters ahead, plotting a course through the dangerous channel and guiding the captain through the enemy ships, slipping in and out of the firmament as needed to ensure safe and silent passage.

His strategy worked perfectly. They slipped through the enemy lines without even being noticed. Alexander breathed a sigh of relief once they were well into the open ocean and sailing north toward Ruatha.

He woke with a start the following morning. Sunlight streamed through the porthole, cutting the dusty air with a shaft of pure white light. He lay still, listening. Another shout of alarm filtered through the deck boards to his stateroom. He sat up and pulled on his boots.

The day was clear but far from calm. A northeasterly wind was driving them across rough waters and the ship was rocking to and fro as it struggled to cut through the waves. Alexander found Kalderson and Jack on the foredeck.

"I don't know how they found us, Lord Reishi," Kalderson said, fighting to keep the wheel steady.

"How many?" Alexander asked.

"Twenty or thirty in a blockade ahead and a dozen behind," Jack said.

"Well, I guess we don't have much choice then," Alexander said. "I'm going to look for a soft spot in their line."

"You mean to run the blockade?" Kalderson asked.

Alexander shrugged. "We're cornered. The only option left is attack."

Several minutes later he saw just how bad it was. They were surrounded and the enemy was closing in. Running their line would just delay the inevitable. Eventually, Kalderson's men would become exhausted and the enemy would board the ship.

After looking at the enemy, Alexander appeared in General Talia's study. The fastidious general officer was reading a history of some battle fought long ago. He looked up, then stood with a smile. "Lord Reishi, I trust you're well," he said.

"I'm afraid not," Alexander said. "I need your help. We're sailing up the east coast of Baden trying to get to Ruatha, but there's a fleet of warships in our way."

"I see," Talia said. "I have eight Sky Knights at my disposal and I can spare a dozen fast-attack boats without diminishing the security of Ruatha's southern coast. Will that be sufficient?"

"It'll have to be," Alexander said. "We can't afford to let Andalia put any more Lancers on Ruathan soil."

"Understood, Lord Reishi. Help is on the way."

"Thank you, General," Alexander said before vanishing.

***

"How can that ship be moving against the wind?" Kalderson asked, shaking his head.

"That's Tyr's flagship," Alexander said. "The wizard on board is pushing them with his magic. Turn toward it and ready the fore ballista."

"I can't," Kalderson said. "The wind isn't with us and the oars won't give us enough speed to stay ahead of the dozen ships behind us."

"Then turn both ballistae toward them and prepare to fire," Alexander said.

"That won't solve the bigger problem," Kalderson said. "They're driving us into the Andalian coast. With this wind, we'll never make it around the horn without slowing down so much that the entire enemy fleet will catch up with us."

"One problem at a time, Captain," Alexander said. "Kill that ship first, then we'll worry about the rest of them. Maybe if they see their flagship sink, they'll lose interest. After all, most of the ships out there are bought and paid for by Tyr."

A warning went up from the crow's nest, drawing all eyes toward the shredder bolt descending on them. It ripped through the mainsail, tearing a gaping hole and slowing the ship significantly.

"Return fire," Alexander ordered.

Both ballistae fired in unison, sending clay firepots toward the enemy vessel. One went wide, but the second shattered against the mainmast, showering the aft deck with fire and igniting the rear sail.

Another shredder lifted off the deck of the enemy ship, arcing through the clear sky. It tore the mainsail nearly in half, slowing Kalderson's ship even further.

Even with the damaged sail, they were able to gain some distance on the single enemy ship within weapons' range, but the dozen ships behind them were closing fast. They would be in weapons' range within minutes.

Kalderson's crew started cutting the mainsail down, preparing to raise the spare, but the damage was done. They were slowing, the gap was closing, and the only possibility of escape was the looming coastline of Andalia—a prospect that Alexander didn't relish.

"Lend me your eyes, Little One."

Chloe buzzed into existence in a ball of light and Alexander sent her his mind, looking at the danger surrounding him through her eyes. The ships behind, driven by the strong wind, were fanning out so each could bring their weapons to bear. The blockade to the north remained in place with the exception of the burning flagship and two ships that were moving to assist. The rocky coast of Andalia filled the eastern horizon.

A whistler arrow shrieked in the distance and a dozen shredders lifted from the fleet behind them, arcing gracefully and silently through the air, crashing into the deck with ruinous effect, tearing holes in the fore and aft sails and killing a number of crewmen where they stood.

"Captain, head for the coast and prepare to abandon ship," Alexander said.

Kalderson looked like he wanted to protest, but couldn't find an argument worthy of putting into words. With grim resignation, he nodded to his first mate manning the wheel and the ship turned east toward the shore while the crew began to make the longboats ready.

"What's happening?"

Alexander's heart skipped a beat. He whirled to find Anja standing next to a hatch on the ship's deck.

"What are you doing here?" he demanded, dumbfounded and chagrined at the same time. She'd made it clear that she wanted to come with him but he hadn't expected her to stow away. Another mistake based on a false assumption.

"I wanted to be with you," Anja said.

"You can't be here," Alexander said to the child-dragon, taking her by the shoulders. "You're not safe here, Anja. You need to change into your true form and fly home right now."

"No," she said, facing him squarely, her chin held high. "I'm staying with you."

Before he could say another word, the sensation of danger flooded his mind. Instinctively, he stretched out with his all around sight and saw the threat descending toward him—another volley of shredders. He grabbed Anja and spun her out of the way as a multi-tined ballista bolt slammed into the deck where they'd just been standing. He pulled her behind the wheelhouse and pressed her against the wall.

"It's not safe here. You have to go home. Please, Anja, do as I ask."

"No, I belong with you."

"Don't be so stubborn, child. We're under attack and we're about to abandon ship in hostile territory. I don't know if I can protect you, and trying to could easily put everything else in jeopardy."

"You don't have to protect me. I can protect myself."

"Please go home," Alexander whispered. "You don't know what you're getting into."

She shook her head slowly, defiantly. "I'm not leaving you."

He closed his eyes and turned away from her, striding purposefully toward his stateroom.

"Where are you going?" Anja asked, trailing behind him.

"Keep an eye on her, Jack," Alexander said, ignoring Anja's question.

She caught up to him and grabbed his arm, turning him toward her.

"Wait, where are you going? What are you going to do?"

"I'm going to talk with your mother. I'm going to ask her to come get you and take you home whether you like it or not."

He twisted his arm free of her grip and left her standing there pouting.

***

"Hello Bragador," Alexander said, a moment after appearing before her. She had been sleeping in her magnificent true form atop a pile of gold and silver coins.

"I had hoped it would be some time before we spoke again."

"Anja has stowed away on my ship," Alexander said. "I just discovered her a few minutes ago. I told her to go home, but she refused."

"I see," Bragador whispered.

"We're under attack. I've ordered the captain to make for the coast of Andalia. We have to abandon ship. If I could turn the ship around and bring her home to you, I would."

"I know that you would, Alexander. I do not doubt your feelings for my daughter."

"Please, come get her," Alexander said. "I can't keep her safe."

"She hasn't listened to my counsel on this matter before. What makes you think she will now?"

"Bragador, I don't care if she listens, just come and get her."

Bragador cocked her head and looked at Alexander quizzically. "Would not such a thing violate the very Old Law that you have argued so forcefully for?"

"Anja is a child. She isn't old enough to know what's good for her yet."

"And yet, she is a sovereign being with free will granted to her by the Maker. Who am I to force her to act according to my will?"

"You're her mother! A child needs limitations and guidance or they could get hurt."

"Perhaps, but I fear nothing short of imprisoning her would keep her here … and I can assure you that imprisoning a dragon is no easy task."

"So what are you saying?"

"I'm saying that my daughter has made her decision and I must honor it because I have no better choice. She will not hear reason and I will not use force against her, even to protect her."

"I don't know if I can keep her safe."

"Nor do I. She was almost murdered before she was even born, and all while under my care and protection. She lives because you risked your life to save her. If I must entrust my child to a human, I could do far worse than you. Please tell her that I love her and that I will miss her every day that she is absent from my home."

Alexander closed his eyes and nodded in resignation.

Bragador settled in to her mound of treasure and closed her eyes, a single tear slipping down the side of her face as Alexander vanished.

***

He stumbled and fell as he came back on deck, the ship lurching violently, a sickening grinding noise reverberating through the hull moments before the keel buckled against a reef several thousand feet from shore.

Anja picked him up and stood him on his feet. "What did she say?"

Alexander regarded her sternly but found his anger evaporating in the face of her childlike naiveté.

"She said she loves you and she misses you," Alexander said, turning away from her, looking for Captain Kalderson.

Alexander found him organizing the loading of the longboats. Alexander grabbed hold of some rigging to steady himself when the ship shifted, listing to one side, water flowing freely into the hold.

Kalderson pointed toward the aft deck and the captain's launch. Alexander nodded, motioning for Jack and Anja to follow him. Several men were already there, waiting for the captain before casting off.

"Shove off," Alexander commanded.

"What about the captain?" one of the sailors asked.

"We'll pick him up at the front of the ship."

Another shredder slammed into the aft deck just above the launch. All hesitation on the part of the crew vanished. Within a few minutes, the sailors had maneuvered the boat around to the front of the ship, using the hull as cover from the increasing barrage of enemy fire.

Kalderson was the last man off his ship, sliding down a rope to one of the longboats and waving for Alexander to make for shore. The rowers rhythmically pulled the launch toward the inhospitable coastline, periodically aided by the waves washing toward the rocky beach. Unwilling to risk their ships, the pirates dropped anchor far enough from shore to avoid the hidden danger of the reef and started putting longboats into the water.

Their caution provided Alexander and his friends a brief reprieve as they quickly moved out of ballista range. Alexander felt an odd sense of calm settle over him, but he knew that it would be shattered all too soon.

"Why did they attack us?" Anja asked.

"Because I'm at war with them," Alexander said. "On board one of those ships are the men who stole you from your mother before you were even born. They used your life as leverage against your mother. And they did all of that to get to me. These people are serious, Anja. They'll hurt you if they can."

The rowers tried to focus on the task at hand, but Alexander could see a mixture of curiosity and intrigue mingle with the fear already staining their colors.

Anja looked out at the enemy ships with a fierceness and intensity that even Alexander found a bit unsettling.

"Not if I kill them first," she said. "If only I could change form without the Temple of Fire, I'd go kill them all right now."

"Anja, you can change into your true form right now and you know it," Alexander said.

"But then I wouldn't be able to change back into a girl. If I take my true form, I'll have to go home."

"Exactly," Alexander said.

She frowned deeply, her brow furrowing under her coppery-red hair, but she said nothing.

"I count seventeen longboats headed our way," Jack said. "Do we run or fight?"

"We run," Alexander said.

"But they tried to kill me," Anja said.

"I don't kill for vengeance, Anja, as much as I might want to. I kill to defend the Old Law. Even if we could kill every one of them without losing a single man, and we can't, it would do nothing to win this war."

"I wouldn't mind seeing Tyr bleed," Jack said.

"I've thought about that too," Alexander said. "But I don't want to kill him until I'm sure he's not the last of his line."

"Why not?" Anja said.

"I don't want to extinguish the Tyr bloodline," Alexander said, patting the hilt of the Thinblade. "This sword is one of only three remaining in the world. In the right hands, it could reunite the Isle of Tyr under the Old Law."

Jack chuckled, taking out his little pad and scribbling notes, nodding to himself.

"You would give away your magic sword?" Anja asked.

"To the right person, yes," Alexander said.

"Why?" Anja asked.

"If I could give the people of Tyr protection under the Old Law for the price of a sword, I'd count that as a bargain."

"But your sword makes you powerful."

"Yes, and I can't think of a better way to use that power."

The beach came into range of Alexander's all around sight. He scanned for danger but found only craggy cliffs populated by gnarled and windblown trees clinging for dear life to the rocky bluffs.

"There," Alexander said to the sailor manning the rudder, "head for that draw. It looks like our best chance to get off the beach."

Several minutes later, they ran aground, the rowers jumping into the water and pulling the boat out of the frothy surf. Many of the other longboats had already reached the shore. Kalderson's crewmen were converging on Alexander's position.

"How long before the pirates reach land?" Alexander asked.

"Ten, maybe fifteen minutes," Jack said, shielding his eyes as he looked out over the water.

Kalderson came bustling up, breathing heavily. "I have seventeen men left from a crew of twenty-nine. Most are sailors but a few can fight if need be."

"I'm hoping to avoid that," Alexander said, trying not to think about the lives that had been lost protecting him.

Chapter 2

Alexander ducked behind a large rock to avoid an arrow just as the last of Kalderson's crew scrambled up the little seasonal waterfall and moved away from the top of the bluff. A dozen or more pirates had reached the base of the draw and the few armed with bows were wasting arrows trying for a lucky shot.

Alexander crouched behind the boulder, watching the pirates with his all around sight. When they began to move up the draw, he smiled to himself, remembering one of his father's lessons: Position matters—where you're standing in a fight can make all the difference.

"Shouldn't we be going?" Kalderson asked.

"Soon," Alexander said. "I need your five strongest men. Send the rest to wait just inside the tree line."

Alexander closed his eyes, watching the enemy advance with his all around sight. When the last of the pirates was well into the narrow confines of the draw, he said, "It's time."

The five big sailors put their shoulders against a boulder perched on top of the bluff and pushed, straining with all their might against the prodigious weight of the stone. Slowly at first, it began to come free of the earth gripping its base, then all in a rush, it gave way and toppled over into the draw, crushing the pirates on its chaotic journey to the beach below.

"That was effective," Jack said, craning his neck to see if any of the pirates had survived.

"It bought us some time," Alexander said.

They quickly moved away from the top of the bluff. The scraggly and windblown trees gave way to a lush evergreen forest that blanketed the foothills of the small mountain range running along the coastline. The forest floor was mossy and cluttered with countless ferns fighting for the little bit of light that filtered through the ancient trees.

The well-shaded forest floor was wet with morning dew. Within minutes, everyone was damp and cold, pressing forward out of necessity and a desire to stay warm. They moved inland along the narrow stream that had cut the draw they were leaving behind.

While they walked, Alexander weighed his limited options and found them to be a list of bad choices and worse choices. He was trapped in enemy territory, being pursued by a superior force and he could see only two ways out: steal a ship or make for the Gate. Neither option seemed like it had a very good chance of success. He decided to wait until he could gather more information before he chose a course of action. Perhaps Talia's people would arrive in time to offer assistance.

"Why are we running away?" Anja asked.

"What choice do we have?"

"We should fight!"

"To what end?" Alexander asked. If Anja was going to stay with him, he decided to educate her as best he could. She was childish and headstrong, but smart and passionate. Mostly, she was possessed of an innocence that he dearly wished he didn't have to take from her.

"If we kill them, then they can't chase us anymore," she said.

"Others would come. If you're going to stay with me then you have to understand this one truth: As long as I'm the Sovereign of the Seven Isles, there will always be people who want to kill me. And, as long as you're at my side, those people will try to kill you too."

"But I never did anything to them," Anja said.

"Doesn't matter. They'll try to kill you for the same reason they tried to kill you before you were even born … to get to me. That's why I keep telling you to go home. You're not safe with me."

She frowned, looking down as she walked, falling silent for several minutes before responding.

"I would rather be happy and in danger than miserable and safe. I'm staying with you."

"I know," Alexander whispered.

Sometime after midday, Alexander noticed several men watching them through the trees. At first, he was alarmed, but a closer look revealed that they weren't pirates or soldiers but hunters, and from their colors, they were just as concerned about Alexander's presence as he was about theirs.

"We're being watched," he whispered to Jack.

"Pirates?"

"No. I don't think they're a threat, but I could very easily be wrong. They're shadowing us a couple hundred feet off to the right. Just keep your eyes open and be ready."

"So just your average afternoon then?"

"Something like that," Alexander said with a chuckle. "We should probably stop for a few minutes so I can take a look around."

The sailors were happy for the break, most being used to hard work but not accustomed to walking for any length of time. All were struck silent when Alexander opened the door to his Wizard's Den. He positioned it carefully behind a large tree to ensure that the four men following them wouldn't see it. Jack handed out some food to the sailors while Alexander sat down in his magic circle and cleared his mind.

He floated through the trees to the place where the men were hiding and he listened to their conversation.

"Who do you think they are?" one said.

Two shook their heads.

The fourth said, "They don't look like Andalians."

"They could be mercenaries."

"They're not armed well enough, and mercenaries would have come from the other direction."

"So what do we do?"

"We watch and wait. Their actions will reveal the truth of them."

Alexander was considering introducing himself when a shout of alarm shattered the tranquility of the forest. With a thought, he was back in his body. He stepped from his Wizard's Den, Thinblade in hand, and found two sailors dead, arrows buried in their chests. Another sailor cried out when an arrow drove through his leg.

The enemy had caught up with them. Several pirates were hiding behind a fallen log some sixty feet away while two of their number attacked with bows and arrows. Alexander was grateful that only two of them were armed with bows; had they all been, the first volley would have killed most of his men.

Alexander charged, racing as quickly as the stiffness in his leg would carry him. One of the archers smiled, releasing an arrow. Alexander took it in the chest, the shaft shattering when it hit his dragon-scale armor. The pirate stopped smiling. His companions raised their weapons to meet Alexander's attack just before he reached the log, leaping atop it, then crashing into their midst, felling the first with a stroke through the skull before he even hit the ground. Alexander's momentum carried him into another man, stumbling when his injured leg failed under the demands he was placing upon it, but not before he swept the Thinblade through another enemy's legs at the thigh.

He fell sprawling face first onto the mossy forest floor, rolling to his back quickly and sitting up, taking another man at the knees with a wild defensive stroke. The man's scream was suddenly drowned out by a guttural, animalistic roar that stunned everyone as Anja leapt over the log, landing on a pirate and crashing to the ground on top of him. The remaining men watched in shock and bewilderment as a girl of a mere hundred pounds repeatedly bashed the man's head into the ground until blood and brains flowed freely.

Alexander used the distraction to regain his feet. In the same moment, the spell of confusion created by the brutality and ferocity of Anja's attack was broken. The nearest pirate raised a broadsword in preparation to cleave her in half, but before he could bring the blade down, he stiffened in surprise and fell to his knees, Jack flickering into view behind him for just an instant.

Three of the pirates faced Alexander, two moving to each side while the man in the middle tried to draw his attention with a feint. Alexander closed his eyes, stretching out with his all around sight, smiling mirthlessly at the looks of triumph ghosting across his attackers' faces just before they rushed him from three sides.

He launched forward with his good leg, cutting the middle man's spear off at the haft, taking several fingers in the bargain, and barreling into him with his shoulder while the two men attempting to flank him attacked the empty air where he'd been standing. Before they could regain their balance, Alexander spun, reaching out with the Thinblade and catching each across the shoulder just deep enough to cut the bones, leaving their arms attached by only muscle and sinew. Facing each other, they screamed in terror and pain before turning in unison and fleeing into the forest.

Anja swept up the broadsword, three inches wide where it met the two-handed hilt, the stout blade nearly four feet long, and brought it around with such force that it cut the nearest pirate in half at the hip. One of the remaining two men moved behind Anja, but she didn't notice … she was totally focused on the pirate in front of her. Alexander didn't fear for her because he also saw Jack moving up behind the man, swift and deadly.

Alexander killed the pirate he'd taken fingers from just before Anja stabbed the last man through the chest with a battle cry worthy of the most hardened warrior. She spun in a crouch, her sword, nearly as big as she was, held in one hand like it was a simple dagger, a streak of blood splatter mingling with the freckles across her nose and cheeks, fury and purpose burning in her golden eyes.

Alexander stretched out with his all around sight. These pirates had come alone, probably scouts sent to track and slow Alexander and his people. More would be coming.

"What about these two?" Jack said, motioning to the two men Alexander had cut off just above the knees.

"Leave them," Alexander said. "I want Tyr's men to see what's in store for them. I want them to be afraid." He picked up the cloak of one of the fallen and cleaned the blood from his sword.

Kalderson's men were standing on the other side of the log looking at the carnage scattered over the forest floor, eyes wide, breath held, fear evident in their colors.

"How many wounded do you have, Captain?"

"Two dead and one with an arrow through his leg."

Alexander went to the wounded man and knelt at his side. "Looks like that hurts."

"Nothing but a scratch," the sailor said through gritted teeth.

"Good man," Alexander said, motioning to the nearest two sailors. "Help me roll him onto his side so I can get the arrow out."

A few minutes later, the sailor was being carried to a bed in the Wizard's Den, the arrow removed, his wound cleaned, treated with the last of Alexander's healing salve, and bandaged. Alexander left another sailor to care for the injured man and closed the door.

As evening approached and the shadows deepened, it started raining—not a downpour but a drizzle, constant and relentless, soaking the world with seemingly deliberate thoroughness. By the time they stopped for the night, everyone was soaked through and shivering.

It was cramped, but all of them were able to find space enough to sleep within the Wizard's Den. While the men were at first awestruck and somewhat fearful of stepping into the magical room, they soon relaxed after Alexander closed the door and built up the fire. Hot tea and a hearty stew erased all hint of fear and replaced it with a symphony of snoring.

"How're you doing?" Alexander asked Anja before going to sleep.

"I'm all right," she said with a shrug. "Why?"

"You killed three people today."

"So?"

"Some people find it hard to sleep after killing, especially the first time."

Alexander remembered the sickening feeling in the pit of his stomach the first time he'd killed a man. It seemed so long ago that he had loosed an arrow in the hallway of some nondescript Southport inn. He still remembered how it smelled, a hint of smoke mingled with sweat and fear. He remembered the mottled color of the walls. But mostly, he remembered the look in the man's eyes in that moment when he realized he was dying.

"They were trying to kill you," Anja said. "I'd have killed the rest of them if you hadn't gotten to them first. And besides, I'm not a person, I'm a dragon." With that she rolled over and closed her eyes.

***

The next morning, Alexander stood to the side of the door before he willed it open. It was raining softly outside, filling the air with the sound of countless droplets falling from the trees above. He stretched out with his all around sight, searching for any sign of the pirates—and he found them. Over a hundred men lying in wait. He looked down at the footprints leading into his Wizard's Den.

"I take it they've found us," Jack said when Alexander closed the door.

"We're surrounded," Alexander said, his brow furrowed in thought.

"Here," Jack said, handing Alexander his cloak. "Slip through their lines and let us out down the road. They'll never know what happened."

"I like it," Alexander said, donning the magical cloak.

"I'm coming with you," Anja said.

"No, you're not," Alexander said. "You're going to stay right here. I'll let you out as soon as it's safe."

"But I can help."

"No, you can't," Alexander said, tossing the hood up and opening the door just long enough to slip out into the world before closing it again. He froze in place, searching for any sign that the enemy had noticed him. They hadn't. Most of the men seemed bored and irritable—all except for Tyr and his wizard. They were both fixated on the spot where Alexander stood.

He moved away slowly, carefully picking each step, sacrificing speed for stealth. By the time he'd passed through their perimeter and reached a safe distance, he had to remind himself to breathe. After another five minutes of walking, he stopped and opened the door to his Wizard's Den.

Anja was waiting for him there, anger flashing in her eyes. "Don't you ever do that again. I'm here to help you."

Alexander stepped through the door, closing it behind him with a thought, causing Anja to back up a few steps.

"Listen well, child." Alexander didn't try to hide his anger from her. "I've told you to go home and you've refused. Fair enough, but understand this. I am at war. More than that, I am in command. You will obey me in battle or I will put you in this Wizard's Den and leave you here until I can take you home to your mother where you belong. Do you understand me?"

Anja's eyes went a little wide and she blinked a few times before looking down.

"I asked you a question, Anja. Do you understand me?"

"Yes," she said very quietly. "I don't like it when you're mad at me."

"Look at me," he said, gently lifting her chin. "I don't want to be mad at you, but there is much more at stake here than just your life or mine, and I cannot allow your willfulness or my feelings for you to jeopardize the future. If we lose this war, then everyone everywhere will lose just about everything and I'm not going to let that happen."

Anja nodded. "I'll try to do better."

"Good," he said, turning to the men watching the exchange. "We're a few minutes ahead of them but we still need to be quiet." He opened the door to the Wizard's Den and everyone filed out.

It wasn't especially cold, but the rain fell steadily. By midday, they were miserable. By dark, they were exhausted and shivering. The warmth and safety of the Wizard's Den was a welcome reprieve from the elements.

When Alexander opened the door the following morning, he was relieved to find that the pirates were nowhere to be seen.

He'd spent the better part of the previous day trying to formulate a plan, and in every course of action that he considered, the first step was to elude their pursuers. With that urgent task accomplished, he could start focusing on getting these people safely to Ruatha.

They set out moving farther inland through the rugged foothills of the coastal range. It wasn't long before the sensation of danger flooded into Alexander's mind.

"Threat!" he shouted, taking cover behind a tree and stretching out with his all around sight. What he saw made him catch his breath. He'd walked them into an ambush. A hundred or more pirates lined the ridge to the right of the trail and the only place they could go was into the ravine to the left of the trail.

Before he could react, Tyr's wizard cast a spell. A blue sphere only an inch in diameter streaked into Alexander's group and froze in space for a fraction of a moment before almost instantly expanding to a diameter of fifty feet, blowing everyone away from the center point of the spell, sending men flying into the woods, breaking small limbs off nearby trees and hurling loose rocks and branches in every direction.

The last thing Alexander remembered before plunging into the dark oblivion of unconsciousness was the sound of the wind in his ears as he flew through the air.

Chapter 3

He woke slowly, confusion and pain competing for his attention. He was being carried over the shoulder of a very large man. Reality and the severity of his situation slowly seeped into his awareness. His hands and feet were bound tightly, a gag cut into the sides of his mouth, and he hurt all over. Each hasty stride of the man carrying him jarred his body, revealing new bruises, each vying for his attention. He remained limp, reaching out with his all around sight, hoping to find something that he could use against his enemies but finding only confirmation that his predicament was indeed as bad as it seemed.

"Are you there, Little One?"

"Yes, My Love. Are you all right?" Chloe's voice was fraught with worry and fear.

"I've been better. What's happened?"

"We were ambushed. The wizard's spell knocked everyone down and then they were on us."

"The Stone ... did they take it?"

"No. Jack told me to hide it in the aether along with your belt pouch. It's in ..."

"Stop. Don't tell me. If I don't know, they can't make me tell them. Where are Jack and Anja?"

"Anja was taken, but Jack got away. He's following in the forest."

"Good. What about Kalderson and his men?"

"The pirates left them when their scout reported that Lancers were coming."

"How long have I been out?"

"About an hour. What are we going to do, My Love?"

"I'm not sure yet, Little One."

The pirates entered a clearing and Tyr called a halt. The man carrying Alexander flopped him onto the ground, insulting his bruises and reigniting his agony. He moaned slightly, trying to rein in his pain, not willing to let his enemies see even a hint of weakness.

"He's awake," the pirate said, rolling him onto his back with his boot.

Tyr stepped up next to Alexander, looking down at him with a mixture of malice and triumph. "You put up quite a fight. I have to say, I've never faced an adversary quite as resourceful as you."

Alexander ignored him, focusing instead on the pain, taking it in and enduring it, facing it in order to master it, setting it aside and regaining his composure and some measure of control over his wounded body.

"Set them up against that tree and build a fire," Tyr snapped to his men. "Where's my scout report?"

Alexander let his head loll forward as he was propped up against the tree, feigning exhaustion and despair, an easy enough task given his circumstances.

They put Anja next to him ... she was still unconscious and bound much more tightly than he was.

Tyr had about thirty men with him, including his wizard.

A man trotted out of the woods and stopped to catch his breath before giving his report.

"Well, where are they?" Tyr snapped.

"Still at the ambush site," the man wheezed, breathing heavily. "You were right. Leaving the sailors alive gave us a good head start."

Tyr snorted, muttering, "Idiots. We'll rest and eat while we wait for the fire to burn down."

His men spread out, some taking positions on the perimeter of their camp while others sat near the fire warming their hands.

"The coals are hot, Lord Tyr," another pirate said after several minutes.

Tyr turned and looked at Alexander, smiling almost fondly as he drew his knife and buried the tip of the blade in the hot coals. "It won't be long now," he whispered, staring into the flames.

Alexander felt his soul quail for just a moment before he steeled himself to endure the coming torture.

"Little One?"

"Yes, My Love?"

"If I don't survive this, promise me you'll help Jack get the Sovereign Stone to Abigail before you join me in the light."

"Don't say such things. I can't bear the thought of you dying."

"Everything depends on the Stone. Promise me, please."

"I promise," she said very quietly in his mind.

Tyr withdrew the knife, the tip glowing orange. He walked slowly toward Alexander, turning the blade this way and that, kneeling in front of him and smiling as he laid it against Alexander's forearm.

He tried not to scream, tried to control the agony, but it was so sudden and so intense that he simply couldn't. His wail carried through the forest, and then the stench of burning flesh reached his nose and he vomited, choking on his own acid and bile. He lapsed into a fit of coughing and heaving that filled his already pain-wracked body with spasms of suffering.

Tyr sat back and watched Alexander try to regain control over his wounded body. "Do I have your attention?" he asked in the same tone one might ask another to pass the biscuits at the dinner table.

Alexander nodded, still trying to regain his composure.

"Good. I thought I might. You don't have to suffer anymore. If you give me what I want, I will make sure that your journey to Phane is comfortable. If you don't give me what I want, well ..." He held up the still-glowing blade, turning it with suggestive malice.

"So, I've already recovered my sword," he said, patting the hilt of the Thinblade at his hip. "But we didn't find the Sovereign Stone, and quite honestly, I think Phane actually wants that more than he wants your head. Tell me where it is and we can be on our way ... and all of this unpleasantness will end."

"I don't know where it is," Alexander said, clenching his teeth in anticipation of the pain he knew his answer would bring, and he wasn't wrong. Tyr slapped the hot blade against his forearm again, this time an inch from the first burn. Alexander tried to scream, but he couldn't draw breath, the pain paralyzing him, overwhelming his senses and threatening to undo his sanity. Then he found himself floating over his body, his limp form slumping over into his own vomit.

Tyr stood up, frowning to himself. "Clean him up and move them both over there. I'm tired of smelling that," he said, pointing at the bile staining the forest floor.

With a flick of thought, Alexander was floating next to Jack, who was watching from a distance, and from the color of his aura looked about ready to burst. Alexander appeared next to him, crouching behind a tree to avoid being seen.

"Alexander, what's happening? Are you dead?"

"I don't think so. The pain just put me out and I found myself in the firmament. We don't have much time. If they kill me, you have to take the Stone to Abigail ..."

He woke sputtering and coughing from a bucket of frigid water splashed in his face. He tried to think back to a time when he'd been this miserable, but the sight of the hot knife, glowing even brighter than before and being held in front of his face, focused his mind on the present.

"This is taking too long," Tyr said, turning to the wizard behind him. "Tell me if he's lying."

"The spell will take a few moments to cast, Lord Tyr."

"Hurry up," he snapped.

Alexander watched the wizard's colors swell with magic when the spell took effect.

Tyr smiled. "I had my court wizard master an aura-reading spell when I learned of your rather intriguing talent, so you of all people should know just how futile it is to lie to me. Now, let's try this again. Where is the Sovereign Stone?"

"I don't know."

Tyr started to bring the hot blade down on his arm when the wizard spoke. "He's telling the truth."

"How can you not know where it is?" Tyr asked. "I saw you open your Wizard's Den. You needed the Stone to do that, so where is it?"

"I don't know," Alexander said. "It's probably back where you ambushed us. I had it before you attacked, but it was gone when I woke up."

The wizard nodded and Tyr shot to his feet shouting a curse at the sky.

"That Stone is worth the entire Isle of Tyr to me and you're telling me you left it lying in the dirt?" He was shouting at the stunned-looking men all around him, his face red, veins standing out at his temples. When no one responded, he surged toward the nearest man, plunging the red-hot knife into the man's gut and pushing him over into the mud.

"Find! That! Stone!" he shouted with such force that his voice broke with each word.

His men stood stock-still for just a moment before they all started gathering their packs and making ready for travel just as another scout raced into the clearing.

"They're coming," he said.

"Who?"

"The Lancers, at least two platoons. They have our trail."

Tyr seemed to struggle against another outburst before mastering himself and turning calmly to his wizard.

"Options?"

"If they've found the Stone, they'll take the pretender and we cannot stop them. If they don't have the Stone, we may yet deceive them."

"How? He's marked. They'll know who he is the moment they lay eyes on him."

"Not necessarily," the wizard said. "I was once scarred badly, an attempt at discipline by my stepfather after a particularly long night of drinking."

"What's your point?" Tyr snapped.

"I created a spell that can erase a scar," the wizard said, "sort of a modified healing spell."

"Do it," Tyr commanded.

Alexander didn't resist. The mark burned into his neck had served its purpose, it was of no further value to him and being less conspicuous while trapped in enemy territory could only help him. The spell hurt, but nowhere near as badly as the hot knife, and the pain faded moments after the skin on his neck had been transformed.

Tyr knelt in front of him, anger and frustration shining as brightly from his eyes as it did from his colors. "Think of it this way, if you tell them who you are, they'll take you straight to Phane, but if you play along, it'll buy you some time. Who knows, you might even manage to escape before I steal you right out from under their noses."

Lancers streamed into the clearing a few moments later, spreading out and surrounding the pirates. Tyr stood his ground, fists planted firmly on his hips, his chin thrust out, a scowl etched into his face.

A big man wearing epaulettes of rank rode into the clearing atop his rhone steed. He sneered at Tyr and then snorted derisively. "I'm Commander Udane. What's your business here, Tyr?"

"That's Lord Tyr to you."

"You know very well that this forested range is off-limits and yet you choose to trespass against the Andalian Empire."

Tyr started laughing. "Your feebleminded king can't even control his own island and yet you insist on calling Andalia an empire."

"Watch your tongue, Tyr!"

"Lord Tyr! And you would do well to watch your tongue. I'm a friend and ally of the Babachenko. Would you like to take this matter before him?"

The commander scowled, then spat at Tyr's feet. "Who are your prisoners?"

"These two stole from me. I wrecked their ship, ran them to ground and now they're mine."

"No, they're not," Udane said. "All castaways that wash ashore on Andalian soil belong to the king. You will surrender them, or I will take you up on your offer to bring this before the Babachenko. I think we both know how he'll decide in the matter."

"They stole from me," Tyr said. "Keep the sailors, but these two are mine."

Udane raised his hand casually and several dozen Lancers dropped their force lances. Every member of Tyr's force was targeted by at least two Lancers.

"How dare you?" Tyr sputtered, his face turning red. "I'm the King of Tyr, wielder of the Thinblade and master of the southern seas."

"You are a small man with a big name," Udane said, "and your name is the only reason you're not flat on your back with my boot on your throat. Leave my prisoners, take your men and get off my island or I will see to it that you spend a month in the mines before anyone even figures out who you are."

"This isn't over, Udane. I'm going to bring this to the Babachenko, and these two will answer to me for their crimes."

"Well, I guess that means you'll have to sail to an approved port where you can apply for travel papers, then you'll have to make your way to Mithel Dour and petition the Babachenko for their release into your custody. By then, I'll have been paid my bounty and I won't care what happens to them."

Tyr seemed to be weighing further threats but stopped short. "Gather your things and make ready to travel," he barked to his men, snatching up his pack and marching into the forest without a second look at either Udane or Alexander. His men scrambled to catch up with him, leaving Alexander and Anja surrounded by Lancers.

Udane dismounted, standing over them. Alexander pretended to ignore the armor-clad commander while studying his base and muddy colors. He feared that things had just gone from bad to worse, but of far more immediate concern was Anja; she was still unconscious. If Alexander couldn't have seen her colors, he would have feared the worst.

"Looks like we got here just in time," Udane said to himself before turning to his men. "Clean and bandage his arm, then cut them loose and get them mounted up. I want to be back at base camp by dark."

Chapter 4

Alexander feigned near unconsciousness while a soldier dressed his burns, searching for a way to escape using his all around sight. What he saw was an impossible situation. There were nearly sixty Lancers in the immediate area and they were all alert and disciplined, professional soldiers who had plenty of experience in the field and who seemed to be particularly adept at securing prisoners.

Just as the soldier finished bandaging his arm, Anja woke with a start. Alexander saw the flare of fear and rage in her colors when she realized her hands and feet were bound. With a battle cry that would have made the most hardened barbarian proud, she broke her bonds and surged to her feet in a crouch, snatching a dagger from the soldier kneeling next to Alexander and plunging it into his neck, then stalking toward Commander Udane. Before she could lunge at him, he raised his hand and a nearby Lancer unleashed his force lance at her, sending her tumbling across the forest floor. A moment later, two men were on her, one snapping a thin metal collar around her neck before she threw them both off of her and sprang to her feet.

Udane smiled, touching his ring. She fell to her knees, gasping for breath and struggling to remove the collar.

"Stop!" Alexander shouted. "Please, don't hurt her. She'll behave if I tell her to, just don't kill her, please."

Udane regarded Alexander for a moment before touching his ring again. Anja gasped for breath, then broke into a fit of coughing and sputtering.

"Anja, listen to me," Alexander said. "Stop fighting. They'll kill you."

She looked up at him and a flurry of emotions cascaded through her colors: fear, anger, despair, loyalty, and finally love. She nodded to him.

"She won't be a problem for you anymore," Alexander said. "Please don't hurt her."

"Hurt her?" Udane said, looking at Alexander as if they were both speaking different languages. "Young women fetch a good price at market, but only if they're healthy, and especially if they have a fiery spirit. She's worth five of you. The last thing I want to do is hurt her, but she will learn obedience or she's worthless to me."

"What do you mean, 'fetch a good price at market'?" Alexander asked.

Udane looked at him again and frowned. "Huh ... well, I guess it's understandable that you're ignorant of our ways, so I'll explain things to you. You'll be sold as slaves at market in Mithel Dour, Andalia's capital city."

"What do you mean 'slaves'?"

"Just that, you'll probably be bought by the Andalian Mining Company along with the rest of the sailors we captured earlier, and she'll probably be bought by some noble or other."

"How can you sell us into slavery?" Alexander asked. "We haven't done anything to deserve this."

"Deserve's got nothing to do with anything," Udane said. "First, the king has decreed that all castaways who wash up on Andalian soil are to be taken as slaves. Second, this province is under a liquidation order."

"What does that mean?" Alexander asked, horror tickling at the back of his mind.

"By order of the king, no subject of the Andalian Empire is permitted to live in mountainous or forested regions because of the difficulty such terrain poses to the daily operations of the Lancers. In short, we can't adequately provide for the safety and well-being of people living in these regions, so they've been ordered to relocate to more suitable areas."

"What if they don't want to leave their homes?"

Udane shrugged, "That's what the sequestration is for."

"What does *that* mean?"

"This province has been cut off from the rest of Andalia. No trade is permitted and all who chose to remain here after the initial relocation period are to be captured as slaves or killed for treason."

"You're starving out this whole province?" Alexander asked, swallowing back the urge to vomit. In that moment, his resolve hardened and his mission shifted. Until the horrible truth of Andalian rule had been made plain to him, his only concern was escaping this place and returning home, but the depravity of the Andalian government's tyranny was beyond evil, their violation of the Old Law so complete, that Alexander silently added another enemy to the long list of those that he intended to destroy.

Udane chuckled. "I didn't think it'd work at first, but the strategy has proven to be remarkably effective. The number of insurrectionist attacks coming from this province has been cut nearly in half just this winter.

"But that's enough talk for now." He held up a metal collar, hinged on one side with a clasp on the other, runes etched into the metal, colors of potent magic radiating from it. "Put this on."

Alexander reassessed his situation: there was still virtually no chance of escape.

Choking down bile, he took the collar and snapped it around his neck.

"That wasn't so difficult, now was it?" Udane said. "I suppose I should tell you how these collars work so you don't get yourself killed out of ignorance. If you wander too far from this ring I'm wearing or if I command it, the collar will choke you. Simple, right?"

Alexander nodded curtly, still struggling to master the rage boiling in his belly.

"I'm glad we understand each other." Then, turning to his men, Udane said, "Let's get mounted up."

"But, sir, she killed Johansson. We should hang her for that."

Udane snorted derisively. "If Johansson was stupid enough to let a little girl kill him, then he wasn't fit to serve under my command."

He stopped, frowning to himself and then raised his voice. "Hear me well, these prisoners belong to me. If any harm comes to them while under your care, I'll kill you myself, and I'll take my time doing it. Understood?"

There was a nervous murmuring of assent.

"I said, do you understand?" Udane shouted.

"Yes sir!" his men responded in chorus.

"Good. Now mount up."

Alexander and Anja each rode behind a soldier on one of the big rhone steeds that Andalia was famous for. The soldiers were experienced riders, comfortable in the saddle and skilled at guiding their mounts through the difficult terrain of the forest, but it was clear within minutes that they couldn't be effective in any real engagement in such terrain, certainly not with the devastating effectiveness they could bring to a battle on the open plains.

"How's Jack doing, Little One?"

"He's struggling to keep up, but your trail is easy to follow."

"Good. Tell him we have a new objective."

"Yes, My Love."

"We're going to Mithel Dour to destroy the Andalian government. Tell him to stay with us as best he can and tell him to stay out of sight. Oh, and tell him he'll need papers to travel safely through Andalia. I'm not sure what that means, but I suspect he's resourceful enough to figure it out."

"I will relay your messages, My Love. Are you all right?"

"I'm pretty beat-up at the moment, but I'll heal."

An hour after they set out, they reached a big meadow where several mountain streams fed into a lake that flowed into a small river. There they joined up with another platoon that had captured some of Kalderson's crew. Only seven remained, including the captain. Alexander hoped the others had escaped into the forest, but he suspected that most were dead.

Udane called a rest break near the river.

Alexander stretched after dismounting. The soldiers didn't seem too concerned that he might run off, maybe even hoped that he would test the collar around his neck.

"Commander, may I go get cleaned up?" Alexander asked, motioning to the vomit still staining his tunic.

"Please let him get cleaned up, Commander," the soldier he'd been riding with said. "If I have to keep smelling him, I'm going to retch myself."

"Go ahead. Just remember," Udane said holding up his ring, "more than a hundred feet and I might not find you before you choke to death."

"I understand," Alexander said. He would execute Udane without a second thought, but he decided that being polite and civil might buy him the leeway he would need to escape when the time was right.

He pushed through the tall grass and found a little pool of still water next to a large tree at the edge of the meadow. After a moment of searching for any soldiers watching him, he was satisfied that they'd left him unsupervised. He stripped off his tunic. Then he took off his armor shirt, rolling up one of his most prized possessions and hiding it under the roots of the tree before thoroughly washing his tunic and wringing it as dry as possible.

"Mark this place, Little One, and guide Jack here. Tell him to wear my armor until he can give it back to me. It'll serve him well."

"But won't you need it, My Love?"

"If they found it on me, it would raise too many questions that I don't care to answer. I'm safer without it for now. Just make sure Jack retrieves it, because I do want it back."

Alexander returned to the Lancers a few minutes later.

"You learn quickly," Udane said. "I expected you to run off."

"Then why did you let me wander away without an escort?"

"The first attempt at escape usually proves to be a very educational experience. We wouldn't want to deprive you of the opportunity to learn your place, now would we?"

Alexander didn't respond to the taunt, but instead dutifully mounted up.

Sometime later in the afternoon, he noticed the colors of several men on a bluff overlooking the trail they were following. A moment later, the sensation of danger flooded into his mind, the coming moments revealing themselves to him all in a rush. He slipped backward off the rump of the rhone and tumbled behind a tree, attempting to make it look like it was a clumsy accident. A moment later, a volley of arrows rained into the side of the soldier and rhone, killing them both. Rocks broke free from the bluff and started crashing into the flank of the Lancers' single-file column, killing two more rhone along with their riders, followed by a second volley of arrows that killed another three Lancers before the attackers vanished into the forest.

It was over before any resistance could be organized. The position of the attackers, coupled with the steep terrain, made it impossible for the Lancers to give chase. Udane rode along the line of his soldiers, inspecting the damage and cursing under his breath.

He stopped and looked down at Alexander, who sat resting against the tree. "Looks like you got lucky today."

"There are a lot of ways I might characterize today ... lucky isn't one of them."

Udane chuckled. "Mount up with another soldier and try not to fall off this time. Hate to have to put you down because you broke your leg."

Just before the sun slipped past the coastal range behind them, Alexander got his first look at the scope of the Lancers' operation. Several hundred feet beyond the wood line, stretching as far as he could see in both directions, was a timber wall. Behind it was a large fortified camp divided into two sections, one with walls to keep the Lancers safe from attack and another with walls to ensure that their prisoners didn't escape.

Despite the blatant immorality and inherent dishonor of the Lancers, they were a well-regulated and disciplined fighting force. Rank was obeyed and they carried themselves with pride. These were professional soldiers, and all the more dangerous because of it.

Alexander and Kalderson's men were taken to the prison camp. While the soldiers certainly didn't show them any respect, they were handled with the kind of care given to a valuable commodity as they were processed and assigned sleeping quarters.

Alexander soon found himself in a large tent with eleven other men, most of them Andalians. A soldier assigned him to his cot and informed him that the evening meal would be served shortly.

He lay down, ignoring the rest of the men in the tent and cleared his mind. Several moments later, he slipped free of his body into the boundless source of all creation and then just as quickly he slammed back into his body again, struggling to breathe, gasping for air, the collar around his neck relaxing its death grip a moment after he returned. He breathed deliberately, filling his lungs to capacity and exhaling slowly until his heart stopped racing.

The next man over was sitting on the edge of his cot looking at Alexander intently. "That shouldn't have happened unless you're a wizard ... and then only if you're dumb enough to try and cast a spell with that choker around your neck."

Alexander sat up shaking his head, the implications of the man's words sinking in even as he floundered for a plausible explanation. The last thing he needed was for anyone to figure out who he really was.

"Udane said he was going to punish me for trying to run," he said, touching his neck tenderly.

"We all try to run."

"Yeah, but I busted him in the mouth when he caught me."

The man looked at him for several moments before a smile slowly spread across his face and he broke into laughter. He was a mousy little man, five and a half feet tall and just over a hundred pounds, but he had curiosity in his eyes and deep turmoil and loss swirling in his colors.

"I'm Hod," he said, extending his hand.

Alexander took it and said, "I'm Alex."

"You don't look like you're from Andalia, Alex."

"I'm not. My sister and I booked passage out of Southport, bound for Baden in Tyr. The war is getting bad on Ruatha and we have kin on Baden. Unfortunately, we were attacked by pirates and our ship wrecked on the reef. We barely made it to shore."

Hod nodded cynically. "Doesn't surprise me. The Babachenko and Tyr have an arrangement. Any ship off our coast that's not flying the Andalian flag is fair game for Tyr. He attacks them, runs them to ground and then lets the crew escape into the forest, while he strips their ship of anything worth taking. Then the Lancers round up the castaways and sell them at the slave market."

"This place just keeps getting better. So who's this Babachenko?"

"You really aren't from around here," Hod said. "He's the Voice of the King, the real power behind the throne. The most important thing to know about him is that you don't want him to know anything about you. Slaves who attract his attention have a bad habit of disappearing."

"Good to know," Alexander said, mentally adding a name to his list.

In the distance, a bell tolled three times and Hod stood, rubbing his hands together. "Time to eat," he said eagerly. "As much as I hate the Lancers, I have to admit they do feed us well. Certainly a lot better than we've had since the sequestration started."

"They feed cows and pigs pretty well, too, right before they take them to market," Alexander said under his breath.

After dinner, the slaves returned to the tent, not because the Lancers required them to, but because they had nowhere else to go. Alexander got the impression that the Lancers were indifferent to the prisoners' conditions. Their only real concerns were ensuring that their merchandise wasn't damaged and didn't escape.

Alexander noted that the women were being kept separately from the men, probably a wise precaution from the Lancers' point of view, but it left him separated from Anja and he was worried about her. For all of her strength and fierceness, she was really just a child and she was very much out of her depth. More calculatingly, Alexander also had to admit that she posed the greatest risk of exposure for him and his identity. At the moment, the only thing they had going for them was anonymity. If anyone even suspected who he really was, things would get much worse very quickly.

He lay down on his cot and reached out for Chloe.

"Have you looked in on Anja?"

"Yes, My Love. She seems frightened and alone. I'm worried about her."

"Me too. When you get a chance to talk to her without others noticing, let her know that I haven't forgotten about her, but that we're going to be here for a while and I need her to be strong, I need her to avoid calling attention to herself and I need her to play the role of the obedient slave."

"I will tell her, My Love. Jack has retrieved your armor and he's also discovered people resisting the Lancers in this area."

"I saw them, too."

"He wants to know if he should make contact with them."

"No. As much as I'd like to help these people, we just aren't in a position to do so right now and I can't risk Jack being exposed or captured. Our objective here is the destruction of the Andalian government and especially the king and his precious Crown."

"I will tell him, My Love."

"One more thing, Little One. I can't touch the firmament with this collar around my neck, so let him know that I'll have to relay messages through you."

"Yes, My Love. Stay safe," she said in his mind.

And then he was alone with his thoughts. "You still awake, Hod?"

"Yeah, it takes me longer to fall asleep here. I guess I just don't feel safe."

"I know what you mean," Alexander said. "Tell me more about Andalia."

"What do you want to know?"

"Why the Lancers are starving out this province, for starters."

"Well, that depends a lot on who you ask," Hod said. "The government says it's to protect the people from bandits and insurrectionists, but most of the people in the areas ruled off-limits say it's to make it easier for the Lancers to collect taxes and dictate terms to the people."

"Who are these insurrectionists?"

"Mostly it's just people who didn't leave their homes when they were told to. When they didn't leave, the Lancers came in and cut off trade, so they turned to banditry to feed their families. The government points to the crime happening in the area as justification for the sequestration that caused the banditry in the first place."

"So this province isn't the first to be starved out?"

"No, this is the third," Hod said. "It all started when Phane woke. The king decreed that all taxes would double to pay for the defense of Andalia against the pretender. The people living in the plains didn't have much choice, but those of us living in more rugged areas mostly ignored the order. Lancers were sent to collect the taxes, but a lot of them never returned. The government responded by stirring up the people in the cities, telling them that the bandits were stealing children and other nonsense. When the people didn't believe them, children started to actually go missing. It wasn't long after that, that the people started demanding emergency measures to deal with the threat.

"That's when the first sequestration started. Thousands starved, more were killed or sold into slavery, but the people in the cities didn't hear about that. What they hear are reports of children disappearing, whispers that the bandits are eating them." He paused for a moment, staring straight ahead. "It scares me the things people will believe, and without even thinking about it for a moment."

"I know what you mean," Alexander whispered, closing his eyes and wishing he could turn off the nightmare swirling around in his mind.

Days passed without event. Each night, Lancer patrols returned with more slaves captured in the forest. A few tried to escape; none succeeded. After a week of waiting, a wagon train arrived, each wagon fitted with a cage capable of transporting eight people.

One by one, the Lancer commanders herded the prisoners into the staging area, lining them up in orderly rows for inspection. A Lancer general walked the ranks, inspecting each prisoner. Behind him, an aide tallied the number of slaves captured by each commander and assigned every slave an estimated value.

As the general approached, Alexander assessed him. His colors were muddy and dark, devoid of humanity, absent of conscience. He might as well have been inspecting bushels of corn.

The general accepted nearly all of the slaves, touching his ring to their collar. The few he deemed to be of too-little value to warrant a place in his caravan were killed on the spot. Once the value of the slaves had been calculated, he paid the commanders and supervised the loading of his purchases into the wagons.

As the Andalians herded the slaves into the wagons, Alexander watched for Anja. She'd been loaded into a wagon with seven other young women. Alexander met her eyes as he passed, mouthing the only thing that really mattered, "I love you."

Chapter 5

Isabel woke slowly, lingering in that place between sleep and wakefulness, unaware of where she was until she opened her eyes and found herself lying on a cold stone floor, dull pain hammering in her head. She pushed herself up to her hands and knees, clenching her eyes against the explosion in her head caused by such sudden movement. She took a moment to breathe, willing her mind to clear and trying to focus.

Very deliberately, she got to her feet and assessed her surroundings. She was in a circular room. Magic circles were etched into both the floor and ceiling. A single window cut through three feet of stone and barred at the midway point provided the only source of light. Opposite the window was a heavy door without a keyhole or latch.

Details began to work their way through the fog of pain in her head. She'd stabbed Phane … but he'd survived. He'd subdued her with poison—a possibility that had never entered her mind. He was an arch mage, yet he'd made preparations to defend himself without magic.

She sat down, the realization settling on her that she'd failed because she had underestimated him. Alexander had warned her, but she hadn't listened.

Then it hit her.

Her hand went to the Goiri bone under her tunic. It was still there. The pain in her head faded, replaced by all of the possibilities racing through her mind. Since she still had the cursed bone, it stood to reason that Phane wasn't aware of it. Surely he'd have taken it from her.

A thrill of fear ran up her spine, quickly spiking into terror so powerful that Isabel found herself cowering on the floor, searching the empty walls for a threat she couldn't name. After a few minutes she regained some sense of awareness beyond the unexplainable fear gripping her soul. The experience had been so intense and so unexpected that she forgot momentarily why she was afraid in the first place. It took a moment of searching her mind before she remembered.

The box.

It was sealed by magic. If Phane got the bone, he could open the box without Lacy—he would have the final keystone he needed to open the Nether Gate.

Isabel surged to her feet, ripping the Goiri bone from around her neck and dropping it to the floor, stomping on it, grinding it into the flagstone with the heel of her boot until it was nothing but powder. Then she carefully scooped up the dust and blew it out the window.

As the remains of the cursed bone swirled away on the breeze, Isabel was thrown across the room as the magic circle reasserted itself in the absence of the null magic field. All vestiges of the fear she'd been feeling faded away in an instant. Then she hit the ground hard and the darkness of the Wraith Queen gripped her psyche once again. She would have screamed if she could have spared the effort, but she knew that any distraction, any slip of focus could lead to ruin, allowing Azugorath into her mind and heart where the demon would take up permanent residence.

Isabel wasn't sure how long she lay on the floor, curled into a ball, fighting to remain in control of her own free will ... it seemed like hours. Moment by moment, she fended off the demonic invasion threatening to take everything from her until the will of the Wraith Queen broke and her push for dominion receded.

Isabel sat up, trying to steady herself, allowing the flutter in her stomach and the energy coursing through her veins to dissipate. With a smile, she tipped her head back and linked her mind with Slyder. He was a long way away, and he was lonely. She could feel his excitement as he took to wing, flying toward her. She knew exactly how he felt. It had been a long time since she'd been able to use her magic, a long time since she'd been able to link with her familiar.

The sound of boots on stone brought her mind back to the circle cell. When the door opened, she remained sitting in the middle of the floor, smiling slightly as Phane stopped at the threshold. Two very large guards stood behind him.

"Hello, Isabel," Phane said, a boyish smile of unabashed joy spreading across his face. "I trust the accommodations are to your liking."

She stood and gingerly pressed against the barrier created by the magic circle. "It's a little too confining for my tastes," she said, meeting his eyes. "I was hoping you'd bled out."

"Charming as ever. The truth is, no one has ever stabbed me before. In fact, no one has ever come so close to killing me before, not even remotely. Quite impressive, really, especially when you consider the magical protections surrounding me. I'm so very eager to learn how you managed to penetrate those defenses."

"I'll bet," Isabel said.

Phane chuckled, not with derision or malice, but with genuine joy. "That's one of the many reasons I like you, Isabel. You are so very defiant ... even in the face of utter defeat, you stand your ground. Such tenacity is to be admired, though not overly so. As you can see, you're all out of moves. I've won. Things will go much better for you once you accept that."

"So, is this where you threaten to torture me?"

Phane actually looked shocked, and even a bit hurt. "Dear Isabel, I wouldn't dream of such a thing. I don't want to hurt you. I want to make you my queen, my Lady Reishi. I can show you how to tap the darkness within you, command it, wield it. I can show you how to bend the netherworld to your will. Kings will kneel before you and tremble."

Isabel started laughing. At first it was slightly forced, but within a few moments, it transformed into a genuine belly laugh that she couldn't stop. Phane's expression morphed from the pure joy of imagining his fantasy to sudden rage, his features contorted and ugly.

With a gesture, he dismissed the magic circle and surged forward, taking Isabel by the throat and lifting her off the ground at arm's length. Still, she laughed past her choking. She watched the struggle play out in his eyes; he wanted to kill her and yet he didn't. Then the rage passed, replaced by cold calculation, and he set her down gently.

"You shouldn't laugh at me, Isabel. It's disrespectful."

She started laughing again.

He clenched his jaw, fury building in his golden eyes, but he retained his composure, glaring at her until her mirth subsided.

"Are you quite finished?"

"For now," Isabel said, focusing her thoughts on the coming moment. He'd already demonstrated that he was unwilling to kill her, a powerful advantage in any fight, especially since her goal in life at this moment was to end his.

"I believe I have a way to persuade you, though I don't expect it to arrive for several days, so we'll resume this conversation then. In the meantime, I'll see about more suitable quarters. You are Lady Reishi, after all, and that must be respected."

"I'm Lady Reishi because I'm married to Alexander, and yet you insist that he's a pretender. How does that make any sense?"

"Simple, Alexander *is* Lord Reishi. He's bound to the Sovereign Stone, and by long tradition of the Reishi family, that fact makes him Lord Reishi, but admitting that to others wouldn't help me, so I've labeled him the pretender." Phane shrugged. "Once he's dead, it won't matter."

"So it's just one more lie then."

"Deception is often more powerful than magic," Phane said, flashing his boyish smile.

When he turned, Isabel started casting her spell. Just before he reached the threshold, her light-lance fired, but it was refracted into a brilliant burst of light before it reached the back of Phane's head, diffusing its power in a thousand directions.

He didn't even turn around, chuckling. "I told you I was well protected." The door closed on his last word.

***

Several hours later, the door opened again. Isabel was sitting cross-legged in the middle of the room staring at the door. She stood when she saw it wasn't Phane, but several other people instead.

The first was an elderly man dressed in simple brown robes. He had sharp features, flat grey eyes, and long silvery white hair but his face was clean-shaven. With a word, he dismissed the magic circle and smiled insincerely at Isabel before bowing formally. "Lady Reishi, welcome to the Reishi Army Regency headquarters fortress. I am Wizard Enu. Prince Phane has assigned me to complete your education in the arcane arts."

A rather severe-looking woman stepped up beside him. She was middle-aged and slender, her hair was pulled back into a tight braid and she wore the drab clothing of a maidservant. "Lady Reishi, I am Headmistress Dierdra. Prince Phane has assigned me to manage your house staff."

"I have a house staff?"

"Yes, Prince Phane has expressed his desire that you should be afforded every comfort. You currently have twelve servants assigned to provide for your needs."

"You've got to be kidding," Isabel said, looking from face to face, searching for some hint of what was really going on.

"I assure you that I am not," Dierdra said, completely unfazed.

Isabel looked past her to the three men standing in the hall. Two were big battle-scarred soldiers wearing armor and carrying spears. The third was slight of build and wore no armor, yet he carried himself with disdain for those around him as though none were his equal. When Isabel saw the ornate black dagger on his belt, she understood—he was wraithkin.

Wizard Enu gestured toward the two soldiers. "A company of the finest Regency soldiers has been assigned to provide you with security. They've already taken up their posts around your chambers. Additionally, Prince Phane has assigned Wraithkin Issa to be your personal bodyguard."

Isabel smiled without any humor and nodded to herself before walking confidently past the wizard and headmistress, stopping in front of the two soldiers and meeting the eyes of the ranking man.

"Take me to my quarters."

"Yes, My Lady," he said with crisp, detached professionalism, before bowing slightly and turning on his heel. Isabel followed without a word, her new and very much unwelcome retinue following behind.

Her quarters were quite some distance from the cell where she'd awoken. The soldier led her out of the building into the afternoon sun. It wasn't a warm day but the air was still and the sky was clear. She breathed deeply, relieved to be out of the confined space of her cell.

The Regency headquarters fortress was really a small city surrounded by an immense stone wall measuring a hundred feet high by a hundred feet thick. Within, the city was laid out on a grid of roads with most blocks occupied by a single building, those on the outskirts constructed in very utilitarian fashion, while those nearer the center were taller and more ornate.

In the very center rose a black tower, two hundred feet on a side and well over two thousand feet tall. It was completely unadorned, the only break in the smooth stone walls being the few windows scattered in seemingly random fashion.

The soldiers led her toward the black tower, but then turned when they reached the base of it, instead taking her to a pyramid occupying the next block over. It rose two hundred feet into the air in five-foot steps toward a large flat top filled with a manicured garden surrounding a beautiful house. Steep staircases ran from the street level to the top on each of the four sides. Soldiers stood guard along the base of the pyramid as well as around the wall surrounding the estate at the top.

Soldiers manning the gate opened it without a word when Isabel approached, bowing deferentially and averting their eyes. The gardens were beautiful yet somehow cold, as if the meticulous grooming made them unnatural and inaccessible. It only served to remind Isabel of how much she missed the Great Forest and all of its wild and untamed beauty.

The house was lavish, gaudy even, filled with works of art from all over the Seven Isles, no doubt looted in ages past. The place was altogether too much. Isabel would have never chosen a house like this. She shook her head, stopping in the foyer to marvel at the ostentatious nature of the whole place. It looked like it was built to display wealth rather than to be lived in.

"Is this not to your liking?" Dierdra asked.

"Doesn't this seem like a little much to you?" Isabel said, motioning to the clutter of mismatched artwork covering the foyer walls.

"You are Lady Reishi. Prince Phane insisted that you be given the most lavish estate in the city."

"I'm surprised he doesn't live here," she muttered to herself.

"Prince Phane resides in the tower," Wizard Enu said, stepping up alongside her. "It is his wish that you be made as comfortable as possible. You are, of course, free to make any changes to the décor that you see fit."

Isabel snorted, shaking her head. "Honestly, I really don't care. What I would like is a bath and a meal."

"I will see to it at once, Lady Reishi," Dierdra said, bustling off into the expansive house.

"Your quarters are this way," Wizard Enu said. "Once you've had a chance to settle in, I would like to discuss your training … at your convenience, of course."

Chapter 6

By the following day, Isabel was about ready to pull her hair out, except she was quite certain that if she tried to, one of her servants would materialize nearby and offer to do it for her. The entire staff assigned to her seemed terrified that she might have to lift a finger on her own behalf. When her maidservant tried to cut a slice of ham on her breakfast plate, Isabel lost her temper, standing so quickly that her chair tipped over backwards.

"Stop it! I am not an invalid. Nor am I a child. Stop hovering over me ..." When she saw the expectant look on Wraithkin Issa's face, she stopped abruptly. He was watching her like he thought she might lash out at one of the servants, as if he hoped she would.

The young woman waiting on her stood stock-still, her face white as a sheet, trembling as she fought back tears.

Isabel released her frustration with a deep breath before putting a slice of ham on a piece of bread, scooping scrambled eggs on top of it and finishing it with another slice of bread. She walked out onto the balcony with her sandwich and leaned against the railing while she ate in peace.

The house was absurd by her standards, but the view was beautiful once she looked past the walls of the fortress. The jungle beyond was lush and green, spreading out to the horizon. As hostile as she knew the jungle to be, she would have gladly traded it for this over-decorated prison cell.

Slyder landed on the railing, cocking his head at her. It had been quite a while since she'd seen him and she wanted more than anything to rub him under the chin, but she couldn't risk Phane and his people discovering her most loyal ally within the fortress walls. With a touch of sadness, she linked her mind to his and told him to fly. He obeyed, but reluctantly.

Not long after breakfast, Wizard Enu arrived, bowing formally before he entered her dining hall.

"Lady Reishi, perhaps we can begin your instruction today."

Isabel schooled her expression and quieted her mind. While the wraithkin posing as her bodyguard was the most overtly dangerous person in the room, Wizard Enu and his intention to teach her to use dark magic was by far the greatest threat to her free will and personal sovereignty. She knew without doubt that touching the netherworld, willfully opening that door within her mind, would expose her to the influence of the Wraith Queen in a way she probably wouldn't be able to resist. Azugorath's presence within her mind had become a constant, gently pushing against her resistance, searching for a weakness, a crack in her resolve. It was in those moments that Azugorath would exert her will, attempting to pry her way into Isabel's mind and assert control.

"What did you have in mind?" Isabel asked.

"Prince Phane wishes me to teach you a most powerful spell he calls 'drain life.' While I've studied the spell extensively, I lack the necessary power to cast it, but he believes that this spell is well within your capability."

Isabel motioned to a chair on the balcony as she sat down in another.

"How is it that you lack the power to cast this spell?"

"I'm not an arch mage," Enu said. "Prince Phane created this spell, though in truth, I don't see the value of it myself. It requires the sacrifice of a child to the netherworld in order to open a conduit to the darkness. Once this conduit is open, the caster then touches a target creature and their life essence is drawn through the caster into the netherworld. The target is killed, and while the majority of the life energy is lost to the darkness, a portion is retained by the caster, healing wounds and boosting vitality, strength, and energy.

"Prince Phane believes that you will be able to cast this spell without the necessity of a sacrifice due to your unique capabilities."

Isabel listened, willing her face to remain impassive, struggling to overcome her desire to throw Wizard Enu off the balcony. While the spell was indeed powerful, the cost was far too great to even entertain the possibility of actually casting it. She understood intuitively that this was just another attempt to gain control of her through the influence of the Wraith Queen.

"I'm not sure Phane really understands my capabilities," Isabel said. "I'm very new to magic and I haven't had nearly as much basic instruction as I would like. Maybe we should start with something less ambitious."

"I'm afraid that your course of instruction has been determined by Prince Phane. He expects you to make progress in your study of this spell."

"He expects a lot of things that he's not going to get," Isabel said, as she stood up and walked away from Wizard Enu. "I don't feel like it today. Come back tomorrow ... maybe I'll feel like it then."

"Lady Reishi, Prince Phane will be most displeased."

"Good," Isabel said, heading up the stairs to her bedroom with Issa silently following her. He tried to follow her into her room, but she stopped him. "I'd like some time alone."

He leered at her but obeyed, taking up a position outside her door.

Alone in her room, she called Slyder to her and spent some time reacquainting herself with her best friend. Once his need for affection was fulfilled, she linked her mind with him and they took to wing. Having accepted that her attempt on Phane's life had failed, she decided to formulate another plan, but before she could do that, she needed more information.

Slyder flew the length of each street, providing Isabel with a good view of the layout of the fortress city and giving her the opportunity to assess troop strength and defensive capabilities. What she saw wasn't encouraging. While an attack with magic might breach the walls, it was virtually inconceivable that any form of conventional attack could succeed.

She spent the better part of the morning exploring the city through Slyder, watching the soldiers guarding the wall, looking at each building to determine its purpose and scrutinizing the outer wall for any type of weakness. She found very little to be encouraged about. The place was indeed a fortress in every sense of the word.

A timid knock on her door brought her back. She sat up and sighed. "Yes?"

The door opened and a young woman entered, eyes down. "My Lady, your lunch is ready. Where would you like to eat?"

"On my balcony," Isabel said, smiling when Slyder landed on the railing.

While she ate, she wondered about Alexander. He hadn't come to her in some time and she was starting to worry. She told herself that he was busy, but she also knew in the back of her mind that something was wrong. He would have come to her if he could have, especially since he knew all too well what her plan had been. The more she thought about it, the more concerned she became.

After lunch, she forced herself to put him out of her mind, then dismissed her servants and propped a chair in front of the door to provide some semblance of privacy, though she knew that the wraithkin could bypass her door with a thought.

She spent the rest of the afternoon working on the shapeshift spell she'd found in Hazel's basement. It was difficult to recall the specifics, but the more she thought about it, the more came back to her. By evening, she felt that she'd made some progress, though it was clear that this spell would take far longer to learn than any of her other spells had, especially without Magda's tutelage. The principles were more complex, requiring a far more detailed visualization of the desired outcome in addition to a durational element.

She drew on memories of her time spent learning from Magda. While her light-lance and force-push spells were almost instantaneous, her shield spell had been far more difficult to learn because it involved an element of time. Shapeshift would require that same component. By dinner, her mind was exhausted and she was ready for a break. She wasn't surprised to see Wizard Enu waiting for her in her dining room.

"Lady Reishi, I have spoken with Prince Phane and he is most insistent that we begin work on the drain-life spell."

"Yeah, I'll bet," Isabel said, seating herself and fending off her servants' interference as she dished hot stew into a bowl.

"We will begin tomorrow," Wizard Enu said. "Please be ready."

She ignored him until he sighed softly and left her in peace. After dinner, she retired to her quarters and started thinking about her next move. Her first objective was to kill Phane, but realistically she had little chance of success, so she began to think in wider terms. Even if she couldn't kill him, she could still hurt him, weaken him, obstruct his plans, or deliver usable information to her allies. The question was: Where was he the most vulnerable?

After Phane, the next most valuable target was Azugorath, but Alexander had already scouted her location and said it was so well guarded as to be virtually inaccessible.

So what then? She could pick at Phane, killing a few of his more important commanders or even Wizard Enu, but those individuals had little strategic value and would only serve to force Phane to tighten his control over her activities. Her opportunities to act would be limited, so she had to make them count.

As she turned the problem over in her mind, she kept coming back to the same idea. While she couldn't kill Phane by herself, she did have an ally who could, provided she could give him the opportunity. Her decision made, she sat down and wrote a note briefly explaining her situation and the beginnings of her plan. With a rub under the chin, she tied the note to Slyder's leg and sent him on his way.

***

"No, no, no," Wizard Enu said, "you have it exactly backwards. I don't know how many different ways to explain this."

Isabel stood up, shoving the book across the table and walking away. "I don't know what you want from me. I'm trying to understand, but these concepts are so advanced." She started crying. It took some effort since she wanted to laugh in his face, but bringing her worry for Alexander to the front of her mind was enough to start the tears flowing. "I just don't understand," she said, punctuating her words with a sniffle.

Wizard Enu sighed in resignation. "Perhaps we should resume tomorrow. A night's sleep may help clarify your understanding of these principles."

Isabel nodded, still struggling with her tears as she headed for her bedroom. Issa followed her without a word, and as always, Isabel stopped him at the door. Once alone, she quickly composed herself and linked her mind with Slyder. She'd sent him north the day before and she wanted to check on his progress. As near as she could tell, he was getting close to the right place … the trick would be finding Ayela, Trajan, and Hector.

By evening, she was watching the world below through Slyder's eyes while he circled over the area where Trajan and his men had been operating when she'd met them. After finding a patrol, she followed them, treetop to treetop, until they arrived at a base camp. She was disappointed to find that it was just a scout base, but it stood to reason. They would have moved their operation to ensure that she couldn't betray them to Phane even if he tortured their location out of her.

A reasonable precaution, but unnecessary since Phane had shown no interest in the House of Karth since she'd arrived. She told Slyder to remain in the area in the hope that she could track the scout soldiers back to the House of Karth's new command facility.

Phane arrived during breakfast the following morning, Wizard Enu trailing nervously behind him.

"Good Morning, Isabel. I trust you're being well cared for."

Dierdra stiffened almost imperceptibly at his question.

"I might be the most well-cared-for prisoner in the history of the Seven Isles," Isabel said without bothering to get up.

Phane smiled brightly, taking a seat at the table and picking up a strip of bacon. "You shouldn't think of yourself as a prisoner. You may go through any door that will open for you within this entire fortress. There is very little here that I will not share with you."

"What do you want, Phane? Do you think you can buy my loyalty or even my love with this over-decorated house? Are you really that delusional?"

The staff and soldiers in the room became very still as if they were trying to avoid any possibility of drawing Phane's attention.

He glared at her, slowly chewing his bacon and shaking his head ever so slightly. "Don't be so ungrateful. I could have easily left you in that cell, and I must say, General Hargrove and his wife were none too pleased when I evicted them from this house."

"So, he's the one responsible for all this clutter," Isabel said, gesturing to the walls.

"More likely his wife," Phane said, then smiled unexpectedly. "You see, we've just discovered something that we agree on. I prefer simple and tasteful decorations in my home as well. Perhaps we have more in common than you think."

"Are you kidding me?"

Phane sighed, looking almost dejected. "You wound me, Isabel. I'm trying very hard to accommodate you in every way and all I get back is mockery and derision. There is only so much a man can take before such rudeness is returned in kind."

Isabel started laughing.

"Enough!" he shouted, surging to his feet. "I will not be disrespected by a guest in my home."

Isabel kept laughing, holding Phane's eyes defiantly.

He returned her glare and started to smile maliciously, gesturing to a guard at the door.

It opened and Isabel stopped laughing, horror and fear filling her in a way that chilled her to the core. She felt the blood drain from her face and her mouth go dry.

Wren stood at the threshold, looking afraid and confused. When she saw Isabel, she wrenched her arm free of the guard and raced to her, both of them breaking down in tears, both for different reasons.

"Isabel, I was so afraid," Wren said. "They took me from Blackstone Keep in the middle of the night and they wouldn't tell me where they were taking me."

"It's going to be all right," Isabel said, hoping desperately that she wasn't telling the girl a lie.

Phane was staring at her smugly when she met his gaze, fury flashing in her green eyes.

"Perhaps you will be more respectful and more forthcoming now that you understand the stakes," Phane said, sitting down again. "Please, child, sit and eat. You must be hungry."

Wren looked to Isabel, who nodded. Wren started timidly, but her appetite got the better of her after her first bite and she ate voraciously. Phane watched contentedly, stopping Isabel from speaking with a raised hand when she opened her mouth, waiting until Wren washed her breakfast down with a glass of juice and looked around.

"Thank you, I was so hungry."

"Rest assured, child," Phane said, "you shall not want as long as you are in my care. And, of course, you're free to roam the city as you please. As I understand it, you're quite a curious young woman, which just so happens to be a trait we share. I encourage you to explore. The soldiers know that you're under my protection. You're safer here within these walls than anywhere in all the Seven Isles."

"Thank you, sir," Wren said.

"What a delight you are," Phane said, turning to Isabel with a bright, boyish smile. "Her manners and courtesy are proof of a good upbringing."

Isabel glared at him but she held her tongue.

"I would say you're a quick study, Isabel, except that Wizard Enu tells me you're having a very difficult time mastering the principles he's been trying to teach you, though I suspect you'll make good progress in your studies over the coming days."

He looked back to Wren with his most charming smile. "If you've had enough to eat, why don't you go with Dierdra? She'll show you to your room and draw a bath for you."

Wren looked from Phane to Isabel and back to Phane. "I'd rather stay with Isabel, sir. If I may?"

Phane smiled disarmingly. "Oh, she'll be here when you're done with your bath, and I think Dierdra has a new dress for you."

"Go ahead, Wren. I'm not going anywhere."

Wren hugged Isabel before she left, looking back once with her big, innocent eyes.

"I must say, Isabel, I've noticed a marked change in your demeanor," Phane said. "Perhaps you'd like to explain how you penetrated my defenses, now that we understand each other better."

Isabel just glared at him, trying to think of a way out, but finding none.

"Shall I have Wraithkin Issa retrieve your friend so that she can participate in our conversation?"

Isabel closed her eyes and clenched her jaw, trying to work through the ramifications of telling him the truth and weighing them against the potential consequences of telling a lie.

"I'm waiting, and Isabel, my patience is beginning to wear thin."

"I used a Goiri bone," she said without opening her eyes.

"Really? I never believed the stories. I thought Siavrax was using the threat of such an unlikely creation as a ruse, as a way of forcing us to respond with a larger troop presence to draw men from other, more important positions.

"Tell me, Isabel, where is this Goiri bone now?"

"Gone," she said, opening her eyes and meeting his. "I crushed it into powder and blew it out the window of my cell the moment I woke up."

"Ah, what a pity," Phane said, shaking his head. "I have a very important use for such an unusual item."

"So did I," Isabel said, holding his eyes.

Phane started chuckling to himself almost good-naturedly.

"I wouldn't laugh too hard, Phane. I almost got you."

"You did indeed, which is exactly why I'm laughing. You are every bit the treasure I was hoping you'd be. Do you have any idea how resourceful you are to have recovered such an item? If I'd been told of your plan before you arrived, I wouldn't have believed it. Yet, you came closer to killing me than anyone before you, and I assure you that I've had my share of very powerful enemies."

"I don't doubt that," she said. "Tell me, why didn't the poison kill you? You managed to stop my blade before I got it into your heart, but there was enough blackwort on that dagger to kill a horse."

Phane laughed again, shaking his head. "You see, this is why you have no hope against me. I'm always prepared. I started taking the antidote for blackwort, as well as a number of other poisons common to this wretched isle, the day I arrived."

"Huh. Well, at least I can take solace in the thought that you know everybody around you wants to see you die."

He smiled his boyish smile again. "Don't you see? *That* is exactly what makes it so delicious."

"You're damaged, Phane."

"Enough distractions. I would like to hear more about this Goiri bone that so effectively nullified my magical defenses. For instance, tell me about the size of the bone you used."

Isabel hesitated, but Phane cocked his head, looking up at the staircase.

"It was a finger bone, maybe an inch long," Isabel said after a moment's more hesitation.

"If I recall correctly, my magic became available to me again once I reached a distance of eight or ten feet from you. Such things usually have power proportional to the size of the item, so it stands to reason that a larger bone might affect a larger area. Does that sound like a reasonable assumption, given your experiences?"

Isabel shrugged. "I suppose."

"Excellent! I find my mind is afire with all of the possibilities this legend-come-true represents, which brings me to my next question. Where did you find the remains of the Goiri?"

Isabel shook her head slowly.

"Let's not forget what's at stake here," Phane said.

"I understand perfectly well what's at stake."

Phane nodded thoughtfully. "I suppose you do, and I can see that I've reached a limit of sorts on your willingness to be persuaded by threats against your friend. Honestly, if I were dealing with almost anyone else, I would have Wren dragged down here and skinned alive on this very table while you watched. Unfortunately, I don't believe doing such a thing would serve my purposes." He regarded Isabel for several moments before nodding to himself. "Well, no matter. I can guess at the likely location of the Goiri's remains. From there, it won't take long to find them. After that, it's just a matter of sending someone to retrieve them for me."

This time it was Isabel's turn to laugh. "Good luck with that. I wouldn't send anyone you can't afford to lose."

Phane smiled his boyish smile. "My Dear Isabel, *I* am the only person that I can't afford to lose."

"And *that* is why you'll never win this war."

He shook his head, feigning sadness. "Don't you see? I've already won. Everything is proceeding according to my designs. Thanks to your rather ambitious attempt on my life, the final keystone is within my grasp. Once I have it, we will travel to the Nether Gate and I will call forth a demonic horde sufficient to scour the Seven Isles of my enemies. This war is nearly over, Isabel, but before it is, everyone you care about will be devoured."

"You keep telling yourself that, Phane. Alexander will defeat you, of that I have no doubt."

"Your confidence in him is touching. One day, I hope you'll hold me in such high regard."

"Now I know you're delusional."

"Don't be so certain, Isabel. Over the course of my life, I've turned many people away from the empty promises of the light. Once people get a taste for the raw power offered by the netherworld, they tend to embrace it with a kind of commitment bordering on fanaticism. I expect you will be no different."

"I'll die before I'll serve the darkness."

"I know you believe that now, but that's exactly why you'll become not just a servant of the darkness, but its champion. At present, your commitment to the light is nearly perfect, so when you fall, your own faith in the light and in yourself will be so shattered that you'll embrace the darkness completely and without reservation because you'll believe that you deserve it, you'll believe that the only punishment sufficient for your crimes is the forfeiture of your soul to the netherworld. And there you will find solace, acceptance, and understanding."

"You have some grand plans, I'll give you that," Isabel said. "The trouble is, I don't see how you plan to get from here to there."

"I'm so glad you asked," Phane said with an unabashed smile. "Issa, go see if the child is finished with her bath. If so, bring her here."

Issa bowed and then vanished, wisps of black smoke dissipating quickly.

"What are you doing, Phane?"

"You didn't think I went to all the trouble of bringing her here just to use as leverage against you in an interrogation, did you? No, I have much bigger plans for her ... and there she is," Phane said, extending his open hand to Wren as she descended the stairs.

"Come here, child."

Wren walked to the corner of the table and stood between Isabel and Phane. "Yes sir?"

"So vulnerable, so young," Phane said softly, motioning to one of the guards. The big, armored man stopped precisely, coming to attention a few steps away.

"What are you doing, Phane?" Isabel said, fear and rage flashing in her eyes.

He ignored her, looking up at the soldier. "Strike the girl across the face with an open hand, hard."

The soldier didn't hesitate, didn't question the order. He hit Wren so hard that she fell sprawling across the floor.

Isabel bolted to her side, rolling her gently over and cradling her head in her lap. "Oh Wren, are you all right?"

She didn't answer, her eyes unfocused, her face red and bleeding from a cut along her cheekbone. Isabel started muttering under her breath, letting Wren's pain fuel her rage. A moment later, she unleashed a light-lance at the soldier, burning a hole through his chest and through the walls of the house until daylight streamed in. The man fell dead without a word.

Phane started clapping slowly, smiling triumphantly. "Well done, Isabel. You've just taken your first step toward the darkness. How did it feel? Did it make you feel powerful?" He leaned forward intently, scrutinizing her while she deliberately let the rage drain away.

"He was just following orders—he was innocent," Phane said. "And you killed him in cold blood."

"No! He wasn't innocent," Isabel shouted. "Any full-grown man who would brutalize a child just because someone told him to isn't innocent. And maybe his violation of the Old Law in this instance didn't warrant death, but his service to you absolutely does. In fact, I'd have no problem killing any of your soldiers—you are the enemy of the Old Law and by extension, so are they. Alexander has already sentenced all of you to death … you just haven't died yet."

Phane tipped his head back and laughed. "Fair enough, I suppose that one can rationalize almost anything—almost." He locked eyes with her, triumph dancing in his golden irises. "You see, the real reason I brought the child here was because I expect you to kill her."

"What!"

"She's the perfect candidate," Phane said with a shrug.

"What are you talking about?" Isabel said, cold seeping into her bones.

"You love her. She's innocent, vulnerable, and completely defenseless in the face of your power. Once you kill her, your spirit will break. You'll no longer be able to look into the light, and if you do, all you will see is condemnation. And in that condemnation, you'll discover the truth of the light … its empty promises will be revealed and you will come to understand that all the light has to offer is judgment.

"You'll struggle against it, but in the end, you'll turn to the darkness and all of your guilt and shame will be washed away. The darkness will never judge you, it will never condemn you. Only then will you truly be free."

"You're insane. I will *never* hurt Wren, and there's nothing you can do to make me."

"I wouldn't be so certain of that," Phane said smugly. "Azugorath is tenacious. Eventually, she will succeed and you will kill your young friend."

"If your pet demon manages to take control of me, I'll just be the weapon, not the murderer."

"You miss the point. The memory of her murder at your hands will live in your mind. You will, no doubt, relive it over and over again until you see it in your sleep. The real question is: Will you ever be able to forgive yourself?

"Ah, it looks like she's waking up. Dierdra, attend to her injuries," Phane said, standing up. He motioned to the dead soldier and his fellow guard carried him from the room.

Dierdra knelt next to Wren and gently inspected her face.

"It doesn't look broken, dear, but you're going to have a nasty bruise. Let's get you over to the couch so I can attend to this properly."

Phane stopped at the door. "Everyone in this fortress belongs to you, Isabel, except me, of course. If anyone displeases you for any reason, feel free to kill them." He left laughing.

***

"I don't understand why he hit me," Wren said.

"Phane's using you to get to me," Isabel said, smoothing her hair back from her forehead. After she and Wren had returned to her bedroom, she'd dismissed her servants and sat down next to Wren on the edge of the bed.

"But why? I don't understand any of this," she said, struggling to keep from crying again. "I'm so scared," she whispered, closing her eyes, squeezing tears from each.

"I know, I'm scared, too."

"Really? You didn't act scared. I remember thinking how brave you were standing up to Prince Phane like that."

"Courage doesn't mean you don't feel fear, it just means you choose a rational course of action in the face of it. Wren, I need you to be brave and I need you to grow up much faster than I would like."

She opened her deep blue eyes and nodded. "I'll do whatever you tell me to."

Isabel shook her head sadly. "No, Wren, I need you to do more than that. I need you to think for yourself. That's the first step. You need to be aware that you're in danger here and you need to be willing and able to make difficult decisions even when you're afraid ... especially when you're afraid."

Wren blinked, then swallowed, nodding timidly.

"I wish I could shield you from all of this, but the truth is, you're the only ally I have here and I need your help. There's so much more at stake than just you and me."

"What can I do?"

"First, you need to understand the situation we're in, so listen carefully. Phane has a very powerful demon, probably buried under that black tower in the center of town, and that demon is trying to get into my mind, trying to control me—and she's winning. She almost made me kill Alexander. That's why I left him and came here, so I wouldn't be a threat to anyone I love, and that's why Phane brought you here. He wants me to kill you."

"Why would you do that?" Wren asked, more tears slipping from her eyes.

"I wouldn't," Isabel said, wiping a tear from her own cheek. "But if I lose control, this demon will make me hurt you."

"But why does Prince Phane care about me?"

"He doesn't," Isabel said. "He wants me to turn against everything I believe in and join him. He thinks I'll do that if he can make me do something so horrible that I would never be able to forgive myself, and he might be right. I don't know how I could live with myself if I killed you."

Wren sniffed back her tears and frowned. "I don't think I really understood what you've been fighting for until right now. I've always thought of evil as something you hear about in stories—make-believe. But it's not, is it? It's real."

Isabel nodded sadly, another tear slipping down her cheek. "This is part of growing up that I didn't want you to have to do, but I'm proud of you. Some people can stare into the face of evil all their lives and never really understand what they're looking at."

"So what are we going to do?"

"I came here to kill Phane. I got a knife into his belly, just not deeply enough. I have a plan to finish the job but I can't do it alone, so I'm trying to call for help. Failing that, we need to escape, and that means we need to find a way out. Since the guards will be watching me carefully, I need you to explore the city for me."

"But won't the guards stop me?"

"No, Phane wants me to kill you; it's an important part of his plan, so he's ordered his men to leave you alone."

"Except when he's ordering them to hit me," she said, touching her cheek tenderly.

"He did that to provoke me, and it worked," Isabel said, shaking her head. "I have to be more careful, I can't let him force my hand like that."

"If you say they won't hurt me, then I believe you, but I'm still afraid of them."

"Good, that fear will keep your mind alert and help you spot danger before it gets too close. I want you to avoid Phane whenever you can, but I need you to explore this place and find a way out of here if there is one. Also, if you can find a knife or two, it would be good to have a weapon."

Wren nodded.

"Tomorrow, we'll go out and look around a bit, both of us. After that, I'll start sending you on errands to get you out of this house and onto the streets."

She nodded again.

"This next thing is going to be hard," Isabel said. "If I don't seem like myself, you need to run away from me and hide until I can regain control. In fact, that's something else I want you to look for, hiding places, both in the house and out in the city."

Wren nodded again.

"You get some rest now. We'll talk more later," she said, offering Wren a reassuring smile.

Isabel went to the balcony and reached out to Slyder. He was perched atop a tree watching the Karth encampment. She sent him into the air, circling higher and wider in an effort to pick up the trail, but the jungle was too thick and the skills of Karth's soldiers were too good to find any trace of their passage. After an hour of searching, she told Slyder to remain in the area, then she returned to her body.

She was sitting on the balcony thinking through her options when Wren joined her.

"I'm not that tired and my face hurts just as much when I lie down as it does when I sit. What're you doing?"

"I was trying to send a message with Slyder, but I can't find my friends."

"When I was in the boat, Lord Reishi came to me and told me he was sending help. Was that just a dream?"

"No, that was him," Isabel said, smiling to mask the lump suddenly welling up in her throat.

"Then why doesn't he come to you now?"

"I don't know," Isabel whispered. "I'm terrified that something horrible has happened."

"Isabel," Wren said, squeezing her hand, "he's Lord Reishi. He's probably just really busy."

Isabel nodded, struggling to keep from crying because she knew that something was wrong. He would have come to her if he could have. The thought of losing him was something she fled from within her own mind. Despair capable of claiming her sanity accompanied that thought—yet another pathway to victory for Azugorath.

Chapter 7

Lacy was miserable. Her hand was healing wrong, leaving it useless and a source of constant pain. She couldn't remember the last time she'd slept through the night. Every time she moved, the pain would wake her and it would be an hour before she could drift back into welcome oblivion. And then there were her dreams. For weeks she'd had visions of her father beseeching her to go to Ithilian, warning her that she was going the wrong way. But nobody would listen to her when she asked to go to Ithilian. Drogan and Commander Arnd had both told her repeatedly that such a voyage was far too dangerous. They assured her that she would be safe on Karth under the protection of Prince Phane and the Regency.

She wasn't so sure. The Regency sailors and now the Regency soldiers had a way of looking at her that made her feel uncomfortable, not the way young men look at young women, but the way the soldiers outside the walls had looked at her the day they'd come to her home and destroyed her quiet little life. At least these soldiers all looked away when Drogan caught them leering at her, but that didn't change what was in their hearts.

The ship had docked at a city on the southwest tip of Karth. Commander Arnd said they would be safer traveling from there to the Regency headquarters fortress. Lacy wanted to ask "Safer from what?" But she knew she wouldn't get an answer, so she held her tongue and waited.

From the looks of the place, the little sea town had recently been converted into a shipyard. The people were busy building more than a dozen warships, and the Regency soldiers seemed intent on pushing the workers to the breaking point. Seeing the working conditions, Lacy began to wonder anew if she was making a terrible mistake by coming here. But then, when she tried to imagine the course she might have taken, she couldn't pick a point in her journey where she would have chosen differently. It was just that so many of her decisions had been made for her, all of them bringing her one step closer to where she stood this very moment.

The journey from the port town took nearly a week. A hundred soldiers rode escort and her covered carriage was armored and well manned. Drogan spent most of the journey with her but he wasn't interested in conversation—not that Drogan was much of a talker in the first place. Lacy passed the time looking out the window at the staggering variety of foliage in the lush jungle.

When they neared their destination, she couldn't see the fortress wall because the carriage didn't offer a forward view, but she did see the heavy stone gates and the array of defensive apertures cut into the hundred-foot tunnel leading through the wall. When the carriage slipped back into the light of day, it turned sharply before coming to a stop. A moment later, a soldier opened the door to the sound of trumpets in the distance.

The soldier offered his hand with a smile and a deferential bow. Unlike the other soldiers, he was wearing a clean and well-pressed uniform with a number of medals prominently displayed on his chest, and was armed with only a bejeweled short sword dangling from his hip.

She took his hand and stepped onto a carpet leading from her carriage to a small white gazebo that was terribly out of place in the austere stone square. Over a dozen high-ranking soldiers awaited her, each accompanied by a woman wearing expensive-looking dresses and jewels. Standing in the center of them all was a very handsome man wearing a dark brown robe that matched the color of his wavy, shoulder-length hair.

"I am Captain Erato," the soldier said, offering her his arm once she'd stepped from the carriage. "Welcome to the Regency headquarters fortress. Please, come with me." He spoke with charm, elegance, and practiced ease. His confidence in such a suddenly formal setting only served to undermine Lacy's.

He walked her to the gazebo, stopping directly in front of the man in the robe. "Prince Phane, Generals and Ladies, it is my honor and privilege to present Princess Lacy Fellenden." With that, Erato stepped back, bowing low and taking a place just outside the gazebo as if standing a ceremonial guard post.

The man in the robe smiled with such pure, innocent joy that Lacy felt a little flutter in her stomach. "I am Phane Reishi. Welcome, Princess Lacy. You are safe. Zuhl and his brutes can't hurt you anymore."

Lacy looked around, a bit bewildered. "Thank you, Prince Phane ..."

"Ah, please call me Phane. It would be so refreshing to dispose of titles and formalities. May I call you Lacy?"

She blinked, looking around at the formality of her welcome and feeling even more unsure of herself. "Of course. I'm grateful for your hospitality, but I've been entrusted with a task by my father and this journey has brought me very far off course."

"Lacy, please," Phane interrupted, "there will be plenty of time to discuss such matters. Let's get you settled in first."

"But," she started to say, emphasizing her frustration with both hands and wincing in pain before she could finish her protest.

"Oh, Lacy, what's happened to your hand? You must be in such agony."

"That's what I'm trying to tell you," Lacy said. "There's something very dark pursuing me. You and your people aren't safe with me here."

Phane smiled like the sunrise, extending his open hand to the wall behind her. "I assure you, there are few who could breach these walls. We are all quite safe here."

Lacy turned and saw the wall for the first time, a hundred feet tall and as sheer as a cliff. From the light at the other end of the tunnel, she could only guess that it was a hundred feet thick as well. She turned completely away from the greeting committee and stared in wonder at the massive fortification. Phane silently stepped up beside her, smiling in feigned wonder.

"How?"

"In truth, I don't really know," Phane said. "These walls were built long ago, though I suspect magic played a role."

"If we'd had walls like these, my people would have survived Zuhl's barbarity."

"Lacy, let me take a look at your hand."

She frowned, hesitating for only a moment before holding up her broken hand for him to examine.

He was gentle, cringing when his probing caused her the slightest twinge of pain. After a moment, he nodded to himself, waving his hand at the open air beside them. A door opened with a soft pop.

Lacy gasped in surprise. She'd seen magic since her ordeal had begun but nothing like this. Phane smiled, stepping into his Wizard's Den and motioning for her to wait where she was. After a few moments of rummaging around, he returned, the door vanishing a moment later.

"Drink this," he said, holding out a vial of pale liquid. "It will numb the pain so I can heal your hand."

She looked at her broken, deformed hand, then back at him, hope shining in her eyes. "You can do that?"

"I can indeed, but it will be a very unpleasant experience without this," Phane said, holding out the vial.

Lacy nodded, drinking the contents quickly, then turning her nose up at the bitter taste.

"I know it tastes bad, but I assure you it will ease the pain. Come, sit with me," he said, motioning to the steps of the gazebo. When they were comfortably seated, he held up a white bandage and started to unwind it. "This is a very special bandage," he said. "It will straighten the broken bones in your hand and then mend them correctly. By tomorrow morning, your hand should be fully healed."

"Really?" Lacy asked, feeling a slight dizziness come over her.

"Indeed. Now, give me your hand."

The rest of Lacy's day was a blur. After Phane wrapped the bandage around her broken hand, he guided her back to the carriage before bidding her goodbye and entrusting her to Captain Erato. Drogan was gone, but his absence seemed like more of a curiosity than anything else.

Rolling down the street in the back of the carriage, she could feel the bones in her hand begin to move. Somewhere very far away, she knew she should be in pain, but she wasn't, or more precisely, she didn't seem to care.

Erato drove the carriage into the courtyard of a beautiful house and escorted her inside. A staff of ten met her in the foyer. They treated her like a queen, bowing and averting their eyes as if she might bite. She would have giggled except nothing seemed real.

One of the servants led her to a lavishly decorated room with a bed even bigger and softer than the one she'd left behind in Fellenden. The last thing she remembered was the servant helping her take off her boots. Then she woke to the light of dawn.

At first she didn't even notice. Then it hit her; her hand was healed. It didn't hurt anymore—not even a little bit. A weight lifted and sudden relief washed over her. She had tried to come to terms with her injury, but all she'd really done was deny the crippling nature of it, until now. Now that her hand was healed, the fear of lifelong suffering she might have endured faded away, leaving only gratitude.

She opened the door leading from her bedroom with a smile and found a young woman waiting for her there.

"Would you like a hot bath, My Lady?"

Lacy closed her eyes, trying not to cry. It had been so long since she'd felt safe, let alone clean. She nodded enthusiastically.

***

"My dear Princess, you are a vision of loveliness," Phane said with a wide smile and a deep bow.

She had spent the day surrounded by dozens of servants as they fussed over her new dress. In her former life, Lacy would have thoroughly enjoyed the attention, but now, after all that had happened, it seemed so unnecessary, so frivolous.

People were dying and she was being pampered like a princess. She had tried to just accept the first dress offered, but the seamstress would have none of it. After several hours of trying on dozens of dresses, Lacy found herself caught up in the process like her old self, only to have reality return with a jolt of guilt.

She was a princess. And that had taken on a whole new meaning. In the past, her title had meant that everything she wanted was offered, that everything she needed was provided, that she needn't lift a finger in her own service. Now she understood. Her station was not a privilege but a sacred burden, a duty to preserve and protect her people no matter the cost to herself.

While Captain Erato drove the carriage to Prince Phane's banquet hall, Lacy reminded herself to be cautious. All evidence to the contrary, she couldn't help feeling that events were out of her control, that there was some larger game being played and that she didn't understand the rules.

The banquet hall was magnificent. Crystal chandeliers filled the long, high room with light, and minstrels filled the air with music over the murmur of the crowd. At a glance, most of the men in the room appeared to be Regency officers and the women, their wives.

The evening started with a receiving line, Phane leading her past each and every officer in attendance. By the time they were seated, Lacy's head was swirling with new names and faces. The officers were mostly dour and serious men, many wearing battle scars like badges of honor. Their wives were another matter. Lacy was ashamed to realize that she saw much of her former self in them. None of them seemed the least bit interested in the historic events unfolding across the Seven Isles, focusing instead on clothes and jewelry, gossip, and their husband's place in the pecking order.

The meal was elaborate and long, each course an attempt to showcase the wealth of her host, though she had to admit, some of the food was quite good. Mostly, Lacy endured the evening, biding her time until she could speak with Phane alone and make her case for transport to Ithilian.

Her time came late in the evening after all of the courses had been served and the guests were mingling. Phane drew her aside and offered her a glass of warm liqueur that smelled of cinnamon. They sat in a pair of comfortable chairs in an alcove off to the side of the banquet hall.

Phane smiled disarmingly. "I trust the cuisine was to your liking," he said.

"Everything was delicious. I wanted to thank you for healing my hand. I've been in pain for so long that I forgot what if feels like to be whole."

"You are most welcome," Phane said. "If I may ask, what led you to leave Fellenden?"

Lacy's mind raced. She realized once again that she was out of her depth and had made no plans for questions like this one. While Phane had been nothing but kind and hospitable, she couldn't help remembering all of the old stories about the Reishi Prince, how he had brought down whole kingdoms with a well-placed lie. She wasn't ready to trust him with her greatest secret, even though she suspected that he already knew all about it.

"I was fleeing Zuhl's soldiers," she said. "When they came, my father sent me to Ithilian, hoping I would be safe there, but I never made it. Zuhl captured me and Drogan at sea. I'd all but given up when your warships rescued us."

"That must have been such an awful ordeal," Phane said. "I'm just grateful that my people were in a position to help you."

"Me too. Thank you," Lacy said, pausing to gather her courage before making her request. "I need to get to Ithilian. Will you help me?"

"Of course, of course. It's just that the oceans are very dangerous right now. Between Zuhl's fleet and the Reishi Protectorate Navy, not to mention the pirates of Tyr, I wouldn't be able to guarantee your safety. At least, not yet anyway."

"What do you mean?"

"Oh, I've been building warships all winter, but my fleet isn't quite ready yet. Once it is, I'll be able to send you to Ithilian aboard an armada capable of fending off any of our enemies."

Lacy frowned, staring into her rapidly cooling drink. It sounded so plausible.

"You spoke of something dark chasing you," Phane prodded gently.

Lacy nodded, her mind focusing on the next lie she was going to tell. "When the soldiers came, they offered us peace if my father would give me over to them. He refused, and I think that made Zuhl mad. He's sent soldiers, dragons, and demons after me ever since. One in particular is especially terrifying. It took control of the wizard I was traveling with and eventually killed him. It said its name is Rankosi."

Phane sat forward urgently, slightly wild-eyed. "Hush. Don't ever speak that name aloud … it can hear you," he whispered, scanning the room.

"What do you mean?" Lacy asked, fear flooding into her belly.

"The creature you speak of is terribly dangerous," Phane said, shaking his head in dismay. "If Zuhl can summon a shade, then things are much worse than I feared."

"What's a shade?"

"There are three of them, brothers, agents of the netherworld, lieutenants of the Master himself," Phane whispered. "Sadly, my father used them to terrible effect in the war. Of all the things he ever summoned from the depths of darkness, the shades were the worst. If Zuhl has discovered the means of summoning such a creature, then he's become far more powerful than I thought."

"Can you defeat him?" Lacy asked.

"I don't know," Phane said after a long pause, shaking his head sadly. "I'm doing all that I can to stand against his unprovoked aggression, but his army is vast and his power ... well, I just don't know."

"But there must be a way," Lacy said. "So many people are suffering. There has to be a way."

"I know how you feel," Phane said, swallowing his sadness with visible effort. "I'd like to show you something." He stood, pausing to collect his emotions before opening his Wizard's Den, taking her by the hand and leading her into the little room.

"This is a very special mirror, made for me as a gift a long time ago. With it, I can see across great distances." He touched the frame and the surface of the mirror shimmered. He concentrated and the image came into focus over Fellenden, rapidly narrowing in on the capital city. Lacy gasped when she saw the scope of destruction that had befallen her home, but then the image came into focus again and she put her hand over her mouth, tears falling from her eyes when she saw her brother.

"He's alive!"

A weight she didn't even know she'd been carrying lifted, leaving her feeling light and hopeful for the first time in a long time.

"Yes, and he's done quite well for your people," Phane said. "The woman seated at the head of the table is my cousin, Queen Abigail Ruatha. She's leading my army against Zuhl's invasion of Fellenden, with significant success, I must say.

"Listen ..." he touched the mirror and Lacy heard her brother speak.

"I would have Fellenden's legions lead the attack."

"Torin, your people have been through so much," Abigail said. "I'm impressed that you've been able to assemble four legions in such short order, but they aren't well trained and they have little experience."

"This is our home," Torin said. "What our people lack in experience, they'll more than make up for in commitment to victory."

"That's what I'm afraid of," Abigail said. "If you throw your people against the walls of Irondale, thousands will die and we can't afford that. We're terribly outnumbered and we need every single soldier we have to survive the day so they can stand with us in the next battle, and the one after that. I know you want blood—if your legions lead this attack, I fear you will have it."

"I concur with Lady Abigail," Magda said.

"As do I," Conner said. "We don't have to fight the enemy, we just have to kill them. That's something Alex—"

Phane touched the frame quickly and the image vanished.

"Who was the older woman?" Lacy asked, reaching for the empty mirror as if she might touch her brother's face.

"Magda Reishi," Phane said. "She's not actually of Reishi blood, but by long tradition, her coven takes the name to honor my mother, the founder of her order."

"They're planning an attack," Lacy said. "How could Torin have raised four legions? Our father only had one legion and most of them died when Zuhl attacked."

"You'd be surprised what people will do when faced with annihilation," Phane said. "I have great faith in Abigail. She'll lead them to victory ... at least in this battle."

"She seems so strong," Lacy said. "She can't be more than a year older than I am."

"I'm very proud of her," Phane said. "For one so young to stand so bravely in the face of such horror ... well, it's inspiring. But even with the sacrifices of so many good people, I fear it won't be enough. If only ..." He stopped, turning slightly away from her and shaking his head.

"Yes? If only what?"

With a gesture, the door to his Wizard's Den closed. "What I'm about to tell you must remain a secret," he said, facing her intently. "If Zuhl were to learn of this ... I shudder to think."

Phane took a deep breath and held it for a moment before nodding to himself and sighing in resignation. "My father created a device called the Nether Gate. A dark and evil creation to be sure, but possessed of such power that I believe it may be the only way to defeat Zuhl. I'm wary of it, afraid even, but I can't think of an alternative, especially if Zuhl has learned how to summon the shades."

Lacy felt a chill crawl up her spine, beads of sweat suddenly rolling down her back.

"What does it do?" she asked, fearing the answer.

"It opens a gate to the netherworld," Phane said, holding her eyes with his.

Lacy shook her head in horror, taking an involuntary step back, entirely unable to disguise her feelings. "How would that help anyone?"

"I understand your fear and I share it," Phane said. "Believe me when I tell you that I've seen enough darkness to last several lifetimes. I would never suggest such a thing lightly. The Nether Gate allows the person who opens it to control the creatures brought forth and then send them back where they belong. With such power, I could end Zuhl's reign of terror in short order." He turned away in exasperation, shaking his head and looking at the ceiling. "Unfortunately, I only have two of the three keystones I need to open it."

A thrill of pure terror raced through Lacy at the mention of the keystone, the very same item that Rankosi was searching for and believed to be contained in the box she was carrying. All of the ramifications of failing her task tumbled through her mind. In the wrong hands, such power could end the world. Even in the right hands, little good could come from the netherworld. The weight of her burden magnified tenfold in that moment. Her father had impressed upon her the importance of her task. Only now did she fully comprehend just how much he had entrusted her with.

Phane was watching her reaction intently, scrutinizing her every gesture. The stories of his legendary deceit played in the back of her mind. She schooled her emotions, willing steadiness into her voice.

"Do you know where the last keystone is?"

"I have my suspicions," he said, "but it's been shielded by powerful magic. Even with my mirror, I've been unable to find it."

"Maybe that's for the best," Lacy said. "It sounds so dangerous." Her knees began to tremble.

"Indeed it is," Phane said. "And perhaps you're right. To my knowledge, my father never actually opened the Nether Gate, so there's no telling what would happen. Tragically, without it, Zuhl will surely wear the world down, starting with the Isle of Fellenden."

He touched the mirror frame again and the scene changed, showing the vast horde of soldiers assembled near Crescent Bay on the Isle of Zuhl.

"He has so many soldiers," Phane said, shaking his head in dismay. "Worse, he's built ships from your own Iron Oak Forest capable of delivering his armies to any shore in the world." The scene shifted to five enormous warships being loaded with supplies and soldiers. "His port is nearly thawed. It won't be long before his army spreads over the Seven Isles like a plague."

Lacy knew Zuhl had a big army, but she never imagined such a horde. She didn't know there were that many people in all the world, let alone soldiers preparing to invade her home. Seeing the vastness of the enemy's numbers, she began to wonder if maybe the Nether Gate *was* the only path to salvation.

"I apologize, Lacy. I meant for this to be a light and joyous evening and I've ruined it with talk of war. Can you forgive me?"

"There's nothing to forgive," Lacy said. "People depend on the decisions we make for their very lives. Our focus should be on their protection rather than our own comfort."

"Spoken like a true princess," Phane said with a warm smile. "So many who aspire to power do so for the wrong reasons. It's refreshing to find a kindred spirit in you. Perhaps together we'll find a way to defeat Zuhl without enlisting the aid of the netherworld."

Lacy's mind swirled with questions during her ride back to her quarters. Phane had been nothing but hospitable, he'd healed her crippled hand, and he'd made her feel safe for the first time in a long time. And yet, the first thing on his mind was the Nether Gate and by extension the box she was secretly carrying.

After returning to her bedroom and changing out of her dress, she dismissed her staff and found her pack, still stuffed under her bed where she'd left it. She pulled the black box from its hiding place. Such a small thing, and yet it contained the future of the entire world. She looked at the box closely, frowning for a moment. She'd been carrying it for so long but had only really looked at it closely once or twice ... and this time it seemed somehow different. Unable to place her odd feeling, she deliberately hardened her resolve, wrapping the box carefully before putting it back in her pack.

She spent several minutes facing her choices … just as they were, ugly and messy. War with men and wizards she could almost understand, but war with the netherworld was the height of madness. Her certainty grew slowly, bubbling up from a place within her that she'd rarely heard from before.

Her father had sent her to take the keystone to Ithilian so the wizards could make sure that it was never, ever used. That was her mission. Keep the keystone in the box. She recommitted herself to ensuring that it was never opened, even if it cost her everything.

A few days passed without event. Phane was entirely absent and her entourage was entirely present, fussing over her comfort, clothes, meals and everything else they could be concerned about until Lacy finally had enough and locked herself in her room for a few minutes of privacy.

Even that didn't last. Not long after she'd escaped the smothering attention of her staff, there was a knock at the door. Lacy didn't anger easily, but her patience was wearing thin. She stomped over to the door and threw it open, expecting to find her maidservant, but instead found herself blinking in disbelief at the person standing in her hallway.

"Lacy? Is that you?" the young woman said, smiling with recognition. She was petite with pale skin, curly black hair, and slate-grey eyes.

"Evelyn?" Lacy said, unsure what to make of the sudden surprise. "Evelyn Ithilian? Is that really you?"

Evelyn threw her arms around Lacy and hugged her tightly. "We've been so worried about you." She held her by the shoulders at arm's length. "How long has it been since we played together as children?"

Lacy's mind reeled. "It seems like forever. Come in."

"Prince Phane went to great lengths to rescue you from Zuhl," Evelyn said, looking at her room appraisingly.

"I'm sorry, what are you doing here?" Lacy asked.

Evelyn giggled with a shrug. "I came here for you."

"What do you mean?"

"When my father learned you'd been rescued by Phane, he sent a small fleet to escort you home. He let me ride along so you'd have a familiar face to greet you. We arrived this morning. Prince Phane was gracious enough to let me surprise you with the news."

"So you're here to take me back to Ithilian?" Lacy asked. "And Phane's all right with this?"

"Sure, why wouldn't he be?"

Lacy shrugged. "No reason. He just said he wanted to wait until his armada was finished."

"He's satisfied that our fleet can protect you, so you're free to come home with me," Evelyn said with a wide smile.

Lacy sat down, feeling a little overwhelmed by the sudden turn of events. She so wanted it to be true.

"There's just one thing, Lacy."

Somewhere in the back of her mind, Lacy noted that her naiveté was beginning to fade.

"What's that?"

Evelyn sat down close to her, leaning in to whisper. "You were sent for a box. Do you have it?"

Lacy got very still.

"My father says it contains a key to part of an ancient weapon we found on Ithilian. It's the last piece we need to make it work. If we had it, Zuhl would be finished for good."

Lacy could feel her heart beating in her head. She hadn't heard this one before. It made her wonder if anything she thought she knew was real.

"Lacy, do you have it?" Evelyn asked, with just a hint of impatience. "If you can just open it, I'll be able to send word home so my father can plan his attack."

So many 'what ifs' tumbled through Lacy's mind.

Finally, she smiled at Evelyn and said, "Do you remember that time we went camping when we were children? Conner caught ten fish that day. Somehow cooking the food ourselves made it taste so much better."

Evelyn hesitated for a moment. "Yes, of course, I remember. It's one of my fondest memories."

Lacy stood, drawing her dagger.

"Who are you? Who do you work for?"

"You are becoming tiresome," she said, the quality of her voice changing. "Open the box. Open it right now."

"Rankosi," Lacy said, shaking her head defiantly. "I'll never open that box."

The woman surged forward, transforming into a man as she moved, taking Lacy by the throat and wrist at the same time, lifting her from the ground.

"Open the box or I will find your brother and torture him to death."

Lacy was choking, trying to get a full breath. She walked up Rankosi's body, planted her feet squarely in his chest and pushed out of his grasp, falling hard. He stood over her, looking down with limitless contempt.

"He'll die anyway if I open that box," Lacy said, her voice cracking.

There was a knock at the door.

"Princess? Are you all right? We heard a commotion. Can we help with anything?" her maidservant said.

"You'll all die anyway," Rankosi said. "I'll be watching. I'll be waiting. And I absolutely intend to take my time with you."

"Princess Lacy?" her maidservant said.

Rankosi left through the window, vaulting over the railing even though her room was on the third story.

"I'm fine, just clumsy is all," Lacy said through the door.

She was anything but fine.

Chapter 8

"Will you look at that," Hod said. "I've heard tell of the city before but I always thought the stories were a bit much … now I know different."

Alexander sent his mind to Chloe to borrow her eyes. After a week on the road, his first glimpse of the Andalian capital city told him it was built with magic.

The city rested in a bowl carved out of the westernmost mountain in a chain of peaks that rivaled the Pinnacles for height, but were much broader at the base.

Steep cliffs rose a thousand feet, culminating in extravagant estates carved into the bedrock edge of the plateau and providing their owners with breathtaking views of the Andalian plains. The entire front half of the city was bordered by these estates, while the rear half was bordered by cliffs rising another thousand feet above the city, culminating in the Andalian palace.

A free-flowing waterfall poured out of the center of the semicircle of estates and fell to the lake below, spraying in the wind and casting a vibrant rainbow in the evening sun. From Alexander's view, it would have seemed magical and idyllic if he hadn't been looking at it through the bars of a cage.

"Impressive," he said. And it was. He doubted that any army could conquer such a place … at least not without the aid of magic.

"It's said that the city was here before men walked the world," Hod said.

"How so?" Alexander asked, his curiosity piqued.

"It's just a folk tale, really," Hod said. "As the story goes, men found the city where it stands, abandoned and empty. Some of the buildings were worn with age but most were still intact, so people just moved in and made them their own. Always seemed far-fetched to me … until now." He looked up at the half-ring of lavish houses lining the front cliffs and shook his head. "Seems hard to believe that men could build such a place."

Alexander just smiled. He knew better, but it wouldn't serve him to speak of it. The wagons rumbled up the road, through a fortress gate that looked rudimentary compared to the city itself, and into a wide tunnel cut into the bedrock of the cliff face. The well-traveled tunnel was dark and dank and appeared to be the road leading to the city above. It ran for several hundred feet, rising on a gradual grade, repeatedly turning back on itself as it continued upward. He counted forty switchbacks before they came to the final ramp leading to the surface of the city.

Finally, the caravan emerged onto a long straight road running beside the canal that fed the waterfall … and into a city from a fairy tale.

Alexander had wondered at the lack of gates until he saw the giant locks set alongside the river. Within minutes, the city's defenders could divert the entire flow of canal water into the tunnel, flooding it completely and ending any chance of invasion by that route.

After marveling at the simplicity and effectiveness of the city's defenses, Alexander started to take note of the buildings themselves. Their construction was unlike anything he'd ever seen, simple yet elegant, the grey stone seeming to flow like water in graceful arches that showed no sign of mortar or seam. It was a blend of artistry and function, beauty and purpose; the entire city seemed to form a whole, as if it had been planned in meticulous detail and then built all at once.

As he marveled at the architecture and wondered at the craftsmanship, he started to notice other things that were less inspiring. A signboard running for several dozen feet along the road was covered with wanted posters, most with sketches of people accused of crimes, some with just a name. When he looked closer, he saw that most of the outlaws were accused of sedition or treason—crimes against the state rather than against other citizens.

The caravan rumbled past a man on a corner wearing a smock emblazoned with the crest of the House of Andalia. "Another child has gone missing," he cried. "The bandit threat has reached into the city and the overseers need your help. Remember, it's your duty to report suspicious activity to the authorities." He paused to catch his breath and then repeated the message.

People stood aside as the wagons passed, some bowing their heads in fear or deference; most of those people were wearing collars like the one around Alexander's neck. The better-dressed people openly watched them roll by, some jeering and taunting, others appraising the merchandise.

When a man wearing a collar stumbled and bumped into a man who was wearing extravagant finery, he apologized profusely, but the extravagantly dressed man shouted obscenities at him until two men in uniform approached. They talked for a moment, then the well-dressed man handed over a few coins. The men in uniforms turned to the man wearing the collar.

"Please, I just stumbled," he begged.

Without a word, the two men in uniform beat him until he was broken and bloody. All the while, the man in finery watched with smug satisfaction.

"All hail the Emperor of Andalia," another town crier shouted as they rolled past.

"How's Jack doing?" Alexander asked Chloe in his mind.

"He's riding on top of your cage, My Love."

"Good. Tell him to get established in the city so he can walk around without being harassed by the authorities. I need him to start gathering information for me as soon as possible."

"I will tell him," Chloe said. "Send me your eyes again. I wish to show you something."

Through her eyes, he saw the palace a thousand feet over the city perched along the top of the back cliff. It was built of the same flowing grey stone but with even more intricate artistry and beauty, especially with the evening sun shining off its walls. Cut in the center of the cliff was a channel guiding a torrent of water flowing from behind the palace into the canal running through the center of the city. Along either side of the waterfall ran a set of tracks. Alexander marveled as he watched a glass-encased carriage being pulled up the tracks by a set of stout ropes.

"That's where the king will be," he said.

"What's your plan?"

"I don't know yet, Little One. I need to gather some more information before I decide. For such a beautiful city, it's inhabited by some pretty ugly people, and I suspect the ugliest of all live up there."

As the caravan turned off the main road, several of the men in Alexander's cage turned toward a commotion at the back of the wagon.

"What was that?" Hod asked.

Alexander just shrugged, smiling to himself as he watched Jack's colors disappear into the side streets. A few minutes later, the caravan came to a stop within a walled square, clearly of later construction since it was made of brick and mortar. Once the entire caravan had entered, the gate was closed and the guards started opening the cages and ordering everyone out into the square. They were brusque and expected obedience but also took care to avoid harming the new slaves as they lined them up in front of a raised platform. A few minutes after the last of the slaves had been organized, a horn blew and the slavers demanded silence.

A man of slight build with a narrow face, oversized nose and angular features stepped up to the podium and surveyed the crowd before him. His short hair was grey and black, his neatly trimmed mustache was silver, and he wore simple grey clothes that would have been almost drab except that they were tailored to fit perfectly and made of very fine cloth. Mostly, Alexander noted the expansive colors surrounding the man. He was a mage.

"I am the Babachenko, the Voice of the King and the First Acuna. Whatever life you had before this day, it has ended. From this point forward, you will have the privilege and absolute security of serving the Andalian Empire.

"You no longer need to fear going hungry. You will never have to sleep in the cold again. All of your needs will be provided for by the generosity of the King. You need not fret or worry over the future because you no longer bear the burden of responsibility for your life. The King will carry that weight for you. You are free.

"So many misguided souls make bad decisions—decisions that lead to ruin for themselves and their families. You no longer need fear your own ignorance for you will be guided by the infinite wisdom and benevolence of the King. You can breathe easy knowing that all of those difficult choices that plague so many of the less fortunate in this world will be made for you, and with far greater care and understanding.

"The King, His Most Merciful and Excellent Majesty, welcomes you into his home and embraces you as his children. All he asks in return is loyalty and obedience, as any father should expect from his children."

With that, he bowed and left the stage. Another man, this one heavy to the point of losing breath from the exertion of walking to the podium, shuffled up and wheezed a few times before speaking.

"Your guild representative will show you to your quarters and prepare your records and papers. Once those tasks are complete, you will be given a meal.

Tomorrow, you will go to auction." He paused, breathing heavily for several moments before continuing.

"Obedience is expected, and remember, the Acuna hears all." With that, he shuffled off, wheezing.

Alexander listened to the entire thing with a sense of dismay and rage boiling in the pit of his belly. He could tell from the Babachenko's colors that he didn't believe a word of his speech, but what really had Alexander concerned was the number of people who seemed genuinely relieved to hear that all of their needs would be provided for … all for the price of their liberty—a price far too many of those around him seemed more than willing to pay.

Several men wearing official-looking uniforms began handing out tiles with numbers cut into them. Once everyone had a tile, one of the officials called for the slaves' attention.

"Around the edge of the square are numbered tables. Go to the table with your number and wait to be called. Be prepared to answer questions about your skills and work history. The clerk at your table will prepare your papers for you. It's vital that you safeguard your papers and keep them with you at all times. Any overseer can ask you for them at any time and you are required to present them or face immediate detention."

What followed was an exercise in frustration. Lines formed amid pushing and shoving for position while disinterested guild representatives asked each person the same series of questions, writing down the answers with almost deliberate slothfulness.

Alexander picked Anja out of the crowd and made his way toward her. He approached the man at the end of her line, smiling amiably. "My sister is in this line and I have a number for that line over there," Alexander said. "I'll trade you numbers. The other line is shorter."

The man frowned at Alexander suspiciously for a moment, looking from Alexander's number to the line and back again before he held out his tile and took Alexander's without a word.

Alexander casually walked to Anja and tapped her on the shoulder. She turned with fury in her eyes that melted into relief.

"Hey, no cutting in line," a man behind her said.

"Never intended to," Alexander said with a smile, motioning for Anja to follow him to the back of the line.

"I don't like this place," she said. "I don't want to be a slave, even if they are going to take care of me."

"I understand completely," Alexander said. "I don't expect to be here for very long, but we might be able to do some good while we're here."

Anja's brow furrowed deeply, but she didn't say anything.

"I need you to behave," Alexander whispered. "Don't draw attention to yourself. Do as you're told. And whatever you do, don't kill anyone. Can you do that?"

"Maybe … it all depends on how they treat me."

"From the looks of things, they actually value their slaves. Just do the work they give you and don't draw attention to yourself."

"I don't want to be a slave."

Alexander just looked at her until she frowned again, looking down at the ground.

"I know, I should've stayed at home," she said. "But I'm glad I didn't. When you decide it's time to kill these people, you're going to need my help ... if I can get this stupid collar off."

"I don't think that'll be a problem," Alexander said.

"What do you mean?"

Alexander just smiled and gave her a wink.

"You mean you could have taken these things off before?" She was starting to get angry again.

Alexander nodded, putting his finger over his lips.

"Why didn't you?"

"Because I decided that I have business here," he said.

"What kind of business?"

"War," he whispered.

That answer seemed to satisfy her. She fell silent for a while as the line slowly moved toward the table.

Then she asked, "What do you want me to do?"

"Mostly, I want you to avoid drawing attention to yourself," he said again. "Aside from that, keep your eyes and ears open. Gather what information you can without getting in trouble. Chloe will pass messages to you. Jack is here as well. Just remember, he's probably going to pretend like he doesn't know you if he sees you, so act like you don't know him either. And if anybody asks, your name is Anja Valentine."

"Next," said a very bored-looking older man seated behind the table. Anja looked back at Alexander, who nodded for her to go ahead.

He could see the frustration building in her colors as the man asked a series of questions, often making up answers for her when she failed to provide an answer that fit his preconceived idea of the available options. After checking and rechecking the documents, he handed Anja her papers and motioned towards the door.

"Next."

Alexander stepped up to the table, and watched as Anja was led away. She looked back before entering the building. He nodded approvingly.

The man looked him up and down.

"Gender, male," he said, checking a box on his form. "Name?"

"Alex Valentine."

"Skills?"

"I was raised on a ranch."

The man looked up, his irritation blunted by his disinterest.

"No call for that ... we'll say you're a miner."

"But I don't know anything about mining," Alexander said.

The man just shrugged, scribbling on the form.

"Here's your guild chit," he said, handing Alexander a tile with a circle engraved on it. "Keep this on you at all times. If you're caught without it, you'll be detained by the authorities. It entitles you to room and board provided by the Slave Guild. Do you understand?"

"Slave Guild?"

"Yes, you're now a member of the Slave Guild," the man said. "Whoever buys you tomorrow will be required to pay your wages to the guild so they can provide you with your necessities. Move along."

The man stood up, gathering his paperwork and motioning Alexander toward the door. A man dressed in a grey uniform stood just inside the entrance. Another stood at the point where the corridor met a hallway. "Move along," he said, motioning for Alexander to turn right.

Down the hall, he came to the end of another line and another uniformed man.

"What's this line for?" Alexander asked.

"No talking," the man said.

"I'm just curious."

"Do you see this emblem?" the man said, stepping closer to Alexander, pointing to the starburst on his collar.

"Sure," Alexander said, working hard to keep his tone amiable.

"This means I'm an overseer. And that means you do as I say, slave. Understand?" He put his hand on the club hanging from his belt.

"Yes, I think I do," Alexander said, stepping into line and reminding himself of his cautionary words to Anja.

The line moved slowly as, one by one, men were admitted to a room at the end of the hall. Finally, the door opened and another overseer looked at Alexander with a sense of relief that he was the last man in the line.

"About time," the overseer behind Alexander muttered.

"Step up to the counter," the overseer in the room said.

Behind the counter stood a completely unremarkable man who looked through Alexander like he wasn't even there.

"Show me your chit," he said.

Alexander placed the tile on the counter. The man nodded, turning to a set of bins behind him. "Get undressed," he said.

"Why?" Alexander asked.

The overseer rapped his club on the counter. "Do as you're told, slave."

Alexander gritted his teeth and started to take off his belt.

The man placed a stack of clothes on the counter. "One pair of pants, one shirt, one smock, one pair of boots. Put them on."

"Why can't I keep my own clothes?"

The overseer jabbed him in the ribs with his club. "Do as you're told or I'll beat you senseless and nobody will buy you tomorrow. If you don't sell, we'll chop you up and feed you to the livestock. Understand, slave?"

Alexander nodded.

"It wouldn't be fair to the other slaves to let you keep your clothes," the man behind the counter said. "Only through equality will everyone's needs be met." It sounded like something he'd said often. "Take off your ring."

Alexander swallowed, looking at the Keep Master's ring, before reluctantly setting it on the counter. The overseer beside him relaxed almost begrudgingly.

"I'm surprised the Lancers didn't take this," the man behind the counter said, pocketing the ring.

"Mark this man, Little One," Alexander said silently. "Tell Jack that he took my ring and I want it back."

"I don't like these people, My Love."

"Me neither."

Alexander tried to put on the boots he'd been given but they were too small for his feet.

"These don't fit," he said.

The overseer bristled, raising his club, but the man behind the counter nodded to himself, motioning for Alexander to give him the boots.

"Try these," he said, handing him a much larger pair.

"They don't fit either," Alexander said, his feet swimming in the oversized boots.

The man shrugged. "Looks like they fit to me. Take your chit and go through that door."

The overseer followed Alexander down the hall to another open door that led into a large room filled with long tables, each flanked by a pair of benches. The overseer just inside the room motioned for Alexander to get into another line wrapping around the walls of the room.

As he walked away from the door, he heard the other overseer say, "Keep an eye on that one, he's a troublemaker." They both glared at him until he took his place in line.

It moved slowly to a row of windows in the wall. "Show me your chit," the man in the first window said, then handed Alexander a bowl and a spoon. At the next window, a man slopped gruel into his bowl. "Move along," he said, without looking up. The man in the next window put a piece of moldy bread in his bowl and motioned for him to continue down the line. The man in the final window handed him a wooden cup half filled with water.

Alexander scanned the room and saw Kalderson. Without drawing attention, he shuffled over to the captain, trying not to trip in his oversized boots, and sat down next to him.

Kalderson started to say something, but caught himself and nodded to Alexander.

"Just keep your head down and be ready," Alexander whispered, tearing off a bit of mold from his bread.

"No talking!" one of the overseers shouted from across the room.

Alexander didn't look up, instead focusing on his meager meal. It was bland and not nearly enough but it was better than nothing. He hoped Anja hadn't lost her temper, but he suspected that he would have heard something if she had.

After their meal, they were led down a corridor lined with locked doors until they reached one that stood open. Inside was a large room with barred windows across the top of the back wall. Hay was piled a foot deep along the sides of the room and there was an overseer standing by a stack of threadbare blankets beside the door.

"Take one and move along," he said, as if those were the only words in his vocabulary.

Alexander found a spot and sat down next to Kalderson, motioning for him to remain quiet. The overseer stood at the door until the room was full, then closed it and locked them in for the night.

"What are we going to do?" Kalderson whispered in the dark.

"Try to keep your men together," Alexander said. "It may take some time to figure this place out, but when I do, I want you to be ready to move."

Kalderson nodded reluctantly.

Alexander lay down, wrapping his blanket around himself. He fell asleep to the sounds of grown men crying quietly in the dark.

The following morning, after a thoroughly unsatisfying breakfast of mush and water, the overseers led the new slaves into the yard, ordering them to line up in orderly fashion. Alexander caught a glimpse of Anja and tried to reassure her with a smile but she just glowered at him.

A number of well-dressed men sat at a table on the raised platform along one end of the yard. Alexander recognized only the one known as the Babachenko. He was wearing the same austere grey uniform he'd worn the day before. The men were eating a leisurely breakfast. Bacon, sausage, eggs, ham, biscuits, potatoes and juice all served on fine silver and crystal. Slaves attended to these men's every need. None of them were bashful about eating their fill, seeming to relish the meal while the slaves assembled before them could hear the rumblings from their own stomachs.

Even after all the slaves had been lined up and stood waiting while dozens of overseers walked among them, the men at the table continued their meal and lighthearted conversation. The few slaves who muttered obscenities under their breath were beaten to their knees and left where they lay. Alexander watched fear and rage ripple through the colors of the men around him while he struggled to school his own indignation. He caught Anja's eye again and slowly shook his head. She looked away, her colors rippling with emotion.

Finally, the Babachenko stood and strolled casually to the edge of the platform, appraising the slaves.

"It is my privilege to introduce to you three of the most distinguished servants of the Andalian Empire. Each of these men has contributed in immeasurable ways to the prosperity enjoyed by every subject of the crown. Their sacrifices are matched only by their loyalty to our people and the Andalian way of life.

"Through these men, you will contribute to our collective prosperity, fulfilling the basic needs of each and every subject, and in so doing, ensuring that all of your needs are met as well.

"I give you Lord Alden Kendrick, holder of the Andalian Shipwright Charter; Lord Nigel Mohan, holder of the Andalian Cartage Charter; and Lord Titus Grant, holder of the Andalian Mining Charter." Each man rose in turn, smiling graciously and bowing slightly. The colors of the first two were about what Alexander expected, muddy and dark. Then the third man stood—he had no colors at all.

Alexander's mind raced at the implications.

"Before we begin," the Babachenko continued, "I would like to share with you a piece of profound wisdom spoken to me this very morning by His Most Excellent Majesty, the King of Andalia. He called me close to him so that he could whisper this eternal secret to me—a secret that I will share with you now. He said: Always remember, service *is* prosperity.

"I share this gift of divine wisdom with you today in the sincere hope that you will think on it often and endeavor to embody the spirit of selfless service exemplified by our humble king."

The rest of the men at the table rose, applauding the Babachenko's speech. Alexander could see from their colors that they were entirely disingenuous, but they did put on a good show.

The Babachenko walked the three nobles down the rows of slaves, while the rest of the men at the table prepared to receive their masters' new acquisitions. They took their time inspecting each slave, asking questions and putting their hands on them as if they were livestock. Sometimes they bickered over price with the Babachenko, bidding between them until one of them won, which was usually followed by the other two suggesting that he'd paid too high a price.

After each purchase, the Babachenko made a note in his leather-bound book and an overseer directed the slave to the correct holding area. The few who were not purchased were directed to return to the slave quarters.

Alexander listened to the nobles and the Babachenko chatting when they got close enough.

"So I hear you lost another shipment of silver, Nigel," Titus Grant said, with a gleam of mischief in his eye.

Nigel Mohan spat in the dirt. "Two days ago. That blasted Nightshade is costing me a fortune."

"Let's not forget, that shipment was wages for my shipwrights," Alden Kendrick said. "They've threatened to strike if I can't make payroll this month."

"Can't say I blame them," Grant said. "After all, nobody likes working for free."

Kendrick scowled at him before turning his attention to another slave and looking at his roster. "Says you're a sailor."

"Yes sir," one of Kalderson's men answered.

"I'll take him." Then turning to the Babachenko, he said, "Surely, you can do something to stop Nightshade from disrupting the flow of commerce. The king ordered those ships built and I won't be able to make delivery at this rate … unless you could persuade the Shipwrights Guild to keep working without pay, just until I can arrange another shipment of silver, of course."

"Now, Lord Kendrick, you know as well as I do that the rights of guild members must be protected," the Babachenko said. "However, I agree that bandit raids on the Cartage Company's shipments are becoming a problem."

"Come now, Babachenko, you know full well that this isn't the work of ordinary bandits," Mohan said.

The Babachenko shook his head slowly, considering the man's words carefully. "I'm still not convinced that this Nightshade even exists," he said, holding up his hands to forestall protest. "It seems more likely that he's a fabrication of the bandits plaguing our lands, a persona they've created to give us a ghost to chase."

"Ghosts don't haul off chests full of silver," Mohan said. "Besides, he left a nightshade blossom, just like before, and he disappeared with my silver in the middle of the night without even being noticed by my guards. Ordinary bandits attack outright."

"The man has a point," Grant said, smiling ever so slightly.

"Don't be so smug, Titus," Kendrick said. "Just because you already got paid for that silver, doesn't mean Nightshade isn't a threat to your interests as well."

Grant shrugged innocently. "What can I say? Whoever's doing this seems to prefer coinage to raw ore. I guess I'm just fortunate to be the holder of the mining charter."

Mohan shook his head, turning back to the slaves. "I'll take these three," he said, pointing to the three men standing next to Alexander.

The Babachenko stepped up in front of Alexander next, looking at him closely, a slight frown ghosting across his face. Alexander schooled his nerves while the Babachenko's colors swirled with curiosity and magic. He didn't know the man's calling, but he did know for certain that he was standing before a mage.

Titus Grant checked his roster and looked at Alexander. "Says here you're a miner."

"That's what it says," Alexander said.

Grant cocked his head and smiled slightly. "Well, I guess if you weren't a miner before, you are now. I'll take him."

An overseer tapped Alexander on the shoulder with his club and pointed at the holding area for Titus Grant's purchases. Alexander dutifully shuffled over to the table. Grant's men questioned him about his experience for a minute and then sent him to await their master with the rest of the day's purchases.

Alexander watched carefully as the last of the men were bought. There were only a handful of women remaining in the yard, all of them looking fearful—all except Anja. She was scowling openly until Alexander caught her eye and slowly shook his head.

Kalderson and his remaining sailors had all been purchased by Kendrick, presumably to be sent to the shipyards.

"I'll take all the women. If you gentlemen have no objection, that is," Grant said. "It's so much easier to find good servants when I buy in bulk and then discard the ones that upset my wife."

The rest of the men laughed, heading back toward the table, now set with a steaming hot lunch.

Chapter 9

Alexander lay down in his bunk, exhausted and sore from a long day's work in the mines. The first few days after being purchased by Titus Grant had involved endless paperwork, assessments of his health and strength, tests of his mining knowledge and finally assignment to a work crew digging deep beneath the city itself. Many of the others bought by Grant had been sent to other mines around the country.

Through Chloe, Alexander had remained in contact with Anja and Jack. He counseled Anja to remain calm and to obey. From Jack, he learned a great many things about Andalian culture and political structure.

In the short time since Jack had arrived, he'd managed to obtain papers and join the Minstrels Guild. While many of the practicing minstrels were none too happy about his musical abilities, the nobles were delighted with his first performance in a concert put on the day after he had obtained his guild chit.

The next day, he had nearly a dozen invitations to perform for various nobles and their guests.

Initially, Jack was concerned that his true identity might be revealed, but after his first private performance, he discovered that no one really cared who he was or where he'd come from. They were far more interested in how his music was received by their guests. Jack made sure they were entertained, and he gained valuable access to the homes of the most influential people in Mithel Dour in the process.

"Are you there, Little One?"

"Always, My Love."

"What have you learned today?"

"I've found the forges," Chloe said in his mind. "It seems that they have two different magical forges, one to create force lances, the other to create slave collars."

"Well done. What can you tell me about them?"

"Both are located under the palace. I heard one of the guards call it Crescent Palace. I believe it's named that because of the shape of the building. It's actually built atop a large dam. I have to admit, the view from the palace is breathtaking. On one side is a placid mountain lake framed by snow-capped peaks. The other side looks over the city itself and off to the western horizon. Sunset is particularly beautiful."

"And the forges?"

"They're in the lower level of the palace, accessible only through a single series of very well guarded passages. Neither of the forges appears to have been used for quite some time."

"I wonder why," Alexander mused. "I have to assume they'd be making more lances if they could, so what's stopping them?"

"I don't know, but I'll keep searching."

"I also wonder if the slave collars are tied to the king's Crown like the lances are. If so, we might be able to undo them all with a single stroke."

"I tried to get close to the king, but there were barriers around his chambers that extend even into the aether."

"Really? I didn't know magic could do that."

"I remember stories from the time before man about races that commanded magic in ways that have been lost. The wards around those chambers are subtle and elegantly woven. I doubt any wizard alive today could reproduce them."

"What about the rest of the city? The stonework is like nothing I've ever seen before and it's clearly ancient. Any insight into who or what might have built this place?"

"No, I don't think anyone really knows."

"Any word from Jack?"

"He's been very busy," Chloe said in his mind. "In between performances, he's been gathering information. Oh, and he got your ring back. The man who stole it took it to the market the very next day and sold it. Jack was able to buy it from a jewelry vendor for a pouch of silver."

"That's a relief. How's Anja doing?"

"She was angry at first, but she's making an effort to fit in and do her work. The lady of the house seems to have taken a liking to her—turns out they both have red hair."

"Good. I've been worried about her."

"How are you doing, My Love?"

"I'm tired. Working in a mine is difficult and dangerous. Supervisor Doyle works us hard, but he's careful to make sure we don't get ourselves killed, probably to protect Grant's investment. Speaking of which, have you had any luck with him?"

"I've been watching him off and on for the past few days," Chloe said. "Titus Grant is very adept at manipulating the system to his advantage. He seems to take great pleasure in beating his rivals and even his associates, always looking for a way to get the better end of the deal in any situation.

"I also noticed him slip a note to another man on the street. It happened so quickly that I almost missed it. They passed each other without even so much as a nod, their hands touching for only a moment. I had to get very close to the other man to confirm what I saw."

"What did the other man do after he got the note?"

"He left the city immediately without even looking at it."

"So, Titus Grant has secrets. Not terribly surprising for a man in his position, especially in a place like this, but still interesting. Let Anja know about his suspicious activities and tell her to pay closer attention to what goes on in his house."

"I will, My Love."

"Good night, Chloe," Alexander said, rolling over and clearing his mind. He was asleep within minutes.

***

The next day, Alexander was working beside Hod and another slave named Benny, digging a tunnel, swinging their pickaxes in dogged rhythm while Supervisor Doyle watched. Doyle was a big man with broad shoulders and burly arms. His black hair was usually coated with dirt and his face was worn and pockmarked. While gruff and quick-tempered, he knew his trade, taking care to ensure that the tunnels and shafts were properly shorn up to prevent a cave-in that might claim the lives of his workers.

"Stop," Doyle said. "Step back and let the shovels clear the debris."

Alexander was grateful for the break. He and the other two pickaxes, as Doyle called them, stepped back and let the team of shovel men dig away the rock and dirt they'd knocked loose. The process was the same all day long. Pickaxe the wall until they were standing in a pile of dirt and rock, then let the shovel men load the material into a cart, clearing the way for them to resume their relentless attack on the wall of earth.

As gruff and hard a man as Doyle was, he didn't care what his men did so long as they got the work done. Alexander, Hod, and Benny sat along the wall behind Doyle while the shovels loaded dirt into the cart.

"Doesn't it strike you as odd that we aren't digging through any ore?" Alexander asked.

Hod just shrugged. "Never worked in a mine before. Not sure I'd know what ore was if I saw it."

"We sometimes come across a vein," Benny said. "They just cart it away like the rest of the dirt and rock."

"So what are we digging for?" Alexander asked.

Benny and Hod shrugged in unison.

"You dig because you're told to," Miles said, waiting by the cart being loaded by the shovels. He was a big man who looked like he'd been born in a mine. "If you do good work for long enough, they'll let you join the Miners Guild. Better pay, better quarters, and no more collar."

"How long does that take?" Alexander asked.

"I've been working for nearly ten years," Miles said. "They tell me I'm almost there."

"How'd you become a slave in the first place?" Alexander asked.

"My parents owed Lord Grant a debt, so they gave me up as payment when I turned sixteen," Miles said with feigned indifference.

Alexander felt his blood start to heat up again.

"How about you, Benny?"

"Oh, I was born into slavery," Benny said. "My mom was owned by Lord Grant when I was born, so I belong to him as well."

Alexander took a slow deep breath. "Does that seem right to you?"

"Hey!" Doyle shouted. "I won't have any seditious talk in my mine. I don't need the Acuna poking around in here, so keep your questions to yourself and get back to work."

Miles gave Alexander a warning look to reinforce Doyle's words as the shovels in his detail started pushing the cart out of the tunnel.

Alexander got to his feet with a dozen new questions swirling around in his head as he went back to work. Not long after, the hard, rocky dirt gave way to softer soil that made for easier digging. No sooner had they started making better headway than the ceiling collapsed. Alexander's magic warned him of the danger a moment before it happened and he was able to grab Hod and pull him out of the way, but Benny was buried alive.

Doyle blew his alarm whistle and started working to uncover Benny, yelling for Alexander and Hod to help him. They went to work almost frantically. Alexander could see Benny with his all around sight and his colors were starting to weaken.

"He's under here," Alexander said, breathlessly scooping loose dirt away with his hands.

Doyle didn't argue, instead shifting his focus to the area where Alexander was working. Miles and his team came running up with shoring beams and went to work stabilizing the tunnel.

It didn't take long to reach Benny's hand and from there dig away the dirt covering his head. He was unconscious but breathing. Moments later, they freed his other hand and pulled him from the loose dirt.

Doyle picked him up with a grunt. "Miles, after you get this section shored up, get out until we can have inspectors take a look. You two, come with me."

Alexander looked back and thought he saw the remnants of some long-buried stonework, but he couldn't be sure in the dark, even with his magical sight. If he could access the firmament and use his clairvoyance, he would have made a note to himself to explore this area later that night, but as it stood he would have to send Chloe to do his reconnaissance for him. Until he was ready to take off the slave collar, his most powerful magic wasn't available to him.

When they reached the main chamber, they were met by a number of healers who went to work on Benny. Not a minute later, a well-dressed man, perfectly groomed, wearing a gold ring on each hand and carrying a finely crafted, silver-shod walking stick, hurried into the chamber.

"Supervisor Doyle, what's happened to my man?" he asked urgently. Alexander could see from his colors that he had little if any concern for Benny.

"Cave-in," Doyle said. "Your man will be fine, Factor Laxman."

"That remains to be seen," Laxman said. "I needn't remind you that mine safety is the responsibility of the charter holder. If you get one of my guild members killed, you're still responsible for paying his wages for a full year from the date of his death."

"I'm well aware of the agreement," Doyle said. "Like I said, your man will be just fine."

"Perhaps the Slave Guild should exercise our right to demand a full inspection of the area in question," Laxman mused aloud. "After all, the safety of our workers is our first concern. One can't be too careful. That would, of course, shut you down for a few days though."

Doyle clenched his teeth and motioned for Laxman to speak with him privately. They walked across the chamber and spoke in heated whispers for a few moments before Doyle handed Laxman a purse. The Slave Guild factor smiled graciously and turned to the miners who'd been called out of the tunnel.

"I am pleased to report that Supervisor Doyle has assured me the mine is safe and work can continue," Laxman said. "The injured miner will receive all of the care that he requires, and more importantly, his wages will continue to be paid by the Andalian Mining Company to the Slave Guild so that we may continue to provide for the well-being of all our valued members." Seeming pleased with himself, Laxman strolled out of the chamber.

Doyle stared daggers into the back of the man's head.

"What was that all about?" Alexander asked Miles, who had returned to the chamber and was resting nearby.

"Factor Laxman represents the slaves in this mine," Miles said. "He heard about the accident so he came to make sure the mine is still safe for us to work. Without the guild looking out for us, we'd all die down here."

Several minutes later, the inspectors came hurrying out of the tunnel and spoke in hushed tones with Doyle. He seemed frustrated with them and was shaking his head angrily, throwing up his hands when they pronounced that the tunnel was unstable. Visibly frustrated, he turned back to his work crew.

"I suggest you men get some rest. It might be a while before we can get back to work."

Alexander closed his eyes and reached out for Chloe.

"Can you take a look at the end of that tunnel? I thought I saw something that looked like worked stone."

"Of course," Chloe said in his mind. A minute or so later, she said, "Send me your mind, My Love. You should see this."

Alexander found himself looking at a finely built, seamless stone wall covered with engraved characters, some of which he recognized from the magic circle. Everything was slightly translucent since Chloe was in the aether, but he could tell at a glance that the chamber was warded—and that the wards extended into the aether.

"Have you ever seen anything like this?" he asked.

"Only the wards surrounding the king's chambers in the palace, but this seems even more ancient somehow."

"Stay away from those wards. I don't want you to get hurt." Alexander returned to his mind and opened his eyes. Titus Grant was speaking with Doyle, but he didn't seem nearly as concerned as Doyle was about the situation.

A few minutes later, the Babachenko entered, followed by four overseers. The miners all whispered urgently to one another for a moment, then fell deathly silent.

"Lord Grant, I hear you've had an accident," the Babachenko said.

"We had a cave-in," Grant said. "One man was buried for a few minutes, but it looks like he'll be fine after some rest."

"I'm glad to hear it," the Babachenko said. "I also hear that you've made a discovery."

"That's what my foreman tells me. I haven't had a chance to take a look myself."

"Then I suggest we remedy that," the Babachenko said.

Thirty minutes later they emerged from the tunnel, the Babachenko's colors swirling with excitement.

"You may have just won this war for us, Lord Grant," the Babachenko said. "I suggest you close this mine except for a few select men—slaves that you can afford to lose."

Grant nodded thoughtfully. "Slaves are expensive. I would hope, given the value of my contribution to the empire, that I'll be adequately compensated."

"Of course, of course. We'll discuss the particulars over lunch tomorrow. For now, this mine must be evacuated until we can determine if you have indeed found what we've been looking for."

"I hate to idle my slaves for too long," Grant said. "They get restless, and I lose money for every day they aren't working."

"We'll discuss that as well," the Babachenko said.

"I only bring it up because we aren't talking about silver or gems," Grant said. "I don't know how to place a value on ..."

The Babachenko held up his hand in stern warning. "Please, Lord Grant, have some discretion. We both know what may lie within that chamber, there's no need to speak of it. Such words may fall on the wrong ears."

"As you wish," Grant said. "I look forward to our lunch tomorrow."

"As do I," the Babachenko said, motioning for the overseers to stand guard at the tunnel entrance before hurrying off.

"Let's get these men back to the barracks, Doyle," Grant said. "This mine is closed."

"You heard the man," Doyle said. "On your feet, leave your tools."

While Alexander was grateful for the reprieve from the hard labor of swinging a pickaxe, he was far more anxious about the discovery his team had unearthed. The Babachenko seemed to believe that whatever was behind the wall they'd found could affect the outcome of the war. Naturally, Alexander's curiosity was eating at him.

He considered having Chloe push his slave collar into the aether so he could use his clairvoyance and fully investigate, but he wasn't ready to make his move yet. Once the collar came off, he would have to move quickly or risk revealing his true identity.

His work detail was locked in their barracks, and except for meals, the guards had left them alone. Most of the slaves saw it as an opportunity to catch up on their sleep, but a few were still awake, Miles and Hod among them.

"So what do you two think is going on in the mine?" Alexander asked.

Hod just shrugged, shaking his head.

Miles started to answer but stopped himself, looking around at the rest of the sleeping miners.

"You know something?" Alexander pressed.

He looked around again, leaning in close. "Not here," he whispered, "the Acuna is watching."

"What do you mean? Who is this Acuna?"

"The Acuna is the real power in Andalia," Miles whispered, barely audibly. "Their spies are everywhere."

"What else can you tell me about them?"

Miles shook his head, fear rippling through his colors. Alexander looked to Hod who just shrugged again.

"All right, what can you tell me about the Babachenko? That's kind of a funny name."

"It's not his name, it's his title," Miles said. "The story says that the greatest mage in the history of Andalia saved the royal bloodline and rebuilt the country after the Reishi War. His name was Gerard Babachenko. He did a lot for the country, set up the government, started the guilds to protect workers, created the charter companies to ensure stable prices … he even rebuilt the Lancers after they'd been all but wiped out in the war. In honor of his memory, the leader of the Acuna takes his name as his title."

"I hear he takes more than the name," Hod said.

"That's just superstitious nonsense," Miles said, shaking his head.

"What?" Alexander said, holding his hands out, urging one of them to continue.

"The story says that the Babachenko doesn't just inherit the name, he inherits the magic of the original Babachenko as well," Hod said. "All the way back, they've been passing along their magic from one to the next."

"That's just a story," Miles said. "Everyone knows that's not possible."

Alexander sat back, his mind alight with the ramifications—wizards passing on their connection to the firmament before they died, ensuring that the next generation would retain the power of the previous.

"Little One?"

"Yes, My Love?"

"I need you to do some more searching for me. I suspect there's a crystal vein with two chambers cut into it somewhere beneath the city or the palace. I need you to find it for me."

"I'll start searching right away."

"Be careful, some of the wards in this city might be able to hurt you."

While Alexander sat against the wall, his eyes closed and mind racing, the ground began to rumble beneath him. All of the sleeping miners woke as the vibrations intensified.

"What's happening?" Hod asked, his eyes wide with fear.

The shaking lasted for less than a minute, but it was strong enough to crack the walls in a number of places. They heard men running past their door. Then the dust settled and the room fell silent again, the other slaves holding their breath as if they were holding back the wrath of the ground beneath them.

Just before lunchtime, Doyle opened the door. "Looks like we're going back to work," he said. "The tunnel we were digging collapsed—killed a whole crew of deep-shaft miners. We're going to dig that tunnel back out and shore it up with stone."

Several of the miners looked to each other, confusion and worry plain on their faces.

"We aren't allowed to work stone," Miles said. "That's mason work."

Doyle gave the man a withering look. "I know that. Workers from the Andalian Masonry Company will be coming in to build the tunnel into a stone corridor as we cut it. The Babachenko ordered Lord Grant to make this tunnel his first priority ... that's just unheard of. They must want whatever's in there real bad, and if I know Lord Grant, they're going to pay dearly for it."

"But the ground just shook," one of the miners said. "How can we know it'll be safe down there?"

"You want a guarantee?" Doyle said. "I guarantee you that someday you're going to die. Other than that, I got nothing. Be ready to go to work after lunch."

***

In the days that followed, Doyle worked them even harder, probably because of the six overseers standing behind him. Fortunately, the dirt and rocks were loose and easy to move compared to the packed earth they'd been digging through a few days before.

While the digging was easier, the forward progress was slower because the masons had to shore up the tunnel every five feet lest the unstable ceiling collapse again. None of the miners complained about the frequent breaks, instead using the time to nap or gossip about the rumors that seemed to materialize out of thin air in Mithel Dour.

Toward the end of the first day, Chloe returned from her scouting. "I couldn't find the chamber you spoke of, but I did find another chamber of interest," she said in his mind. "It looks just like the place where we found the heartstone of Blackstone Keep, but the crystal shattered long ago."

"Where is this chamber?" Alexander asked.

"Directly under the forges," Chloe said. "I believe it used to provide the magic to power them."

"Interesting ... and you said the forges don't look like they've been used for some time. Does it look like they've been unused since the crystal failed?"

"No, My Love, the forges appear to have been active within the past few years."

"So how are they powering them without the heartstone? And why aren't they using them to build more lances right now?"

"I don't know."

"I know, Little One. Just thinking out loud, as it were."

"Back to work," Doyle shouted, more for the benefit of the overseers than for the men.

***

Alexander slept like the dead that night, his body sore and tired from exertion. The next day wasn't any better.

He spent most of the work breaks watching the masons. He'd never worked with stone before, so he found the methods used to move and maneuver large blocks of granite fascinating. The masons were masters at using leverage and counterweights to manipulate carefully cut blocks of stone and set them into place. While they seemed to work slowly and very deliberately, Alexander was impressed with how quickly and efficiently they were able to transform the earthen tunnel into a stone corridor.

During one of the breaks, Alexander could hear the overseers having a conversation that he found particularly interesting.

"I hear the king's sister is pregnant again," one overseer said.

"So soon after she lost the last one?" another said, shaking his head.

"I hear it's the king's," yet another said in a guarded tone.

"Maybe that's why she keeps losing them."

"Hey!" the lead overseer said, approaching his men quickly and talking in a harsh whisper. "The Acuna hears all. Do you really want your idle speculations about His Majesty to get back to them?"

All of the other overseers fell silent, looking about furtively.

"Break's over!" Doyle bellowed.

One day ran into the next, each more grueling than the last. Alexander considered escaping several times, but he was far too curious about the warded stone wall he and the other miners were digging toward. The Babachenko seemed to believe that whatever was behind the wall would tip the scales in the war raging across the Seven Isles. If that were indeed the case, then he had to stay the course.

After a week of digging, the crew came to a body buried in the dirt.

"Supervisor Doyle," Hod called out. "I found a body." He backed away from the corpse.

"Dig him out and load him into the cart," Doyle said.

The hour that followed was gruesome. The bodies of six men, buried alive and crushed from the weight of the cave-in, were exhumed, one after the other. Once the grisly task was complete, the masons went to work again.

Hod sat down next to Alexander and Miles, shaking his head in dismay. "That could have been us in there."

"No," Miles said without elaborating.

"What do you mean?" Hod asked.

"We were pulled out of there for a reason," Miles said.

"What are you saying?" Alexander asked.

"Deep-shaft miners are political slaves," Miles said. "People who speak out against the king or make trouble for the powers that be get assigned to the most dangerous work. Really just a death sentence without saying as much."

***

Alexander lay down that night thinking of Isabel. He was torn between his need to discover the secrets behind the ancient wall and his desire to see his wife. Her plan had either worked or it hadn't. If not, she was probably being held by Phane. Either way, she would be expecting him to reach out to her … and she would be worrying that he hadn't. He could go to her right now, but that would mean removing the slave collar, and once it was off, there was no practical way to get it back out of the aether and around his neck again, since it could only be opened with the master ring it was bound to—the one worn by Titus Grant. He had to be ready to make his move before he removed it and he didn't have enough information yet.

Benny came back to work the next morning, his injuries healing but still causing him some pain. Of far more interest to Alexander were the ripples of fear in his colors every time the man looked at him. Something had changed.

During the first break that morning, while the masons did their work, Benny sat down next to Alexander.

"So, you never did say where you're from."

"No, I didn't," Alexander said, closing his eyes.

Benny hesitated, his colors swirling with fear and anxiety.

"Well, where are you from?"

Alexander sighed, opening his eyes. "I'm tired, Benny. If I tell you, will you let me rest?"

"Sure," Benny said a little too eagerly.

"I was born in southern Ruatha. My sister and I fled the war and got attacked by pirates. Our ship sank off the coast of Andalia and we ended up here," Alexander said, closing his eyes again but watching Benny's colors intently.

"What did you do on Ruatha?"

"I thought you were going to let me rest."

"Back to work," Doyle said.

At the next break, Benny sat next to Alexander again.

"So you have a sister," he said. "What's she look like?"

"She's too young for you, Benny."

"Oh … I … well, I didn't mean that," he said. "I was just wondering. Trying to make conversation."

"She has coppery red hair and freckles across her nose and cheeks," Alexander said.

Benny frowned in confusion. "But I thought she had blond hair." No sooner had he spoken than his colors flared with alarm. "I mean, don't most women from Ruatha have blond hair?"

"No, not really," Alexander said. "I suspect it's just like anywhere else." While he remained outwardly calm, his mind raced to understand exactly what was happening. Benny had never been this inquisitive before and both his colors and his knowledge of Abigail betrayed him. Alexander suspected that the Acuna had paid him a visit while he was recuperating from his injuries—but how had they come to suspect Alexander's true identity?

It was entirely possible, given Andalia's relationship with Phane, that the Reishi Prince had used his mirror to locate Alexander and then sent word to the Babachenko. But if that were so, why hadn't they come for him? Surely, Phane would demand that he be captured at once.

Whatever the case, Benny's knowledge of Abigail's blond hair was alarming and it was good reason to make his move sooner rather than later.

That evening, the crew reached the warded wall. The moment it became visible, Doyle halted work, pulling the detail out of the mine and sending everyone back to their barracks. Six overseers took up guard positions around the tunnel entrance after the miners and masons filed out.

Chapter 10

"Alex Valentine!" Doyle bellowed over the din of breakfast.

"Here," Alexander said, raising his hand.

"Finish up. Lord Grant wants to see you. The rest of you will be reassigned to other mines outside of the city."

"Why?" Miles asked. Many of the other miners nodded, wondering the same thing.

"This mine has been closed by order of the Babachenko until additional safety measures can be put in place," Doyle said. "Factor Laxman is making a big stink about the men who died down there the other day so we're shut down."

"Where will we go?" Benny asked.

"Lord Grant will have your assignments after breakfast," Doyle said. "You'll all know soon enough."

Events were starting to move more quickly. Alexander had no doubt that he'd been singled out for reasons that had nothing to do with mining. He finished his gruel and reported to Doyle.

"Ah, there you are," Doyle said. "Follow me."

He led Alexander out into the yard in front of the slave barracks. A number of wagons equipped with cages were being prepared while Grant sat at a table off to the side, reviewing documents. He looked up with irritation when Alexander and Doyle approached.

"Here's the man you asked for," Doyle said.

"Oh ... your sister says you know horses."

"Yes sir, I do. We grew up on a ranch."

"Good enough," Grant said, turning in his chair. "Rollins!" he shouted across the yard. A man attending to the tack and harness of one of the horse teams dropped what he was doing and trotted over to the table.

"Yes, Lord Grant?"

"Here's your new man. Put him to work. Once you're done with the wagons, take him to the house and get him settled in."

"Yes, My Lord," Rollins said, not waiting to be dismissed. Grant went back to his papers without a second look. Alexander felt a keen sense of blindness at not being able to see Grant's colors. He'd relied on his magical insight for so long that he wasn't entirely sure what to make of the man—except that his lack of colors was of great interest in and of itself.

"Come on, come on," Rollins said over his shoulder as he hurried back toward the team he'd been hitching to a wagon. "You have to keep up, especially on a day like today."

Alexander trotted behind him. Rollins was a tall, lanky man with a completely bald head and a neatly trimmed white beard and mustache. His eyes were brown, his hands work-worn, and his face ruddy with exertion. His colors were those of a man who had a job to do and no interest in other matters. That suited Alexander just fine. Whatever game was being played behind the scenes, Alexander doubted that Rollins had any part in it.

That still left plenty of things for him to worry about and more than enough unanswered questions, but Rollins didn't give him a moment to think about either. The man was driven and he demanded that his stable hands work at least as hard as he did. By the time they were finished hitching all of the wagons, Alexander was starting to wonder if working in the mine hadn't been easier.

Once the last of the wagons loaded with Grant's slaves rolled out of the yard, Rollins took a deep breath and let it out slowly.

"You ... what was your name again?"

"Alex."

"You did well enough for your first day, Alex, but I'll expect better from you as you learn the job. Come with me and I'll get you settled in at Grant Manor.

"First things first," Rollins continued while they walked through the ancient and hauntingly beautiful architecture of Mithel Dour. "That collar around your neck will let you have the run of the city, but if you try to leave, it'll kill you. Lord Grant will need you to run errands for him on occasion, so it's best for you to learn the streets and the customs."

Two overseers were walking down the street toward them. As they neared, Rollins stepped up against the wall, pulling Alexander with him, and looked down, averting his eyes. Alexander mimicked him, watching the flare of smug satisfaction and power in the overseers' colors as they marched past.

"Let that be another lesson," Rollins said with just a hint of acid. "Don't give the overseers any reason to question you. They can beat you to death in the street or activate your collar and let you choke while they laugh ... and no one will even ask them why."

Alexander just nodded, not trusting himself to speak lest he betray his true feelings.

"Truth be told, you've been given a gift," Rollins said once they were well out of earshot of the overseers. "Working in the stables is a far better life than working the mines—just remember, as long as you wear that collar, you can always be reassigned.

"Now don't get me wrong, Lord Grant is a fair master. If you do a good job, after ten or twelve years, he may allow you to buy your freedom; although, I wouldn't recommend it unless you've been accepted into a guild first. Free men don't stay free for long around here unless they have guild protection."

"Hear one, hear all," a crier shouted. "The Acuna has uncovered a new threat, a conspiracy of such evil that it threatens our very way of life. The Ruathan scourge has invaded our home and is sowing the seeds of treason on Andalian soil. The enemy has joined with the criminals and brigands in the sequestered territories to challenge our enlightened way of life and cast our civilization into darkness. The king calls on one and all to renew your commitment to service, to embrace the necessary sacrifices so that we may all survive this terrible threat. Most of all, the king commands you to report any suspicious activity at once."

Rollins didn't give the crier a second look, though there were a few people who had stopped to hear his words. Anxiety lit up their colors as they conferred with one another about the new development.

Alexander smiled inwardly. He suspected that his message to General Talia during the fight with the pirates had prompted him to move into Andalia. While the number he'd sent was undoubtedly small, they would probably be working to incite resistance within the people of Andalia against their own government. Talia was a student of war and an avid reader of history. He would design his strategy to cause maximum disruption at a minimum cost.

"What do you think about what that man was saying?"

"Not much," Rollins said. "As in, I wouldn't give it a second thought. Of course, I wouldn't say that too loudly either. The walls have ears around here."

Alexander waited for him to continue but he just walked on without another word.

"How do you mean?"

Rollins looked at him and then looked around carefully before speaking. "The man who used to have the job you're taking—he liked to talk about the powers that be, used to speculate about their goals and such. Two nights ago, he vanished ... went to his bunk that night and simply wasn't there the following morning. You'll find that's the way of things around here. Talk too often or too loudly about important people, and like as not, you'll disappear too."

"Where do they go?"

"Don't know and don't care to know," Rollins said.

They walked on, Alexander pondering the nature of Andalian society in silence until he caught a glint of silver out of the corner of his mind's eye. A coin lay in the gutter. He started to reach for it, but Rollins roughly pulled him away.

"Don't ever do that," he whispered. "If the overseers catch you, they'll beat you to death for treason."

"But it's just a coin."

"No, it's not," Rollins said, pointing to a wanted poster tacked to a nearby bulletin board. The picture was only a silhouette of a head but the name read: Nightshade. "The most wanted criminal in all of Andalia is fond of taunting the authorities. He steals shipments of silver bound for the war effort and then scatters the coins around the streets for people to find like hidden treasure. The king has decreed that picking up a coin on the street is stealing from the people and punishable by death."

"Seems I have a lot to learn," Alexander said.

"Here's a good rule of thumb," Rollins said, "do only what you're told to do and nothing else. Remember that and you'll stay out of trouble."

Alexander held his tongue and walked on until they came to a beautiful four-story manor house built into the stone of the cliff wall looking out over the plains of Andalia below. The sun was just setting, casting an orange glow over the fluid arches and seamless stonework. The property was surrounded by a high wall and flanked on either side by similar estates.

A pair of private guards nodded to Rollins as he passed under the arched entry into a courtyard bounded by perfectly manicured gardens.

"Stay out of the main house unless you're told to go inside," Rollins said. "The stables have quarters above. You'll share a room with another of my hands, a man by the name of Ritter. He's not terribly friendly; likes horses more than people."

"I can identify with that," Alexander said.

"In that case, maybe you two will get along just fine, but I doubt it."

A clanging rang out over the yard and Rollins frowned, checking the position of the sun.

"Didn't think it was so late already. That was the supper call. We'll eat and then I'll show you the stables."

The meal was better than he'd had working in the mines but it was still not quite enough. The dining hall was full of estate hands with only two private guards at the door, both looking bored. The majority of the people in the room wore slave collars.

"Meals are served three times a day," Rollins said. "If you miss a meal, you go hungry, so listen for meal call and come here when you hear it." He was finished eating before Alexander was half done. "You'd better hurry up, there's still work to do."

Alexander choked down the remains of his dinner and followed Rollins out into the paddock.

"Lord Grant owns one hundred and eighty-seven horses at present, but not all of them are stabled here ... just the finest. Most are used to haul wagons for his business, so more often than not, the majority are on the road.

"Wagons come and go every day so we're constantly stabling horses for the night, then turning them around the next day for a new job." He pointed to a smaller but much nicer barn. "The riding horses are stabled in there while the work horses live in the big barn. You'll be working in there. That means the small barn is off-limits. Understand?"

"Sure," Alexander said with a shrug.

"Good, follow me and I'll show you around."

Alexander spent the next hour becoming reacquainted with the workings of a stable. In many ways it was refreshing and familiar, reminding him of his childhood, but he kept his purpose firmly in mind, noting the layout of his new, and very temporary, home should it become important in the near future. Rollins ended the tour at the door to Alexander's room.

"Ritter, this is your new bunkmate," he said. Then he turned to Alexander and said, "Breakfast is at sunup. Don't be late."

Alexander nodded. "Got it. Thanks for the tour."

"Well, close the door already," Ritter said. "That's your bunk, keep your mess on that side of the room."

"Shouldn't be a problem," Alexander said. "I don't have much to make a mess with."

Ritter's colors were those of a man who'd lost everything except his bitterness—not evil, just broken and angry. Alexander could sympathize; the collar around his neck looked old and worn.

Ritter just grunted, glowering at Alexander for a moment before rolling toward the wall. "Turn out the lamp already."

Alexander doused the light and lay down. In the darkness, he began to see the glimmer of light. Tiny points of magical color glowing in the dark, scattered haphazardly around the room, floating in the air as if suspended in time. He'd walked through several and had felt nothing. They were so dim that he hadn't even seen them until the room was dark and then only barely. But they were there and they were magic.

Yet more questions.

It was nearing time to make his move. He'd been here for weeks, and while he hadn't learned everything he wished to know, he'd discovered enough. He had two objectives: destroy the Crown and discover what lay in the depths beneath the city. He began thinking about a plan. Force wouldn't do, at least not entirely. Stealth was his best option. Before he drifted off to sleep, his thoughts turned to Isabel. He was becoming more and more anxious to go to her, just to see her, but he knew that he had to wait until he was ready.

The next morning he and Ritter were assigned to retrieve a string of horses from the mine yard. Alexander tried to make conversation, but Ritter just ignored him. The morning was crisp, clear and calm. Alexander focused on his surroundings, soaking up all he could about the people. Most were just people, though more fearful and beaten down than Alexander had ever seen before.

Most of them shied away from overseers and nobles with practiced self-debasement, almost cowering, many with genuine fear. The powerful walked the streets as if they owned them and everyone nearby as well. Alexander followed Ritter's lead, imitating him at every encounter with those who thought they were better than a lowly slave.

They arrived to find several slave wagons, all empty but still hitched to teams of horses.

"I wonder why they brought in a load of slaves," Alexander said.

"Why's that important to you?" Ritter said, eyeing him closely.

"Just seems odd since they closed the mine."

"Stop wondering and get to work."

As they guided their string of horses down the road on the way back to Grant Manor, a crier ran past them, taking his post on the street corner.

"The crown princess has been murdered!" he called out, catching his breath and shouting it again.

"That ought to stir things up," Ritter muttered to himself.

They passed a crier on every other corner, all shouting the same thing. Alexander was quite sure that everyone in the entire city had been made aware of the development by the time he and Ritter reached the stables.

That evening, after a day of hard, yet fulfilling work, Grant came into the refectory, trailing another man in an official-looking uniform, though different from those worn by the overseers. The idle conversation over dinner died out quickly.

"You've no doubt heard the disturbing news," Grant said. "New details have come to light that the Acuna feels are important to communicate to the people." Grant stepped aside and introduced the man in the uniform with a gesture that was at once deferential and slightly dismissive.

"Thank you, Lord Grant," the man said, turning to the crowd and regarding them with a grave expression. "The enemy is in our midst. We have reason to believe that the pretender himself is within our great city. He has poisoned the Crown Princess, murdering her and the unborn heir to the throne. As you well know, without the Crown to protect us and our enlightened way of life, we will surely be overrun by the enemy in his mad quest for total power.

"If you ever had any doubt of his power, let the heinous murder of our beloved Crown Princess set your mind right. He has penetrated our defenses and lives within our walls even as we speak, yet his powerful magic protects him from detection. It is for this reason that the Acuna comes to you with great humility. We need your help. The Babachenko can see farther and better than any man alive with the aid of his powerful magic and yet he is blind to this enemy, unable to find him even though he stalks our streets in the night. We come to ask for your eyes and ears. We come to beg that you will watch and report anything that seems suspicious.

"Such is the sworn duty of every Andalian subject, yet we all know that not everything that should be reported is brought to our attention. That must change if our children are to survive this war. Our King, His Most Excellent Majesty, has chosen to send the bulk of our forces against the enemy in faraway lands to prevent them from bringing this battle to our shores, but alas, war has come into our home and dealt us a grievous blow.

"But do not despair, our King is still strong and virile, he is committed to the future of our great country more than ever before, he has felt the evil of the enemy we face in the most personal way possible, and he stands firm, unwavering in the face of nearly impossible odds. I am here to ask you to stand with our brave King. Help us bring the murderer to justice and end this terrible war."

He finished his speech with his head bowed in sadness, yet his colors revealed only a desire to put on a good performance. The man didn't seem to have any interest in the truth of the words he spoke, only that he delivered them convincingly.

Alexander sat very still, scrutinizing the men in the room with his all around sight, looking for any indication that he was being singled out. He felt an almost uncontrollable urge to bolt, to run for his life before they could find him, yet he held still. The men in the room were busy discussing the news while the man from the Acuna stood near the door with Grant.

It wasn't long before a stable hand approached them, speaking in hushed tones for a moment before pointing out another man in the room. Two overseers entered as if on cue and dragged the man away while he protested his innocence. A few minutes later another man stood and pointed out someone else, claiming that he'd been acting suspiciously. That man was dragged out of the room as well. Alexander sat quietly trying with all his might to be invisible.

Five men in all were removed by the overseers, each having been accused of various suspicious activities. Alexander could tell from their colors that the accusers were lying and the accused were innocent. Once five men had been rounded up, the Acuna and Grant exchanged pleasantries and left the rest of the men to finish their meal.

His appetite gone, Alexander left the refectory, going to a small balcony adjacent to the paddock that overlooked the plains a thousand feet below. He leaned against the low wall separating him from open sky and tried to process what had just happened. The evening was cool but pleasant enough, the sun having just set. He needed to think.

The Acuna mouthpiece had said that the Babachenko could see farther and better than any man alive. In his mind's eye, Alexander compared the colors of Mage Jalal and the Babachenko to confirm his suspicion and his fear. While Jalal was a good man and the Babachenko was not, they shared the same calling: divination. Both specialized in magic that provided information.

Alexander knew he wasn't immune to magical sight … Phane had spied on him often enough. The inescapable conclusion that sent icy chills up his spine was that the Babachenko knew who he was and where he was. Reason demanded it, yet he hadn't been dragged off with the others—why?

"Alexander?" a voice whispered from the shadows.

He didn't turn, but instead reached out with his all around sight to identify the source before confirming his identity.

"Hello, Anja, it's good to see you."

She raced out of the shadows and hugged him. "I've done like you said. I've obeyed even though I want to eat some of these people."

"Good. I'm proud of you."

"They know we're here," she whispered urgently. "They just told us that you killed the crown princess and they're looking for you."

"They're lying," Alexander said, focusing on his all around sight, looking for any sign of magic or people before continuing. "They know exactly where I am."

"I don't understand."

"I can only guess that they want the Stone and they know I don't have it, so they're trying to flush me out, force me to make a move."

"Wouldn't they just torture you?"

"If the Babachenko is what I think he is, then he probably knows why he can't find the Stone, and he also knows that torture wouldn't work."

"So what do we do?"

"Nothing. Just be ready. When it's time to move, we'll have to be quick about it."

"I'm ready right now."

"I know. Oh, and thank you." He kissed her on the forehead.

"For what?"

"For getting me reassigned to the stables."

"But I didn't. I wanted to say something to Lady Grant but I was afraid it would draw attention."

"Huh, that's interesting. One more thing to think about."

"Oh, I almost forgot," Anja said. "Jack will be singing for Lady Grant tomorrow evening. He seems to be making a name for himself."

Alexander chuckled. "Why doesn't that surprise me. Let him know we need to talk, and keep doing what you've been doing."

She stood on her toes to kiss him on the cheek before melting back into the shadows. He waited for a few minutes longer, leaning against the railing, trying to decide how to proceed, when two men came into view behind him, crouching behind the bushes that bordered the little balcony. He slowed his breathing and focused on the threat, waiting for them to make a move. Their colors were calm and steady, eager even, those of men accustomed to violence, though thankfully, neither showed any trace of magic.

They started to move, very slowly, never rustling the bushes any more than the occasional breeze might have. One of the two wrapped a length of rope around each hand as he crept up behind Alexander. The second stopped ten feet away, waiting for his companion to strike. Alexander inventoried the nearest man's weapons: sword, dagger, boot knife. He studied his colors and scrutinized his face without providing even a hint that he was aware of him. The moment seemed to slow as the enemy drew near, and then he saw the attack unfold in his mind's eye ... in that timeless place where his magic lived, Alexander watched the man loop the rope around his neck and pull him over backward.

When the man moved, Alexander ducked under the rope, grabbing it with one hand while lunging into the man's midsection with his shoulder, quickly removing the dagger from his belt before grabbing him by the legs and tossing him over the wall. The second man was so surprised by the sudden turn of events that Alexander had him flat on his back with the dagger to his throat before he could react.

"Who sent you?" Alexander whispered.

The man stared back in blank surprise, still too shocked to process what had just happened. Alexander pressed the flat of the blade to his throat.

"Tyr ... Lord Tyr sent us."

"What were your orders?"

"To capture you alive and bring you to him."

"Where is he?"

"Here, in the city."

"Do the Andalians know he's here?"

"Yes, he's an ally of the king. He has a house just down the road."

"What were you supposed to do if anyone caught you?"

"Kill them. Leave no trace."

"Good. Get up," Alexander said, hauling the man to his feet and walking him toward the balcony wall with the blade still to his throat. The man's eyes went wider until he was staring at Alexander with nothing but the fear of death. When he reached the wall, Alexander grabbed the man by the belt and tossed him over without a moment's hesitation. He considered keeping the dagger but decided it was too great a risk, so he threw it over as well.

He returned to his room and went to bed as if nothing was out of the ordinary, deciding to wait until he talked to Jack before he chose his first target. He wanted to make a move against the king, but he knew he would have a far better chance if he could use all of his magic to plan his attack first, and that would take some time—time spent without the slave collar.

That left the mine.

"Chloe?"

"I'm here, My Love."

"Can you go to the mine for me?"

"Of course," she said. Several minutes later she touched his mind again. "I'm here, My Love."

Alexander looked through her eyes down the tunnel. Black scorch marks marred the wall, but it remained intact. Three magical circles had been inlaid in silver into a slab of stone laid near the wall. Each circle overlapped equally, creating a space within the center that was protected by all three. Around the three was another circle. Alexander had never seen magical circles arranged in such a way, each lending strength to the others. Six overseers stood guard at the entrance to the tunnel, but otherwise it was empty.

"Looks like they've been busy," Alexander said.

"And yet, they haven't gained entry," Chloe said. "Maybe they won't be able to get in."

"From the looks of those circles, I bet they break through tomorrow."

Chapter 11

Alexander had just started his work the following morning when Grant entered the stables with Tyr and his wizard.

"I have many fine horses, Lord Tyr," Grant said. "For the right price, I would consider selling any of them."

Tyr scanned the room, locking eyes with Alexander, rage boiling in his colors. He tried to remain calm, struggled to contain his anger, but it seeped through into his voice and bearing.

"I'll take those two," Tyr said, stabbing his finger toward two horses without really even looking at them. "And I'd like to buy a slave to care for them. He'll do." Tyr pointed at Alexander like he was aiming a weapon.

"Come now, Lord Tyr, you know as well as I do that the slave trade belongs to the Babachenko. Records must be kept, fees must be paid."

"Formalities," Tyr said. "I'll give you gold."

Grant held up his hands in a helpless gesture, shaking his head. "Lord Tyr, again, you know as well as I do that all transactions must take place with Andalian silver crowns. Gold is strictly forbidden."

"Don't play with me, Grant," Tyr nearly growled.

"I mean no offense, but our laws are dear to me," Grant said. "Only through the careful order of Andalian society can all be assured equality and prosperity."

Tyr's bald head started to turn red. Alexander went about his work, pretending to ignore them while watching the exchange with his all around sight. Tyr walked away, breathing deeply and deliberately, then turned back and stalked up to Grant, his hand resting on the hilt of the Thinblade.

"Name your price."

Grant regarded him thoughtfully before smiling amiably. "Perhaps I do have a slave or two that I'd be willing to sell without all the official hassle. Why don't we go take a look at them?"

"No," Tyr said. "I want that one." He pointed at Alexander again.

"Fancy that one, do you?"

Tyr glowered at him.

"I've just acquired him," Grant said. "If I sell him so quickly and the Babachenko finds out about it, I could be charged with illegal slave trading. That's a very serious crime." He leaned closer, lowering his voice. "But I do have two men outside without proper documents on record. I'd be happy to sell you either of them."

"I! Want! Him!" Tyr shouted at the top of his lungs.

Grant stepped back, blinking in confusion. "My Lord Tyr, I'm afraid I can't help you."

Several privately employed guards armed with crossbows entered the stables a moment later, all of them looking to Grant for instructions. He forestalled any action with a gesture, but they fanned out around the walls, just in case.

"I believe it's time for you to be going, Lord Tyr," Grant said.

Tyr started shaking, then spat at Grant's feet before storming out, cursing with every step. Alexander kept working as if nothing had happened.

Later that morning, Rollins pulled him aside. "I told you to avoid attention."

Alexander just shrugged.

"Lord Grant wants to see you in the riding stables. Right away."

Alexander nodded, heading toward the much smaller but better-built barn.

"Be ready, Chloe. We might have to move fast."

"Yes, My Love."

Alexander stepped inside.

"Close the door," Grant said from the shadows.

"Yes, My Lord," Alexander said.

"Can you tell me what that was about this morning?"

"No, My Lord."

"You're not a very good liar," Grant said. "After Tyr threw his tantrum, I did some looking into you. It's really quite odd. My wife told me that your sister, her new maid, recommended you, and yet your sister denies it. Normally, I would conclude that your sister is a liar, yet I detected no guile in her when I questioned her, so I enquired further. It seems that your sister was in the kitchen at the very same moment that she was also speaking with my wife about you. Now Tyr shows up demanding to buy you. Who are you?"

"Just a cowhand that got pressed into slavery," Alexander said.

"So you say," Grant said, eyeing Alexander the way a cat eyes a mouse. "You're reassigned as my personal valet. I want to keep an eye on you." He stepped into Alexander's space, close to his face. "I will learn the truth of you."

"As you wish, My Lord," Alexander said, bowing his head and averting his eyes.

"Come with me," Grant said. Alexander followed without a word. Grant led him toward the main house, but stopped suddenly when the city shook. A loud crack reverberated through the stone beneath their feet, followed by a rumbling that slowly diminished over the span of a minute or so.

Grant spun toward Alexander with a fierce smile. "Well now, this seems like the perfect opportunity to find out who you really are." He touched his ring to Alexander's collar. "Follow me and stay close or you'll choke to death."

"Stay close, Little One."

"Always."

Alexander followed Grant back to the riding stable. "That one's yours." He looked up just long enough to point out a dappled mare. "Be quick about it."

Alexander went to work calming the horse and preparing her to ride. She was a fine animal, spirited and strong, but still a little skittish from the ground shaking beneath her. Alexander was ready to mount before Grant, but he waited.

Grant led him onto the road that ran along the cliff bordering the row of estates. When they reached the main road that ran down the central canal, Grant rode with all the speed he could coax from his horse. Alexander stayed right behind him. Each time they passed an overseer, the man would start to protest until he saw that it was Lord Grant, at which point he would abruptly lose interest.

Grant stopped at the mine entrance, dismounting quickly and surveying the yard. A number of horses were picketed nearby. He nodded to himself as he headed inside. Rather than take a direct path, he led Alexander to an office, gesturing for him to close the door once inside. Grant surveyed the room and smiled, moving a small table away from the wall and opening a secret panel. He motioned for Alexander to get the lamp and they entered the passage, closing the secret door behind them. The passage was low and narrow, unused and filled with dry, stale, dust-laden air.

After several minutes of choking on dust, Grant opened a panel at the other end of the passage and stepped into a large room, once the top of a mineshaft but now abandoned and sealed except for the hidden passage.

Grant led the way down a set of wooden switchback stairs leading down a very old mineshaft. Several minutes into their descent, he stepped through a broken board but recovered with remarkable dexterity, catching himself and pulling himself to safety without a word.

Alexander proceeded with greater caution, but the rest of the stairs were solid. Once they reached the bottom, Grant took the lamp from Alexander, raising it high to get a better look at the tunnels leading away into the darkness.

"Stay close and stay silent," he said.

Alexander followed through the darkness, stretching to see as far as he could with his all around sight. The tunnel was old and cut through worthless rock and dirt. After twenty minutes, Grant stopped and doused the light.

"We're going into the chamber behind that wall you found," Grant said. "The overseers will try to stop us if they see us so we're going to slip by without being seen. Just follow me and stay close. If they do catch us, keep your mouth shut."

Alexander walked carefully, trying to avoid noise with every step. All the while his mind fumbled with what was happening. He was having a hard time understanding Grant's motives, especially since he couldn't see the man's colors, but regardless of his motives, he was taking Alexander exactly where he wanted to go.

They reached an opening to the main shaft that led to the tunnel Alexander had helped excavate. Two overseers stood guard at the entrance almost fifty feet across the room. Grant stopped briefly, assessing the rest of the room carefully, before heading directly toward the two overseers. He walked across the room quickly, not bothering to hide in any way.

Alexander hesitated momentarily until Grant looked back, beckoning him to follow. Alexander watched the two overseers, expecting a sudden reaction, mentally preparing for a fight, but Grant walked right between the two of them with Alexander a step behind him and they didn't even notice. Alexander's estimation of how much trouble he was in grew immeasurably as Grant strode down the tunnel like he owned it.

At the other end of the tunnel stood a wizard in the exact center of the magic circles. A hole had been blasted through the ancient wall by tremendous force, opening into a chamber larger than the wizard's lantern light could illuminate. A number of overseers and wizards lay scattered around the magical circles—dead from some cataclysmic force.

Grant skirted the magical circles without hesitating, walking right past the wizard with Alexander in tow … the wizard didn't even notice them. The room beyond the breach was a hundred feet on a side. Four stone columns supported the ceiling, each nearly a perfect replica of a fir tree.

The workmanship could only be magical. Each tree was beautiful, reaching straight and tall to the ceiling, each a work of art worthy of the greatest king's hall. Grant walked between the trees toward the opposite end of the room. He seemed impressed by the pillars, yet not nearly as much as Alexander was.

Once across the room and into the opposite corridor, Grant lit the lamp and led on into a perfectly cut stone corridor that looked for all the world like two hedges that had grown together overhead. The branches were natural-looking, the leaves perfect in every detail.

Several hundred feet into the corridor, they came to a balcony with five broken bridges leading away into a black expanse. An enormous chasm several hundred feet wide and far longer and deeper than light could reach stretched out before them. Above and below were several balconies, platforms and buildings set into the walls, all separated by the open air and connected by bridges that looked more like ribbons of stone than viable pathways.

Grant lifted the lantern and started searching the platform. He went immediately to a nearby pile of dirt and stone. It looked like the beginnings of a stalagmite, but without its counterpart. He kicked it over and a crystal almost a foot long and two inches wide went skittering across the floor.

He picked it up and dusted it off, appraising it tenderly before putting it in a bag. What struck Alexander were the crystal's colors—bright and vibrant, rich and multihued … almost lifelike. Grant found another mound of dirt and another crystal within it, then another. With three of the crystals in his bag and no more mounds of dirt on the platform, Grant left without a word, returning the way they'd entered.

Alexander suspected that the crystals were indeed what the Babachenko was after, but the discovery had only led to more questions. He wanted to delve further, look across the bridges, find some answers he could use, but he dared not get too far from Grant lest his collar start choking him.

Before he reached the entrance to the tunnel, Grant handed Alexander the bag, then stopped at the threshold, glaring at the wizard standing guard, who saw them immediately this time.

"I demand an explanation!" Grant said. "I hold the mining charter, yet this mine has been worked without my permission or knowledge and without the knowledge of the Miners Guild. I demand that you send for the Babachenko, the

High Overseer and the Master of the Miners Guild at once. Serious crimes have been committed here and I will have justice."

"How did you get in there?" the wizard asked, seeming a bit alarmed by their sudden appearance.

"We slipped past while you were napping," Grant said. "The better question is, why are you trespassing in my mine?"

"I'm here by order of the Babachenko, as you well know."

"Well, I guess you'd better send for him."

The wizard seemed torn, but finally raised a horn to his lips and blew one long blast that reverberated down the tunnel. Grant gave Alexander a look of smug satisfaction and sat down on the edge of the platform to wait.

Not long after, one of the overseers guarding the entrance to the tunnel came trotting up to the wizard, giving Grant a suspicious look, before leaving with a note. Alexander sat down next to Grant.

"Now what?" he asked.

"Now we wait, and then I find out who you really are," Grant said, smiling at him like he'd just sprung a trap.

"I told you who I am," Alexander said.

"Stop talking."

Grant didn't say another word, apparently content to wait in silence while the wizard resumed his post in the center of the circles as if nothing had happened. Nearly an hour passed before a group of men came parading down the corridor flanked by six overseers, all carrying lanterns.

"Here we go," Grant said, getting to his feet but remaining on the platform just behind the shattered wall. "Don't say anything unless you're asked a direct question."

"Lord Grant, what is the meaning of this?" the Babachenko said, his eyes flicking to Alexander and his colors rippling with calculation and deceit.

"I must ask you the same question," Grant said. "As you well know, I hold the mining charter. You have no right to do mining work without my knowledge or sanction. Further, you have no representatives from the Miners Guild, whom I see have not been summoned."

"Please, Lord Grant," the Babachenko said, climbing up onto the platform where he could face him on level ground, "I understand your anger, and it is warranted, to a degree. By the letter of the law, you are correct. However, the decree of war issued by the king could be construed to supersede your rights, in very limited circumstances, of course."

"Is that a precedent you want made public to the other charter holders?"

"No, no, of course not," the Babachenko said. "They'd be impossible. I'm sure we can work something out."

"I was hoping you would say that," Grant said, taking the bag from Alexander. "You see, I think I've found exactly what you are looking for." He held up one of the crystals.

The Babachenko's colors surged with excitement and the promise of power. Even his face gave him away, though he tried mightily to hide it.

"Perhaps you have, though I would have to do some tests," he lied.

"Of course," Grant said. "I stand by the product of my mines. As a show of good faith, I'll give you these three crystals for your testing. Once you've confirmed their value, we can have a chat about price. After that, I can have a crew working day and night by week's end."

"About that," the Babachenko said, looking intently at Alexander. "There are some security concerns that need to be addressed, starting with him. Who exactly is he?"

"Oh, him? He's just a slave I picked up at the auction a few weeks ago," Grant said offhandedly, while scrutinizing the Babachenko carefully. "Although something strange did happen today with this particular slave. Tyr came to buy some horses from me. Then he decided he wanted to buy this slave … and all without cutting you in. Of course, I refused. I wouldn't dream of infringing on *your* business rights."

"Well, you know Tyr, always trying to violate the rules," the Babachenko said, his eyes never leaving Alexander. "Perhaps it would be best if I took this slave into custody … for security reasons."

"If he's a security risk, then he needs to be put down," Grant said. "If not, then taking him into custody is just taking my property."

The Babachenko bored into Alexander with his grey eyes. He was sure the man knew exactly who he was so he kept his head down and avoided eye contact.

"If you're really concerned about it, I'll put him down," Grant said, touching his ring. Alexander's collar began constricting around his neck, bringing him to his knees in moments.

"I'm coming, My Love."

"Wait! But stay close." Alexander fell over on his side, struggling for a breath, the world starting to go dark. In the distance, he heard the Babachenko.

"Stop!"

Grant released the collar at once. "So he isn't a security risk then?"

"No, I don't believe he is. We will speak about price tomorrow." With that, the Babachenko turned on his heel and strode away trailing his overseer guards.

Grant looked at Alexander as he regained his feet, still struggling to breathe past the violence done to his throat. "Now, I wonder why he did that. Care to shed any light?"

Alexander shook his head, rubbing his throat.

"No? I didn't think so. Stay close. I'll never hear the end of it if I'm not home in time to hear this new minstrel my wife is pining over." He led the way out of the mine, this time taking the main shaft and the counterbalanced lift to the surface.

When they returned to the manor, Grant showed Alexander to a small room adjacent to the master chambers, telling him to get cleaned up before dinner. Then he was taken to the kitchen and assigned the task of bringing Lord Grant his meal courses during a formal dinner his wife was hosting for nearly twenty guests.

He spent the evening keeping his head down, except to wink at Anja once when no one was looking. Jack ate with the guests, regaling them with stories of events that Alexander was quite sure had never happened about people that Alexander had never met. All of the stories had a single theme in common—the heroes were always Lancers, overseers or the Andalian King himself. For the entire meal, Jack never once looked directly at Alexander.

Music followed the meal. Jack performed a number of traditional Andalian songs, most praising the courage and sacrifice of kings past. While his lyrics were, no doubt, sanctioned and approved by the authorities, his musical embellishments and fluid, easy play captivated the audience. He switched from a lute to a whistle and back again, enjoying each song as much as his audience did.

After the musical entertainment, spirits were served and the nobles spent an hour or more talking very seriously about nothing of consequence—affairs, scandals and other safe but unimportant topics. Alexander followed Grant around and made sure his beverage was regularly replaced even though he rarely took a drink. In due time, Grant came around to a circle of people talking with Jack.

"You play quite a song, Minstrel," Grant said, bowing ever so slightly.

"You're too kind, My Lord," Jack said with a deliberate, formal bow.

"And where are you from?"

"In truth, I don't even know where I was born," Jack said. "I've traveled the Seven Isles for my whole life, picking up stories and songs along the way, but I must say, Andalian music has a charm all its own."

"Indeed," Grant said. "What brings you to our city at such an historical time?"

"Why, it's that very history you speak of, My Lord," Jack said, leaning in slightly and lowering his voice before continuing. "First, wars are fought by better men than me, so I thought it prudent to be on the right side when everything settles down, if you know what I mean." Grant smiled without humor and a few of the women tittered. "Second, this great city will be right at the heart of the war that decides the next age, and I mean to be the one who sings that story for all the world to hear."

"How very ... plausible."

"Dear, don't be rude," a very attractive woman said, stepping up next to Grant with a gracious smile. She was tall and held herself with deliberate poise. Her eyes were blue and her hair was red fading to brown and tied back in an elaborate braid with strands of silver woven through it.

Grant smiled at her with genuine, unguarded joy. Since Alexander had met the man, every action, every word, every gesture had been calculated and deliberate, yet the smile he gave his wife was spontaneous and real.

"Forgive the inquisitiveness," Grant said, bowing in deference to her. "With all that's been going on, I'm afraid I'm a little uneasy."

"There's nothing to forgive, Lord Grant," Jack said with another bow. "You are right to be vigilant."

"I have some friends who need to leave but haven't had a chance to meet you yet, Master Colton," Joss Grant said. "May I steal you from my husband for a moment?"

"With your permission, Lord Grant."

"Of course," Grant said, giving his wife's hand a squeeze as she turned to leave with Jack. He watched them go for a moment before commanding Alexander to follow him with a look. He took him inside and downstairs, deep under the manor house, until they reached a large, bare room with a magic circle inlaid into the floor. Grant dropped the bar on the door and pulled Alexander into the circle with him before saying another word.

"Nobody can hear us here," he said. "Tell me who you are. Tell me why Tyr wants you. Tell me why the Babachenko didn't let me kill you ... that's ... that's just unheard of."

Alexander stood mute, weighing his options.

"Here's how I see it," Grant said, starting to walk in a circle around Alexander. "Something about you is important, and that means you have value. Since I paid for you, I want to maximize my investment, which means I have to know what you're worth to make the best deal I can. I would prefer to come to some kind of agreement with you, but you should know that I'm not above bringing your sister down here."

Alexander couldn't help but smile, just a little.

"Something about that funny?" he said, stepping close to Alexander, invading his space, then stepping back deliberately and reining in his hostility. "Let's consider other options, shall we? Now, we both know you're not the pretender. He'd be a fool to come here ... and besides, he has bigger problems, if I hear right. So that leaves a whole range of options. You could be Acuna, but Tyr wouldn't care about that. In fact, he wouldn't care if you were a spy from any organization on Andalia.

"That narrows it down quite a bit. Then there's the Babachenko. He would kill a slave just as soon as look at one, and yet he stopped me from killing you, even though you'd seen something of the utmost importance to the war effort. You're clearly a security risk. As a slave, that means a quick death, no question.

"Yet here you stand ... and I want to know why."

Alexander faced him silently, relaxed and poised, ready to act should the attack come ... but it didn't.

"Perhaps we could help one another," Grant mused. "If I had to guess, I'd say you're one of the pretender's agents come to take the Lancers out of the war. Eliminate the Crown ... or the king ... and the force lances lose their magic. Andalia's greatest vulnerability. What if you and I wanted the same thing?"

Alexander wished to the Maker that he could see this man's colors.

"I'm a merchant," Grant continued. "All my life, the Lancers have ruled the roads with unchallenged authority, exacting bribes when and how they please, dispensing justice at their whim. The Lancers have no authority within the cities where countless factions vie for power and wealth, but trade requires transport over the roads.

"When the war started, the king sent the bulk of the Lancers to Ruatha, where they're laying waste as we speak," he said, watching Alexander carefully.

Alexander schooled his expression, hoping with all his might that Grant was lying, yet knowing full well that he wasn't.

"Since most of the Lancers shipped out, my profits are up dramatically. I can get shipments through for a fraction of the cost. That got me to wondering about what might be possible if the Lancers were gone forever."

"You speak treason," Alexander said.

"Treason for me, war for you. We both get what we want."

"I'm not at war, My Lord," Alexander said. "I don't know why Lord Tyr wanted to buy me, and I'm not sure he knew why either, only that he did and that he couldn't get his way. And I don't know why the Babachenko stayed my execution, though I'm grateful that he did."

Grant stared at him, clenching his jaw, openly appraising Alexander like a piece of meat. Alexander looked at the ground, but he was watching Grant closely with his all around sight.

"I could pay you."

Alexander looked up. "Pay me for what?"

"Killing the king," Grant said.

"How would I do that? I'm just a ranch hand."

"Pity, I was hoping we could work together," Grant said. "I guess the best I can do is turn you in to the Acuna as a spy. I hear they draw the end out as long as possible. You'll stay here tonight. I'll send for them in the morning."

Alexander waited until he left, extinguishing the lamps and plunging the room into darkness, before testing the boundary of the magic circle. He quickly stepped back inside when his collar began to constrict. Then he sat down in the center of the circle reached out to Chloe.

"Lead Jack and Anja here if you can, Little One."

More than an hour later, Jack slipped into the room, shrouded by his cloak but clear as day from his colors. Anja showed up soon after.

"We have a lot to talk about," Alexander said, once they were all seated within the circle. Chloe buzzed into existence and floated to the floor in front of Alexander. "Why don't you start, Jack."

"All right … on the way to the city, I left the caravan and obtained some official papers, then went straight to the Minstrels Guild once we arrived. It took me a day to learn the requisite song lyrics, really a pathetic set of pandering blather set to ancient music. Didn't take long to get my chit after that. I've used that cover to gather quite a bit of background information about Mithel Dour.

"In truth, this place is like nothing I've ever seen. There's a strict class system, with a very definite hierarchy. Privileges flow from rank; law is applied not based on the crime committed but upon a combination of the crime and the ranks of the criminal and the victim. Bribes are common and even expected.

"For me, the most frightening aspect of this city is the total lack of thought people put into the claims made by the government. For well over half of the people, if the government says it's so, then it's so, even if their own eyes tell them otherwise.

"In many ways, a bard is a propagandist, a teller of stories who mixes truth with fantasy to create a version of reality that makes an argument. And in all my life, I've never seen a people so unskeptical, so unquestioning, and so pliable as these people.

"I can only guess that they've been conditioned to believe the authorities and trained to avoid thinking about any subject with a critical eye. That leaves the rest of the people, self-interested criminals all, to take advantage of the sheep without challenge."

"No wonder this place is so broken," Alexander said.

"From an operational perspective, I've obtained lease to two residences and a bakery with a basement that accesses one of the underground passage networks. I have modest stockpiles of food and water, so you both have a place to hide when you decide to move."

"Nice."

"Spending time entertaining the nobility has given me the opportunity to gather some potentially useful information. It seems that General Talia has launched a rather effective insurgency within the western province where you were captured. They have begun to coordinate attacks against the slave camps and caravans while avoiding or ambushing the Lancers in the forest. There are also stories that the rebels have magical support ... as well as reports of dragons. As I understand it, the Babachenko isn't pleased with this development."

"What do you mean, dragons?" Anja asked.

"I'm certain people are mistaking wyverns for dragons," Jack said.

"They wouldn't if they'd ever seen a real dragon."

"You're probably right," Alexander said. "Anything else, Jack?"

"This character Nightshade is a frequent subject of hushed conversations in the upper circles. He's been stealing shipments of silver bound for the shipyards along the northern coast. The effect has been to financially weaken the Andalian Cartage Company as well as the Cartage Guild, precipitate a work stoppage in the ports backed by the Shipwrights Guild, and undermine confidence in the Lancers and therefore in the king's ability to protect trade routes. I presume the stolen silver is an added bonus. We might consider reaching out to him. Some of his goals seem to coincide with our own."

"The thought crossed my mind," Alexander said. "Anja, what have you learned?"

"Only that Lady Grant was really unhappy about the death of the crown princess, but when I asked how long she'd known her, she said they'd never met. It didn't make sense. Other than that, I've been a servant ... and I'm getting tired of it."

"There's more to the death of the crown princess," Jack said. "The word on the street is that the king impregnated his sister, which is the long tradition of the Andalian royal line so as to maximize the purity of the bloodline. Apparently the Acuna is very concerned about the viability of the Crown. In fact, it's a common theme of some of their more stock propaganda.

"The interesting thing is, Joss Grant is a cousin of the king."

"And you think she's afraid the king will claim her to produce a pure blood heir."

"I know she's terrified of it because she brought it up to me," Jack said.

"Interesting," Alexander said. "Considering Grant's recent activities, I wouldn't be surprised if her fear isn't well founded. These people have a maddeningly complex array of rules and laws that seem more designed to control than protect, but they do respect them … at least the more prominent citizens do."

"Seems only natural," Jack said. "The rules provide them with their wealth and power, and the more complex they can make them, the harder it is for people of lesser means to understand and therefore comply. That way, powerful people can always find some legal justification for persecuting those of lesser rank. Large numbers of complex rules also enables corruption to thrive."

"Corruption is certainly alive and well here," Alexander said. "I think it's time for us to move. Titus Grant just tried to make a deal with me. He said he thinks I'm one of the pretender's agents sent to stir up trouble. He wants me to kill the king so he can make more money … trouble is, I can't see his colors. I can see him with my all around sight like I can see anyone else, but he just doesn't have any colors, so I don't know what to think about him."

"Don't trust him," Jack said.

"No, but he might be useful."

"If he doesn't have colors, he's dangerous."

"There's more. He can make people not see him … or those with him."

Anja and Jack looked around the room.

"I don't think he's here," Alexander said.

"So he has something like my cloak?"

"No, he can make people not even perceive that he's there, like he's reaching into their minds and blocking out his very existence from their awareness."

"That makes for a very short fight," Jack said.

"True, but I think it might be worth the risk, especially if he really does want the king dead. Either way, he's going to force the issue. If I don't agree to work with him, I'll have to kill him, and that could be a problem given his rather unique talents."

Jack and Anja both nodded reluctantly.

"There's a lot more …" Alexander spent nearly an hour explaining the mine, the crystals, the Babachenko, and Tyr, briefing Jack and Anja about everything that had transpired and warning them to be prepared to move quickly. Finally, he outlined his plan and objectives.

After they left, Alexander sat in the middle of the circle and brought himself to the edge of the firmament, then held himself there, focusing his mind and freeing himself of all thought at the same time. He balanced on that edge until it felt natural, sitting in that state when Grant entered the following morning.

He wasn't in the firmament, yet his all around sight was perfect, clear with vibrant detail, reaching out farther than ever before. He was sitting quietly, his mind poised on the very edge of the collar's control, at the precipice of the firmament, yet still present in his own mind, and the moment felt like he owned it, as if he could bend it to his will with a thought.

He opened his eyes and focused on Titus Grant with his entire awareness.

"Decision time," Grant said.

Alexander stood up slowly, settling into a stance that was at once relaxed yet tense, and faced Grant very deliberately.

"I have terms."

"I'm listening."

"Remove the collars from me and my sister, give me a thousand silver crowns and papers for us both, plus a hundred thousand silver crowns once the king is dead. Oh, and I'll need your help in gaining access to the palace." Alexander stopped talking and held his breath.

Grant stared at Alexander as if thinking through his options. "That's quite a change of heart."

Alexander shrugged, "You forced my hand."

"Perhaps you're just telling me what I want to hear. I mean, I'm good at reading people, but not that good. I can't help but wonder if there isn't another explanation for you being here—one that I haven't considered."

"Oh, you were close. I *was* sent by Lord Reishi but I'm not one of his agents; I'm a hired assassin."

"Would he really entrust such an important task to one with such fickle loyalty? Doubtful."

"That's assuming I'm the only assassin he's hired for the job," Alexander said. "There are twelve others. The one who returns with the Andalian Crown gets paid, the rest get nothing. I've already killed two of them, but I'm afraid a few the others are getting close and I have no intention of letting them collect my reward."

"That's a bit more plausible, though still unlikely. He has to know how difficult it would be to kill the king. It's far more likely that he would send his very best ... and I seriously doubt that his best would wind up here wearing a slave collar."

"Like I said, he's sent others, probably more than just the other assassins I'm competing with. And keep in mind, Andalia isn't his only concern. As for winding up here, it seemed like a good plan—get close to a powerful noble and leverage his access to infiltrate the palace."

Grant's eyes narrowed as he regarded Alexander skeptically.

"Come now, Lord Grant," Alexander said. "What do you think that show with Tyr was really all about? I paid him handsomely to take an interest in me, knowing full well that his interest would pique yours."

"You played me," Grant said.

"Perhaps a little too well," Alexander said, gesturing to the magic circle he was standing in.

"That still doesn't explain the Babachenko," Grant said. "Why would he spare you?"

Alexander frowned, looking away in feigned frustration. "I don't know and I'm a bit concerned about it."

"You should be," Grant said, starting to pace, then stopping abruptly to face Alexander again. "Fifty thousand silver crowns, no more."

"What about everything else?"

"Done, but you need to be ready tonight. The king is very well protected, so access is difficult and limited. Fortunately, the crown princess must be mourned, tradition demands it. There will be a banquet in her honor tonight at the palace. You and your sister will accompany Joss and me as our personal servants. That's the best access I can give you."

"Good enough," Alexander said, tapping the collar around his neck.

"It has to stay on if you're going into the palace," Grant said, shaking his head. "Powerful wards guard the inner chambers where the king lives—wards that can detect a slave collar. If you try to enter with a fake collar, the palace guard will be alerted immediately."

"That wasn't part of the deal," Alexander said.

"I can either take your collar off or give you access," Grant said with a helpless shrug.

"If you take it off, can you put it back on?"

"Of course."

"Then take it off for the day and put it back on before we go to the palace. I need time to prepare and this gets in the way."

"So you're a wizard then," Grant said, nodding thoughtfully. "As soon as I put the collar back on, your magic will be useless."

"Not entirely," Alexander said. "I have a number of very useful spells that last for quite some time. Once I cast them, their effects will remain even with the collar blocking my access to the firmament."

Grant hesitated.

"This was your idea. If you want it to work, then this is how it has to be."

"Very well, but you'll understand if I ask you not to leave the grounds."

"I don't intend to," Alexander said. "In fact, I don't plan on leaving this room, although I would appreciate it if you'd send down some breakfast."

Grant chuckled as he touched his ring and closed his eyes. A moment later, Alexander's collar popped open and he handed it over, rubbing his neck.

Chapter 12

The firmament came easily. Always before, it took an effort … calming his body, clearing his mind, entertaining thoughts just to acknowledge them so that he could dismiss them one by one. It had been weeks since he'd been able to touch the firmament and it seemed closer than ever.

He thought of Isabel and the world flashed past him.

She was alive. For several moments he simply looked at her, marveling at her beauty and wondering at her courage. She was in an overly decorated room, sitting at a table with an older man cloaked in the colors of a wizard. Of far greater concern were Isabel's colors. The Wraith Queen's grip was tightening.

"It just doesn't make sense to me," Isabel said.

"But it's so simple!" the wizard said, throwing up his hands.

"Maybe for you, but you've been studying magic for years," Isabel shot back. "I just went through the mana fast less than a year ago."

"These are the most basic concepts. You should have learned them before even attempting the mana fast."

"Yeah, well, it didn't work out that way," Isabel said, walking away from the table.

Wren came in from the balcony as if she lived there. Surprising, since the last he knew, she was imprisoned in the hold of a ship.

"Is it time to eat yet?" she asked.

"Perhaps a break would be in order," the wizard said, collecting his hat and staff before leaving.

"You're a lifesaver, Wren. I don't know how much longer I can play dumb with that man."

Alexander materialized, laughing.

"Oh! Thank the Maker, you're alive," she said, stepping toward him with tears welling up in her eyes, both hands covering her mouth.

"So are you," Alexander said. "I wish I could touch you."

She nodded, tears spilling down her cheeks.

"I don't have much time … I just needed to know that you're safe."

"Phane told me you were dead," she said, wiping her cheeks. "He said he couldn't find you with his magic and that could only mean one thing."

"He's a liar," Alexander whispered.

"I got a knife into his gut, but it wasn't enough," she said, struggling to collect her emotions. "So much has happened. Phane has me and Wren. He's trying to make me use the darkness … I'm fighting it, but I'm terrified that it's only a matter of time before I lose control."

"I believe in you, Isabel. You can do this."

"There's another problem," Isabel said. "Phane just sent an expedition to retrieve the Goiri's remains. I sent Slyder to find Ayela in the hopes that she can stop Phane's people, but she's nowhere to be found."

"I'll deliver the message," Alexander said. "I'm coming for you, Isabel, just as soon as I can."

"I know … I love you."

"I love you," Alexander said, fading back into the firmament. He turned his thoughts to Ayela and found himself in an underground room, where she and Severine Karth were sharing a meal.

"Hello, Ayela."

"Lord Reishi?" she said, standing in a rush. "Phane has Isabel."

"I know," Alexander said. He turned to Severine, who was staring at him like he'd seen a ghost. "Forgive me, Lord Severine, I would prefer a less dramatic introduction, but circumstances are forcing my hand. Phane has sent an expedition to retrieve the rest of the Goiri bones. If he succeeds, he'll win this war."

"But how? How are you even here?" Severine asked.

"Magic, Father," Ayela said, "but that's not important. We must stop Phane, and we will, Lord Reishi, but there's something else. My brother Trajan has a Goiri bone and I fear that it's driving him mad. He's fled into the jungle and we can't find him."

Alexander nodded thoughtfully. "I won't be able to find him as long as he has that bone. Fortunately, neither will Phane, at least not with his magic."

She sat back down, deflated. "I understand. We'll do everything we can to stop Phane from getting the bones."

"Thank you, Princess," Alexander said with a bow as he vanished, slipping back into the firmament and then appearing on the battlements of Fellenden City right next to Abigail and Anatoly.

Abigail did a double take. "Where have you been? I've been worried sick."

"It's good to see you too, Abby. I'm on Andalia … and I'm planning to assassinate their king tonight."

"Are ya now?" Anatoly said, leaning over the railing to look around Abigail.

"Believe it or not, I didn't go looking for this particular fight … they dragged me to it."

"So you and Jack are just going to stroll into the Andalian palace and kill the king while his royal guard watches?" Abigail said.

"Actually, Anja and I …"

"Wait … Anja, the dragon whelp?" Anatoly asked.

"She stowed away in human form when I left the dragon isle. Bragador knows, and she isn't coming to eat me, at least not yet anyway."

"So where's Jack?" Abigail asked, a hint of fear in her voice.

"He's playing the role he was born to play—the most popular minstrel in all of Andalia, maybe in all the world."

Abigail smiled, struggling to contain her emotions.

"I'm glad to hear that Master Colton is well, but let's get back to this assassination you're planning," Anatoly said. "After you kill the king, assuming you manage that, then what?"

"Then we leave," Alexander said. "This isn't why I'm here. I need to know what Zuhl's up to."

"We'll get to that in a minute," Anatoly said. "I'd like to hear your plan for getting out of the Andalian palace after you've killed their king."

"All right … Anja can turn back into her true form whenever she wants, but then she'd have to go home and she doesn't want to do that, even though her mother and I both agree that it would be for the best. Once we kill the king, there'll be only one way out—for her to fly us out. We escape and then Anja goes home where she belongs."

"Huh … well, it's not a perfect plan, but it is a plan, provided the dragon isn't too stubborn to cooperate," Anatoly said.

"About Zuhl?"

"We have reports that the northern ocean is navigable, but dangerous," Abigail said. "We had snow last week, the last of the season according to Mage Jalal. He predicts warmer weather over the coming days, so we're preparing to move north. Zuhl's force has abandoned the shipyards and withdrawn into the walls of Irondale. I suspect they'll receive reinforcements before we arrive, so I've called on the Ithilian Navy to sail north and blockade the city."

"Where's his countermove?" Alexander muttered.

"I've been wondering the same thing," Anatoly said. "We hit him pretty hard. He has to be looking for a way to hit us back."

"What does he want?" Alexander asked.

"Iron Oak ships," Abigail said, "but he hasn't even tried to rebuild his shipyard."

"Not that one, anyway," Alexander said. "I'll be right back." He vanished, moving his awareness to the Iron Oak Forest in a blur. Once there, he moved to the point where it met Irondale and the ocean, then followed the coastline west as fast as he could while still registering the landscape.

"He's got five more shipyards," Alexander said, reappearing beside his sister a few minutes later. "Each looks just big enough to build one ship; all five are along the northern coast. The terrain is so rugged it would be difficult to get enough men to any of them over land."

"Well, at least we know what he's doing," Abigail said. "I'll send scouts to map their exact locations and then we'll get to work. Stay safe, Alex."

"You too," he said. "Oh, I almost forgot, Phane has Isabel and Wren. They're both safe for now, but his plans for them aren't good."

"How did that happen?" Abigail asked, alarm in her voice.

"Isabel pretended to switch sides so she could get close enough to stab him in the belly."

"You did well with that one, Alexander," Anatoly said, nodding approvingly.

"Unfortunately, Phane survived and she was captured. Then he abducted Wren from Blackstone to use as leverage against Isabel."

"What are we going to do about that?" Abigail said.

"I'm working on it."

Abigail nodded as Alexander faded away.

Next, he appeared in a war council room with a dozen officers, including his father and Hanlon. Both looked like they'd come from the battlefield several hours before and hadn't bothered to get cleaned up.

Duncan looked up, confusion ghosting across his haggard face, and then he smiled. "I've been worried about you, Son."

"I got sidetracked," Alexander said. "Abigail is in Fellenden City with Anatoly and the rest of her army. She's planning to move against Zuhl's forces in Irondale soon. Phane has Isabel. She's safe ... for the moment."

"What does that mean?" Hanlon asked, worry evident in his voice.

"He's trying to turn her to the darkness, so he's treating her like royalty. I don't believe she's in any immediate danger."

"I hope you're right," Duncan said, straightening up. "I'm sorry to say we've lost Warrenton, Buckwold, and Headwater. We suspect the Lancers will regroup before attacking New Ruatha ... at least that's been their pattern."

"Casualties?"

"The bulk of our losses have been soldiers ... we managed to get most of the people out before winter's end," Duncan said. "We've been fighting a retreating action since winter broke in the east. The first battle went our way—a lot of Lancers fell, but those that got through managed to break our lines and cripple our defensive emplacements. We retreated when they fell back to regroup.

"Over the winter, we built a series of defensive positions between Buckwold and New Ruatha where we could make a stand against a charge. It's been costly ... we've lost nearly a legion, but we've killed a legion of Lancers as well. It also slowed their advance, giving us the time we needed to relocate the people. They're not happy about being refugees, but they're alive."

Alexander nodded sadly. He felt like he should be doing more, like he should be with his father, leading the fight for his home.

"I'm in the capital city of Andalia right now. If my plan works, the force lances will lose their power tonight."

"I wondered why General Talia thought you were on Andalia," Hanlon said, sitting forward. "As soon as Commander P'Tal heard where you were, he left Glen Morillian to find you. I wouldn't be surprised if he shows up any day now."

"That's good news. I could use his help."

"Back to your plan," Duncan said.

"I don't have time to explain it right now, Dad," he said. "Just be ready if the force lances stop working. It's good to see you both. I wish I could stay longer, but I have a lot to do."

"Stay safe," Duncan said as Alexander vanished.

He found Jataan next, standing impassively outside a large tent in the midst of a hastily built camp, deep within the forests of the western province of Andalia.

"Hello, Jataan."

"Lord Reishi," Jataan said with a slight bow but almost no surprise.

"Report," Alexander said with a smile.

"I arrived on Andalia with a company of General Talia's best soldiers and a squad of Sky Knights two weeks ago. The soldiers have been organizing the local population into resistance units with significant success. The people who remain in this area are very motivated to fight but lack training and leadership. With our help, they've managed to destroy three slave camps and draw a number of Lancer patrols into ambushes. At present, the Lancers have consolidated into two large camps along the edge of the forest and have stopped patrols within.

"Where are you, Lord Reishi? I've healed and I'm ready to stand with you."

"I'm in Mithel Dour at the moment, but I plan on leaving tomorrow. If everything goes well, I'll make contact with you before I leave. If you don't hear from me by tomorrow night, make your way into the city and look for Jack."

"Understood."

"I'll be glad to have you back at my side, Jataan."

Alexander returned to his body and opened his eyes to a mild headache. After a few minutes of quiet meditation, he returned to the firmament and thought of Tyr.

The bull-necked man was looking at a number of suits of clothing being presented to him by a tailor while his wizard sat nearby.

"I hate fancy clothes," Tyr said.

"Your customary attire would be considered an insult to the king," the wizard said.

"What about your robes?" Tyr shot back.

"I'm a wizard … my robes are fashionable in any situation."

"Be careful, Edric."

"Of course, My Lord."

"Tell me again why I have to go to this thing."

"It's known that you are in the city," Edric said. "It would be considered a snub to the king if you did not attend."

"The king's an idiot," Tyr said. "He won't know one way or the other."

"But the Babachenko will."

Alexander floated out of Tyr's manor house and moved his focus to the palace. It was an enormous structure built into the top of a dam that held back a sizable mountain lake. The stonework was certainly accomplished by magic. The entire palace had a fluid, graceful design that was as beautiful as it was functional. At the very center sat a banquet hall built almost entirely of glass. Only the side walls were stone, while the ceiling, front and back walls were transparent, allowing an unobstructed view of the mountains reflecting off of the calm water to the east and the sun setting over the city below to the west.

Water flowed from the lake into the palace through myriad conduits, some for consumption, some for utility, and some for power. The only ways in were the twin elevators powered by the controlled flow of water through an array of paddlewheels.

Deeper within, Alexander found the forges, both coming to life as workers prepared to put them into service after so many years of disuse. He moved closer and discovered what he'd feared. The crystals Grant had found in the mine were being prepared to power the forges in a vastly scaled-down version of a heartstone chamber. The ranks of Lancers would soon begin to expand.

He spent over an hour exploring the palace while servants worked frantically to prepare for the banquet. The guards wore different uniforms than the overseers or the Lancers, and they were alert and well organized. Still, their number was limited. Given the difficulty of reaching the palace in the first place, a large guard force didn't seem warranted.

Most of the upper chambers and passages were busy with servants and functionaries, but the palace had many levels below that were used for storage or simply not used at all. What he couldn't find was an escape route. In every keep he'd ever seen, there was always some form of hidden way out, yet this palace seemed entirely cut off except through the twin elevators.

Next, he went to the king's chambers but slammed back into his body the moment he tried to pass through the wards protecting that part of the palace. His hope of hiding in the palace and killing the king in his sleep diminished. If he couldn't move through the barriers around the king's chamber with his clairvoyance, he knew without a doubt that he wouldn't be able to physically enter that part of the palace. That left the banquet itself. Not his first choice, but the best chance he would probably get, all things considered.

He calmed his doubt and returned to the firmament, this time going to the mine and the darkness within. He found an ancient city carved into the stone on many levels, with countless rooms, buildings, and bridges. The central chamber where he and Grant had turned back was a great chasm nearly three leagues long, reaching deep into the heart of the mountain. All along the chasm walls were structures built into the stone, some were platforms jutting out into the black with buildings resting upon them that could only be described as works of art, while others were vast networks of chambers cut into the stone with delicate grace yet structural soundness. As Alexander explored, he found many more of the crystals that glowed with the colors of life—the crystals that the Andalians were using to make force lances and slave collars.

He delved deeper, finding chambers and statues that looked like they'd been created for the artistry of it rather than for any functional purpose. One enormous room held a forest, accurate in every detail, down to the needles on the fir trees and the birds on the branches, yet everything in the room was made entirely of stone, silver, and gold. Alexander could have spent hours in that room alone just marveling at the detail of it all.

Occasionally, he came across creatures in the dark that he couldn't identify, some so well-hidden that he would never have seen them were it not for their colors.

Many of the areas in the vast network of chambers were lit by eerily glowing stones set into the walls and ceilings that cast just enough light to see by, while other places were black as pitch.

As Alexander neared the far end of the chasm, he started to see the faint glow of light in the distance. Abandoning his cursory search of the underground city, he flitted to the light with a thought. A stone platform seemed to float in the darkness; the single bridge that used to link it to the rest of the structures had long since vanished, leaving only the abutment. Seven pillars of stone once stood in a circle on the platform. Six topped with softly glowing orbs remained, while the seventh lay broken and scattered in chunks. Just within the pillars was a magic circle cut into the stone, but instead of the customary seven symbols, there were dozens of symbols crowded between the inner and outer boundary lines. Near where the pillar had fallen, the stone floor was melted and deformed, wiping away a section of the magic circle.

In the center of it all rested a low altar cut from a vein of quartz shot through with gold. Atop it was a broad bowl carved from the same piece of quartz. Alexander had seen something like this before. He approached and found the bowl empty except for dust and a few pieces of stone debris.

As he was examining the altar, a mound of dirt that he hadn't given a second thought to stood up, taking the form of a crudely sculpted humanoid.

"Why are you taking them?" he pleaded. "They've done nothing to harm you. Please bring them back."

Alexander materialized before the three-foot-tall humanoid, wondering how the creature had been aware of him. "Hello," he said.

"Why are you taking them?" the humanoid said with such forlorn sadness that Alexander couldn't help but feel sympathy.

"I haven't taken anything, but maybe I can help you. My name is Alexander."

"I'm called McGinty, or I was. Now I'm just alone in the dark. They made me too well and now they've gone."

"Who's gone?"

"The fay."

"I don't know who the fay are."

"They're the makers."

"They made all of this?"

"No, they made those that made all of this."

"And who are they?"

"The Linkershim. Why are you taking them?"

"I'm not."

"But you're a fleshling. You dig and you dig until you find the Linkershim and then you kill them. They've never done you any harm, yet you kill them. Why?"

"Who are the Linkershim?"

"They are the builders made by the makers."

"So the makers are the fay."

McGinty nodded.

"What happened to them?"

"They died," McGinty said, sitting down dejectedly. "When the light went out of the world, they all died."

"When did this happen?"

"Before," McGinty said.

"Before what?"

McGinty seemed confused … he was hard to read, since his colors were so faint as to be almost invisible and his facial expressions were made of clay. Alexander waited.

"Before the fleshlings came."

"And I'm a fleshling."

"Yes. Why have you taken them?"

"I haven't taken anything."

"But you have ... I saw you. You took three of them."

"The crystals are the Linkershim?"

"Yes, why did you take them?"

"I was with a man who took them, but I didn't know what they were ... I'm still not sure I do."

"You are a fleshling, and you took them. I tried to keep you out. I shook the world and I warded the entrance, but still you came. More will come and more Linkershim will die."

"The crystals are alive?"

"They are Linkershim—they are all alive."

"How?"

"Magic ... the fay made them."

"But they're just crystals, they can't do anything."

"Not anymore," McGinty said, starting to cry, though without tears. It seemed very odd for such an inhuman creature to behave with such humanity.

"McGinty, tell me what happened."

"The first fleshling happened. He came into the underdark and took the memory. I tried to stop him, but I couldn't—his magic was beyond me, beyond the defenses. When he left with the memory, the Linkershim stopped building, stopped moving ... just stopped. I've been alone ever since."

"What's the memory? I don't understand."

"It was there," McGinty said, pointing at the crystal bowl without looking. "I was made to protect it, to preserve the memory of the world, and I failed."

Alexander stared at the altar while the implications swirled around in his mind. The blood of the earth *was* the memory of the world, and he had a drop— just one, but Balthazar had said that a single drop was enough, that the blood of the earth was all one thing, one entity, separated by distance yet connected completely.

One of the paths to Isabel's salvation depended on the blood of the earth.

"Who took it?"

"He told me his name, told me he needed the memory more than I did, told me it would win a war. I tried to stop him."

"And his name?"

"Siavrax Karth."

"Siavrax Karth was the first fleshling?"

"Yes," McGinty said, nodding. "After the fay left, the Linkershim lived here, building, always building, but never venturing above. And then the first fleshling came and took the memory and they stopped building."

"How did they build? They're just crystals."

McGinty stared at him, his head slowly tilting this way and that until he very deliberately shrugged.

"They told the earth and stone what to become," he said, finally.

"And the earth and stone obeyed?"

"Yes," McGinty said, standing up, raising his hands and head, looking around at the underdark as if it were the whole of creation.

His hands and head fell like he'd suddenly run out of energy. "But now the earth and stone are silent and still."

Alexander went to the crystal bowl. "Is this where the memory of the world was kept?"

McGinty frowned, seeming to process the question. "That is where it resided," he said.

A whole race of intelligent beings subjected to forced hibernation for millennia.

"What would happen to the Linkershim if the memory of the world returned?"

McGinty looked up at Alexander, his clay face struggling to produce a coherent expression.

"The Linkershim would awaken."

One fewer chance for Isabel.

"What would the Linkershim do after they woke?"

"They would build."

"What about the fleshlings?"

McGinty hesitated again, shaking his head slowly. "They are very angry with the fleshlings for killing them."

"How could you know that if they haven't moved for so long?"

"I can hear their song, beautiful and complex, infinitely varied, yet unique. When one Linkershim dies, the song changes, forever adding death and loss where once there was life and creation."

"They're mourning their dead," Alexander whispered.

"Why do you take the Linkershim?"

"Some of the fleshlings use the Linkershim to create weapons," Alexander said. "But fleshlings are not all the same."

"All fleshlings I've seen are the same," McGinty said. "There are differences in appearance, but you are all made the same, except you, since you aren't really here."

"You can tell I'm an illusion," Alexander said. "Huh ..."

"I would not have allowed a fleshling to get this close to the well of memory, not again ... never again."

"When I say that all fleshlings aren't the same, I mean they don't all want the same things. Some fleshlings are good and others are evil ... most of us are just trying to survive."

McGinty didn't answer, his head cocked to one side and a semblance of a frown creasing his unfinished face.

"There are only a few fleshlings who've hurt the Linkershim," Alexander said. "Most of us are innocent. If the Linkershim woke, would they hurt the innocent?"

"What is innocent?"

"Fleshlings who've done nothing wrong."

"Fleshlings killed Linkershim."

"Some did ... most didn't."

"But you are all fleshlings."

"Let's try this a different way," Alexander said. "If I returned the memory of the world to the well, would the Linkershim go to war against the fleshlings?"

"No," he said, after a long pause as if he were listening to something only he could hear. "They would build."

"After that, what would happen when the fleshlings tried to take a Linkershim?"

"The Linkershim would stop them."

"What would they do to the city above us?"

McGinty paused again, listening.

"Unbuild it," he said.

"Would they let the fleshlings leave first?"

"Yes ..."

What would Isabel counsel him to do if he could tell her about the blood of the earth? If he could explain everything, what would she tell him to do?

A whole race of intelligent beings capable of building on a grand scale, but also capable of art and beauty like nothing he'd ever seen before.

What would she say if he saved her with the blood of the earth and then told her about the Linkershim?

"McGinty, I want to help you, and I think I can, but you'll have to help me get here with my body. I don't know the way through the underdark."

"You are a fleshling."

"I know, and I want to help you. I have a drop of the memory of the world. I'll bring it here if you'll help me navigate the underdark."

"Why would you help us?"

"Because the Linkershim are alive," Alexander said with a shrug. "And because I want to see Mithel Dour be unbuilt."

McGinty tried to frown, tilting his head to one side. "Bring the memory of the world to where the fleshlings entered and I will help you, but only after I'm sure you have the memory."

"I will," Alexander said, vanishing and returning to his body.

His list had gotten long, and as with all such lists, some tasks would be easier to accomplish before others.

Chapter 13

Jack slipped into the room and barred the door before tossing his hood back.

"It's good to see you both," he said, taking a seat in the circle with Alexander and Anja.

"You too, Jack," Alexander said. "Before we get started, I have Chloe watching the door. If anyone comes, she'll let us know so you can hide. I don't want anyone to know we're allied."

"So what's the plan?"

"The short version: we're going into the palace to kill the king tonight."

"Ambitious," Jack said. "I've already secured an invitation to the banquet. I figured I might learn something useful … that and the invitation read more like a summons, so I thought it best to attend."

"Good. Make sure you maintain your cover," Alexander said. "If things go badly, I want you to escape and look for Jataan; he'll be coming to the city if I don't make contact by tomorrow night."

"Understood," Jack said. "There's something else. I received this letter today. It was on the table in my residence with a dried nightshade blossom on top of it."

"What's it say?"

"It offers to pay me quite well if I will report that I saw suspicious activity at a particular house."

"I wonder what he's up to," Alexander said.

"Probably a number of things," Jack said. "First, he's is trying to determine if I can be useful to him. Second, he's trying to eliminate a rival. Third, he's trying to get dirt on me to use as leverage in later negotiations."

"Sounds like you've given this some thought."

"A bit, yes."

"I don't see an upside," Alexander said.

"On the contrary. I should absolutely do as he asks. I've been looking for a way to reach out to him, and what better way than letting him reach out to me?"

"I don't trust him."

"Nor should you," Jack said. "But he clearly has resources and knowledge we lack. Whatever his motivations are, he could be an extremely useful ally."

"All right, but be careful. This might be a trap," Alexander said. "Once we've killed the king, we'll head for the western province. Talia has a company working with the locals to disrupt the Lancers' slaving operation, but more importantly, that's where Jataan is."

"That's good to hear. He's not much of a conversationalist, but he's nice to have around in a fight."

"Who's Jataan?" Anja asked.

"Jataan P'Tal is the General Commander of the Reishi Protectorate and my personal man-at-arms," Alexander said. "He is, quite possibly, the most dangerous man alive in a fight."

"I want to meet him."

"You will," Alexander said. "So the plan hinges on Tyr ..."

***

Lord and Lady Grant arrived at the palace elevator station in a carriage driven by Alexander with Anja at his side. Both still wore their collars, but Alexander had a dagger hidden in his boot.

The atmosphere was festive, excited even. Nobles mingled with one another while they waited for the elevator to return. Alexander idly wondered who had really killed the crown princess while he watched the crowd without appearing to do so.

Most guests wore the muddy, base colors of those who pursue power before all other things, but there were a few notable exceptions, mostly among the slaves and servants. Every now and then, Alexander would see a person with the colors of magic, most from some enchanted item or other, but a few were wizards, though you wouldn't know it from their behavior or attire.

After nearly an hour of insufferable conversation about the most meaningless things, the elevator settled into its cradle and the double doors opened. Within were four palace guards, each armed with a nasty-looking mace sporting five spikes twisted to make them look almost like a crown. More importantly, each of their weapons glowed brightly with magic.

The guests and their servants stepped into the lift, which was a simple room filled with rows of comfortable chairs and lined with windows on three sides. The doors closed and the operator pulled a lever. With a shudder, the lift began rising along its thousand feet of vertical track. It took several minutes, during which time the view became progressively more spectacular.

When they reached the palace, everyone stepped out of the elevator and into a security line that ran along a balcony overlooking the city. Alexander was startled to discover that he could actually see that far. Before, his all around sight could only reach several hundred feet. While he still couldn't see the horizon, he could see parts of the city a thousand feet below.

They reached a broad entrance flanked by six guards. Spread across the entrance was a field of slightly glowing yellow light. An officer and a well-dressed servant stood at a podium in the exact center of the path.

After Grant presented his invitation, everyone in his party was instructed to touch the stone on top of the podium. Alexander did as he was told and felt a chill of magic race over his skin, followed by a tingling sensation when he stepped through the shield.

"Touch the stone before you go through that shield, Chloe," Alexander said in his mind. "Just to be safe."

The corridor stopped at the entrance to the crystal ballroom where a man was waiting to announce the arriving guests.

When Grant and his wife stepped up to the entrance and waited for their introduction, another man pulled Alexander and Anja aside. "Servants' entrance is down there," he said. "Just tell them who you belong to and they'll make sure you get where you're supposed to be."

Alexander obeyed without a word and was quickly swept up in the chaotic swirl of the kitchen. Within minutes he was carrying a pitcher of wine out to Lord Grant with strict instructions to pour a cup, then stand against the wall behind Grant until he was summoned. Once Alexander had completed his task and was standing next to Anja, he carefully surveyed the room while appearing to look at the floor.

As he'd seen from his reconnaissance, the two side walls were made of stone, while the front and back walls, as well as the ceiling, were made of crystal panes laced together with stone in a graceful pattern that seemed almost organic. The setting sun lit up the room with brilliant orange light.

Jack was already there, tuning his lute while a number of young, unattached noblewomen sat around him giggling. Most of the people in the room were mingling in small groups.

Guests were being announced in a steady stream as they made their way to the ballroom. Alexander picked out the Babachenko making the rounds, chatting amiably with the guests, welcoming them to the palace. Another man caught his eye as well. He was big—barrel-chested, and nearly seven feet tall. If his colors hadn't given him away as a wizard, his position near the only door on the opposite wall and his relentless scrutiny of the guests would have given him away as the king's protector.

"Vasili Nero, envoy of Prince Phane Reishi," the announcer said above the din of conversation. Alexander's breath caught in his chest. Without moving his head, he reached out and looked at Nero. What he saw sent a chill up his spine—Nero had become a wraithkin. He was smiling coldly to the Babachenko, who'd come to greet him personally.

"Master is not pleased," Nero said.

"He soon will be," the Babachenko said with an equally humorless smile. "I have matters well in hand."

"We shall see."

Alexander thought furiously. Adding Nero to the mix was bad enough— he could identify Alexander on sight. Their first meeting in Buckwold had gone badly for Nero; he wouldn't easily forget Alexander. His transformation into a wraithkin was a potential disaster. Even worse was the idea that the Babachenko did have things well in hand, and Alexander was missing some vital piece of information. If that was true, this night was going to end very badly.

Tyr entered next without pausing for the man to announce him. Alexander let his breath out when Nero sat facing away from him along the same side of the table where Grant was seated. Unfortunately, Tyr sat on the opposite side of the table, but he looked bored and inattentive, not bothering to talk to any of the nobles and deliberately ignoring Grant.

A bell chimed and the servants started to move to the kitchen for the first appetizer course, several large shrimp on a skewer, wrapped with bacon and drizzled with cheese sauce. A few of the guests required their servants to taste the food before serving it. Alexander was mildly disappointed that Grant did not.

A few moments after the appetizer was served, a large bell tolled and all of the guests stood, dutifully facing the single door on the wall opposite Alexander. After everyone had waited an uncomfortable amount of time, the door opened and an impeccably dressed little man with a completely bald head and a ruddy face stepped forth and stopped, surveying the crowd deliberately before clearing his throat.

"Lords and Ladies, I present His Most Excellent Majesty, the First Lancer, Giver of Charters and Founder of Guilds, Lord Gervais Andalia, Our Beloved King." The little man stepped aside, bowing deeply, holding his pose until the king entered the chamber.

The "Beloved King" was fat, blubberous and lumbering. His lips protruded, glistening with spittle, and his jaw hung slack. He was dressed in velvet red robes trimmed with entirely too much gold and he wore a jewel-encrusted baldric supporting a sword that looked almost exactly like a Thinblade, except its colors were dead. His stringy, unkempt hair was receding, his eyes were unfocused and dull, his hands (that he seemed to wring as a matter of habit) were soft and pudgy. On his head rested a golden Crown with colors that screamed of power, ancient and potent, yet the colors of the man wearing it revealed a small mind, an ailing body, and a vicious heart.

"Your Majesty," the little man who'd introduced him said, motioning to the head of the table.

The king labored to walk across the room, a faint wheeze emanating from his chest. When he reached his oversized chair, he stopped to catch his breath before flopping himself into it. The protector and the servant took up station behind him just before an army of servers filed past, setting a feast before him. He started eating as if he hadn't seen food in a week.

The guests took their seats and resumed their conversations, largely neglecting their now-cold appetizers and ignoring the overt display of wanton gluttony taking place at the head of the table.

The king seemed oblivious to his guests, gorging himself on a steady supply of different dishes placed before him. The service bell chimed again and the main course was served, roasted boar with rich brown gravy and crusty bread. Alexander was careful to ensure he didn't draw undue attention as he delivered the plate of food to Grant.

The meal progressed, one course after the next, most dishes returning to the kitchen only a bite or two lighter. Alexander had marked all of the dangerous players in the room: the protector, the Babachenko, Nero, Tyr, and several other nobles who were also wizards, plus the twelve palace guards interspersed around the periphery of the room. He knew he could probably kill the king with the knife in his boot before anyone knew what was happening, but he wasn't sure he'd be able to escape now that he was faced with the reality of the situation.

Then he considered the alternative—the damage the Lancers were doing in Ruatha. So many lives lost. He decided that taking action was worth the risk. As he fetched Grant's dessert, he had Chloe send his collar into the aether, stopping

Anja on her way to the kitchen to free her as well and hoping that nobody would notice two slaves without collars.

Midstride, he slipped the knife out of his boot and held it with the blade along his wrist while he served Grant his pastry. He stood, focusing on the king, gauging distance, looking for any hint of magical protection and finding none aside from his bodyguard.

The king sat back and belched loudly, then leaned forward with both hands on the table and stared at Tyr.

"I want the Thinblade!" he shouted, pointing at Tyr as he tried to stand quickly, but losing his balance in the bargain and falling back into his chair.

Alexander cautiously returned to his place along the wall.

Tyr's reaction actually surprised him.

"Your Majesty, I have humbly offered to give you my Thinblade several times," Tyr said with sweetness dripping off his tongue. He stood and smiled as he approached the king, unbuckling his belt and holding the hilt of the sword out toward him.

Before Tyr could reach him, the king's protector stepped between them, barring the way and slowly shaking his head.

"Enough!" the Babachenko said. "I've warned you about this, Lord Tyr."

"I want the Thinblade!" the king said, drool escaping from the edge of his mouth.

"I'm just trying to please the king," Tyr said, feigning innocence.

"I want it," the king said.

"Your Majesty, Lord Tyr holds the Tyr Thinblade," the Babachenko said. "It's tied to his bloodline just as the Crown is tied to yours."

"But I'm an Island King. I should have a Thinblade!"

"Perhaps someday, Your Majesty, but Lord Tyr's Thinblade would kill you."

The king crossed his arms and sat back, pouting and glaring at Tyr. For the first time since Alexander had met Lord Tyr, the man actually seemed happy.

Once Tyr had returned to his seat, the Babachenko stood and addressed the room.

"Lords and Ladies," he said, raising his glass until everyone stood. "We have come here today to mourn the loss of the crown princess. Pray that the Maker has taken her into his warm embrace." Everyone raised a glass, standing, heads bowed with mock solemnity, while the king sat petulantly glaring at Tyr.

"As you well know," the Babachenko continued, "the Andalian bloodline must remain as pure as possible to ensure the viability of the Crown. We are currently in the process of examining lineage records to identify who will have the privilege of serving as king's consort."

A number of women around the table tensed, their colors flaring with fear.

"Of course, if any of you believe you have a greater claim … or perhaps a lesser claim that warrants special consideration, I welcome your petitions."

There was a collective sigh from the women around the table. The Babachenko smiled slightly, motioning for the music to begin. Jack played an ode to the king, singing the praises of his courage and gallantry in battle. While the words were ridiculous, Jack's delivery was superb, drawing in even the most jaded guests in the room.

The Babachenko led the applause, standing to honor Jack and remaining standing after the rest of the guests had taken their seats.

"As I understand it, many of you have had the privilege of listening to Master Colton before. I now understand why he is so highly regarded, but I have come to learn something about him that isn't widely known … he is a true and loyal servant of the Andalian Crown.

"Just this afternoon, he reported suspicious activity to the authorities. He saw something out of the ordinary and he reported it. So new to our city and yet a model citizen.

"What he wasn't aware of was that the house he reported was a secret store for the notorious criminal Nightshade." The Babachenko stopped, nodding to the crowd. "We discovered hundreds of thousands of silver crowns, all stolen from shipments bound for the shipyards. It didn't take long from there for the overseers to determine who owned the house."

The Babachenko looked straight at Nigel Mohan, holder of the Cartage Charter, and shook his head sadly. "An outsider, doing his duty to the crown, has unraveled one of the most dangerous criminal enterprises in the empire, and I'm sad to say that Nightshade is, in fact, Lord Mohan."

Mohan stood, eyes wide, mouth working furiously without making a sound and his head shaking quickly back and forth.

"Lies," he managed to sputter. His wife started slapping him on the shoulder and berating him while two palace guards stepped up behind him.

"We will soon know the truth," the Babachenko said. "All of it. Take him away."

"No!" the king said, standing with visible effort, leaning heavily on the back of his chair.

"Your Majesty?" the Babachenko said.

"He's a traitor," the king said, motioning for the palace guard to bring Mohan to him.

The moment Mohan was close enough, the king quickly pulled a thin-bladed dirk from his sleeve and unceremoniously stabbed Mohan in the heart. He didn't look the man in the eyes, or even seem to notice that he was a human being. It was as impersonal a thing as Alexander had ever seen. The table fell silent as Mohan crumpled to the ground, his face a mask of confusion and disbelief. The king flopped back into his chair as if he'd just climbed a mountain, huffing loudly to catch his breath.

Grant stood up, drawing the Babachenko's attention. "I will buy the Cartage Charter."

The room fell deathly silent for just a moment before it erupted into chaos.

"I'll pay more."

"He can't own two charters."

"Dissolve the Cartage Charter and let us transport our own goods."

"No one's ever held two charters before."

"Preposterous!"

"Silence!" the Babachenko shouted, waiting for the room to quiet. "The Cartage Charter is not for sale until we can put it up for auction."

"I can pay more than anyone at this table," Grant said. "I will give the entire contents of the underdark for it."

There was a gasp, and then the room erupted again.

"That's not fair."

"You can't let him get away with this."

"Only silver crowns are money."

The shouting escalated even as the Babachenko tried to get the room to quiet down. When he was unsuccessful, he started casting a spell—a bubble quickly floated off his outstretched hand, rising into the air over the table where it burst like a clap of thunder, rattling the glass walls and ceiling and momentarily stunning everyone in the room.

Before the Babachenko could assert his authority into the vacuum, Grant pressed his offer. "I can offer something that no one else can."

"And what might that be?"

"Assassins who've come to kill the king," Grant said, pointing straight at Alexander and Anja.

"Now, Chloe."

Two of the palace guards had dragged Mohan's corpse out of the room while another had escorted his distraught widow away—that left nine plus the Lord Protector. All nine guards unhooked their maces and started to converge on Alexander.

Many things happened at once.

Tyr stood up, knocking his chair over and grabbing for his belt.

"Who stole my sword?!" he shouted at the top of his lungs, his face going red, veins popping out at his temples. His wizard stood as well and began casting a spell. Tyr grabbed the nearest guard and slammed him into the wall, taking his mace and brandishing it at the next guard. "Who! Took! My! Sword!" he shouted so forcefully that his voice broke with each word.

Alexander dropped his boot knife into his hand just as Nero turned to face him.

"Pretender!" Nero shouted, pointing at Alexander and drawing his long black dagger.

Alexander threw his knife. It flew true, burying to the hilt in the king's throat. He held his neck, gurgling blood, frothy and red then slowly slumped out of his chair and under the table, his eyes frantic with pain and surprise. Grant's head snapped around so quickly that Alexander thought it might unscrew and fall off on the floor. He stared at Alexander with total shock and growing horror, but Alexander ignored him … he had other concerns.

Time seemed to expand, stretching into the coming moments, giving him a glimpse into what might be, but there was so much danger coming his way, and all of it happening at once, that he couldn't focus on everything, so he let go and gave himself over to the moment, reacting without thought, letting instinct and the simple need for survival guide him.

The nobles began to panic, many of them racing for the single exit, while others tried to find sanctuary at either end of the room. Their sudden, confused rush in every direction only served to amplify the chaos.

Two palace guards were pushing through the crowd toward Alexander, while another two were trying to shove their way through the stream of nobles crowding the door. The Lord Protector was quite suddenly wearing a suit of black wispy plate mail that looked translucent and yet Alexander had no doubt it would stop any blade.

The Babachenko snatched the Crown from atop the dead king's head and ran for the door to the king's chambers.

Nero appeared in front of Alexander, but he'd seen him coming and was already moving, pivoting to one side, grabbing Nero's blade hand at the wrist and following through with a hard punch to the side of his head. Alexander stripped Nero's blade out of his hand a moment before Anja grabbed him by the throat with one hand and flung him over the table; he vanished before he hit the ground.

Alexander spun to meet the attack of two palace guards, slicing the first across the throat, then sidestepping to put the dying man between himself and the second guard. Anja snatched up the dead man's mace and advanced on the other guard. He smiled—she snarled. Alexander left them to it, turning toward Tyr's seat and leaping onto the table, the guard behind him screaming in agony.

Within one stride across the table, he saw the threat, but there was nowhere to go … he was in the open, exposed, and the Lord Protector was pointing his mace at him. A moment later, he was blown halfway down the length of the table, landing on the end and toppling over into the trample of fleeing nobles.

Stunned and disoriented, he struggled to regain his senses, clambering under the table and crawling toward the chair where Tyr had been sitting.

"Now!" he thought urgently.

Chloe flashed into view for just a moment, bringing the Tyr Thinblade, scabbard and all, with her from the aether. Alexander emerged from under the table, blade drawn and ready. Tyr saw him almost instantly and his rage spiked, battle frenzy and pure fury giving him the strength to toss aside the two guards standing between him and Alexander.

In that instant, Nero appeared on the table behind Alexander, looping a length of rope around his neck and pulling him backward. Before his feet could be pulled from the floor, Alexander shoved backward, both to loosen the rope and to gain distance from Tyr. Thankfully, before Tyr could reach him, the Lord Protector blasted the pirate across the floor with his mace. In the back of Alexander's mind, he imagined that the mace functioned on the same principle as the lances, though that thought didn't intrude for long.

He stabbed up and back with the Thinblade, aiming for Nero's head, but slicing through his shoulder instead. Nero's scream was cut short when he vanished. Alexander scrambled back across the table toward Anja. The crowd was thinning … most had already fled the banquet hall, giving the guards more room to work.

One was charging Anja, mace poised to strike. Alexander reached the other side of the table, sliding forward, kicking a chair into the guard's path and slicing him in half when the man stumbled over it. Anja had killed three, and another three were surrounding her, trying to get past her guard, but she had her back to the wall and was lashing out at them whenever they got too close.

Alexander moved behind the one in the middle, killing him and drawing the attention of the other two—a distraction that proved fatal for them both. Anja clubbed one in the head, crushing his skull and splattering a line of blood diagonally across her face. Alexander cut the other man's mace and stepped into his guard, stabbing him through the heart.

The Babachenko returned, entering the room with both hands raised, chanting ancient words under his breath. Palace guards started pouring out of the door behind him. They quickly subdued Tyr, his wizard standing down and raising his hands in surrender as soldiers filled the room and started flowing around the table toward Alexander.

The Babachenko loosed his spell, a wave of crackling bluish energy emanating from his hands and washing over both Alexander and Anja. Alexander went totally blind when it hit him, his all around sight failing, his aura-reading gone, even his precognition vanished.

"Take them alive!" the Babachenko commanded.

Two men grabbed Alexander by the wrists, stripping the Thinblade from his grasp before he realized what was happening. His magic was gone … how, he didn't know.

"What have you done to me?" Anja said, her voice beginning as that of a young woman and ending as that of a dragon. Alexander and the men nearby were shoved to the ground by her abrupt transformation. The men farther away stopped in their tracks, scrambling backwards when they were suddenly confronted by a dragon.

Alexander knew better. Her scales were not yet hard enough to stop steel and her breath was only hot enough to scorch; certainly not the dragon fire of legend. She was vulnerable … and she was the biggest target in the room.

The Lord Protector unleashed his force mace at her, blasting her a dozen feet away from Alexander. She roared. Alexander felt the warmth of her fire, but it wasn't hot enough to kill any but those closest to her. Still, it did seem to instill a sense of caution within the ranks of the palace guard.

A collar snapped around his neck and started constricting.

"Run!" he shouted to Anja before his voice failed him.

She roared in defiance, whipping her tail around. Two more men screamed.

The Lord Protector hit her again with his force mace.

"Run!" Alexander tried to shout.

Pain exploded in his head, accompanied by a bright white flash followed quickly by oblivion.

Chapter 14

Abigail nudged Kallistos into a shallow dive, Magda riding her right wing, two more Sky Knights in formation trailing behind them. This was her favorite moment. They'd been flying for hours, gliding on the wind, covering distance to the coastline and then floating above the shore toward the first of the shipyards. Tipping her wyvern forward, feeling the exhilaration of acceleration, the wind drowning out everything but her thoughts, leaning into her steed's neck, descending toward her target, she forgot all of her concerns—the present moment eclipsed past and future, thrusting her into a place where there is only now.

With a slap against his coarse hide, Kallistos flared his wings, rapidly slowing their descent until he was nearly hovering on the wind. It was crushing, but Abigail expected it; she pressed herself against her wyvern's neck and waited out the pressure of such sudden slowing, then sat up into the calm that followed, throwing her firepot very deliberately before coaxing Kallistos into a climb just moments after it was away. She watched the clay pot filled with liquid fire shatter harmlessly against the shield covering the single-berth shipyard cut into a secluded cove on the north coast of Fellenden.

She turned away, back toward Fellenden City, still looking over her shoulder as her scout team followed her lead. A dozen drakini tried to give chase, but the wyverns easily outpaced them.

***

"It is as we feared," Abigail said. Her most trusted advisors were seated around the long table, and scores of officers lined the walls of the room. "Zuhl has established at least five shipyards along the northern coast. Each is protected by a powerful magical shield and several drakini."

"Beg pardon, My Lady," said a commander in the Fellenden legions. "What's a drakini?"

Abigail nodded to Magda.

The Reishi triumvir stood, prim and with perfect poise, nodding deferentially to the officer who'd raised the question, then facing the assembly with grim purpose and sobering presence. "Drakini are a creation of Zuhl, the blending of dragon and man. They stand seven feet tall with blue-scaled hide that's proof against steel. They have broad powerful wings, a long snout lined with needle-sharp teeth, and claws capable of rending flesh from bone. Also, they breathe frost cold enough to paralyze even the most hearty warrior."

"How do we fight such a thing?" another commander asked, this one from the Ithilian Army.

"Most of you won't," Abigail said. "Prince Conner will lead the bulk of our ground forces against Irondale. We'll leave two legions of the Fellenden Army commanded by Prince Torin to guard the city, while the remainder of our forces will move to destroy Zuhl's best foothold on Fellenden. Nine wizards, including Mage Dax and Wizard Sark, will lend support to the assault along with two wings of Sky Knights.

"Forty-seven ships of the Ithilian Navy left Elsmere three days ago. Two wings of Sky Knights, led by Flight Commander Corina will coordinate with them to systematically destroy Zuhl's shipyards ... and his ships, if the opportunity presents itself. These wings will include nearly all of the witches in the flight, since they'll need magic to defeat the shields.

"Zuhl outnumbers us. His army is bigger than all other armies in the Seven Isles put together. As long as his soldiers remain on the Isle of Zuhl, they're no threat to the world. Let loose, they're the end of us all.

"The attack on Irondale is cleanup work, necessary and vital, but not worth one single life on our side. Zuhl has abandoned over four legions of his men, choosing to send his ships to establish other shipyards rather than reinforce his foothold on Fellenden.

"He's forsaken those men, but we have not. Play on their fear, poison their courage with messages of the truth, tell them in every way possible that Zuhl has abandoned them. Use their doubt against them to break their resolve and gain entrance to the city ... then kill them all.

"Zuhl cannot be allowed to control Irondale. His men hold to a code of conduct that does not accept surrender—they will fight to the death, and that makes this a hard business. I would burn Irondale were it not for the countless innocent people within its walls living in terror of Zuhl and in hope of our arrival.

"That leaves brute force ... or something else. I'm hoping that Conner and the wizards under his command will find that something else."

"I have something in mind," Conner said, with a polite nod.

"I suspected you might," Abigail said. She had worked closely with both Conner and Torin over the past weeks; both men had proven to be dedicated to the Old Law and willing to learn at every opportunity. Both had become her friends, familiar and close, trusted and relied upon. She feared for them both, even as she placed them in harm's way.

"The Ithilian Navy and the Sky Knights will bring the fight to the shipyards and destroy them one after the next," Abigail said. "Good hunting."

***

Abigail floated easily on the high winds, Magda at her right, looking down at two wings of Sky Knights lining up to begin their attack runs. Nearly fifty wyverns flying in two strict V-formations began to shift into four columns.

As the attack began, each Sky Knight in the first wave cast a spell ... a blue orb shot forth from each in turn, each orb hitting the shield and weakening it. A single witch wouldn't be able to collapse such a powerful shield, but two dozen, each casting the spell in succession, brought the shield down on the first pass.

The next wing threw firepots into the recently constructed berth, igniting it with dozens of orange splashes of liquid fire. Nearly a thousand men scattered into the forest, fleeing the rapidly growing conflagration. A lone figure on the shore of the cove launched a string of ice shards at the Sky Knights, while drakini started rising into the air. One of the wyverns in the middle of the attack run took three hits to one of its wings and broke formation, beginning to spiral toward the ground.

Another of the Sky Knights matched the wounded wyvern's speed and course from above, while the Knight below guided the rescuing wyvern's claws into the harness of her saddle. Together, they turned south, one wyvern supporting the other.

Abigail wanted to dive toward the enemy, to bring the fight to Zuhl's priest on the ground and to the drakini rising toward her, but it would serve no real purpose. The ship berth and the bare skeleton of the warship growing within had been destroyed—that was the objective. She would leave it to the Ithilian Navy to mop up the enemy.

***

Anatoly was waiting for her when she landed. Snow still blanketed the ground in northern Fellenden, so the army was moving slowly. The bulk of the forces were encamped on the plains just south of the Iron Oak while the Rangers had moved north to scout the city and establish a forward operating base.

Abigail and her Sky Knights had succeeded in burning all five of the shipyards along the northern coast, but the Ithilian Navy had reported that the soldiers and workmen had disbursed into the forest. That left nearly five thousand enemy personnel, led by priests and supported by drakini, running loose in the Iron Oak.

Anatoly rode up leading her horse as she fed Kallistos.

"What's happened?" she asked, after one glance at his grim expression.

"Prince Torin has gone missing. We have conflicting reports, but the one thing they all have in common is a woman."

Abigail left Kallistos to a handler and mounted her slightly skittish horse, patting her on the neck. Magda joined them and they made their way to the command tent.

"I trust you've heard the news," Conner said when they entered.

"What do we know?" Abigail asked, taking her seat at the head of the table.

"In simplest terms, a woman arrived, talked her way into a meeting with Torin and then left with him and six of his personal guards," Conner said. "The odd part, aside from Torin leaving his command, is the differences in the reports. The men all said that the woman was more beautiful than any woman they'd ever seen, but the women all said she was hideous and demonic-looking."

"Sin'Rath," Magda said. All eyes turned to her, most of them blank with confusion.

"I thought the Sin'Rath were on Karth," Abigail said.

"They are, or they were, at any rate," Magda said. "For centuries, the Sin'Rath and the Reishi Coven had an agreement—we would not set foot on Karth if they did not leave Karth. Isabel broke that agreement."

"But she didn't know," Abigail said.

"No, but that's of no consequence to the Sin'Rath," Magda said.

"Why do they want Torin?" Conner asked.

"For his blood," Magda said. "I suspect that they've become aware of the Nether Gate, and more importantly, the magical box containing the last of the keystones."

"There's no way Phane is going to let them get hold of the other two keystones," Abigail said. "They have to know that."

"Not necessarily," Magda said. "The Sin'Rath are insane. Their reasoning is often not entirely reasonable. Unfortunately, Phane is well aware of this."

"You think he put them onto Torin," Anatoly said.

"I do," Magda said. "If he can get the Sin'Rath to steal the box from Lacy and then have Torin open it … collecting the keystone would be a simple matter."

"That seems like a lot of trouble," Conner said.

"If Phane gains control of the Nether Gate, he wins," Magda said. "In truth, this is probably one of several paths that he might travel to reach his goal. He is, no doubt, pursuing them all."

"Well, we're going to make sure he doesn't succeed on this particular path," Abigail said. "I'll have Captain Sava ride south and send a pair of Sky Knights to scout for him."

"That won't work," Magda said. "Men are useless against the Sin'Rath."

Anatoly cleared his throat, frowning at her pointedly.

"Men are charmed by their very presence," Magda said with a shrug. "Every man we send will simply join the witch's ranks. We must send women."

Anatoly grunted, shaking his head, muttering, "Magic," under his breath.

"Pick two experienced witches from the ranks of the Sky Knights," Abigail said to Magda. "The four of us will fly at dawn. Anatoly, I'd like you to ride to Fellenden City and assume command as Regent until either Torin or Lacy returns."

"You know I don't know anything about running a city, right?"

"Just keep the people safe," Abigail said. "It's only temporary."

***

Handlers approached Kallistos moments after he landed in the makeshift aerie within the walls of Fellenden City. Abigail had scarcely dismounted when a commander in the Fellenden Army rode in with a dozen men riding two abreast behind him.

He dismounted, handing the reins to his nearest man and bowed formally with a smile that was entirely too bright for Abigail's mood.

"Lady Abigail, I am Commander Ash. Until Prince Torin is found, I have assumed command of forces within the city and assumed the duties of Regent. How can I be of service today?"

Abigail's eyes narrowed slightly. She was trying to learn temperance, trying to be less rash and more measured, so she found this situation particularly trying.

"Tell me, Commander, how did your prince disappear from under your nose? And why aren't you out looking for him?"

Ash lost a little of his good cheer. "We woke to find Prince Torin missing, and I assure you we are doing everything within our power to find him."

"Tell me about the woman."

His smile brightened and he actually blushed. "She was beautiful ... more beautiful than any woman I've ever met. Truthfully, I don't blame Prince Torin for leaving with her." He smiled wistfully and shrugged. "Between us, I bet he'll return from his dalliance in a few days."

Abigail took a deep breath and reminded herself that these men were under the influence of magic. "I see," she said with a forced smile. "In that case, we'll just go get cleaned up while we wait."

"Of course, Lady Abigail," Ash said. "I've taken the liberty of providing an honor guard for you."

"That won't be necessary."

"Oh, but I insist. If we're wrong about Prince Torin, and the enemy really is in our midst, then I'd be remiss in my duties if I didn't provide you with adequate protection."

Commander Ash and his men accompanied Abigail and Magda to the keep. While one soldier remained with the horses, the rest escorted the two women inside.

Abigail's quarters were just as she had left them, but cold and neglected. She'd chosen a small room off the main meeting hall, more for convenience than for any other reason. She closed the door before one of the guards could follow her inside. She and Magda shared a worried look.

Only a moment after she closed the door and dropped the bar, there was a loud pounding from outside.

"Lady Abigail," Commander Ash shouted through the door. "I really must insist that you allow my men into your room ... for your safety. The enemy could strike anywhere at any time."

"No," Abigail said.

There was a long pause and then he knocked again. "We need to keep you in sight," he shouted, a slight edge of panic in his voice.

Abigail ignored him, turning to Magda. "How many do you think she turned?"

"At least those dozen men, maybe a few more."

"How do we get them back?"

"Time," Magda said with a helpless shrug. "As we understand it, a Sin'Rath naturally charms any man close enough to see her, but that charm doesn't last for long once he leaves her presence. Their venom is how they create lasting power over their victims. Hopefully, it will wear off in time."

"We don't have time," Abigail said. "We need to find enough soldiers who haven't been bitten to contain this lot, so we can figure out where Torin was taken."

"Agreed," Magda said. "First, we'll need to elude them."

Ash pounded on the door again. "Lady Abigail, Lady Abigail, I've just received word that Prince Torin has been spotted in an abandoned part of the city."

"I'll bet," Abigail said to Magda. "How do we get out of here?"

"What's on the other side of this wall?" Magda asked, placing her hand on the bare stone.

"I think it's a storeroom."

"Is there a way out of that room that will get us past the soldiers?"

"I think so," Abigail said, drawing the Thinblade.

"That won't be necessary," Magda said, beginning to cast a spell. Nearly a minute later, the wall became transparent in an area about the size of a door. Magda walked through, motioning for Abigail to follow. It was an odd sensation, like walking through thick air. When they were both in the room on the other side, the wall became opaque again with a single word from Magda.

The room was dark and filled with crates stacked along the walls. A service stair led to the level above. Abigail and Magda moved quietly up the stairs to a balcony running the width of the council chamber that Abigail had used to coordinate the efforts of the army over the winter.

The far wall was lined with windows every ten feet, the first being accessible from the balcony. Magda opened it carefully, peering out before pushing the shutters wide. Abigail looked down into a service alley several floors below.

"Take my hand and jump when I do," Magda whispered. "And don't let go."

Abigail nodded, holding Magda's hand and climbing up onto the window ledge. Magda muttered a few words before stepping off the ledge. They fell fast, air roaring past their ears for just a moment before the featherlite spell slowed their descent and set them both gently on the ground.

They moved cautiously, sticking to the alleys and avoiding notice as much as possible, until they came to one of the main barracks housing several hundred soldiers.

Abigail stopped at the side door for a moment. "I hope the Sin'Rath's influence is as limited as we think or this might go badly."

"Just stay near the door," Magda said. "Your soldiers will fare better if we run from them rather than fight them."

Abigail nodded, then slipped into the barracks. Over a hundred men were sleeping, the sounds of snoring reverberating throughout the large room. She went to the nearest bunk and shook the man awake. He blinked several times, rubbing his eyes in confusion.

"Who are you?"

"I'm Abigail. Where's your commanding officer?"

"He's in the room at the end of the barracks, probably sleeping since we just ended our guard shift at dawn."

"Tell me about the woman Prince Torin left with."

"She was pretty. I only saw her from a distance, but I understand why the prince left with her." He sat up, looking at Abigail more closely, realization seeping into his consciousness the more fully he awoke. "You're Lady Abigail."

"Yes."

He stood up quickly, sleepiness replaced with sudden nervousness.

"Forgive me, My Lady, I didn't recognize you."

"Nothing to forgive, soldier," Abigail said. "Wake the rest of your men while I go speak with your commander."

She didn't wait for him to obey, instead heading to the end of the barracks. The soldier started yelling at the men nearby while pulling on his boots. The commander came out of his room, disheveled and half asleep.

"What's going on out here?" he bellowed. Then he stopped and stared, trying to blink away his confusion.

"Lieutenant, do you know who I am?"

"Lady Abigail, what are you doing here?"

"I need your help, right now. Wake your men and get them ready."

He hesitated, seemingly stunned by the abrupt awakening and the presence of Abigail.

"Now, Lieutenant."

He nodded quickly and started shouting. Within a few minutes he had over a hundred men up, dressed and gathered around Abigail and Magda to hear their orders. Abigail explained the situation quickly and impressed upon the soldiers that the men they were going to detain were not the enemy.

She went back to her quarters, followed by a company of soldiers, citizens moving hastily out of their way. Just before they reached the council chamber, the roar of a wyvern shattered the late morning air.

Abigail looked at Magda, concerned for the two witches who had remained with the wyverns.

"Amelia and Jillian are in trouble," Magda said.

"We have to contain these men, then we'll go to the aerie."

Ash smiled brightly when he saw Abigail, then abruptly snarled when he saw soldiers flow into the room behind her.

"You can't do this! Mistress commanded us to stop you." He drew his sword, his men following his lead.

"Take them without hurting them if you can," Abigail commanded. "Disarm them and detain them under close guard."

The company of soldiers swarmed into the room, surrounding and cutting off escape for all of the soldiers under the Sin'Rath's spell. Ash and his men lashed out but their blows fell on shields, few doing any damage. One by one, they were disarmed, tied up, and lined against the wall.

"You can't do this," Ash pleaded. "Mistress commanded us to stop you from following her. We can't fail her." He started crying uncontrollably.

"Lieutenant, keep these men here. We'll be back soon," Abigail said.

She and Magda ran through the streets toward the aerie. They arrived to the sounds of a pitched battle … Amelia, Jillian, two message riders and the handlers on one side and six soldiers on the other, with several more already down, dead or unconscious.

Abigail and Magda came in behind the Sin'Rath-charmed soldiers just as Amelia knocked one sprawling with a force-push. Magda started casting a spell, her voice building from a whisper to loud forceful words that culminated in a shout. A wave of force, similar to a force-push but much wider, emanated from her hands and hit all five of the remaining soldiers, blasting them forward and tossing them onto the ground at the feet of the Sky Knights, who quickly bound their hands and feet.

"We caught them trying to kill the wyverns," Amelia said. "Fortunately, Kallistos was still awake."

"Is he all right?" Abigail asked urgently.

"Yes, his warning brought us quickly enough to stop them," Amelia said.

"We'll lock these men up with the rest," Abigail said.

***

"I've never seen anything like it," the young woman said. "It wasn't human. It looked at me and smiled, like it knew what I was seeing, but also like it knew that none of the men would believe me. And they didn't. I tried to warn them and got this for my trouble," she said, gently touching the swollen red bruise on her cheek.

Her account only reinforced what Abigail had learned when she interrogated the men under the Sin'Rath's spell. They were distraught that they had failed to stop Abigail, some of them breaking down in tears, sobbing uncontrollably. Abigail found it to be a chilling display of power.

"Do you know where they took Prince Torin?" Abigail asked, leaning closer and taking the woman's hand.

"I don't know where they were going, My Lady," she said, shaking her head, "but they left out of the south gate. I followed them to the wall and watched them ride south. I wanted to stop them, all of the women did, but there wasn't anyone able to stand up to them, and they were all so bewitched by that thing that none of them would listen to us."

"It's all right, dear, you've done well," Abigail said.

"It makes sense," Magda said. "The witch would probably want to take Torin back to Karth. The ports along the south coast are her best bet for getting a ship."

"So we fly south," Abigail said.

Chapter 15

They'd been searching the roads south of Fellenden City for three days without any luck when they spotted a group of riders on the road to Sochi. The sun had just slipped past the horizon, casting the world into growing shadow.

Abigail signaled Amelia and Jillian to make a pass. When their wyverns both roared, confirming their target, Abigail and Magda tipped into a dive, while Amelia and Jillian circled, gaining altitude for an attack run.

Moments after the wyverns roared, the horses broke into a gallop, all of them angling for a sparse grove of trees alongside the road. Abigail loosed an arrow, missing narrowly, but drawing the witch's attention. Magda fired a light-lance, burning a hole through the rump of the Sin'Rath's horse. The dying animal's squeal seemed to linger on the wind as the wyverns banked to circle for another pass.

Looking over her shoulder, Abigail watched as the witch tumbled from her horse and started barking orders at the men. Two headed for the grove of trees while the other five reined in their horses and spread out to meet the next attack, each nocking an arrow while the witch started chanting guttural, almost animalistic words that carried into the darkening sky.

Amelia and Jillian lined up for a run, gaining speed, diving toward the witch. Amelia sent a blue sphere streaking toward the Sin'Rath. It hit her shield and seemed to flow over the surface of it, weakening her magical bubble of protection. Jillian followed with a string of five wedges of blue magical force, one after the other. The first three hit the shield, dissipating with the impact … but the fourth broke the magical barrier and the fifth grazed the witch across her shoulder.

Her guttural chanting culminated with a shriek followed by a streamer of black smoke rising from her outstretched hands toward Jillian. It moved quickly, separating into several tendrils as is neared, then wrapped around the wyvern's wings, binding them to the beast's body. Abigail heard the staccato popping of Jillian's locking bolts coming loose just a moment before she leapt from her saddle. Her wyvern hit the ground with a terrible crash; the sounds of bones snapping and flesh rending filled the night.

Jillian landed gently several moments later, her featherlite spell slowing her descent. As she ran toward her dying steed, Abigail heard her yell, "No! No! No!" She felt a pang of sympathy for her as she nocked another arrow and focused on the task at hand.

With the soldiers' arrows rising toward her, she couldn't slow to take careful aim so she released her arrow too soon, missing again. Magda cast another spell, an orb of light growing in brightness as it streaked through the air, but rather than hit the witch, it stopped a dozen feet above her head, freezing in place, and then beginning to get brighter. The Sin'Rath snarled a curse, shielding her eyes from the light with one hand while pulling a human skull from her bag with the other. She began to shake the skull like a rattle. Even with the wind roaring in her ears, Abigail could hear a clatter of bone on bone.

Amelia formed up on Abigail and Magda for another pass, but before they could get lined up, the witch threw the skull to the ground, shattering it into pieces and releasing a darkness that seemed to seep out of the remnants of the bones, forming into a dozen distinct shadows, each with wing and claw and fang. From her vantage point, it was difficult for Abigail to make out exactly what they were, but she could see at a glance that they were not of this world.

The creatures rose into the air with a howl, their wings black as night, yet not entirely solid, their eyes glowing red with malice and hate, their open maws lined with needle-sharp teeth. Several went to the light floating over the Sin'Rath, swarming it and extinguishing it even as it burned them from existence, plunging the world back into dusk.

The rest flew toward Abigail and Kallistos. She sent an arrow at the nearest, finally scoring a hit. It dissipated like smoke on a breeze. She dropped her bow into its sheath and drew the Thinblade, coaxing Kallistos to gain altitude … but it wasn't enough to evade them. The creatures were closing fast. Another vanished in a flash of light, then another as both Magda and Amelia fired light-lance spells. Then the five that remained were on Abigail, tearing at her steed's wings and clawing at his flesh.

She lashed out at the nearest, her sword passing through it like it wasn't even there, yet the creature vanished a moment later. Kallistos roared, snapping at another clamped onto his wing. Abigail watched it fade away like he'd bitten down on a puff of smoke.

Another hit her from behind, coldness seeping into her bones, claws digging into her shoulders. Before it could bite, she thrust back with the Thinblade and it vanished in a cloud of noxious smoke. One whiff sent her into a fit of coughing and gagging.

With a snap of his tail, Kallistos killed one clawing at his belly. The final creature shrieked one last time before vanishing on its own, why Abigail didn't know or care … Kallistos was injured, a series of tears in both wings sending him toward the ground. She composed herself and guided him into a shallow dive that wasn't nearly shallow enough. He was going in too fast, heading for a hard landing.

Magda's wyvern quickly moved overhead, extending his talons. Abigail had only trained on the maneuver once, but she knew what to do. She grabbed Taharial's left talon and pulled it into her saddle strap, then slapped the top of his foot. He gripped the strap, taking care not to injure Kallistos any more than he already was. When the second talon was locked in place, Magda guided them into a landing that brought them down near Jillian and her dying wyvern.

The impact was jarring, but they landed without causing Kallistos any more harm. Magda released at the last moment, gaining altitude while Amelia floated overhead providing cover, even though there was no need. The Sin'Rath and Torin were gone into the woods, lost in the night.

Abigail slipped out of her saddle, soothing Kallistos and inspecting his injuries, sickness growing in her stomach. He was in no danger of dying, but his wings were injured severely enough that he would need time to heal, even with the aid of magic.

After patting him on the jaw and offering a few soothing words, she went to Jillian, warily watching the shadows in the forest for any sign of the enemy.

"I'm so sorry," Abigail said.

Jillian was sitting next to her steed's head with a hand laid tenderly on his snout. Tears flowed freely down her face, but the look in her eyes was one of murder and vengeance more than sadness and loss.

"He was a good steed. I'll miss him," she said, dashing the tears from her face. "How's Kallistos?"

"He'll live but he won't be flying anytime soon."

Jillian nodded, seeming to come to her senses, remembering that they were still in potential danger, even though the enemy had fled.

Amelia continued circling overhead while Magda landed nearby. She came to Jillian without a word and took her into her arms, letting the younger witch cry while she held her.

Abigail's emotions roiled within her. She was sad for Jillian, worried about Kallistos, and furious at the Sin'Rath. And behind it all was a crushing sense of duty, an obligation to press on, give chase, rescue the Prince of Fellenden from a kind of slavery that was so complete it made her skin crawl—and do so before he could be used to release a darkness like nothing the world had ever seen before.

Kallistos was licking his wounds, one wing splayed out, still too tender to be folded against his body.

"We have to move," Abigail said, looking sadly at her wyvern.

"I know," Magda said, separating herself from Jillian.

The younger witch nodded tightly, a lock of sandy-blond hair falling into her face. She brushed it back, wiping away fresh tears. "I'll tend to Kallistos as best I can, then I'll walk him back to the city," she said.

"Amelia will stay with you while Magda and I go find that witch," Abigail said.

Another tear slipped from Jillian's eye. "When you find her, if you can make it painful, I'd appreciate it."

Abigail hugged her without a word.

Within minutes, she'd transferred her pack and weapons to Taharial and they were in the air, following the road by moonlight. Abigail knew they would be able to easily overtake the enemy in the air, but it would be nearly impossible to find them under cover of darkness, especially if they were traveling in the forest, so she opted to get in front of them.

Not an hour after lifting off, they came to a village at the intersection of the road and a fast-moving river full to the banks with snowmelt. The place looked like the home of five hundred souls, but more importantly, there was a bridge—a choke point. Abigail tapped Magda on the shoulder and she nodded, banking away from the village toward a rocky knoll in the forest about a mile from town. After a silent pass, Magda landed her steed gently on the secluded hill.

The half-moon was enough to see by, but just barely. Abigail moved slowly and cautiously through the woods, one hand out in front of her face to

avoid branches that might blind her. Magda offered light, but Abigail didn't want
to alert the enemy of their presence. Surprise was a prerequisite for an effective
ambush. She smiled, remembering a lesson from so long ago, a lesson she'd tried
to sneak into just to be with her brothers. Anatoly had caught her ... then told her
she could stay, but only if she paid attention. She did.

They reached the outskirts of town within half an hour, certainly well
before the Sin'Rath and Torin could have arrived, even at a gallop. The streets
were mostly empty, the windows of nearly every building were glowing, and the
chimneys were sending streamers of smoke into the sky. Moving quietly to avoid
contact, they made their way to the bridge in the center of town.

It was a simple structure built of stout timbers lashed with rope and was
just wide enough for a wagon. The river roared beneath, swollen with icy water.
Abigail and Magda waited in the shadows of an alley between two nearby houses.

After they'd waited for several hours and not a single soul had crossed
the bridge, Abigail whispered, "They should've been here by now."

"I know. I suspect they've stopped for the night," Magda said.

Abigail nodded to herself, weighing her options. "The question is, where?
I could really use Alexander's help right now. I hope he's all right."

"Your brother is quite resourceful; I'm sure he's fine. As for the
Sin'Rath, it's hard to say where she might be."

Abigail sighed and sat down, pulling her blanket out of her pack. "I guess
we wait then."

They took turns watching during the cold night. Abigail got some sleep
but not much. Each time she woke, she was sore and cramped from sitting on the
cold ground. Finally, as dawn neared, she packed her blanket and started pacing,
partly from anxiety and partly to loosen her sore muscles and to warm herself.

"Have you thought about your future?" Magda asked.

Abigail frowned, stopping to consider the question. "Not really, I mean
not past this war anyway."

"I only ask because I have a vial of Wizard's Dust set aside for you, but
we've never discussed it."

"Honestly, I'd forgotten about that. Now that you bring it up, I'm not sure
that I really want it."

"May I ask why?"

Abigail hesitated, her frown deepening. "It's a really big decision, and it
would change everything—if I survived."

"I'm confident that with the proper preparation, you would succeed,"
Magda said. "But I sense there's something else."

"Jack," Abigail whispered. "I'm not sure I want to outlive him."

Magda nodded with a sad smile. "That is one of the more significant
sacrifices a witch or wizard must endure. However, I suspect that Jack would be
welcome to undergo the fast if he wished to."

"I hadn't considered that," Abigail said, but before she could finish her
thought, the sound of horses clopping through the streets broke the morning calm.
It was just before dawn, only the brightest stars still piercing the deep blue sky. A
few windows were starting to glow as the village's residents began their day.

Abigail nocked an arrow and peeked around the corner.

"It's them," she whispered. Magda started casting a spell.

A party of eight, the witch, Prince Torin and six of his royal guard slowly and cautiously rode through town, looking this way and that for any sign of danger. Abigail caught her breath when she saw the Sin'Rath witch for the first time. She looked vaguely human but with grey skin. Long, sharp canine teeth protruded past her lips, leaving raw, red sores where they rubbed against her chin. Her eyes were completely black. A single horn jutted from the right side of her forehead, curving up over long, greasy jet-black hair.

With a single word, the men surrounding the witch stopped before the bridge. Her barbed tail flicked about nervously like a cat's. Abigail withdrew around the corner.

"She's not human."

"No," Magda said. "I could unhorse them all, but my spell might injure Torin, possibly even kill him if he falls wrong."

"I don't have a clean shot," Abigail said. "Torin's guards are in the way. Go ahead with your spell."

Magda crept up to the corner and began whispering. Several moments later, she stepped out and released a pea-sized sphere of bright blue light that streaked to her target and then stopped, hovering in the midst of the guards for just a moment before expanding to twenty feet in diameter in an instant, toppling horses and tossing everyone to the ground, shattering the morning stillness with shouts of surprise and panic.

Abigail stepped out and raised her bow, but the enemy was scattered across the road, all of them still down. She raced onto the bridge, angling for a clean shot at the witch, with Magda following close behind her. They stopped when the Sin'Rath regained her feet, cackling with a mixture of glee and malice.

"I've waited a long time to face one of the Reishi Coven," she said in a very reasonable tone, motioning for a guard who had regained his feet to attack. Abigail drew but couldn't get a clean shot past the charging soldier until Magda knocked him over with a force-push.

The arrow flew true but turned suddenly a few feet from the witch, clattering harmlessly onto the road, a plane of shadowy grey magic no more than a foot in diameter becoming visible for just a moment where the arrow had been deflected.

The witch laughed. "Your weapons are of no use against me," she said, raising her clawed hand toward Abigail. Magda stepped forward just in time to take a swirling bolt of black magic, wispy like smoke yet unnatural. It hit her shield and splattered away, dissipating a moment later.

Abigail sent another arrow at the Sin'Rath, using Magda's shield as cover, but the result was the same. Several more of Torin's men were coming to their senses and beginning to form up in front of the witch when Magda launched her next spell. A constellation of seven points of brilliant light, each trailing a shower of sparks, formed in front of her, then rose overhead, spinning around a common point until they reached a height of a hundred feet. They held there, spinning faster and faster for several seconds before, one by one, they targeted the

Sin'Rath, slamming into her shield and exploding in a shower of sparks with each hit.

The witch shrieked in fury. Each blinding explosion illuminated another panel in her dark and angular shield. It looked like a swirling collection of panes of glass, each joined with the next at a seam much like stained glass, each shaped differently, many with five or six sides and each imbued with powerful dark magic … but not powerful enough. With each impact, a pane shattered, leaving gaps in the Sin'Rath's defenses.

Abigail took careful aim, threading the needle between two of Torin's guards and timing her shot to coincide with an opening in the rotating shield. Perfect calm flowed into her, confidence in her skill as an archer filled her mind. She released her arrow into that stillness and it flew true, slipping past the charmed soldiers, through the narrow opening in the shield, into the witch's left eye socket and out the back of her head.

What happened next threatened Abigail's sanity. Her perfect shot should have killed the creature, but instead, the witch froze as if time itself had stopped, and then she exploded into a cloud of locusts, black and angry, thousands strong, all trace of her true form vanishing into the swarm. Abigail watched in stunned amazement as the swarm of devouring insects wrapped itself around Prince Torin and carried him away into the morning sky, over the river and into the forest south of the town.

The guards watched as well, a mixture of fear and revulsion soaking into them after the insects vanished from sight. The lead man looked at Abigail and Magda, confusion vying with growing awareness in his expression.

"Lady Abigail? What just happened?"

"Captain, you and your men have been under the influence of a witch."

"Where's Prince Torin?" he asked, alarm rising in his voice.

"She took him," Abigail said.

The captain turned to his men. "Round up the horses and prepare to ride."

"No, Captain," Abigail said.

"But we're sworn to protect him."

"Yes, and you are all powerless to do so."

"I don't understand."

"Tell me about the witch," Magda said.

"Mistress Peti? She's not a witch, she's the most beautiful woman I've ever met."

"And yet, she just transformed into a swarm of insects and flew away," Magda said.

The captain shook his head, trying to reconcile recent events with his understanding of the world.

"How is that possible?" he asked

"It had to be a constructed spell," Magda said.

"I don't understand."

"Some spells are cast in the moment they are required, while others are cast well before they're needed and set to be triggered by an event or a command. Such spells can be extraordinarily powerful because the caster has much more time to visualize a desired outcome. Constructed spells are typically linked to an item that is often destroyed in the activation of the spell."

He shook his head, still confused.

"It felt as if obeying her commands was the very definition of morality," he said. "How could we all be deceived so easily?"

"Deception is often at the heart of dark magic," Magda said. "Contrary to commonly held belief, evil does not wish to destroy so much as it wishes to corrupt good, to turn those who hold life and liberty sacred against those very beliefs. Lies are their stock in trade, and dark magic can turn a simple lie into something else entirely."

A crowd was starting to gather, some holding a variety of garden tools, but a few armed with swords. One man wearing a badge of office and carrying a stout staff pushed through the onlookers.

"What is the meaning of this?"

"Captain, gather your men and your horses," Abigail said. Then she turned to the approaching constable. "I'm sorry for the disturbance. We'll be on our way shortly."

"You'll answer my question or you'll not be going anywhere."

Abigail nodded to herself, reining in her desire to speak her mind, stepping in close to the constable. "My name is Abigail Ruatha and I'm in pursuit of a half-demon witch that has abducted Prince Torin," she said quietly enough that only he could hear her.

He seemed incredulous until he noticed the Thinblade on her belt and then his face went pale and he stepped aside, nodding slowly.

"Captain, bring me Torin's horse," Abigail said, turning back to the Fellenden royal guard. "Take the rest of your men north along this road. When you overtake the two Sky Knights walking an injured wyvern back to the city, you will stop and offer them your assistance. Then you will accompany them, taking your orders from either of them. Is that understood?"

"Prince Torin is our charge; we'll not abandon him."

"And how well have you protected him so far?" Abigail asked, her temper slipping. "You can do no good against this witch … she'll just charm you again and set you against everything you hold dear. Leave her to us and do as you're told."

The captain clenched his jaw but nodded while one of his men brought Torin's horse forward, handing the reins to Abigail.

"Good man," Abigail said, mounting the horse and offering Magda a hand up behind her. The crowd parted as she spurred the animal into a gallop. Once they reached the open range south of the village, Magda cast a simple spell that was answered by a roar in the distance.

"I'll look from the air while you search for any sign on the ground," she said, dismounting. "If you see anything, send up a whistler. I won't be far."

"Good hunting," Abigail said, spurring her horse toward the thin forest running between the road and the foothills of a mountain range a league to the east.

The ground cover beneath the fir boughs was sparse and the few shrubs she saw were devoid of leaves. Under the shade, the air was cold but still and moist with the morning dew. Abigail guided her horse cautiously, searching for any sign of passage but finding none. The swath of forest was miles wide and crisscrossed with animal trails and a few hunting paths, none bearing any sign of recent traffic. As the morning wore on, she became convinced that finding them within the woods was nearly impossible given the sheer size of the area to be searched. On top of that, she had no idea how far the witch had carried Torin in her flight from the village, nor what other capabilities her enemy might possess.

Reluctantly, she guided her horse out of the forest and back to the road. She had just cleared the tree line when she heard Taharial roar in the distance. She spurred her horse into a gallop, racing south toward Magda, slowing when she crested a gentle rise.

Then she saw the enemy. The witch was standing in the open, atop a small hill beside the road. A goat was hogtied on the ground in front of her, and she was chanting while holding a dagger over the helpless animal. Torin stood behind her, seemingly oblivious to the events swirling around him.

Abigail surged forward, leaning into her horse's neck and trying to coax more speed from him even as his strength waned. Magda released a bubble of liquid fire the size of a man's head toward the witch, but the Sin'Rath ignored it, continuing to chant the words of her spell as the fire burst against a half-sphere shield covering the entire hilltop where she and Torin stood, dripping orange flames to the ground in a circle surrounding them.

Magda banked sharply, wheeling for another attack run when Peti shouted the final word of her spell and plunged her dagger into the goat, its bleating scream carrying on the wind until it exhausted its final breath. Moments later, sooty black streamers began seeping up from the ground, rising up over Peti's head and coalescing into a whirling cloud of darkness. With a menacing cackle, she pointed at Magda, and the darkness shot forth with terrifying speed, lifting toward Taharial, striking the wyvern full in the chest and soaking into the beast like water into a sponge.

Abigail watched helplessly as Magda's steed turned jet black, freezing solid as if he'd been turned to stone. A moment later, Taharial shrank out of sight, leaving Magda strapped to her plummeting saddle.

Unable to help her friend and mentor, Abigail turned her attention to the Sin'Rath, sending an arrow at her while still on the run, knowing full well that it wouldn't penetrate the shield, but trying nonetheless. After her arrow shattered against the magical barrier, Abigail slung her bow and drew the Thinblade.

Magda pulled her release cord, the locking bolts popping free, allowing the saddle to fall away from her while she cast her featherlite spell and landed gently. Moments after reaching the ground, she unleashed a light-lance that was brighter than any Abigail had ever seen. The shield protecting Peti faltered, flickering out of existence a moment later.

Then Peti cast another spell. Abigail saw no visible effect until the ground around Magda started growing into a patch of barbed tangleweeds that wrapped around her, immobilizing her within seconds.

Abigail drew closer but the witch just cackled, beginning to cast yet another spell. Abigail was only a few dozen feet away when her horse stopped charging and started bucking, dancing and trying to throw her. She leapt clear in a desperate effort to control her fall but still hit hard, dropping the Thinblade and tumbling to the ground.

Shaking her head, she struggled to recover, unslinging her bow and nocking an arrow, but Torin was riding behind Peti, blocking her shot. She heard the witch laughing as they rode south. Still entangled, Magda loosed a spell at the Prince of Fellenden, a small sphere of translucent yellow light striking him squarely in the back but seeming to have no effect.

After retrieving the Thinblade, Abigail cut Magda free of the tangleweeds, each stalk turning to black smoke as it was severed. Magda was bleeding from a dozen places, but her eyes showed only rage.

"I'm going to kill that witch if it's the last thing I do," she said, stepping free of the thorny growth, "and then I'm going to find her sisters and rid the world of their taint once and for all."

"I'm sorry about Taharial," Abigail said.

"I don't think he's dead, but I can't be sure."

"I don't understand."

"The witch used a transformation spell," she said, looking about and walking quickly to a small object on the road. She picked it up with a humorless smile. It was a perfect replica of a wyvern, cast in black metal. "If I can figure out how to reverse the spell, I think I can bring him back. Unfortunately, that will take some time and research to accomplish."

"At least he's not dead."

"No, but he won't be helping us for a while," Magda said, wiping blood from one of the scratches on her arm.

"You take care of your injuries while I get our packs from your saddle," Abigail said. "My horse was exhausted before they stole it, so they won't get too far before they have to start walking. If we hurry, we might be able to catch up with them, provided they don't vanish into the forest again."

"That won't be a problem," Magda said. "I hit Torin with a tracking spell. I'll be able to determine his direction and distance with a simple incantation anytime I like."

"How long will it last?"

"Several weeks, certainly long enough."

"Well, that's the best thing I've heard all day."

Chapter 16

The horse's tracks followed the road and it looked like he was being run ragged. Confirmation came when they found the animal, collapsed and left to die where he fell. Abigail shook her head sadly, kneeling next to him. His body was still warm.

"They're not far, maybe an hour or so ahead of us."

Magda nodded, muttering a few words under her breath. "About a league south," she said, looking up at the steel-grey sky. "Only a few hours of light left."

They moved quickly, pushing themselves to cover greater distance, but as fast as they were, Magda reported that Torin remained a league out of reach.

"Why didn't she bite Torin's guards?" Abigail asked while they walked.

"That's hard to say. It could be that her venom is limited and she used so much of it to turn so many soldiers back in the city that she didn't have enough left. Or it could be that those charmed by venom lose some essential aspect of their free will, making them less useful to her in a fight. The truth is, we don't really know for sure how their venom works."

"Do you think she's bitten Torin?"

"I doubt it. Over the years we've done what we could to gather information about the Sin'Rath without violating our truce. It seems that they don't bite those in positions of power whom they wish to influence. Instead, they reserve their venom for those that they deem expendable. I suspect that the influence of the venom diminishes one's ability to think rationally and thereby diminishes one's usefulness."

"I hope you're right," Abigail said. "She should be dead. I put an arrow right through her head. If that won't kill her, what will?"

"As I said, she survived your arrow because of a very powerful constructed spell. One that I'm quite sure she hasn't had the time to replicate. Another such well-placed arrow would be the end of her."

"I've seen a lot of things over the past year, but that swarm of locusts made my skin crawl."

"It was disturbing."

They walked on in silence, the forest to their left thickening and eventually overtaking the rangeland that had bordered the road on their right, creating the effect of a tunnel with a ceiling of fir boughs. Magda stopped a dozen feet before entering the gloaming pathway before them, her eyes narrowing.

"What is it?" Abigail asked, unslinging her bow and looking around warily.

"I'm not sure. Something's not right here."

"It just looks like a forest road to me."

"Yes, but …"

An arrow whizzed past Abigail, grazing Magda on the shoulder, her riding armor deflecting the shaft but not before it managed to cut a shallow gash across her outer arm. She cursed, then began casting a spell.

Abigail nocked an arrow, searching the woods for any sign of movement. A rustling in the bushes caught her attention. She fired blindly into the foliage, eliciting a cry of pain. Three men emerged from the woods, two charging toward them while the third walked around in a circle, trying to reach the arrow sticking out of the back of his shoulder, yelling in pain with each attempt.

Abigail dropped her bow and drew the Thinblade, swinging it wildly to ward off the man charging at her, cutting him in half from the ribcage to the shoulder with one stroke. His torso fell into her and nearly knocked her over, staining her armor with blood.

The other man ran headlong into Magda's newly erected shield, bouncing off it in stunned amazement, then turning toward Abigail with almost desperate urgency. She pointed the Thinblade at him and shouted, "Stop!" but he charged right into it, impaling himself on the blade while still trying to stab her with his dagger. She spun away, drawing the Thinblade through half of his torso and narrowly avoiding the blade plunging toward her.

The third man had fallen to the ground and rolled onto his back, breaking the arrow off with a horrific scream before staggering to his feet and advancing toward Abigail with a knife. Magda knocked him over with a force-push. His landing stunned him for just a moment, but then he scrambled to his feet and charged again, wild-eyed and driven by something unnatural.

Abigail clenched her teeth and set herself to meet the attack, sidestepping to her right and spinning, lashing out with the Thinblade. A foot of the magical blade passed through the man's upper arm and his chest, cutting through his heart and lung. He fell in a heap, bright red blood gushing from his wound in decreasing surges until the ground beneath him was soaked red.

Abigail's heart was pounding in her head from the sudden violence. She searched the darkening forest for more threats, but the calm of the late winter day settled over the battlefield in stark contrast to the carnage scattered across the road.

"How did you know?"

"I cast a number of spells every morning as a matter of course," Magda said. "One such spell warns me when danger is near ... at least most of the time. As with everything else in life, spells sometimes fail."

"Well, I'm glad it worked today."

Magda knelt next to one of the dead men, pulling his collar down and nodding to herself. "He was bitten."

"Three dead ... and all of them innocent."

"We should proceed with caution," Magda said. "These are probably not the only men she'll send against us."

"I wish we had time to bury them," Abigail said.

"As do I, but every moment we delay ..."

"I know. Let's at least move them off the road into the woods."

After the grisly task was done, they continued south, walking briskly into the growing darkness of late evening. When night fell, Magda conjured three

softly glowing orbs of light that hovered over their heads, providing enough
illumination to travel by without drawing undue attention. They walked well into
the night until exhaustion overtook them both.

Morning came much sooner than Abigail would have liked. She was sore
from walking so many leagues, but her sense of urgency overpowered any
discomfort she felt. They ate a cold breakfast on the move, picking up their pace
after their bodies warmed and limbered from exertion.

The forest remained thick and overgrown on both sides of the road as it
meandered along a path cut to avoid the ups and downs in the terrain until it came
to a stream where it turned and followed the water. Not an hour later, the road
crossed the stream over a bridge that looked in need of repair, many of the timbers
rotting from the constant moisture. A village was nestled against the far side of the
river.

As they approached, a man on a platform in a tree overlooking the bridge
blew a horn, and seemingly every able-bodied man in the little hamlet took up
makeshift arms and came rushing to the bridge. Pitchforks, shovels, and axes were
the most common, though a few had spears, and one, the biggest among them,
carried a broadsword. He stepped through the crowd of men arrayed on the
opposite side of the bridge and planted the point of his sword in the ground,
resting his hands on its pommel.

"You shall not pass!" he shouted over the low roar of the water.

"This is getting old," Abigail muttered, stopping a step short of the
bridge.

"Indeed, yet it does pose a problem," Magda said. "I count nearly thirty
men."

"And all of them are dupes; not a one deserves to die."

"Agreed. Perhaps they would be open to reason."

"I doubt it, but it's worth a try," Abigail said, holding her hands up and
open in a gesture of peace, while walking to the middle of the bridge. Magda
waited on the far side, softly casting her shield spell.

The big man's eyes narrowed suspiciously but he approached after a brief
internal struggle, stopping several paces from her.

"You shall not pass," he said, planting his sword point in the bridge
planks as if punctuating his statement.

"You said that already," Abigail said. "I would ask you to hear me out."

He frowned as if her request was unexpected. Then he nodded.

"Prince Torin is under the influence of a witch. We are trying to rescue
him."

"Nonsense! Lady Peti is his betrothed and he's a lucky man to have her.
She'll make a fitting queen."

"You've been duped—deceived by witchcraft. Peti is not a lady, she's
demon spawn and she has her claws in your prince."

"He said that you would come and he said that you would lie, but I didn't
think your lies would be so obvious. You are fair by any man's standards, but
Lady Peti makes you look plain by comparison."

"This is getting nowhere," Abigail muttered, shaking her head. "Do you have a wife?"

"What's that ..."

"Answer my question," Abigail interrupted.

"Yes," he said, seeming somewhat taken aback by her demeanor.

"Did she see Lady Peti?"

His brow furrowed and he spat. "Yes, but she was jealous of her—kept going on about her not being human and such. Utter nonsense."

"Perhaps she saw true."

"I'll believe my own eyes before I believe the addled ramblings of a woman."

Abigail took a deep breath to steady her growing anger, looking up and down stream for another place to cross.

"Don't think to pass elsewhere," he said, raising his sword point it at her. "I am the protector of this village and I will obey my prince."

"You are a fool," Abigail said, her temper finally slipping out of her control, "a dupe who betrays your prince and threatens the future of the very people you profess to protect."

"I think you need a lesson in manners, woman," he said, advancing toward her. "I command you to lay down arms and surrender."

The rest of the men started forward onto the bridge while Abigail started backing away.

"Submit or die!" the village protector shouted, bringing his broadsword up over his head.

Abigail stopped, grasping the hilt of the Thinblade and standing her ground, anger flashing in her pale blue eyes.

"So be it," he said, bringing the sword down.

Abigail drew, slipping to the side and cutting his broadsword off at the hilt, then bringing the flat of the Thinblade down on his shoulder. He froze in shock and disbelief, the men rushing in behind him stopping uncertainly.

"Your witch-blade will not prevail here," he said, though with somewhat less certainty. "You may kill me, but ..."

"Shut up! Back away! Right now!"

Confusion and relief danced in his eyes as he slowly stepped backward, out from under the threat of the Thinblade, still holding the useless hilt of his broken broadsword.

Abigail swept her blade through the timbers under her feet, then turned and ran. The bridge creaked and groaned for a moment before the timbers gave way and the bridge collapsed, spilling several of the men into the water. They flailed against the strong current even though the stream was only a few feet deep. The rest of the villagers scrambled to pull their friends out of the frigid water.

Abigail didn't say a word, stalking past Magda, turning into the forest heading downstream and trying to master her temper but mostly taking it out on the brush in her way. A hundred feet from the edge of the village, she stopped and sliced through a tree with a single stroke. It wobbled for a moment before slowly crashing across the stream.

"Once we're across, we'll double back into the village, get some horses and be on our way."

"The fallen tree is likely to draw attention," Magda said.

"I know, just try not to kill anyone," Abigail said, stepping onto her makeshift bridge.

Within minutes, the villagers were converging on the place where the tree had fallen, but Abigail and Magda had already moved through the forest to the road and were running back into the village.

A startled woman was the first person they saw. She eyed them warily.

"Where's the stable?" Abigail asked.

The frightened woman pointed farther into the village. They continued without a word, finding the building and slipping quietly inside. A woman cleaning out one of the stalls froze when she saw them, staring like they might be death itself.

"We won't hurt you," Abigail said. "We need two horses with saddles." She held up a coin purse, rattling the contents. "We'll pay."

The woman nodded tightly but didn't move.

"You have nothing to fear from us," Magda said gently.

"It's just that ... the last travelers to pass this way weren't natural."

"We know," Abigail said. "We just need horses."

She seemed to relax a bit until several of the men searching the woods shouted that they'd found tracks.

"We don't have much time," Abigail said. "These two look like fine horses. How much?"

"I don't know. My husband always does the business, but he's been acting so strange since they arrived. The one that came with the prince ... she looked like something out of a nightmare. She just smiled at me like she knew I could see her, like she knew none of the men would believe me."

"I know," Abigail said. "Here are six gold coins for the horses and saddles."

The woman stared at the gold that Abigail dropped into her hand, quickly nodding her agreement. Abigail and Magda went to work saddling the horses and attaching their packs.

"Will you help us?" Abigail asked.

"What can I do?"

"Go toward the bridge and shout for help. Say you saw us in the woods."

"We don't want to hurt your men, dear," Magda said. "But they aren't themselves right now, and we can't afford to let them delay us any further."

"All right, but you have to promise me you won't kill anyone."

"Agreed," Abigail said, leading her horse to the barn door and opening it just enough to peek outside. "Looks clear."

They waited until the woman started shouting before leading the horses out. They had just mounted when one of the men saw them, shouting to the others. Abigail cursed under her breath, looking over her shoulder at the man running toward them.

"Time to go," Magda said, spurring her horse.

Several more men emerged from the forest in a vain attempt to stop them, but they weren't willing to risk being trampled by the two galloping horses.

Ten minutes later, well south of the village and out of immediate danger, they slowed their pace to preserve the strength of the horses.

"How far is Torin?"

"Just over a league, still nearly due south," Magda said.

"It's a good bet they got horses in that village, too."

"Agreed."

They'd been traveling for about an hour when they heard the thunder of hoof beats growing in the distance behind them.

Abigail shook her head, sighing heavily. "It's never easy."

The forest was still thick, tall firs lining each side of the road, their boughs reaching across overhead and mingling with those from the opposite side. Abigail suspected she could get her horse through the brush on either side of the road if she led her, clearing the more stubborn shrubs with her sword, but she knew it wouldn't be quick. She reined in her horse and dismounted.

"What do you have in mind?"

"I'm going to fall a few trees across the road; see if I can slow them down. Maybe they'll lose interest."

Magda shrugged, nodding her approval. "Better than killing them."

Abigail selected trees just off the path, cutting them carefully with the Thinblade to fell them diagonally across the road, taking three from each side but alternating them so that each toppled over the last, creating an interlocking obstacle completely blocking passage.

Nearly twenty men from the village arrived just after she felled the last tree. Magda chuckled, handing Abigail her horse's reins and they continued south, shouts and curses fading into the distance behind them with each passing moment.

By evening the forest had thinned, once again opening to rangeland on the western side of the road while the east remained blanketed with trees. Just before dark, they came upon a dead horse left in the road where it fell.

Abigail shook her head sadly. "Poor thing."

"Seems like Peti's in a hurry."

"Yeah ... good thing for us she has no idea how to get the most out of a horse. If she took care of her animals, they'd carry her a lot farther."

Magda nodded, gently patting her steed on the neck. Abigail handed over her reins and dismounted, kneeling next to the dead horse.

"He's still a little warm. If they're doubled up on an exhausted horse, they'll be on foot before long."

Magda nodded, muttering the words of a spell under her breath. Three softly glowing orbs of light materialized overhead, circling in a lazy orbit.

"We should press on for a few hours," she said. "Maybe we'll get lucky and catch up."

They rode into the night, well past dark until they came upon a second dead horse.

"Let's bed down a few hundred feet up the road," Abigail said. "We'll have a better chance of tracking them in the light, and our animals are tired."

"I know how they feel," Magda said. "For what it's worth, we've narrowed their lead. They're less than half a league ahead, and I think they've stopped for the night as well."

The next morning brought an overcast sky and fits of gentle rain. They set out just before dawn, eating jerky and dried fruit for breakfast. Had they been relying on footprints, they would have been traveling blind, but Magda's tracking spell guided them nearly due south. Abigail was all but certain that Peti was headed for Sochi, the port city on the southern tip of Fellenden. From there it would be a simple matter for her to charm the captain and crew of any ship she liked. After that, catching up with them would become much more complicated.

They made good time through the morning in spite of the weather. By midday they were wet and cold from the intermittent rain. They stopped to rest their horses and eat a hasty lunch atop a hill overlooking a broad valley. It was an idyllic setting. A stream ran out of the foothills, winding through verdant fields crosshatched with farm plots. In the distance, a small castle perched on a bluff overlooked the road below, which was bounded on the opposite side by the stream. It was a natural choke point—the only way around was to ford the stream and cut through the farmland blanketing the flood plain on the other side. The road forked before the bluff, the new road winding up a series of switchbacks to the castle.

"There they are," Magda said, after casting a spell.

"I don't see them," Abigail said. "Are you sure?"

"Yes, they're on foot about half a league from the castle road."

"Good. Let's end this."

They mounted up and rode hard, pushing their tired animals nearly to their limit. The road wound down into the farm fields and leveled out as it straightened. Within a few minutes, Abigail spotted the two figures walking in the distance. Not long after, Peti and Torin stopped.

"Looks like they see us," Magda said, slowing her horse to a trot. "Peti will be making preparations; be on your guard." She started casting a spell, then another while they rode toward battle.

Abigail released an arrow at the limits of her range, sending the shaft in a high arc toward the witch, but it went wide by a dozen feet. Peti's cackle carried through the damp air, followed by an unnatural darkness oozing away from her across the ground. It looked like sooty smoke but it moved like a living thing, gaining speed with each passing moment. Magda cast a light-lance at it but it simply flowed around the brilliant shaft of white-hot light.

It didn't seem to have substance or form, moving like sentient smoke until it reached them, still covering only a few inches of the ground, surrounding them, flowing under their horses. Abigail's sense of alarm peaked when the smoke seemed to flash with a pulse of darkness and then it was gone. The horses screamed in pain, toppling to the ground and throwing them both. Abigail's leg was pinned under her terrified horse. She cried out in pain, trying to disentangle herself from the panicked animal.

Scrambling away, she saw with horror what had befallen the horses. The dark smoke had cut their hooves off when it vanished, leaving each horse with four stumps where its feet used to be. Choking back sadness and sickness, she staggered to her feet, drawing the Thinblade. With grim resolve she took her horse's head, silencing the panic and pain with a stroke.

Magda had managed to get clear of her steed but fell hard. She was lying still while the animal struggled to regain its feet, screaming in pain with each attempt, thrashing around in wild panic. Abigail killed the mare a moment later. Distant cackling drifted into the sudden silence.

Magda shook her head, rolling to her belly and lifting herself to all fours, trying to regain her senses. Abigail sheathed the Thinblade, checking the enemy as she went to Magda.

"Are you all right?"

"Just dazed. What's the witch doing?" Magda asked, squeezing her eyes shut and shaking her head again.

"They're heading up the castle road."

"I was afraid of that."

They took a few minutes to gather their gear and regain their senses. Magda had a red-and-purple bruise on the right side of her forehead and Abigail was limping. Doggedly, they pursued the enemy toward the castle, knowing with certainty that they were walking into a bigger fight than either of them was ready for. Peti and Torin reached the castle well before them. Abigail and Magda took pains to approach with caution, unwilling to underestimate Peti's power yet again.

After rounding the final switchback, both of them stopped in their tracks. Set in the middle of the road not two hundred feet from the drawbridge was a woman impaled on a pike. A man in scale armor with a spear stood beside her.

"You will come no farther!" he shouted. "Turn back or all of the women within this keep will be killed."

"Dear Maker," Abigail whispered.

Peti and Torin stood on the wall of the gatehouse, the witch's cackle taunting them.

"This certainly complicates things," Magda said.

"Let's fall back," Abigail said. "We need a plan."

"Agreed."

They withdrew around the bend and out of sight. Abigail sat down on a rock, rubbing her leg and shaking her head.

"How do we get to her without causing a bloodbath?" she asked.

"I'm not sure we can. If she sends the keep's soldiers against us, we'll have little choice."

"So we hide until dark and then sneak in," Abigail said.

"That may work, assuming she chooses to remain within the keep."

"You think there's another way out?"

"Of course," Magda said. "And if not, she can always use her magic to reach the road below."

"Maybe we should make our way south and try to ambush her again," Abigail said.

"Getting past the castle without being seen will be impossible. I suggest we move to those rocks and wait for her to make the next move. If she's still in the castle after dark, we go in after her."

Abigail nodded, looking at the rocky outcropping near the switchback. Several large boulders offered ample cover and a defensible position should Peti send soldiers to attack. They carefully picked their way across the steep hillside, sliding a few times in the scree but eventually reaching their destination. From within the shelter of the boulders, they had a view of the battlements atop the gatehouse, but not of the gate itself.

It wasn't long before a horn blew from within the castle. Soon after, a score of men came over the rise on foot, all of them armed and a few armored. Most looked like working men, armed with pitchforks and woodcutting axes, but there were a few soldiers armed with spears and swords. Behind them, a dozen men on horseback rode escort for Peti and Torin.

Peti picked them out in the rocks and pointed her clawed finger at them. "Kill them!" she shouted.

The men on foot gave a battle cry that was far more enthusiastic than one might expect from a bunch of workmen and started charging toward Abigail and Magda. The horsemen surrounded Peti and Torin while they rode around the switchback and down toward the main road below.

Abigail tried to find an open shot, but the charmed men surrounding Peti rode too closely together, shielding the witch completely.

"I'm really getting tired of her," she said, relaxing the tension on her bowstring.

As the men on foot negotiated the steep scree-covered hillside, a few fell, sliding down to the plain below. Magda started casting a spell, releasing a pea-sized blue orb several moments later. It struck the hillside just above the approaching men and rapidly expanded to a diameter of twenty feet, shoving them all off balance and loosening the already unstable scree beneath their feet, sending all twenty sliding to the base of the hill.

"Nice," Abigail said. "Let's go see if there are any horses left in the castle."

Chapter 17

They climbed higher to avoid the area of hillside that Magda's spell had disturbed and reached the road without difficulty.

The man who had warned them earlier not to enter the keep was still with the woman impaled on the pike, but now he was kneeling before her, sobbing uncontrollably.

"What have I done?" he asked when Abigail and Magda reached him. "Why would I kill my own wife?" He leaned forward, mewling in abject misery, putting his forehead on the ground before her, shaking as he cried.

Abigail and Magda shared a look of sympathy and anger but left the man to mourn his loss. The drawbridge was still down, spanning the gap between the road abutment and the rocky outcropping that the castle was built upon. Several frightened women were in the courtyard.

"Who are you?"

"What do you want with us?"

"Leave us be."

Abigail raised her hand to forestall any further questions. "Who is the lady of this keep?" she asked.

An older woman with grey hair pulled back into a braid, wearing a simple grey dress, stepped forward.

"I am," she said. "What is your business here?"

"We're hunting the witch that took your men."

She met Abigail's eyes, taking her measure before nodding curtly. "My own husband couldn't see that thing for what it was, none of the men could. How is that possible?"

"Magic," Magda said, "dark and evil magic."

The woman swallowed, looking at the ground for a moment as if afraid to put words to her fears. "Will our men return?" she asked very quietly.

"The ones who left on foot will return within the hour," Abigail said, "though some may be injured. As for those on horse, I don't know."

She nodded tightly, a tear slipping down her cheek. "My husband was among those on horse. Why did that monster come here?"

"She's fleeing us, and we need to catch her as soon as possible," Abigail said. "Do you have horses?"

"No, she took them all … made a point of it."

"Show us to the ramparts overlooking the road," Magda said.

The woman frowned. "I don't understand."

"You don't need to understand, you just need to show us to the ramparts overlooking the road."

"Quickly," Abigail said.

After a brief moment of indecision, the woman motioned for them to follow her, leading them up a flight of stairs to the top of the wall and then up another to the western wall of the keep. The cliff was several hundred feet high with the natural stone flowing seamlessly into the wall.

"There," Magda said, pointing. "They've just reached the main road. Give me your hand and don't let go."

"Really? Are you sure that spell will work at this height?"

"Quite sure," Magda said with a reassuring smile and an outstretched hand.

A few moments later, they leapt off the battlement and fell into the sky, wind roaring past them, the ground rushing toward them with terrifying speed, but their descent slowed rapidly when they approached the base of the cliff and they landed as if jumping off of a table.

"Huh, I guess that would come in handy, especially if I fell off Kallistos," Abigail said. "Maybe I'll give the mana fast more thought."

"I encourage you to do so, but not right now."

The sound of Peti and her charmed horsemen approaching carried on the damp air. With the cliff on one side and the river on the other, Abigail and Magda stood in the middle of the road preparing to meet the attack.

"I'd rather not kill those men," Abigail said, nocking an arrow.

"Nor would I, but it may become necessary," Magda said. "I'll spook their horses … be ready to take your shot."

Abigail nodded, putting tension on her bowstring and setting herself to draw and fire quickly. When the horsemen saw them, they spurred their horses into a charge while Peti and Torin fell back, separating from their unwitting protectors.

Magda began her spell.

The air filled with the thunder of horses' hooves as the men drew closer. Magda released her spell with a clap of her hands, producing a thunderclap that struck fear into the horses charging toward them. Several turned aside, bolting toward the river; a few went toward the cliff, then turned again and ran back the way they had come; a few more started bucking wildly, filled with panic, desperate to dislodge their riders.

Through the chaos unfolding before her, Abigail loosed her arrow. It flew true, but Peti saw it coming and turned aside just enough to avoid a killing blow, instead taking the shaft through the outside of her shoulder. She snarled, then began barking the words of a spell in some ancient and unclean language. Abigail's next arrow was deflected by the witch's many-paned shield.

Magda sent five shards of blue force at her, one after the next, but none could defeat her shield, each striking with a loud crack.

"I'm sorry," Abigail whispered before releasing her next arrow, driving the shaft into the throat of Torin's horse. The animal squealed in shock and pain, bucking and throwing Torin before toppling over and thrashing around on the ground, desperately trying to flee death's inevitable grasp.

One of the men from the castle had regained his feet and was charging toward them with his sword drawn. Abigail had just nocked an arrow meant for Peti's horse, but she knew the charging man would be on them before she could nock another, so she sent it into his leg. He crashed into the dirt, screaming and writhing in pain.

Torin gained his feet and Peti began casting another spell. Her words were laced with anger and filled with malice as she spat them into the world. She reached out with her clawed hands and swirling blackness gushed forth, splattering onto the ground before her and taking shape as rats with coarse black fur, red beady eyes, and long sharp fangs. Dozens, then scores, swarmed toward them, racing across the ground.

"Run!" Magda shouted, pointing toward the river.

Abigail hesitated just long enough to send another arrow into the fray, the shaft plunging into Peti's horse, driving into its right eye and killing the beast instantly.

When the rats reached the man that Abigail had felled in the middle of the road, they swarmed over him, devouring his flesh. He screamed in terror and agony ... and then fell silent.

Abigail ran for the water, not daring to look back. The sounds behind her filled her with a kind of fear she didn't know she could feel, yet she retained mastery over her will, focusing on putting one foot before the other. She heard a roar behind her, like fire consuming a great pile of dry tinder, followed by snapping and squealing, but she didn't look back until she reached the river bank.

Magda was standing her ground, a gout of flames jetting from her hands, scorching the plague of rats swarming toward her, the dangerous little vermin vaporizing in sooty black smoke when the fire washed over them, but it wasn't enough. A dozen got past her fire, swarming around her feet, climbing up her legs, biting and clawing, bringing her to the ground with a defiant battle cry. In the distance, Peti laughed with maleficent glee.

Abigail turned as quickly as she could, scrambling in the loose dirt, nearly falling but regaining her footing and sprinting back toward Magda, drawing an arrow as she ran.

The rats swarmed over Magda, biting and clawing while she tried to roll away from them, killing several with her body, but leaving others scurrying after her with single-minded viciousness. She staggered to her feet before unleashing her quickest spell, a force-push, into the midst of the few remaining rats, blasting them away, killing the last of them before she collapsed.

Abigail loosed an arrow at Peti, but it bounced harmlessly off her shield. Dropping her priceless bow, she drew the Thinblade and ran toward the witch with all the speed she could muster. Peti's dark eyes widened, realization of what she faced ghosting across her face. Abigail was closing fast, gaining speed with each stride.

Peti didn't cast a spell, but instead withdrew a jar from her bag and tossed into Abigail's path. It tumbled through the air, shattering on the road and releasing a dark and squirming mass of something unnatural. In that same moment, a ballista bolt drove into the ground not three feet from Peti, sending her scrambling away and snarling at the ramparts above.

Before Abigail could react, the squirming mass of darkness that Peti had cast before her grew into a patch of black tentacles rising up out of the ground, flailing about in search of a victim. Several tentacles wrapped around her legs, then her waist, all of them trying to pull her to the ground. She struggled against them, slashing this way and that, desperately trying to cut her way free, but with each severed tentacle, another grew to take its place.

A second ballista bolt nearly impaled Peti, disrupting the spell she was attempting to cast. She growled, barking in fury before grabbing Torin by the collar and pulling him toward the river.

"I'm going to kill you, witch!" Abigail shouted, still hacking at the tentacles, freeing herself just as Peti and Torin reached the riverbank.

She cast about looking for her bow, racing around the flailing tentacles to retrieve it, but when she looked back, Peti and Torin were both on the opposite riverbank … how they'd gotten there she didn't know. She took careful aim, loosing her arrow into that moment of stillness that always accompanied a perfect shot, but the arrow was turned aside by Peti's shield. They fled on foot into the farm fields along the other side of the river.

Abigail froze, caught in a moment of indecision. Rage compelled her to give chase, but the river was moving too swiftly with early spring runoff to hope to cross safely. And more importantly, Magda was still down.

She went to her friend's side, rolling her over and catching her breath at the sight. The High Witch, Triumvir of the Reishi Coven, was stricken with some magical ailment beyond Abigail's understanding.

At each bite mark, her skin was black with tiny veins of darkness spreading from the wound.

"Oh Magda, what am I going to do?"

Several men approached, surrounding her on all sides; she ignored them, focusing on her worry for Magda.

"Stand away and answer for your crimes," one man said.

Abigail felt ice-cold rage spread from her spine out to her hands and feet, calm settling over her and filling her with resolve. She stood, drawing the Thinblade in one fluid motion, leveling it at the man who had spoken.

"Attack and I will kill you all," she said with deadly calm.

The man looked at her sword, a frown furrowing his brow.

"A Thinblade—how?" he said.

Before she could answer, another ballista bolt struck near the road, startling the men, drawing all eyes up toward the ramparts of the castle.

"Are you the lord of that keep?" Abigail asked.

"I am," he said, still filled with confusion.

"My name is Abigail Ruatha. The creature you saw as a beautiful woman, the one you fought for, is actually a half-breed demon witch. She charmed you— took your free will and used it as her own. She put your life in jeopardy and discarded you when it suited her. I, on the other hand, am offering you choices: You can help me, you can get out of my way, or you can be my enemy. Choose!"

"Ruatha? You're Lady Abigail, Commander of the Reishi Legions, those who saved our homeland from Zuhl's horde?"

"Yes, I am. Now make your choice … I'm pressed for time."

His confusion and the Sin'Rath's charm seemed to break at once.

"I'm Sir Raban, at your service, My Lady."

"Outstanding. Have your men carry her to the castle," Abigail said, pointing to Magda. He nodded and several men gathered around and carefully picked her up.

"Do you have a wizard?"

"No, My Lady, but there is a shaman who lives in the wilds. He practices the arcane arts."

"Send for him immediately," Abigail said. "Do you have any women who know how to fight?"

"None. But why would you need women? I have many strong men who would serve you."

"Never mind. Gather your men and send a rider ahead for a wagon to carry Magda."

"Lady Abigail, if I knew more, perhaps I could be of greater help."

"Do you know anything of magic?"

"No."

"Then you can help me best by getting my friend to your castle so your healers can attend to her and by sending for this shaman you speak of."

Raban seemed to struggle with his curiosity for a moment before he turned to his men and started shouting orders.

***

"How are you feeling?" Abigail asked.

Magda worked her tongue in her mouth before shaking her head, struggling to open her eyes, then clenching them shut.

"Here's some water."

Abigail trickled a few drops into her mouth, letting her work it around before offering more. Magda rubbed the crusted tears from her eyelashes and tried to sit up.

"Easy ... here, let me get you another pillow," Abigail said, helping her sit up against the headboard.

"How long?" Magda asked, her voice breaking.

"Five days," Abigail said, offering a cup of water.

"You should have gone on without me," she said before gingerly taking a sip.

"Nonsense, you almost died. I wasn't about to leave you in this condition."

"Peti?"

"She escaped with Torin."

Magda closed her eyes and shook her head. "We failed."

"Not yet," Abigail said. "I sent riders north with a letter for Anatoly. Help should be on its way soon."

Magda took another drink, draining the cup slowly.

"What else has transpired?"

"Sir Raban, the lord of the keep, has taken us in. He summoned a shaman from the nearby mountains, a strange little man … I think he's been on his own for a very long time, but he knew enough to make a poultice that drew out the poison. I used the last of my healing salve on your wounds and we've been waiting for you to wake ever since.

"Aside from that, I've had a few conversations with the people who live here. They're starved for information about the war and afraid for their children. I can't say I blame them."

Lady Raban entered quietly, smiling brightly when she saw that Magda was awake.

"Oh, thank the Maker, we've been so worried about you. You must be hungry, let me get you something to eat," she said without taking a breath and then she was gone.

"They seem eager to please," Magda said.

"Yes … it took a few days for the truth to sink in for the men, but once it did, they became very repentant. Many have expressed shame and guilt for succumbing to Peti's charms. I tried to explain but I don't think my words did much good. Since then, just about every man in the castle has come to me and offered to help when we resume our pursuit. And the women were so grateful to have their men back that they've been almost annoyingly helpful."

Magda chuckled, lapsing into a fit of coughing, clearing her throat several times before she could speak again, nodding her thanks to Abigail when she offered another cup of water.

Lady Raban returned with a tray of food. "The castle is abuzz with your waking," she said, carefully setting the tray over Magda's lap. "If it weren't for Myron standing watch over your door, I fear you'd have a roomful by now."

"Myron?"

"The man who killed his own wife," Abigail said. "He's been guarding the door since we brought you in."

"I don't know if the poor man will ever forgive himself," Lady Raban said. "I fear something inside him has broken."

"He wants to come with us when we go after Peti," Abigail said.

Magda sighed. "So much tragedy."

Lady Raban offered her a spoonful of broth.

"Oh, that's good," Magda said with a warm smile. "I'm suddenly very hungry."

By evening two days later, Magda was almost fully recovered and the entire keep was brimming with anticipation. Abigail and Magda shared a smile when the warning horn blew and they saw four wyverns floating overhead. Everyone came outside to watch them land as they carefully set down on the towers and the gatehouse, folding their wings and settling in for a rest while their riders conferred with Abigail and Magda. The children squealed and laughed with delight, while the adults were a bit more dubious about the new arrivals.

Amelia strode up to Abigail and Magda, bowing respectfully. "Mistress Magda, Lady Abigail, Master Grace dispatched us within an hour of receiving your letter. We had just returned to the city and I'm happy to report that Kallistos is healing nicely. He should be back in the air within the month."

"Thank you, Amelia," Abigail said. "I've been worried about him."

"Mistress Magda, has Taharial fallen?"

"In a manner of speaking," Magda said, withdrawing the figurine of her wyvern. "The witch transformed him into this. I'm hoping that I can reverse the effect, but I suspect it will take some time and study."

The other three wyvern riders arrived a moment later, lining up behind Amelia. "Per your instructions, Master Grace has sent four witches: Bree, Dalia, Kat, and me. In addition, he sent message riders to Ruatha via the fortress island to pass word of this new threat and to seek assistance or advice from Mage Gamaliel and the Wizards Guild."

"Good," Abigail said. "The Guild Mage might be able to send something that could even the odds."

"Also, Master Grace wished me to deliver a report on the battle for Irondale," Amelia said. "Prince Conner has taken the city with minimal casualties. The few enemy soldiers who survived have fled into the forest."

"That's welcome news," Abigail said. "How did he manage such a decisive victory with so few losses?"

"As I understand it, an elderly woman living in one of the nearby villages that had been pillaged by Zuhl's horde came to him with knowledge of a nonlethal, yet highly debilitating toxin made from a locally available type of moss. Prince Conner led a small team into the keep and poisoned the cistern. Within a day, most of the entire population was too sick to fight. Mage Dax breached the wall and our soldiers flooded into the city, killing the barbarians without mercy or quarter."

Abigail sighed, nodding to herself. "Well done, Conner," she whispered sadly.

"Unfortunately, the Ithilian Navy didn't fare as well," Amelia said. "Zuhl's five ships engaged them along the northern coast and sank half the fleet before they scattered. Some that survived reached Irondale and we presume more fled to Elsmere. We have scouts looking for them."

"I see," Abigail said. "Did they sink any of Zuhl's ships?"

"No, their weapons were no use against his shields."

"Thank you, Amelia," Abigail said, falling silent and nodding to Magda.

"Ladies, we face a most dangerous adversary. This Sin'Rath witch has bested us three times, killing one wyvern, injuring another, transforming a third, and nearly killing me with one of her dark spells. Abigail put an arrow through her eye and out the back of her head, yet she lives. We must find her, we must kill her, and we must preserve Prince Torin's life in the process. I've placed a tracker spell on the prince. When last I checked, he and Peti were already on the water, many leagues from shore. When we overtake them, we will disable the ship without sinking it, board the vessel, and kill her. The men aboard will resist us—use what force is necessary without killing them, if at all possible."

All four of the witches nodded.

"Excellent," Magda said. "Abigail will ride with Amelia and I'll be riding with Bree."

Abigail turned to their hosts. "Sir Raban, Lady Raban, your assistance and hospitality has been invaluable. We are in your debt."

"If you are ever in need of safe haven, our home is always open to you, Lady Abigail," Sir Raban said.

"Thank you."

Myron pushed through the crowd. "I would ride with you. I have a score to settle with this demon-witch."

"I know you do. And if it were any other enemy, I would welcome your help, but this is beyond you … she would just use you against us. Stay here and protect these people."

He swallowed his emotions with a visible effort, then bowed formally.

A few minutes later, four wyverns launched into the evening sky, gaining altitude for the journey to Sochi.

Chapter 18

At first Wren had been timid about venturing out into the city without Isabel, but after several afternoons of cautious exploring, she came to understand that the soldiers would ignore her ... at least most of the time. The first day a few gave her challenging looks, but she just kept her head down and tried to stay out of their way.

One soldier did bother her though. She caught him staring at her in the market. He looked familiar, though she couldn't place where she'd seen him. The thing that really bothered her was the look of recognition on his face when she looked directly at him. He was gone a moment later.

On her third day of exploring, she decided to be bold and tried to enter the black tower. The big, armored man guarding the door just shook his head when he saw her coming. She didn't press the issue.

Isabel had sent her to the market nearly every day with lists of things to buy. Phane had told the merchants that Isabel was to be given anything she wanted, with the exception of weapons or armor, and by extension, Wren was given nearly anything she asked for.

Mixed in with several new dresses for them both, Wren had obtained everything on Isabel's list: packs, bedrolls, waterskins, belts, pouches, boots, cloaks, and two changes of sturdy clothes for each of them, along with cooking utensils and a bag of dried food.

She'd explored a portion of the city between their manor and the nearest wall. Most of the buildings were barracks, some were residential buildings with floor after floor of identical living quarters for workers, while others were warehouses and businesses.

She'd found a few places to hide and even a couple of abandoned passages, both leading to unused basement rooms under barracks buildings. From the decaying weapon racks lining the walls, it looked like the basements had once been used as armories. She had chosen a broken old cabinet within one of these rooms to hide the equipment that she'd gathered, adding to it a bit at a time to avoid suspicion.

She'd managed to steal a knife from the house kitchen, and although it was small and ill-suited to fighting, the blade was sharp and it fit neatly inside her boot.

Isabel had told her to keep her efforts a secret from everyone, even her, and Wren had dutifully, though reluctantly, obeyed. She wanted to tell Isabel about her progress, describe the musty old basement where she'd hidden the gear ... she wanted to hear Isabel tell her that she'd done well, but she told herself that this was part of the growing up that Isabel said she needed to do. So she kept her work secret.

In the few weeks since she'd arrived, Wren had watched Isabel become more detached and distant, often waking in the night screaming, then crying quietly. More than anything, Wren wanted to help her, but she didn't know how, and Isabel had begun to withdraw, seeming to spend as little time with her as possible. She told herself that Isabel was afraid she might lose control and hurt her, that she was just trying to protect her the only way she knew how, but that didn't take away the loneliness and isolation she felt.

She had just added a length of rope to her hidden cache of equipment when she heard an odd noise, muffled and distant. She froze, listening intently, holding her breath until she heard it again. Very quietly, she tiptoed across the room, away from the light of day streaming through the door she'd left ajar and into the shadows. She heard it again, coming from the corner of the room. Holding her breath, she crept closer until she walked on a section of floor that felt different.

Searching the darkness on hands and knees, she found a trapdoor. She pulled on the ring, gently at first, then harder when it didn't budge, and then with all her might. All at once it broke free and she fell backward, knocking her wind out and leaving her sitting on the floor struggling for breath. When she was finally able to draw air, she nearly vomited from the fetid and rotting stench emanating from the hole in the floor.

She sat still for several minutes, regaining her breath and listening. The noise she'd heard didn't come again, but the passage she'd found was an opportunity she couldn't afford to pass up. As unpleasant as it smelled, whatever lay below might be the best chance she had for discovering a way out of the city. That task had been ever in the back of her mind—find a way to escape.

As her eyes adjusted to the darkness, the faint glow of green lichen growing on the walls of the shaft provided just enough light to make out the ladder leading down into the stench. Fear crept into her mind, poisoning her resolve with all manner of foul possibilities, but she set it aside, choosing instead to remember Isabel's lesson on courage. They needed a way out … she couldn't abandon that necessity out of fear.

She tested the first rung and it held, then the second. Slowly, testing each rung before committing her full weight to it, she descended into the bowels of the city. The putrid air burned her eyes and turned her stomach, but she held her course until she reached the last rung and stepped onto a ledge that ran along a canal filled nearly full with slow-moving sewage. The light offered by the glowing lichen wasn't enough to see by, so she picked a direction and began to feel her way along the wall. When she heard a noise echoing from behind her, she reversed course, her heart hammering in her head and her breath so loud in her chest that she was sure it would give her away.

In the dark, she couldn't be certain of her direction but she thought she must be moving toward the city wall, and it seemed that she was following the flow of sewage, though it was difficult to tell because it moved so slowly.

When the wall she had been following abruptly disappeared, she stopped in her tracks, straining to see in the dark, then feeling for the wall and finding that the passage had turned, or perhaps intersected with another, though she couldn't be certain. Cautiously, she reached out with her foot and found cold, hard stone. After several minutes of feeling her way in the dark, she found a bridge across a smaller canal that fed into the long canal she'd been following. Not long after that, she saw light … not the eerie light produced by the lichen, but white light.

She slowed her pace even further, focusing on moving without a sound, stopping when she heard voices. One was raspy and hoarse, the other merely a whisper. Light was coming from an open door in the passage wall. She crept closer, reaching the doorframe and peeking around with one eye. There were two figures standing in a small room with several large levers and hand-crank wheels set into one wall.

The first was a man wearing a Regency uniform with the rank of captain. He was holding a lantern. Wren edged an inch further and froze in fear when she saw the other figure. She was hunchbacked, leaning heavily on a stout cane with an oversized hand covered in scales, hooked bone spurs protruding from each knuckle. Her head was oversized and looked as if it had been sculpted from wax and then just slightly melted on one side, creating a hideous deformity. Warts and sores pocked her face and a forked tongue darted between her lips when she spoke.

"Lady Reishi is of no consequence … for the time being, anyway," she said, her voice raspy as if it took a great effort to speak. "Kill the princess and bring me the black box she carries."

"Yes, Lady Druja," the man whispered, bowing respectfully to her. "Would you like her to suffer?"

"Yes, but it isn't necessary," Druja said. "Of utmost importance is that she not be allowed to open that box for Phane. Also, take care to avoid being caught."

"I understand. Do you have any other tasks for me?" he asked, his eagerness to please such a creature beyond understanding to Wren.

"I would meet this Wizard Enu," Druja said, "but not yet. For now, watch his movements, identify his patterns of behavior and learn his habits. Once I know his routine, it will be a simple matter to place myself in his path."

"As you wish."

"Go now, and close the door," Druja said, turning away from him. He bowed deeply.

Wren withdrew into the shadows, panic welling up in her chest. She crouched in the dark, hoping beyond hope that he wouldn't notice her … and he didn't, turning away from her and lighting his way down the narrow ledge, opposite from the way she'd come.

Wren was torn, fear told her to retrace her steps, return to Isabel and tell her about what she'd heard. Isabel would know what to do. But another part of her told her to follow the man. Isabel had said that she should make her own decisions, base them on rational thought, especially when she was afraid. She was afraid now. After a brief internal struggle, she set out to follow the man, staying well behind him but keeping the light of his lantern in sight.

He seemed to know where he was going, turning this way and that, crossing over a narrow bridge at one point before coming to a ladder leading to the surface. Wren waited until he'd ascended into the shaft before hurrying to catch up.

She reached the base of the ladder just in time to hear him slide the sewer grate back into place, then she waited for the sound of footsteps before she started climbing, nearly falling when she trusted a rung without testing it first and it gave way. She clung to the ladder, her heart pounding and her breathing heavy while she struggled to regain her courage. After a few moments, she continued until she reached the grate. Only then did she discover that it was heavy, too heavy to lift with her arms, especially at such an awkward angle.

Her mind raced. The man was getting away. If she didn't reach the street soon, she would lose him and someone—no, not just someone—a princess would die. She wasn't sure why the distinction seemed to matter, but it did. She tested the rungs at the top and found them sturdy, then braced her back against the grate and pushed up. It lifted a little. With a heave, she raised it a few inches further and twisted her shoulders, sliding it off her back.

She emerged in an alley between two buildings occupying one block. Looking this way and that, she saw several boot prints leading away from the sewer grate, fading with each successive step. She raced out to the street looking for the man and found him rounding the corner a block away. She ran after him. A soldier frowned at her, scrutinizing her closely before deliberately looking away. She turned the corner and slowed to a walk, her quarry only half a block ahead.

She hadn't explored this part of the city yet, but she could guess at her location from the position of the black tower. She followed the man through the streets until he turned into the courtyard of a beautiful estate occupying half an entire city block. The wall around it was painted white and stood only four feet high. The gardens within were well cared for and the house itself was ornate and ancient, yet looked to be in pristine condition.

Wren climbed over the wall, keeping a bush between her and the man, darting to another bush that was closer still. He was chatting with a guard at the main door.

"Good talking with you, Captain Erato," the guard said just before the man entered the house, clapping the guard on the shoulder.

Wren skirted the main entrance, slipping past the lone guard, using the ample foliage for cover on her way to the kitchen entrance. She was familiar with the inner workings of a kitchen and knew how to blend into the background. The staff didn't even seem to notice her, especially after she scooped up a tray of food and slipped out of the kitchen into the hall, where she stopped, looking this way and that until she saw a guard at the end of the hallway sitting lazily in a chair.

"Excuse me, sir," she said, looking down timidly. "I'm new to this house and I can't remember the way to the princess's quarters. Would you help me, please?"

"Take the service stairs up two flights … it's the door at the end of the hall," he said, leaning his head back against the wall and closing his eyes before he even finished speaking.

Wren raced up the stairs, slowing to a fast walk once she came to the top floor, nodding respectfully to an elderly cleaning lady she passed in the hall, while watching Captain Erato enter the princess's quarters and close the door.

Wren wasn't sure what she was going to do once she reached the room, but she found herself setting the tray down on a small table along the wall and slipping her knife out of her boot, flipping it around in her hand so the blade ran up against her wrist, just the way Commander P'Tal had shown her back in Blackstone Keep.

She opened the door a crack.

"Where is the box?" Erato said, quietly but threateningly.

"I told you, I don't know what you're talking about," a beautiful woman with fair skin and strawberry-blond hair said, backing away from him. "When Prince Phane finds out about this …"

"He'll never know," Erato interrupted.

Wren slipped into the room on her tiptoes, carefully closing the door behind her and turning her knife back around in her hand.

The woman looked past the man, frowning in confusion. "Who are you?" she asked.

"Nice try, Princess," Erato said. "We're all alone here and I can kill you long before any help will arrive."

Wren put her finger over her lips, holding Lacy's eyes urgently, drawing closer with each passing moment, sacrificing speed for silence. Commander P'Tal's voice played over and over in her mind: If you have to stab a man in the back, aim just above the belt and to the side of the spine. Wren picked her target, focusing her mind, trying to remember every detail of her brief knife-fighting instruction.

"Tell me where the box is and I'll make this quick and painless," Erato said.

Lacy shook her head. "You won't get away with this."

"Who's going to stop me?" he asked, mockingly.

Wren lunged, stabbing with all her strength through Erato's leather armor, the blade of her knife thin and sharp. Her target was standing still and unaware, then he stiffened in shock, unable to utter a single word, frozen on the end of her blade.

"She is," Lacy said, drawing her dagger.

Wren pulled the knife sideways, just like Commander P'Tal had taught her, slicing through the side of the man's back. He toppled over into a growing pool of blood.

Everything caught up with Wren in that moment. She slumped to her knees, dropping the knife in a clatter and burying her face in her hands, crying uncontrollably. All of the bottled-up fear came pouring forth, overwhelming her deliberately self-imposed courage and reducing her to wracking sobs.

"Hush, it's all right," Lacy said, laying her trembling hands on Wren's head. "You didn't do anything wrong." She knelt next to Wren for several minutes until her crying subsided and she looked up, sniffling and wiping the tears from her face.

"I'm Wren," she said, her voice cracking.

"I'm Lacy. I don't know how I can ever thank you. He would have killed me if it weren't for you."

Wren sat up, frowning first in confusion and then in growing realization. "Wait, you're Princess Lacy? Lacy Fellenden?"

Lacy frowned back. "How do you know my name?"

Wren shrugged. "Sometimes the adults talk about important things while I'm in the room. They've been trying to find you. They said you're in danger and that you may hold the key to something called the Nether Gate."

Lacy grabbed her by the shoulders. "You know about the Nether Gate? Who are your friends? Where are they?"

Wren blinked, somewhat taken aback by Lacy's sudden intensity.

"My friends are Isabel and Abigail. Isabel is here in the city; Phane's holding her prisoner. Abigail is on Fellenden, fighting Zuhl's army."

"Abigail—Phane's cousin Abigail?" Lacy said, letting Wren go and frowning in confusion. "Phane said he sent her to protect my people against Zuhl's aggression."

"What?" Wren said. "Phane didn't send Abigail to Fellenden, Alexander did—her brother, Lord Reishi."

Lacy put her hands on her head. "I'm so confused. Phane showed me Abigail in his magic mirror—tall, silvery blond hair, blue eyes."

"That's her, but she would kill Phane in a heartbeat. She hates him."

"But ... he's been nothing but kind to me. He healed my broken hand and saved me from Zuhl's men."

Wren stopped, blinking again, her mind racing. She didn't know what to think, didn't know if she should trust Lacy or not, didn't know if Lacy would betray her to Phane.

"I should go," Wren said, getting to her feet and backing away.

"Wait, I won't hurt you. You saved my life," Lacy said, looking down at Erato's corpse. "I don't even know why he attacked me. He was supposed to be the captain of my guard detail."

"I saw him talking with something in the sewers," Wren said, "something that wasn't human ... something evil. He called her Lady Druja. She told him to kill you and take the box. You're not safe here, Princess Lacy. Don't trust anyone."

She turned to go.

"Wait ... I don't know what to believe."

"Please don't tell Phane I was here," Wren said before she opened the door, then she turned back as if remembering something urgent. "If you open the box, the world will die," she said, then slipped out the door.

Lacy sat down on her bed, trying to process everything that had just happened. Coldness seeped into her bones as the very real possibility that she'd been duped by Phane began to sink in. All of the old stories said he was a deceiver, that he'd unmade whole countries with nothing but a well-told lie. What if everything he'd said, everything he'd done was a lie?

She didn't even know the waifish girl who'd appeared at just the right moment, her moment of need, and saved her life, but she knew with perfect certainty that Wren had saved her. Whatever she did, she wouldn't repay her with betrayal.

She looked down at the corpse and nodded to herself, drawing her own dagger and stabbing him in exactly the spot where Wren had, drawing her blade out his side just as she had only slightly deeper. She took Wren's knife and wrapped it in a scarf, then hid it under her bed before going to the door.

"Guard!" she shouted.

After some very suspicious and threatening house guards disarmed her and sat her down at the end of a sword, they called for Phane. He arrived half an hour later, casually strolling into the room, then stopping in his tracks, assessing the situation in a glance.

"Why are you holding the princess with weapons drawn?" he snapped.

"Prince Phane, she killed Captain Erato. We thought ..."

"Silence!" Phane said. "You are dismissed. You will wait for me in the courtyard. If I find that you have mistreated the princess in any way, you will pay dearly."

Both men turned white, snapped to attention, saluting crisply, if not a bit forcefully, before scurrying from the room.

"Princess, I hope you will accept my sincere apology for the unacceptable behavior of my men." He had gone from stern and angry to contrite and remorseful in an instant. "Please, tell me what happened."

"I'm not really sure," Lacy said, her voice shaking. "Captain Erato came into my room and drew his sword, leveling the point at me. I could see in his eyes that he meant to kill me."

"It's all right, you're safe now," Phane said. "Take your time."

She nodded, taking a deep breath to calm her nerves. The residual fear of the brief struggle was still with her, but more than that, she was planning to lie to Phane and lying always made her terribly self-conscious.

"He lunged at me, but he tripped on the edge of the carpet and fell forward into me, knocking me down against the bed. Before he could get up, I stabbed him in the back." She looked up from the table. "Prince Phane, why would he try to kill me?"

"I don't know, Princess, but perhaps I can discern something by examining the body."

Lacy remained where she was, terrified that he'd seen through her lie, but relieved that he seemed to believe her.

"Quite a well-placed strike," he said, almost to himself before he started murmuring a few words under his breath. "Interesting." He pulled away Erato's collar and nodded.

"Well, this is certainly disturbing," he said, motioning for Lacy to come closer. "See here, these bite marks? Captain Erato wasn't acting of his own accord. He was doing the bidding of another, a very dangerous enemy of mine called the Sin'Rath." Phane stood abruptly, pausing to think for a moment. "At the end of the Reishi War, I banished a very powerful demon known as Sin'Rath, the Succubus Queen. What I didn't know at the time was that she had spawned offspring. Apparently, her line survives to this day.

"I'll be making some changes to your guards. I don't know why the Sin'Rath have taken an interest in you, but your safety is paramount. This is important, Lacy—trust no man save me. The Sin'Rath can charm almost any man alive. A few, such as myself, are capable of defending against their black magic, but not many. Your staff and guards will be comprised of women from now on. If any man enters this estate, call for help immediately."

Lacy nodded, wide-eyed.

"Did he say anything? Anything at all?"

"It all happened so fast. I don't remember him saying anything."

"Can you think of any reason why the Sin'Rath are interested in you? Any reason at all?"

Lacy's mouth went dry. "No," she said, looking up for only a moment.

Phane remained silent but Lacy could feel his stare boring into her. She glanced up again. In that glance, she knew she'd been caught.

"Princess Lacy, we live in difficult times. Allies are far too rare. Are we allies?"

She looked up again, nodding tightly. "Yes, Prince Phane. I'm so grateful for all you've done for me."

"Then why are you hiding something important from me?"

Lacy just stared at him.

"I can't help but notice that an alarming number of very powerful parties have taken an interest in you. I would know why. I give you shelter and protection. At the very least, you can provide me with insight into the enemies I am facing on your behalf."

Lacy tried to swallow but her mouth was too dry. She was trapped. Any further attempt at deception would surely fail.

"I don't know, Prince Phane," Lacy said, after working up enough saliva to speak. "I don't know why so many people are trying to kill me. I wish I did, but I don't."

He took a step forward, anger flashing in his eyes. "Don't lie to me!"

She was stunned speechless.

Phane shook his head and turned away from her, raising his hands and speaking in some long-forgotten language. Several moments after he stopped speaking, he dropped his hands to his sides and sauntered over to her bed, reaching underneath and retrieving her backpack, holding it up for her to see before dumping it out on the bed.

It felt like slow motion, or a dream where she was trapped in place and couldn't flee the approaching menace. She wanted to protest, to scream, to shout, to stop him, but she was powerless to do anything but watch.

The little black box came to rest atop a pile of her clothes and traveling gear.

Phane picked it up and set it in front of Lacy, taking a seat across from her at the table.

"Is this what you're protecting?"

She nodded.

"Open it."

She shook her head.

A frown crossed his brow, followed by a warm and genuine smile.

"Princess, I apologize for yelling at you and for invading your privacy, but you must understand that I have countless people depending on me to protect them. I can't afford to allow such dangers as this," he gestured at the box, "into my city without my awareness."

Lacy didn't say anything. Her face felt hot and her heart was racing.

"What's in the box?"

"I don't know," Lacy said.

He nodded, appraising her intently.

"How did you come by this box?"

"My father sent me to find it and take it to Ithilian," Lacy said, feeling both a flutter of relief that she could answer a question truthfully and a thrill of fear that she was revealing too much.

"I see," Phane said, a hand covering his mouth, a frown furrowing his brow for a moment before he continued. "Did you retrieve this from your family crypt on Fellenden?"

"How could you know that?"

Phane sat back with a wistful look on his face.

"Lacy, within this box resides the third keystone to the Nether Gate." He shook his head, his smile turning into laughter. "All this while, salvation for the entire world is right here, safe within my walls."

Lacy just looked at the box, shaking her head with a mixture of dismay and revulsion.

"Oh, Princess, you should rejoice in this," Phane said. "We now have the power to save your people, but we must hurry. Open the box and we'll set sail within the week."

Lacy looked up at Phane, continuing to shake her head.

"No. I will never open this box."

His smile fell into a look of pure dismay. "But, Lacy, we could save everyone."

"What's in that box won't save anyone; it will only doom them."

"No ... it can save us all. I wouldn't expect you to understand the principles of magic, but one of the most important is to always maintain positive control over your magical manifestations. My father was very careful about that, hence the three keystones. I can promise you, we can control it, we can use it, we can close it, and then we can destroy it forever."

She shook her head very deliberately.

"You can't be serious, Princess. I saved you. I brought you here where you're safe, I healed your hand. What more can I do to earn your trust?"

"It isn't about that. You've been most gracious, but the whole idea of the Nether Gate is beyond insanity. I can't be a part of bringing that kind of darkness into the world—I won't."

Phane closed his eyes sadly and slowly shook his hanging head.

"Then I fear a bad end for us all," he whispered.

He left, looking dejected, like a scolded puppy, not meeting her eyes again, his entire demeanor a study in sadness.

Chapter 19

"Are you allied with the Sin'Rath?" Phane said, barging into Isabel's library while Enu tried to teach her a spell she didn't want to learn.

"What are you talking about?"

"Answer my question!" he shouted, extending his hand toward Isabel and lifting her three feet into the air with his magic, then slamming her against the wall hard enough to knock the wind out of her and rattle her teeth. He held her there against the wall, splayed out and helpless.

She felt a flutter of fear in her stomach. She'd been pushing Phane over and over, trying to see just how much he would take and what he would do about it. Now, she wasn't so sure that had been wise. Anger and murder flashed in his eyes as he marched up to her while she struggled to draw a breath.

"I won't ask you again."

Isabel tried to answer but the pressure holding her against the wall was so great she couldn't speak. Seeing her soundlessly working her mouth, he released his magic and she fell to the floor, toppling forward onto her hands and knees, gasping for breath. He gave her a few moments before lifting her into the air once again, this time holding her a foot off the floor.

"Well?"

"No."

"Then explain why one of those infernal demon-spawn witches is lurking in the sewers under my city?"

"How should I know? Why don't you go down there and ask her yourself?"

He released his magic, dropping her by surprise. She stumbled but caught herself before falling again.

"Ever defiant," he said, shaking his head and walking away several steps before turning back.

"Tell me what you know of the Sin'Rath, and I'm warning you, Isabel, I can tell when you lie to me."

She glared at him, returning to her chair and regaining her composure before answering.

"Before I came here to kill you, I helped the House of Karth kill ten of the Sin'Rath. Three escaped—I haven't seen any of them since."

He blinked, frowning momentarily, then smiled so disarmingly that she almost forgot how dangerous he really was.

"How wonderful," he said, plopping down in a nearby chair, his anger completely transformed into childlike glee. "I hate the Sin'Rath. I would see them exterminated entirely … yet another piece of common ground between us. Tell me, how did you defeat so many of them? Whatever else they are, they do not die easily."

"The Goiri bone," Isabel said.

He nodded thoughtfully. "Well then, I'll let you get back to your lessons." With that, he left, whistling to himself.

"Shall we continue, Lady Reishi?" Wizard Enu asked pointedly just before Wren burst into the room, stopping in her tracks when she saw that Isabel wasn't alone.

Isabel rubbed her shoulder and looked at the wizard. "I think I need a break and it's almost time for lunch."

"Very well, I'll return in an hour."

Wren looked at Issa, then back to Isabel.

"I think we'll take lunch on the balcony of my room," Isabel said. As usual, Issa followed until she shut the door in his face.

Once they were alone, Wren swallowed hard, her eyes going wide and welling up with tears. "I killed someone," she whispered.

Isabel led her to a chair and sat her down. "Tell me what happened."

Wren described her morning in detail, recalling every event as accurately as she could, starting with her cache of equipment, explaining how she found Druja, followed Captain Erato to Lacy's quarters, snuck in and killed him. She finished her story by recounting the warning she'd given Lacy about the box.

Isabel let her talk without interrupting, processing each new piece of information and trying to piece together the puzzle she'd been presented. When Wren finished, Isabel hugged her and then held her at arm's length with a smile.

"Well done. Killing is always difficult; it *should* always be difficult, but sometimes it's necessary. Today was one of those times. Lacy is at the center of events ... saving her life may have saved us all."

"I was so scared," Wren whispered.

"I know," Isabel said, hugging her again. "But you acted decisively in spite of your fear. That's courage."

Wren nodded, smiling a little even though tears ran down her face. "What was Druja?" she asked. "She was so hideous."

"She's a very powerful witch spawned from a demon," Isabel said. "I helped kill most of her sisters before I came here, so she's going to try to kill me soon. This is important, Wren. She can charm men—make them do whatever she wants them to do, so you can't trust any man in this city."

"I already don't trust anybody in this city but you."

"Good. Just remember that Phane is trying to make me turn to the darkness, so you can't fully trust me either. I want you to make friends with Lacy. Build a relationship with her. She's all alone here; she needs a friend and so do you. Just don't let Phane find out about it. The two of you talking is liable to make him nervous."

Wren nodded. "She seemed confused when I told her the truth about Phane. He told her that Abigail was working for him on Fellenden, showed her Abigail and Prince Torin working together against Zuhl."

"That bastard can twist just about anything to his own purposes," Isabel said, shaking her head. "Tell her we know the shade is after her. Tell her that she's been having dreams of her father telling her to go to Ithilian. Explain that those dreams are really Alexander posing as her father because Torin told him that she's

a terrible liar and he didn't want to put her in the position of having to lie to
Phane."

"Do you think she'll believe me?"

"I don't know, but it'll definitely get her attention and maybe cause her to
doubt Phane enough to keep that box shut no matter what lies he tells her."

Wren nodded, hesitating for a moment. "Then what? We're not safe
here—none of us are."

"I know. I was hoping to have another stab at Phane, but he's too well
protected." She thought for a moment. "We need to escape, especially now that we
know Lacy is here with the keystone. Go to her now, gain her trust, explain
everything. I'll go into the sewers and look for a way out."

"But what about Druja? Isn't she dangerous?"

"In the extreme, but if she got into the city through the sewers, then we
can get out the same way. I just have to find it."

There was a knock at the door and Dierdra entered with lunch. Wizard
Enu was waiting in the hall.

"I will await you in the library," he said. "We must continue your lessons.
Prince Phane is becoming impatient with your progress."

Isabel snorted. "I'll bet."

Wren caught her eye. She was suddenly afraid.

"I'll be down right after I eat," Isabel said dismissively to Enu.

"As you wish."

"I forgot," Wren said, after Dierdra and Enu had gone. "Druja told
Captain Erato that she wanted to meet Wizard Enu."

Isabel looked at the door. "That's good to know. With the captain dead,
Druja will be looking for another proxy."

After lunch, Wren left on her errand while Isabel went to the library,
entering warily, watching Enu for any hint of danger, but saw none. Still, she
remained vigilant, taking the chair closest to the door and watching his every
move. For the first time since she arrived, she was actually relieved to have
Wraithkin Issa in the room.

"You seem tense, Lady Reishi. Is something wrong?"

"You mean besides the fact that I'm being held prisoner by a madman
who wants me to learn black magic against my will?"

Enu smiled mirthlessly, seating himself across the table from her.

"Your resistance is to be expected, though I assure you, it is only
delaying the inevitable. Prince Phane has been working diligently to devise a
means of circumventing your defenses. I have every confidence that he will
succeed even if I fail."

"Doesn't that make you nervous? Failure, I mean. Phane isn't known for
his forgiving nature."

"Were I any other, I would be very concerned, but I happen to be the only
wizard other than Prince Phane on this entire isle."

"That's interesting. How did you manage to avoid the Sin'Rath for all
these years?"

"Simple. I arrived from Andalia just last summer. Now, shall we begin?"

Isabel nodded, mentally steeling herself. She had been resisting in every way she could, but Azugorath was becoming more and more powerful within her mind. It seemed that the exercises Enu was teaching her were designed primarily to help Azugorath learn how to overcome her will.

At first, her unwanted tutor had focused on teaching her the drain-life spell that Phane wanted her to learn. When that proved futile, he switched to teaching magical principles in an effort to help her comprehend the intricacies of the spell. After a while, it became obvious that she was failing deliberately, so he switched tactics yet again.

"Close your eyes," Enu said. "Relax and clear your mind."

Isabel had no sooner obeyed his seemingly harmless command than Azugorath thrust into her psyche with all her might, severing Isabel from her will and casting her adrift within her own consciousness. Always before, she'd been able to fight it, struggle against it, but this time she'd been caught completely off guard.

Her eyes opened, unbidden. She was within her body, could see and hear, feel and smell, but she had no control. Enu stood before her, holding his staff over her head, a faint darkness emanating from it.

She stood. It was a strange sensation, to feel her body moving without having any control over it.

"Where's the girl?" she heard herself ask. Terror gripped her, filling her soul with unbridled panic. Somewhere, she heard laughter, unclean and maleficent.

"Running errands," Enu said.

"You fool! How can I kill her if she isn't here?"

Isabel struggled, her rage rising into fury. The laughter grew with it, mocking her, taking malign glee in her helplessness.

"I will send for her immediately," Enu said.

Isabel let go of her emotions, calming herself and willing her mind quiet. The laughter turned nervous, then became taunting and insistent. Isabel ignored it. Instead, she thought of Alexander, seeing his face in her mind and focusing on her love for him.

Azugorath berated her, shrieking within her psyche, daring her to fight, baiting her with images of horror from her own worst nightmares ... but Isabel ignored her, choosing to feel only love for her one true love.

Light started to shine in her mind again, the barrier that was sealing off her connection with the realm of light started to fray, allowing streamers of healing light into her soul. She reveled in it, holding on to her love for Alexander and ignoring the atrocities Azugorath was projecting into her mind.

And then, as suddenly as it had begun, the attack ended. The Wraith Queen retreated into the depths of her subconscious mind and the barrier blocking her link with the light slammed firmly into place again. Isabel slumped to her hands and knees, breathing hard, trying to understand what had just happened.

Enu returned. "The watch has been alerted. The girl will be brought as soon as she's found."

Isabel stood, scooping up a lamp in one fluid motion and hurled it at him. It shattered against his shield, spreading burning oil over it in an instant. He muttered a single word, then hit the floor with his staff and a sudden gust of wind spread away from him in all directions, extinguishing the fire in a whoosh.

"I see you've returned, Lady Reishi. No matter, we've made progress worth reporting to Prince Phane. I shall leave you to contemplate your fate."

Once he'd left, Isabel sat down heavily, her mind racing, trying to find a way out of the trap that was rapidly closing around her. She replayed the experience in her mind and found that she'd been suddenly separated from her will. In that moment, no doubt caused by Enu's spell, Azugorath had gained control.

But there was more. When Isabel fought against her with rage, her grip had only tightened. Yet, when she fought with love, the Wraith Queen had struggled to hold on, until the light began to shine through and then her grip had faltered completely. Isabel played the experience over and over in her mind, searching for some lesson she could use to fight the darkness and finding only one … love.

She returned to her bedchamber, locking Issa in the hall outside her door as usual, knowing full well that the lock, or the door for that matter, was meaningless to the wraithkin.

She put her forehead against the closed door and took several deep breaths to steady herself, then went to her bed and sat down, still shaking from the ordeal with Azugorath.

Slow, creeping despair started building in the back of her mind. When she thought of Wren … of killing Wren … she felt a kind of wild panic screaming from a place so deep inside her that she knew her spirit would break, knew her soul would be scarred beyond forgiveness. Others might try to forgive her, but she knew she would never, ever forgive herself.

That self-loathing would be all the Wraith Queen needed to use her at will.

Phane would win.

In that moment, everything came into clear focus—all of the soldiers fighting battles all across the Seven Isles, all of her friends and loved ones in harm's way, the future hanging in the balance.

She'd lost perspective.

She'd come here for more than one reason. Killing Phane was why she'd wanted to come here, but that was really nothing more than a way of finding the good in a bad situation. She'd really come here because she was dangerous to those she loved, more so now than ever.

Wren had to leave.

Isabel had obligations, duties she'd taken upon herself willingly and even joyously, despite the burden they'd been. There were many threats arrayed against the Old Law, but only a few were within her power to fight. Lacy Fellenden carried a keystone that could never be allowed to fall into Phane's hands. Isabel could do something about that.

Lacy had to leave, too, and that box with her.

Isabel sat down at her desk, summoning Slyder with a thought. She felt a pang of guilt as she wrapped the note around her hawk's leg. Sending him off with an affectionate scratch under the chin, she returned to her room and stood before her dressing mirror.

She'd been working on the shapeshift spell every available moment since she'd arrived in the fortress city. Her last attempt had nearly succeeded. Today, it actually mattered. Rather than use anger, she opted to use love as her distraction emotion, more to see how it would affect Azugorath's interference with her link to the light than for any other reason.

It took a long time to get into the right emotional state of mind, violent thoughts bubbled up to distract her, but she finally reached the right degree of emotional intensity needed to attempt the spell. However, once she'd fully visualized the desired effect, she'd lost her emotion.

It took an hour before she finally succeeded, transforming her appearance into that of Dierdra, her maidservant. She inspected the face staring back from the mirror and smiled; it was a perfect likeness. After several minutes, the spell broke and Isabel reverted back to her own appearance.

She opened her door a few inches. "Send for Dierdra. I need help drawing a bath."

"It's the middle of the afternoon," Issa said.

Isabel just glared at him and closed the door. Dierdra arrived a few minutes later. Isabel followed her into the bathing chamber, quietly stepping up behind her, slipping her arm around Dierdra's neck, under her chin, locking it in place with the other arm, then drawing her backwards to the ground and choking her until she fell unconscious.

She worked quickly, tying Dierdra's hands and locking her in the bathing room before casting her shapeshift spell again. This time it worked much faster and the results were just as accurate. She checked her appearance in the mirror, smiling to herself.

"She says she doesn't want a bath now, she's going to take a nap ," Isabel said to Issa on her way out of the room.

He shrugged indifferently.

She made it out of her estate house and into a nearby alley before the spell ran its course and her appearance reverted to normal. Taking a moment to get her bearings, she set out toward the barracks buildings where Wren had stashed their gear. Isabel drew a few looks from soldiers and tradesmen while walking through the streets, but she ignored them, and they seemed entirely unwilling to confront her, which suited her just fine.

It wasn't long before she found the empty basement and the stash of equipment, just where Wren said it would be. Isabel took a lantern and left everything else where she'd found it before going to the trapdoor in the corner.

The stench emanating from the sewer was foul. She steadied herself, letting a wave of nausea wash over her before testing the rungs and descending into the dark. At the base of the ladder, she held up her lantern, assessing her surroundings, then drew a careful map of the area in a little notepad she'd taken from her desk. Once satisfied that she'd sketched every important feature nearby, she picked a direction and set out until she'd traveled far enough to warrant adding to her map.

She followed the flow of sewage, knowing that it would have to go somewhere, hopefully outside the walls. The canal ran straight and just off level. Other narrower canals intersected it at even intervals from both sides, all angled to feed into the large canal, and each bridged by a span of stone as wide as the ledge. Only the occasional rat running from her lantern light interrupted the eerie solitude. Eventually, the canal came to an intersecting corridor and a grate covering a ten-foot-wide drain tube running off at a slightly steeper angle into the dark, sewage flowing through the lower half.

The grate was stout and sturdy, two-inch bars welded into a grid with less than a foot of space between each. As with the canal she'd been following, a ledge ran along the drain passage. Isabel picked a bar and burned through it with a light-lance spell, then another and another until she'd opened a hole large enough to crawl through. She marked it on her map, then filled in the corridor running perpendicular to the canal she'd been following, the right passage crossing the canal over a stout bridge attached to the grate. She went left.

It wasn't long before she found another similar grate leading to a similar drain tube, being fed by a similar canal running parallel to the one she'd initially traveled along. Looking at her map, she discerned a pattern—long canals running the length of the city with side passages between them to balance the flow, water coming in one end of the fortress city and sewage going out the other, two sets of grates. She burned a hole in the grate, marked it on her map, and made her way down the corridor toward the next.

A noise ahead made her freeze in place. She dimmed her lantern, listening for a second occurrence, straining to sense anything out of the ordinary. After a moment of hyperawareness, she relaxed and continued down the corridor running along the down-water boundary of the fortress city. At the next grate she found a ladder. She linked with Slyder and scouted the buildings above.

More barracks. Dangerous territory.

She marked it on her map and continued, slowing when she heard another noise in the darkness. She shuttered her lantern, moving slowly, using the wall as her guide, straining to hear between each cautious footstep.

"They took my sisters," a raspy voice said.

Isabel froze, schooling her breathing, listening with complete attention.

"We'll take everything from them for what they did to us."

She knew where the witch was—in a small room just this side of the next grate.

The witch chuckled, her menacing laugh transforming into a fit of wheezing that culminated in several barking coughs before she finally cleared her throat and fell silent.

Isabel knew who she was … Druja, a Sin'Rath witch, one of three remaining. If Isabel caught her by surprise, hit her hard, then hit her again … and again, she might kill her … but it could very easily go the other way.

"All of them. Every single one of them," Druja said, clearing her throat for several protracted seconds.

Isabel held perfectly still, calming her breathing and listening.

"Peti's plan is a good one. By the time they see what we've done, it'll be too late." She cackled madly, her shrill laughter echoing down the sewer passages.

Isabel wrestled with the thought of attack, surprising Druja and killing her … but Druja was powerful, more than a match for Isabel. Even with surprise, Isabel was doubtful about the outcome.

"Once we have an army," Druja said, wheezing a few times, "we can take everything a piece at a time."

Isabel took a step back.

"The Reishi Coven made a mistake coming here. We were content with our island, but now we'll take it all."

Another step.

"Where is Enu?!" Druja howled, followed by a fit of coughing.

Isabel hurried away, as quietly as she could, retracing her steps, not daring to risk more than a sliver of light from her lantern until she was a grate away. Then she opened the shutter wide and ran to the next grate.

Druja had control of Enu.

Isabel turned up the main canal she'd come down, running toward the ladder leading up and out.

She had to warn Lacy … and Wren.

Once she was safely back in the barracks basement, she summoned Slyder and went to work on a note and a map showing the way out and where Druja was hiding. She put the map and the lantern into the cabinet and replaced the note on Slyder's leg with the new one, sending him into the sky.

She didn't make it far on the street before a guard spotted her and blew his horn. More than a dozen soldiers converged on her very quickly, respectfully but insistently escorting her back to her house.

Chapter 20

Phane was waiting for her in her dining room when she arrived.

"Oh, Isabel, you stink," he said, covering his nose with a napkin. "Go get cleaned up. We have a lot to discuss and dinner will be served shortly, so be quick about it."

She didn't answer except by obedience, more because the idea of a bath and clean clothes was appealing than for any other reason. Feeling much better after changing, she went to face Phane, wondering what he wanted this time.

He seemed to be in a good mood, but Isabel had come to understand just how quickly and how violently that could change. She was on guard. A few moments after she sat down, dinner was served ... roasted game birds with potatoes and some type of green vegetable cooked into mush.

"So, where to begin," Phane said. "Let's start with how you managed to elude Issa. He tells me he found your maidservant tied up in the water closet."

"That's where I left her," Isabel said with a shrug.

Phane chuckled, shaking his head.

"Issa also swears to me that he saw your maidservant leave the room—even claims she spoke to him."

Isabel smiled slightly but remained silent. She didn't want to reveal her new spell, but Phane was like a dog with a bone—he wasn't going to let go until he was satisfied.

"Have you taught yourself another spell? A shapeshift spell?"

"I starting working on it before I arrived," Isabel said.

"I see, you're capable of teaching yourself a new, and quite complicated spell, without tutelage, and yet you're unable to learn the most basic magical principles from Wizard Enu."

"He's not a very good teacher."

"Don't try my patience, Isabel."

She stared at him silently.

"Well, no matter. Enu tells me he's made a breakthrough. He said he spoke with Azugorath through you after casting a new spell he's devised. Not exactly the complete success I'm looking for, but it's a significant step forward.

"Speaking of which, where is your little friend?"

"I sent her out on some errands."

"Good. Then I suspect she'll be back just in time. Enu will come by after dinner to cast his spell." Phane stabbed a piece of meat with his fork and smiled suggestively at Isabel before eating it. He took his time chewing, watching her intently like a cat watches a mouse, then washed his food down with a long pull from his wine flagon and sat back with satisfaction.

"Wren will die tonight."

Isabel closed her eyes, pretending to shut out Phane and his assertion, but really linking her mind with Slyder and directing him to Lacy's balcony. Relief washed over her when she saw both Wren and Lacy sitting on the bed talking softly. After Wren saw Slyder and retrieved the message, Isabel broke the link and returned.

"… no choice in the matter," Phane was saying.

"There's always a choice," Isabel said.

"Not for you," he said. "Enu assures me that his spell will allow Azugorath to gain control, even if only for a few moments."

Isabel just glared at him.

"We'll revisit that topic after Enu and Wren arrive. There are other matters I wish to discuss. My expedition to retrieve the Goiri bones has failed."

"I'm not surprised."

"I don't imagine that you are, especially since I suspect you and your beloved had something to do with the ambush that killed my people."

"Flattery will get you nowhere, Phane."

He stared at her for several moments. She glared right back.

"Fortunately, the expedition was not a total loss. Those few who survived captured part of the ambush party. Most were Karth family soldiers, but one man in particular stood out. I believe you know him … he said his name is Hector Lal."

Isabel closed her eyes, sighing heavily. Hector had already been through so much, lost so much. She had no idea what Phane might do to him.

"Good … you do know him. I thought we might have a chat, just the three of us," Phane said, snapping his fingers.

Both doors swung open, revealing Hector, beaten up and broken-spirited, flanked by two soldiers.

"Come in, sit down, have something to eat," Phane said jovially.

Hector moved woodenly, as if he was just going through the motions. He sat and ate without looking up.

"Tell me, Hector, was it you who sent that stalker demon after me?" Phane asked, leaning in with interest. "It caused quite a bit of excitement, killed almost a hundred of my soldiers."

Hector looked up, his eyes sunken, heavy dark bags underneath them.

"Honestly, sending that demon to kill you was an afterthought," Hector mumbled. "It wasn't really about you at all."

Phane's eyes flashed with anger, he started to raise his hand toward Hector, but then reined in his ire, taking a deep breath before speaking again.

"If killing me wasn't your purpose, then what exactly did you hope to accomplish?"

"I wanted to kill Hazel the same way she killed my brother," Hector said.

Phane sat back, smiling boyishly. "Ah … vengeance. Now we're getting somewhere. I understand vengeance." He looked at Isabel meaningfully. She ignored him.

"So you sacrificed the witch and commanded the demon to kill me just as she had sacrificed your brother to kill whom, exactly?"

"One of the Sin'Rath," Hector said. "I don't know which one."

"And all of this took place in Siavrax Karth's ancient fortress at the center of the swamp, yes?"

Hector nodded.

"Where you assisted Lady Reishi in retrieving a bone from the long-dead Goiri."

"Don't tell him any more," Isabel said.

"Don't be foolish, Isabel. Can't you see, he's a broken man. He knows what will happen if he resists."

"Don't listen to him, Hector."

"I've already lost everything, Phane. Why don't you just kill me and have done with it?" Hector said, his voice a monotone, devoid of emotion.

"You see there, Isabel? Broken," Phane said, holding out his hand toward Hector as if he were introducing him for a speech.

"What if I could help you get back some of what you've lost?" Phane asked, leaning forward with genuine excitement.

"You can't," Hector mumbled.

"Oh, but you're wrong, Hector. I'm an arch mage. I can do many things."

Hector looked up, frowning, a spark of hope and interest in his eye for the first time since he'd arrived.

"Don't listen to him, Hector," Isabel said, leaning forward and putting her hand on his forearm. "He's a liar. No good will come from bargaining with him."

Hector's brow fell and he looked down at the table again.

"That's quite enough from you, Isabel. I'd like you to sit there quietly now. Can you do that for me?"

"What do you think?"

Phane smiled insincerely, raising his hand toward her, pressing her into her chair with his magic and binding her wrists and ankles to the arms and legs of the chair. She tried to protest but found that she couldn't speak—she could try, but no noise came out.

"Now, isn't that better?"

She struggled in vain for several moments, finally stopping because Phane was enjoying it too much.

"Now, where were we? Oh yes, I can help you, Hector. If you help me."

"Horace is dead," Hector said with a shrug.

"I just so happen to know a thing or two about death," Phane said. "For example, most people believe that death is final ... and yet, it isn't. For the right price, anything is possible, even bringing back the dead."

Isabel wanted to scream, to shout, to shake Hector, but she couldn't move or speak ... she could only watch, horrified by what was taking place right before her.

"You could bring my brother back?" Hector asked, a spark of hope now fully ablaze in his eyes.

"Yes," Phane said.

"How? How is that even possible?"

"As with anything involving magic, it's possible because we will it to be possible and reality bends to our will. The real question is, do *you* have the will to bring your brother back from the dead?"

Isabel felt sick as Hector leaned forward, all vestige of his malaise replaced with blind and reckless hope burning in his eyes.

"I'll do whatever you ask."

Phane smiled like the sunrise.

"Good, let's start with a conversation. Tell me about your experiences in the swamp and the fortress. Take your time; don't leave anything out."

Isabel closed her eyes in defeat when Hector started recounting their journey together, step by step, in detail. He told Phane everything from Hazel's hidden sanctuary to the threats they faced along the way to how the fortress was laid out, where they entered and what they found within.

Phane was particularly interested in the crystal chamber, questioning Hector extensively about it. He took note of the cave-in blocking the room with the Goiri bones and the traps in the black-and-white room.

He seemed especially pleased to learn that Trajan had taken a large Goiri bone and was hiding somewhere in the jungle.

After Phane had thoroughly questioned Hector about every aspect of the journey, he sat back and took a few moments to digest what he'd learned.

"Here's what I propose," he said, smiling at Hector. "You will accompany an expedition force of adequate size to the fortress, where you will help them retrieve the remains of both your brother and the Goiri. When you return, I will raise your brother from the dead."

"Bargain struck," Hector said, standing and holding out his hand to Phane.

Isabel fought back tears as Phane escorted Hector to the door and saw him off, patting him on the back on his way out. After he'd gone, Phane released the spell holding her in the chair.

"You bastard!" she shouted, surging to her feet. "You lying bastard!"

"Really, Isabel, what do you expect? He was so ripe for the picking," Phane said, chuckling. "People are never more susceptible to deceit than when they're desperate. Did you see the moment? The moment when he turned? His eyes came alight and he suddenly had perfect clarity. It was ... delicious. Soon, Isabel, you'll have that kind of clarity as well."

Isabel had never felt so powerless in her whole life. She wanted to kill Phane where he stood, strike him down without mercy, but she couldn't and she knew it. Worse, from the look on his face, he knew it too and reveled in it.

"Sit down, Isabel, we still have things to discuss," he said, meeting her challenging glare with the smug satisfaction of a man who knew he held the upper hand.

Isabel sat, willing her anger into the background.

"It seems you've been holding out on me. I guess that's to be expected, given the circumstances, though it makes me wonder what else you know."

Isabel glared at him.

"It pains me to see you so miserable ..."

She laughed in his face. "You don't care one bit about how anyone else feels and you probably never have. How old were you when you realized that you're different?"

Phane's face contorted into sudden rage but he didn't draw on his magic, instead backhanding Isabel across the face hard enough to send her sprawling. Bright flashes of light exploded in her head when he struck her and again when she hit the floor. She lay still for a moment, her ears ringing ... then the pain came, slamming into her, full force. She groaned.

"You will learn respect ... one way or another. Now get up and sit with me."

Isabel rolled to her knees and staggered to her feet, still a little unsteady, willing the pain aside. A few wobbly steps and she was sitting at the table, still slightly dazed from the blow. Somewhere in the back of her mind, she made note of his strength, strength far greater than that of any ordinary man.

"As I was saying," he said, all vestige of anger gone, "your misery stems from your unwillingness to accept that you have already lost. And now the inevitable string of betrayals and defections has begun. I've seen this sad tale play out before. When high-minded principles come up against cold, hard reality; when men see the suffering they'll bring down on their families, or worse, experience it; when they realize that they're fighting for a lost cause ... well, they lose hope. They falter.

"In that moment of weakness, there is such profound opportunity. Just the right combination of words, delivered just so, and you can shift the tide of history. I've done it, more than once. In fact, I may have just done it again with poor Hector."

Isabel worked her jaw, tenderly probing her face. It was swelling and felt hot, but nothing was broken. That didn't stop it from hurting, though.

"That's the wonderful thing about turning someone, it's almost like unwrapping a gift ... you never know what you're going to get. For example, I didn't know about Trajan Karth and his Goiri bone. This entire war might hinge on that simple piece of information. I also didn't know about the crystal chambers in the abandoned fortress. While unlikely to provide any immediate value in this war, it has effectively solved a dilemma I've been struggling with for some time now—namely, how to live forever.

"So you see, in addition to enlisting one of your personal bodyguards into my service in pursuit of a goal that may prove pivotal, I've revealed two additional opportunities. Magic is powerful, but I know of no spell that could have accomplished so much for so little—nothing more than the right promise made to the right person at just the right moment. Words."

"So you took advantage of a man who's already lost his brother ... that's not really much of an accomplishment, Phane."

"I took advantage of a situation," Phane said. "And it has paid off richly."

"At what cost?"

"Like I said, a few words—empty promises."

"It's like I'm talking to a tree," Isabel said, shaking her head sadly.

"Hmm, that reminds me, have you had contact with any dragons since you left Tyr? The truth now." He sat forward, scrutinizing her intently.

"What? No. Where did that come from?"

"Never mind, just following up on a report," he said, sitting back again and glancing at the door. "I expected Enu to be here by now, not to mention your little friend." He looked at Isabel suggestively. "Your time is running out, or rather her time is. I have to warn you, it will be difficult at first, but I'm here to help. You're not the first I've mentored through this process."

"That's comforting," Isabel said without looking up. Slyder had delivered his message. With any luck, Wren and Lacy would be in the sewers already.

"I was speaking with Azugorath about you earlier today. It seems that she has to focus a large amount of her energy into blocking your link with the realm of light. In fact, she believes that she could control you at will if your link with the light were eliminated altogether. Perhaps an enchantment could block the link … or a potion. But I'm getting ahead of myself. If Enu's boasting is even half accurate, his new spell may be the key to your transformation."

Isabel was ignoring him, facing her situation with cold hard honesty. She would probably not survive Phane. The best she could hope for was to prevent the keystone from falling into his hands. Maybe, if she was lucky, she might get another shot at him, but she doubted it.

"What's wrong, Isabel? You aren't your usual pithy self today."

She didn't bother acknowledging him.

"Can you feel the anticipation building? I can." He looked at the door again, frowning. "We're about to take a monumental step together. I've been working toward this since your beloved pretender murdered Kludge." Phane stopped talking, crossing his arms over his chest and sulking while she continued to ignore him as best she could.

He huffed. "They really should be here by now."

Isabel didn't look up.

"Enu had better have a good explanation. And your little scullion, too."

Isabel couldn't help but laugh softly to herself.

"What's so funny?"

"You wouldn't understand," she muttered. She could feel him glaring at her.

"My patience is at an end," Phane said, opening his Wizard's Den and going to his mirror. Isabel quietly followed him in.

"This was a gift from my father," Phane said, caressing the edge of the mirror. "It took three arch mage enchanters over a month to create it."

As he focused, the mirror rippled, then became clear, revealing a bedroom. Lacy and Wren stood at the foot of the bed, facing Wizard Enu.

"Where's the box? Hand it over and I won't hurt you," Enu said.

Phane leaned forward. "Well, isn't this interesting."

"Does Phane know you're here?" Wren asked.

"The whelp asks a good question," Phane muttered, engrossed in the scene unfolding within his mirror.

"Does he know you're here? With the princess?" Enu shot back.

"Get out or I'll call for my guards," Lacy said.

"Go ahead," Enu said. "Do you think I'd be foolish enough to come for you without first incapacitating your house guard? I assure you, Princess, we're all alone."

Lacy looked about quickly, fear dancing in her eyes.

"Give me the box," Enu said, stepping forward and raising his staff.

"No!"

As he pointed the tip of his staff at Lacy, the stone embedded in it began to glow, red and menacing. He pronounced a word, and she collapsed on the floor, gasping in pain, writhing around in a desperate attempt to escape the agony of Enu's torture spell.

Wren darted in and tried to stab Enu but his shield turned her blade aside.

"I'm beginning to see why you like her," Phane said, chuckling, thoroughly enjoying the events playing out before them, even as horror gripped Isabel.

Enu released his spell, leaving Lacy trembling and sobbing on the floor and raising his staff toward Wren, madness and murder in his eyes. A sudden gust of wind from the balcony distracted him. A moment later, a man strode into the room, unleashing a jet of fire from his outstretched hands at Wizard Enu.

At first Enu's shield held, but the fire continued, second after second, pouring heat into the wizard's magical barrier, driving him back until the shield failed and he was blasted against the wall, burnt into an unnaturally contorted, charred husk of a corpse.

Rankosi casually stepped over Lacy as she recovered from Enu's spell. He snatched the bag from under the bed, dumping the contents out on top of her.

"Pick it up."

"No."

"Pick it up and open it."

"No."

"I'll kill your friend," Rankosi said, pointing at Wren, who backed away, holding her knife up like a ward.

Lacy picked up the little box and staggered to her feet, then sat heavily on the edge of the bed.

"If I open this, you'll kill everyone."

"Yes, but I'll save you for last."

Lacy shook her head, helplessly looking up at Wren. "I'm sorry."

Wren's eyes widened when Rankosi slowly raised his hand toward her.

"This is quickly getting out of control," Phane said, stepping inside a magic circle carved into the floor of his Wizard's Den.

He spoke a word and erected a shield around the circle. Another few words and he was standing stone-still within the circle, while a perfect likeness of him appeared in the room with Lacy, Wren, and Rankosi.

Isabel looked around at the contents of his Wizard's Den, calculating how she could hurt him the most.

"Hello, Rankosi," Phane's projection said.

"Don't have the spine to come in person, I see," Rankosi said.

"I have a proposal for you," Phane replied, ignoring the jibe.

Rankosi lowered his hands. "I'm listening."

"I want you to shapeshift into Wizard Enu and take the box to the Sin'Rath witch in the sewers."

"Why would I do that?" Rankosi asked.

"Because her sister has Torin Fellenden under her control. He'll open the box for the Sin'Rath and then we can all fight over the keystone. At least that way, we can actually lay our hands on it, since it's pretty clear that our dear princess here isn't going to open the blasted thing for us."

"You'd let me leave with the keystone?"

"Don't sound so surprised," Phane said with a boyish smile. "Once it's out of the box, I'll come to collect it."

"You'll try," Rankosi said. "What aren't you telling me?"

Phane held up his hands in a gesture of helplessness. "Only that the princess and her friend are not to be harmed."

Rankosi glared at Phane as if he knew he was walking into a trap, yet he couldn't resist.

"Give me the box," he said to Lacy, holding out his hand. She shook her head, tears streaming down her cheeks as she clenched it to her chest.

Rankosi put one hand on her face, pushing her back on the bed while pulling the box free of her grasp with the other hand.

"No!" Lacy shouted, bouncing back off the bed and charging him. He backhanded her, sending her sprawling on the floor, then left without a word.

"Well now, that worked out well," Phane said. "You ladies wait right here while I send someone to fetch you."

Isabel watched the entire encounter. The moment Phane's image began to waver, she picked up the magic mirror and raised it over her head, then smashed it to the floor with all her strength, sending glass shattering in every direction, leaving only a mangled frame as evidence that it had once been a mirror. Faint light flickered from the edges of the shards of glass a moment after they settled to the floor ... and then they went dark and transformed into fine sand.

When Phane returned to his body, his eyes went wide in disbelief, his mouth working to create a sound. He locked eyes with Isabel. She thought she might have actually pushed him too far this time.

"You wretched harlot! That was irreplaceable!"

Isabel just held his glare. He reached out with his magic and lifted her off her feet, propelling her backward, out of his Wizard's Den and toward the wall with crushing acceleration. She expected to die—any moment now. She expected to smash into the wall with such force that it would crush the life out of her in an instant, but then she slowed so quickly that she nearly lost consciousness and reversed direction until she came to a jarring stop floating in front of him. He held her there, her toes six inches off the ground, her arms bound to her sides, her chest constricted so tightly that she could barely breathe.

"I have tried to be patient. I have tried to tolerate your constant insolence. I have been a gracious host, but this ... this goes too far."

He slapped her across the face. White light exploded in her head as it snapped to one side. He hit her again, open-handed but hard, much harder than a man should be able to hit. Blood sprayed across the floor. He hit her again. Another flash of light, another concussive detonation in her head. Again. Blackness started to envelop her. She welcomed it. One last flash of light … and then nothing.

Chapter 21

"We have to run ... now," Wren said, when the door closed behind Rankosi.

All trace of hesitation evaporated. Lacy started stuffing things into her pack.

"I can see soldiers coming," Wren said from the window. "Hurry."

"I'm ready," Lacy said.

They left the room quietly, slipping into the corridor and racing to the nearest corner on tiptoes. Wren peered around cautiously before she started to move.

"Wait, the way out is this way," Lacy said.

"No. We'll go through the kitchen and out the back."

Lacy frowned, falling in behind Wren. They'd spent the afternoon talking, Wren answering every question Lacy posed as best she could. Her head was swimming in new information, most of which she had no way of confirming. What she did know for sure was that Wren had risked her life to save her and that Phane was working against her. His appearance and bargain with Rankosi had confirmed it.

Things were happening quickly. She'd lost the box. The Sin'Rath had Torin, a fact made all the more horrible by Wren's limited description of the true nature of the demon-spawn witches.

Following Wren into the service corridors of the house, Lacy came back to her chosen purpose and made up her mind to go after the box. Escape wasn't enough. If the Nether Gate was opened, there'd be nowhere to hide.

That left the how. She was no match for either the witch or the shade. She needed help, and the more the better.

They reached the kitchen and slipped through it mostly unnoticed. Some of the staff looked up long enough to recognize Lacy, but they looked down just as quickly. Wren led her out into the grounds where they climbed a small tree to get over the low wall. Once on the street, Wren led her by way of alleys rather than streets to avoid scrutiny as much as possible.

Lacy wished she'd listened when Wren had first taken the note from the hawk's leg. It all seemed so surreal, the idea that this waif of a girl, her wispy hair floating around her head like a halo, was receiving directions from Lady Reishi. The note said they should run. Wren wanted to leave right away, but Lacy had resisted, still clinging to the hope that Phane might be a powerful ally. Now she knew better, now that she'd lost the box, now that she'd failed her father's trust.

With an effort, she pushed that out of her mind and tried to stay alert. Wren seemed to know where she was going, but Phane would send people to look for them the moment he realized they were missing. They had to get outside the fortress walls as quickly as possible.

Lacy struggled to come to terms with her radical new understanding of the conflict she was reluctantly at the center of. She had believed so many things that weren't true. She'd been duped by Phane so thoroughly that he might have succeeded, if he'd just had the patience to wear her down.

Wren stopped at the corner of a building and peeked around it, pulling back quickly and motioning for silence, then retracing her steps back into the alley.

"What is it?" Lacy asked.

"Wraithkin," Wren whispered, ducking into a doorway and pulling Lacy along with her. "We'll wait for him to go away."

"What's a wraithkin?"

"Dangerous." Wren put a finger to her lips, her eyes going wide when she heard footsteps entering the alley. The sound stopped briefly, then resumed, coming closer. Again, the sound of footsteps stopped, and a man appeared not ten feet from where they were hiding. Lacy started trembling when she saw him appear out of nothing, but she didn't make a sound. The wraithkin took a few steps and vanished. Wren motioned for silence. Lacy nodded tightly, her eyes still wide and filled with new fear.

After several minutes, they ventured out of their hiding place, creeping along the wall to the corner of the building, peeking out into the street.

"Follow me," Wren whispered, then dashed across the street into the opposite alley. Once safely within the shadows between the two buildings, she looked up and down the street again before motioning for Lacy to cross.

When they finally reached the dark undisturbed subterranean room, Lacy felt a great sense of relief. But as evening slipped into the darkness of night, the number of soldiers searching for them seemed to grow rapidly.

"I was hoping Isabel would be here already," Wren whispered on her way to the cabinet containing her supplies. "We should probably get ready so we can leave as soon as she gets here."

She frowned when she opened the cabinet door and saw a note resting atop her supplies. She picked it up and read it.

Dear Wren,

I can't come with you. Take Lacy and flee the city. I've drawn a map of the sewers showing the way out. Also, there's a witch down there—I've marked her last known location on the map as well. Avoid her at all costs. Once you're out of the city, find someone from the House of Karth and tell them to take you to Princess Ayela. Tell her everything. She'll help you.

I'm going to miss you.

Love,
Isabel

Tears rolled down Wren's cheeks as she read the words.

"What's wrong?" Lacy asked, a hint of alarm in her voice.

"Isabel isn't coming," she said, handing her the letter.

Lacy read it, shaking her head. "I don't understand. Why can't she come with us?"

"Phane," Wren said, sniffing back her tears. "I'll explain it as best I can later. Right now, we have to go." She started preparing her pack.

Lacy wrinkled her nose when Wren opened the hatch to the sewers, but she didn't say anything, smiling to herself as she descended the ladder after Wren. Not long ago, the mere idea of venturing into a sewer would have made her nauseous. She'd come a long way in a short period of time, and yet she still had so far to go.

She took a moment at the bottom of the ladder to let her eyes adjust and to master her queasy stomach. The stench was almost unbearable, but she endured it better than she thought she would.

Wren opened the shutter on the lantern just enough to let a sliver of light out, then handed Lacy the map. Together they oriented themselves to the sewer canals and made a mental image of the way out. Wren led the way, silent as a mouse, the sliver of light shining backward toward Lacy while Wren used the wall as her guide.

The sporadic drip, drip, drip was unnerving, especially since Lacy knew there was a witch somewhere in the darkness, but after several minutes, it faded into the background and she began to worry instead about the jungle beyond the walls.

When they reached the end of the canal, Wren stopped at the corner, quickly shuttering the lantern. Through the gentle rustling of the foul water sliding past and the incessant dripping of condensation from the ceilings, she could hear voices in the distance. She and Lacy both froze in place, straining to hear, but the voices were too far away.

"We should just go," Wren said.

"But what if they have the box?"

"What if they do? What can we do about it?"

Lacy shook her head in frustration, her eyes burning from the tears that were about to come anew. "My father entrusted me with that box. I have to do something."

"If we confront them, they'll kill us."

"Then we'll follow them."

"Isabel said to find the House of Karth. We should do that first, then go after the box."

"By then it might be too late. I have to do this, Wren. And I really need your help."

Wren nodded in the darkness. "All right, but we have to be quiet and we can't use any light."

"Agreed."

Wren led the way down the corridor running along the down-water edge of the city. The voices grew louder as they drew closer. Dim light filtered into the tunnel from the distance. Two figures were standing on the bridge spanning the canal just before the second outflow grate that Isabel had cut a hole through. Wren slowed, placing each step with care. Lacy crept along behind trying not to breathe too loudly and feeling slightly deprived of air for her efforts.

Wren stopped. Lacy knelt down and took several slow deep breaths before focusing her attention on the two figures standing not a hundred feet away. A thrill of fear jolted her when she saw Druja for the first time. In that single glance, she understood the malice bound up within the Sin'Rath. Sudden fear for her brother nearly made her cry out.

"Your next task is the death of the Reishi witch," Druja said, clearing her throat noisily, then spitting into the canal.

"Yes, My Lady," Rankosi said, looking just like Wizard Enu.

"Once she's dead, you'll travel north to Stobi, where I will await you. Phane will send soldiers to pursue me. Kill them along your way." Her words trailed off into a wheeze followed by a hacking cough that reverberated in the sewer tunnels.

"Understood."

Light erupted from the canal, followed by a gout of fire. Rankosi turned toward the fire with contempt, while Druja transformed into a cloud of black smoke just a moment before the flames engulfed them. The roar and the heat and the light assaulted Lacy and Wren as they huddled together along the wall, well out of reach of the flames.

When the fire subsided, Druja was gone, but Rankosi was still there, unscathed.

"Hello, Tasia," he said. "You're too late. But more than that, you're just not relevant." He smiled maliciously before transforming into a large snake, then he slithered into the sewer canals and vanishing under the sludge.

"Blast! I thought I had her."

"I'm just glad the shade didn't breathe fire back at us. I wasn't looking forward to taking a swim."

Two other people, a woman and a man who was dressed in the uniform of Phane's soldiers, walked out onto the bridge. The woman was holding her palm up and a lick of flame was floating just above it, illuminating the nearby area.

"Who are they?" Lacy whispered.

The woman's head snapped around, and she peered into the darkness, looking straight at them.

"Wait, I know him," Wren said, standing up.

Lacy grabbed her arm. "He's been chasing me."

"Show yourselves or I'll light you on fire," the woman said.

"What is it?" the man asked, unslinging his bow and nocking an arrow.

"We're being watched."

"We have to run," Lacy said.

"No. That's Captain Wyatt," Wren said. "He'll help us."

The woman sent a ball of brightly burning orange fire down the center of the tunnel, illuminating them as it passed.

"You can't escape me," she called out. "Stand forth or burn."

Wren opened the shutter on her lantern and held it up. "Please don't hurt us."

"Wren? Is that you?"

"Yes, Captain Wyatt," she said as she walked toward them, leaving Lacy standing in the dark, torn and afraid.

"You, as well, come forward," the woman said.

Lacy hesitated a moment more before deciding to trust Wren. When she stepped into the light, the man in armor frowned for a moment, then smiled broadly.

"Tasia, may I present Princess Lacy Fellenden and Wren, a friend of Lady Reishi's."

"How do you know my name?" Lacy asked, anxiety flooding into her stomach.

"There's no need for alarm, Princess. We're here to help you. I'm Captain Wyatt of the Ruathan Rangers and this is Tasia. I was charged by Lady Abigail Ruatha with finding you and bringing both you and the box you carry back to Fellenden."

Tasia looked at Wyatt with a faint air of disgust. "Perhaps we should find a more suitable place to have this conversation."

"We have to go after Druja," Lacy said. "She has the box. If you're really here to help, then help me get it back."

"Captain Wyatt, Phane is looking for us," Wren said. "Will you help us get out of the city?"

"First things first," Wyatt said, "I like that. Once we're in the jungle, it will be a simple matter to find the witch. We need to get to the surface."

"No," Wren said, pointing at the hole burned through the nearby outflow grate. "Isabel cut a hole through that grate so we could escape."

"Wait ... Lady Reishi is here?" Wyatt asked, alarm in his voice.

"Yes," Wren said. "Phane has her."

Wyatt put his hand on his forehead and turned around whispering to himself, "What do I do?"

"You do as you were charged to do," Tasia said.

"If Lord Reishi knew she was here ..."

"He does," Wren said. "We can't try to rescue her, if that's what you're thinking. She wouldn't want us to."

"How can you be sure?"

"Because she told me," Wren said sadly.

"I don't understand. Why wouldn't she want us to rescue her?" he asked.

"Phane is slowly gaining control over her free will," Wren said, a slight tremor in her voice. "Once he has her, she'll be a threat to all of us and she doesn't want that."

Wyatt seemed to struggle for a moment before he nodded resolutely. "I see. We should go then."

"Are we certain where that leads?" Tasia asked, eyeing the outflow drain suspiciously.

"No, but it's the only way out of the city besides the main gate," Wren said.

"No, it's not," Tasia said. "We'll do better to head for the surface and make our escape from there."

"But how?" Wren said.

Just then, Lacy saw a faint glow in the distance. "What's that?" she asked, pointing down the tunnel. The glow vanished momentarily, then appeared slightly closer.

"Wraithkin," Wyatt said. "We have to move … quickly."

He set out toward the center of the city with Tasia bringing up the rear. Not fifty steps into the tunnel, another light came into view ahead.

"Soldiers," Wyatt said, unslinging his bow. "Douse your light."

Wren shuttered her lantern.

"I count six," Wyatt whispered.

A roar of fire erupted behind them, drawing everyone's attention, as Tasia directed a jet of blue-hot flame at the wraithkin who had just appeared not twenty feet away.

In the sudden light, Wyatt loosed an arrow at the first soldier in the file. A moment later, darkness engulfed them, a muffled splash reverberating softly down the tunnel. The soldiers started shouting, the sound of their footfalls growing quicker and louder.

Light bloomed again, this time in the form of three fiery orbs, each about a foot in diameter, one hovering over Tasia, the second moving down the tunnel behind them and the third moving toward the soldiers.

"The wraithkin is gone," Tasia said.

"He'll be back soon," Wren said.

Wyatt killed another soldier, causing the next man in line to trip and fall over his dying companion, splashing into the muck. The remaining three men clambered over the fallen men in a rush. Wyatt felled another, leaving him howling in pain. His cries drew shouts of alarm from yet more soldiers searching other parts of the vast sewer network.

"That drain is starting to look like our best chance," Wyatt said as he sent another arrow at the enemy. He scored only a glancing blow against the lead man's shield, now held high to protect the advancing soldiers while more men raced to back them up.

Suddenly, the wraithkin appeared next to Wyatt, slashing at him viciously with his long black dagger. Wyatt blocked with his bow, defending against a fatal wound, but taking ruinous damage to his bow. He dropped it, drawing his sword, but the wraithkin disappeared, reappearing in front of Tasia and stabbing at her savagely. Quicker than a cat, she caught his wrist and jerked his thrust wide of her belly, at the same time grabbing him by the throat with the other hand, spinning him off his feet and propelling his head into the wall with such force and speed that the back four inches of his skull caved in, spraying blood across Lacy and Wren. Tasia casually tipped his corpse into the canal and slipped past the three of them to face the oncoming soldiers.

She raised her hands and unleashed a gout of flame that filled the entire tunnel for a hundred feet or more, waves of heat washing back over them, the roar echoing throughout the sewer system. When the dragon fire subsided, all that remained of the onrushing soldiers were charred husks, warped so grotesquely that it was hard to imagine they had once been human.

"Follow me," Tasia said.

Wyatt dropped back to cover the rear as they set out toward an exit and the surface. Shouting soldiers were converging on their position, but Tasia calmly proceeded onward with seemingly little concern.

Lacy, on the other hand, was terrified. She didn't know these people, and even though they were fighting to protect her, she couldn't help but realize that she was utterly at their mercy should they choose to turn on her, especially Tasia. Lacy hadn't seen a demonstration of such profound power since the dragons had attacked her ship en route to Karth.

At the first ladder, Tasia started climbing. Lacy was relieved to see slivers of daylight through the sewer grate in the road above. When they surfaced in an alley, Tasia melted the iron grate into place to stymie any pursuers before heading toward the nearest road.

"Now what?" Lacy asked.

"You'll see, Princess," Wyatt said.

"I don't like this," she said. "I want to know how you plan on getting us out of here, and I'm not taking another step until you tell me."

Wyatt considered her words, openly appraising her.

"Very well, Tasia is going to take her true form and fly us out of here."

Lacy stood dumbstruck, looking at Wyatt as if the world no longer made any sense.

"What are you talking about?"

"That," Wyatt said, with an admiring smile.

Tasia was standing in the middle of the road, facing what sounded like a platoon of approaching soldiers. Her form seemed to become indistinct momentarily ... and then she morphed into a beautiful, terrifying silver dragon, filling the entire road with her bulk and filling the air with her roar. The angry shouts coming from the approaching soldiers abruptly turned into cries of panic that retreated into the distance.

"Dear Maker," Lacy whispered, cocking her head in recognition. "Wait ... she was the one who saved our ship from the green dragon."

"One and the same," Wyatt said. "Let's go."

Lacy felt a surreal sense of detachment come over her. She was running toward the dragon, yet a part of her was screaming in terror. Fear bubbled up from some ancient place within, deeper and older than conscious thought—born of pure animal instinct, it seemed to know at a visceral level that the dragon was the ultimate predator, that she was nothing more than prey. She stopped running and started backtracking. No sane person would willingly run toward a dragon.

"Lacy, what are you doing?" Wren shouted.

Lacy couldn't get any words out past the constricting fear closing around her throat. All she could do was shake her head in denial.

"Wyatt!" Wren shouted.

He looked back, scrambling to change directions when he saw Lacy was trying to run away.

She turned just in time to see a wraithkin appear not ten feet in front of her, faint wisps of black fading quickly in his wake. She screamed. He smiled.

Wyatt's throwing knife caught him in the shoulder and he vanished. Wyatt grabbed Lacy and pushed her up against a wall, standing in front of her, guarding her and preventing her from escaping at the same time, his sword drawn and his head snapping this way and that, looking for his enemy.

"Tasia!" he yelled.

The dragon's long neck coiled back, bringing her head into the alley a moment before the wraithkin appeared again. He was facing Wyatt and Lacy ... and his back was to Tasia.

She darted forward and bit his head and shoulders off with a single snap of her powerful jaws, chewing once before spitting parts of him into the alley as if he tasted foul.

"Hurry," she said. "Phane will come himself when he learns that a dragon is loose in his city."

Lacy was trembling. She couldn't seem to make her mind work right. Things that shouldn't be possible were happening around her with alarming frequency and she was powerless.

"We have to go, Princess," Wyatt said.

When she didn't move, he sheathed his sword, picked her up over his shoulder like a sack of potatoes, and carried her to Tasia. Wren climbed aboard without hesitation and helped Wyatt get Lacy into place on Tasia's back.

"Go!" he shouted.

Tasia launched into the air with a powerful thrust of her wings, carrying them straight up past the windows of the buildings surrounding them until she was in open sky. Lacy felt the crushing weight of acceleration as they ascended into the night, then cool air when they began to fly away from the city and Phane.

In all of her life, she had never once even imagined that she would find herself riding a dragon. That thought replaced the irrational terror that had gripped her just moments before with a kind of giddy optimism. She was riding a dragon— if she could do that, she could do anything.

Chapter 22

As exhilarating—and terrifying—as riding a dragon was, Lacy was relieved when she slipped off Tasia's neck into the little clearing where they'd landed.

A moment after her passengers dismounted, Tasia transformed into a woman and Wyatt led them into the jungle.

"Where are we going?" Lacy asked.

"My men are hiding nearby," he said. "Stay close."

He led them through the dark, following a path that Lacy couldn't discern. Within a few minutes, they descended into a narrow crevasse not four feet wide. It led thirty feet below the surface of the jungle and into a network of washouts and caves that offered ample shelter from the elements as well as concealment from all but the most thorough searchers.

Four men with weapons drawn and ready seemed to materialize out of the shadows.

"Captain Wyatt?"

"Report," Wyatt said.

The men sheathed their weapons, and the lead man stepped forward. "Our position is secure, and Princess Ayela has arrived, along with a dozen of her men. We've gathered ample supplies and replenished our stock of arrows."

"Good. I'll need a bow before we leave," Wyatt said. "Take us to Ayela."

"Yes sir."

Lacy felt like she was floating in a river, at the mercy of the currents around her and powerless to change them, so she decided to accept her situation while she looked for a way to impose her will on it. She was a princess, a title that had taken on a whole new meaning the day her father had entrusted her with her family's greatest charge. She decided anew to start living up to her duty rather than allowing fear and circumstance to dictate her course.

They led her into a cave that flowed into another, larger cavern. A soldier held back the blanket hung across the narrow entrance, and the sudden light of lanterns and a cook fire made her eyes hurt.

The cavern was filled with men, most dressed in leather armor and armed with bows and swords, while the rest wore light clothes fashioned from leather and were armed with spears, javelins, and blowtubes.

A beautiful young woman with dark eyes and hair, rich golden skin, and a bright unabashed smile approached.

"Captain Wyatt?"

"Yes."

"I'm Ayela Karth. We came as soon as we received Lady Reishi's message. My men and I are prepared to help you in any way we can."

By the time Lacy lay down to sleep that night, she felt warm and full and safe for the first time since she'd left her home. She had spent the evening listening to Ayela and Wyatt recount their experiences fighting beside Lord and Lady Reishi. More than anything else, their loyalty and love for the sovereign and his wife shone in their eyes, a testament more compelling than any words.

Lacy questioned them relentlessly, piecing together the puzzle of what had really happened to her home, her family, and her life. She was dismayed to discover just how thoroughly Phane had deceived her and relieved to hear how Lady Abigail had routed the barbarian horde rampaging across her homeland.

She fell asleep with growing confidence in her new allies. They had pledged to help her recover the box she'd been entrusted with. More than anything else, that simple fact gave her hope.

***

"I will go alone," Tasia said.

"No!" Lacy replied, a bit more forcefully than she would have liked. Somewhere in the back of her mind, a voice of caution was warning her to be careful, but she ignored it. "Protecting that box is my responsibility."

"Yes, and look how well that's worked out," Tasia said.

"Some backup couldn't hurt, Tasia," Wyatt said.

"I agree, yet in this circumstance, who would you send? You? The witch would turn you in a glance. Look around you. Everyone here capable of fighting is a man. You would ask me to take two women and a girl into battle? What of their safety? And what could they possibly do to aid me against the Sin'Rath?"

"Please take me with you," Lacy said. "I can't fail in this. There's too much at stake."

"Indeed, there is," Tasia said. "You have no idea how fortunate you are, human. Lady Bragador had a plan that would have ended this threat, but she let young Alexander talk her out of it … and the cost has been terrible."

"I don't understand … what plan?"

"Bragador was going to send Aedan to kill you and your brother, thereby ending the threat of that infernal box ever being opened. And now Aedan, my friend and my kin, is likely lost to the darkness, and all for the sake of two fragile and ephemeral human lives."

Lacy stared in shock and dismay while possibilities tumbled through her mind, all of them leading to one inescapable conclusion.

"Oh, Dear Maker … Bragador was right. With my brother and I dead, the world would be safe." She walked away from the fire into the shadows.

"Huh," Tasia said, openly appraising the princess.

Lacy spun around quickly. "Why would Lord Reishi risk so much to protect me?"

"He wasn't protecting you," Wyatt said. "He was protecting the Old Law."

"At what cost?" Lacy said, a haunted look filling her eyes. "As long as my brother and I live, the Seven Isles are at risk."

"You're wrong," Ayela said. "There's another way to open the box—the Goiri bones. Your death would be meaningless."

"Sounds like we're back where we started," Wyatt said.

"Indeed, we are," Tasia said. "I shall go retrieve this box and bring it back to you, Princess." With that, she turned on her heel and strode out of the cave.

"Wait," Lacy called out, following behind her. "Take me with you."

Tasia ignored her, transforming into her true form and launching into the sky as soon as she had the space to unfurl her wings.

Lacy raced back into the cave and started gathering her pack. Wren began packing her things without a word.

"What do you intend to do, Princess?" Wyatt asked.

"I'm going after her," Lacy said without looking up.

With a nod from Ayela, her men began to break camp. Wyatt just shook his head, gesturing for his men to make ready as well. Within half an hour they were on the move through the jungle. It didn't take long for Lacy to realize just how foolish it would have been for her to set out alone. She didn't know the first thing about the jungle. Were it not for the guidance of Ayela's men, she would have quickly fallen victim to any number of seemingly benign dangers, from quagmires to poisonous flowers.

By midafternoon, the Rangers had acquired Druja's trail. While Ayela's soldiers knew their jungle intimately, they were no match for the Rangers when it came to tracking. From the looks of the witch's stride, she was moving slowly, probably due to her many deformities.

Not long after they found her tracks, they heard the roar of a dragon in the distance and made for the top of a nearby knoll that offered a vantage point above the canopy. Lacy caught her breath when she saw two dragons launch out of the jungle, one dark green, the other brilliant silver.

Even at this distance she could almost feel the ferocity of the battle taking place. It reminded her of two cats fighting, with all of the speed, viciousness and intensity … yet this fight was taking place in the air, between two creatures each as big as a house. The fury of the battle shattered the relative calm of the jungle, sending every other creature to ground, even the most fearsome predators.

As furious and frenetic as the fight was, it lasted only a few minutes before the shade-possessed dragon pinned Tasia's wings to her body and drove her into the ground. He burst from the jungle moments later, roaring into the afternoon sky in triumph.

"Tasia," Wyatt whispered.

"We have to see if she's still alive," Lacy said.

Ayela nodded, gesturing to three of her men to run ahead. They vanished into the jungle a moment later. It took the better part of an hour before the rest of the party reached her. She was sprawled out awkwardly in a trampled patch of jungle, blood staining her brilliant silver scales.

Wyatt ran to her, closing his eyes in relief when he felt warm breath at her snout.

"Tasia, how badly are you hurt?"

"Bad enough," she said weakly. "The shade is protecting the witch. He left me to die slowly—said it would hurt more that way."

"Can you transform into a woman again?" Ayela asked.

"To what end? I'm more vulnerable as a woman."

"Yes, but we can care for you and shelter you as a woman. As a dragon, we can't move you."

"I guess I don't really have much choice," Tasia mumbled, closing her eyes and whispering words in some ancient tongue. A few moments later, she morphed into a woman, severely injured with a deep set of gashes across her side and one arm broken so badly that bones were protruding from her flesh. She gasped in pain and fell unconscious.

Ayela's men were already busy preparing to carry her to safety, lashing several blankets to two stout poles they'd cut and stripped bare. Ayela knelt next to Tasia, examining her wounds before opening her bag and setting out several jars.

"This is going to take some time," she said, "but it has to be done or she'll die."

"If the shade is protecting the witch, we're going to need a plan before we do anything, anyway," Wyatt said, kneeling next to her. "How can I help?"

"Help me roll her onto her back ... carefully."

Tasia moaned but didn't wake. Ayela opened a jar of white powder and poured half its contents into the gashes along her side, packing it into the wounds. The bleeding began to subside as the powder mixed with blood and started to clot. Next she scooped out a generous dollop of salve made from deathwalker root and carefully applied it over the powder before dressing the wounds with clean bandages.

"That should keep her from bleeding to death," Ayela said, turning to the broken arm and sprinkling some of her white clotting powder on it. "I'm glad she's unconscious, because this is going to hurt a lot."

She gently dabbed healing salve on the jagged ends of the protruding bones. Then she took a deep breath, seeming to settle her nerves.

"Sit beside her," she said to Wyatt, "then put your foot into her armpit and take hold of her wrist. When I tell you to, pull her arm straight and don't stop until I say so. We need to set the bones or she'll heal wrong."

Wyatt swallowed hard, but nodded, getting into position and looking to Ayela. She knelt beside the arm and examined the break closely one last time before nodding to herself.

"Wren, I need you to be ready with the clotting powder. Pour it onto the wound when I say, then hold the wound closed until the bleeding stops."

Lacy watched with a mixture of horror and fascination as Ayela went to work. When she nodded to Wyatt, he began to pull gently but firmly, extending Tasia's arm while Ayela guided the bones back into place, her delicate fingers reaching into the gashes, guiding the jagged ends back together. Blood flowed freely, dripping into the dirt. Tasia moaned.

"Slowly ease off the pressure," Ayela said. Once Wyatt had released the arm and Ayela was satisfied that the bones were set as well as possible, she nodded to Wren and pulled her fingers from the wound.

Blood began to gush. Wren quickly dumped the jar of clotting powder onto the wound and covered it with her hands, trying to stem the flow of red while Ayela smeared some healing salve onto a bandage. On her order, Wren let go and Ayela quickly pressed the bandage into place, tying it firmly around Tasia's arm. Blood seeped through but seemed to be subsiding. Ayela wrapped another bandage around the first and set the arm in a splint before her men carefully lifted Tasia onto the makeshift litter.

"She needs better care than I can give her," Ayela said, worry in her voice.

"What more can we do for her?" Wyatt asked.

Ayela shook her head, shrugging helplessly. "Just take her someplace safe where she can heal."

"If that's all we can do, then that's all we can do," Wyatt said. "We'll leave four of my men and two of yours to carry her to safety and tend to her until she heals."

When they set out tracking Druja once again, it suddenly occurred to Lacy that she would probably be very dead right now if she had accompanied Tasia. A fact that reminded her yet again just how little power she had in comparison to her many enemies. And yet, here she was, surrounded by soldiers risking their lives in pursuit of her goals. It was a sobering thought that made her reconsider the nature of power itself. While she couldn't hope to stand against Phane or Rankosi or Druja alone, she could build alliances and forge relationships that would bring allies to the battlefield in defense of their common interests.

Her mind wandered to thoughts of her father and his customary style of leadership. He always sought to include those with a stake in the outcome of an enterprise, whatever that may be, from delivering clean water to the people to establishing trade relations with neighboring territories. By presenting his interests honestly and without apology, he gained the trust and respect of those he dealt with. By respecting the interests of the other parties at the table, he earned their loyalty and friendship. While they walked, she tried to glean lessons from his many negotiations that she could apply to her current situation.

The trouble was, she faced threats greater than any he had ever faced, with the sole exception of his last stand against Zuhl—the outcome of which didn't bode well for Lacy's hopes that she could find a way to protect her people and the Seven Isles through alliances and negotiation alone.

A Ranger's hasty appearance from out of the jungle brought her back to the present.

"We're being followed," he reported to Wyatt.

"How many?"

"Dozens, maybe more. They seem to be keeping their distance."

Ayela sighed, shaking her head sadly. "It's probably my brother." She motioned for two of her men to fall back and confirm her suspicions.

"Do I need to be concerned?" Wyatt asked.

"I don't think so," Ayela said.

"I'm going to need more than that, Princess," Wyatt said. "Is he a threat?"

"I don't think so," Ayela said, helplessly. "Ever since he brought that cursed bone back, he's been paranoid and irrational, spending more and more time in the jungle with his most loyal soldiers.

"I went to his camp a few times to try to talk him into coming home, but he wouldn't listen to me. It's like he's becoming a different person. We used to be close, but now he doesn't trust me anymore, doesn't trust anybody except his men, and they all seem to be losing their minds as well.

"When I suggested that he destroy the Goiri bone, that it was making him crazy, he became furious, accusing me of plotting against him. He said it was the only weapon capable of scouring magic from the world once and for all. After that, his men escorted me back home and told me never to return."

Sadness filled her voice and clouded her eyes, a sense of helplessness seeming to settle over her. "I wish I could help him."

"We can't let him get anywhere near the box as long as he has that bone," Lacy said.

Wyatt thought for a moment. "This might be an opportunity. If this Goiri bone functions like you claim, we could use it to destroy the keystone itself."

"We'd have to take it out of the box first," Lacy said. "What if it doesn't work? What if we open the box, but the keystone still can't be destroyed? Phane would come for it ... he'd win."

"I agree with Lacy," Ayela said. "The risk is too great."

Wyatt nodded to himself. "In that case, we may end up in a confrontation with your brother."

"I know," Ayela whispered.

Wyatt regarded her for a few moments. "Lady Reishi chooses her friends well," he said.

One of Ayela's men materialized out of the jungle. "It's Trajan with nearly forty of his men. They're staying about five minutes behind us."

"No sense in provoking them" Wyatt said. "We stay the course."

"I agree," Lacy said.

Ayela just nodded, worry creasing her brow.

They traveled for the rest of the day, with Trajan trailing behind them, though never too closely. From the tracks they were following, the Rangers were able to determine that they were steadily gaining on Druja.

By nightfall, Lacy was so exhausted she fell asleep within moments of lying down and without the usual struggle to quiet her mind. She woke with a start sometime in the dead of night, a hand clamped over her mouth. Panic surged into her belly, only subsiding slightly when she heard Wyatt's voice.

"We have to move, quietly," he whispered, waiting until she nodded her head before taking his hand from her mouth.

"What's happening?"

"Soldiers are coming. Gather your things quickly."

Within minutes, they'd broken camp and were moving through the jungle in four single-file columns, each person walking with a hand on the next person's shoulder for guidance through the pitch black.

When Lacy looked back, she caught a flicker of torchlight in the distance but then it was gone. They moved slowly but steadily for over an hour before the sky began to lighten and they could pick up the pace. Lacy was sore and tired but determined to keep up no matter how much she hurt. They ate on the move and didn't stop for a break until the sun was high in the sky and even then only because there was a small butte rising up out of the jungle that offered a good view of the surrounding area.

"It's hard to tell for sure, but our scouts estimate there are a thousand men moving toward us from the Regency fortress," Wyatt said. "Also, we lost the witch's trail in the night."

"Why would he send so many men?" Wren asked.

Lacy looked up sharply, a thought occurring to her suddenly. "What about Trajan? We didn't warn him."

"No, he warned us," Ayela said. "I wouldn't worry about those soldiers finding my brother."

"You don't understand," Lacy said, alarm building in her voice. "Phane has a magic mirror. He could be watching us right now, which means he knows about Trajan … he knows about the Goiri bone. Those thousand soldiers aren't here for us, they're here for your brother."

"She's probably right," Wyatt said. "If I were Phane, I'd have sent wraithkin after Lacy and Wren, but they'd be useless against your brother."

"My brother may be losing his mind, but that hasn't diminished his knowledge of the jungle. If my family has had one advantage against the Regency, it's always been the jungle. They won't find him unless he wants them to."

"I hope you're right," Lacy said.

"Me too."

"So where does that leave us?" Wyatt asked.

"Right where we started," Lacy said. "Chasing after the witch."

"It might be difficult to pick up her trail again without Phane's soldiers catching up with us," Wyatt said.

"She's trying to get to Ithilian, so she has to be heading for a port," Lacy said.

"That would be Stobi," Ayela said. "It's probably a day and a half away if we head straight there."

By the following morning, Lacy was starting to fear that she wouldn't be able to keep up any longer. She was exhausted and hurting all over, especially her feet. It was hard to imagine how Ayela's men could move so quickly for so long wearing only sandals. Despite her pain and exhaustion, she didn't fall behind, willing herself forward, step by step, until they caught sight of Druja.

She was nearing the outskirts of Stobi, walking as briskly as her deformed body would carry her. They only spotted her because she was walking down the main road between the Regency fortress and Stobi, apparently unafraid of encountering any of Phane's men or agents.

"If we run, we can get ahead of her and lay an ambush where the road rounds that bluff," Ayela's lead man said, pointing into the distance.

Lacy felt like she was going to cry. She could barely keep up at the grueling pace they'd set … running was beyond her at this point.

"We'll send half of the men ahead," Wyatt said. "The rest of us will come up from behind in case she escapes."

Ayela nodded her approval and the men separated into two forces, half of the Rangers and half of her men in each group.

Lacy felt a wave of relief. She couldn't bear the thought of Druja escaping because of her.

Each group set out, the ambush team running through the jungle toward the bluff, while Ayela, Wren, and Lacy went with Wyatt and the remaining soldiers on a course that brought them to the road.

Ayela looked around nervously.

"What's wrong?" Lacy asked.

"The Regency uses roads; we use the jungle," Ayela said.

"Right now, we'll make better time on the road," Wyatt said. "Just keep your eyes open and be ready to retreat into the jungle if we see soldiers."

Traveling on the relatively even surface of the road was so much easier than moving through the jungle, but Lacy also felt exposed and couldn't help looking around nervously for signs of a threat. Everyone stopped in their tracks when the dragon roared.

Ayela put her hand over her mouth as Rankosi floated over the men poised on the bluff. Time seemed to slow—helplessness flooding into Lacy. A great gout of fire spewed forth from the dragon, igniting the jungle and scouring the bluff of life, leaving it smoldering and charred. She knew that no one could have survived such an attack.

It felt like she'd been punched in the gut. The horrible truth began to sink in—she'd lost the box and she simply didn't have the power to take it back. Her feelings of despair transformed into terror when Rankosi turned his attention toward them, rising higher into the air with a thrust of his wings and then diving toward them with alarming speed. Everyone stood stock-still, frozen like prey as the moments ticked by until Rankosi flared his wings and landed in the road before them.

Fear broke. The Rangers fanned out, nocking arrows in preparation for a wholly suicidal attack.

Rankosi flicked his tail out, quicker than a cat, stabbing one of the Rangers through the chest, then casually bringing the warm corpse up to his mouth and slowly chewing the body before swallowing in exaggerated fashion. The rest of the Rangers backed away.

"You will come no farther," Rankosi said. "Were it not for the princess in your midst, you would have already suffered the same fate as your ambush party."

His head darted forward with blinding quickness, snapping up another man, this time one of Ayela's. Again, he took his time chewing.

A volley of arrows rained against his scales, bouncing harmlessly away.

Rankosi laughed, a deep rumbling sound filled with derision, cut short when he snatched up another man. The Rangers backed farther away, sending another volley of arrows, this time aiming for the eyes. Several would have hit, except Rankosi simply blinked.

He reared back in preparation to lunge into the mass of men arrayed before him when Trajan came racing out of the jungle, screaming incoherently, charging the shade-controlled dragon with reckless and wild abandon. Rankosi looked bemused, redirecting his attention to Trajan, waiting for him to get close enough to eat, but then he flinched, a yelp of fear escaping from him as the null magic field brushed up against him. He tumbled backwards away from Trajan, scrambling desperately, rolling onto his feet and running several giant steps before taking flight, frustration and rage in his roar.

Trajan stopped in their midst, his men flowing out of the jungle to stand with their leader. Rankosi tipped his wing and dove, breathing a gout of orange-red fiery death at them. Lacy fell to her knees, throwing her hands over her head in expectation of sudden annihilation ... but it didn't come.

She heard the roar of the fire, saw the light glow brightly all around her, even felt hot air flow over her ... but she wasn't dead. She looked up just in time to see the last of the dragon fire washing over a perfectly spherical half-shell surrounding them. Only the few men standing outside the thirty-foot range of Trajan's Goiri bone died in the attack.

Rankosi roared again, floating out over the jungle before turning toward Stobi, apparently abandoning his attack.

Trajan stalked up to his sister like he was going to hit her, then stopped, his expression morphing from one of fury to one of great relief, tears welling up in his eyes.

Ayela hugged him, then held him at arm's length, appraising him with a mixture of hope and worry.

"Thank you, Trajan. That's twice you've saved our lives in as many days."

"Many soldiers come for you and Lady Reishi's friends."

"No, they're coming for you and the bone," Ayela said. "You have to flee. Go north to more familiar jungles. Phane cannot be allowed to get that cursed bone."

Trajan smiled confidently, holding up the femur and testing its weight. "He won't—at least not like he wants it."

"Trajan, you promised me you wouldn't go after him," Ayela said, sudden alarm in her voice. "He has too many soldiers."

He frowned, scratching his head. "I forgot about that."

"I know," Ayela whispered. "Go north."

"No, I'll stay with you in case the dragon returns."

"Might not be a bad idea," Wyatt said.

"If Trajan gets too close to the box, it'll open," Lacy said. "We can't risk it."

"And how will you stand against a dragon without me?" Trajan shouted, suddenly furious. "I alone can defeat magic!"

Lacy was taken aback and a bit fearful. Wyatt eased closer to her, his hand on the hilt of his sword.

"Trajan!" Ayela snapped.

He seemed suddenly surprised by her presence, then he started looking around quickly, his head jerking this way and that before he fixed on a point in the empty air, staring at it as if there was a dragon poised to strike. He turned and ran screaming into the jungle, terror and madness fading with each stride. His men followed without a word as if such occurrences were not uncommon.

"He's getting worse," Ayela said.

"What do you mean?" Lacy asked.

"Ever since he took possession of that bone, he's been slowly losing his mind. I'm afraid it might already be too late to get him back."

"I'm sorry," Lacy whispered, putting her hand on Ayela's arm.

"Me too," she said with a forced smile. "We should go; the road isn't safe."

They moved back into the jungle and turned north toward Stobi, traveling parallel to the road but far enough away that they couldn't be spotted through the dense foliage. Again, Lacy found herself searching her mind for a strategy or tactic that would lead to success against the witch and the dragon, but she couldn't find a single one.

The depressing truth was, she was simply outmatched. A Sin'Rath witch against a hunting party comprised of mostly men had a decisive advantage, and confronting a demon-possessed dragon was nothing short of suicidally insane, yet she and her companions pressed on until they stepped past the edge of the jungle into the farm fields surrounding the medium-sized port town of Stobi.

Lacy stopped, frustration and hopelessness finally overcoming her drive toward a potentially fatal confrontation. The death of half of the men she'd been traveling with weighed on her conscience. She had enlisted their assistance, she had set their course, she had delivered them to their doom.

"What are we going to do once we find her?"

The rest of her company stopped.

"I was thinking we'd kill her and take the box, then commandeer a ship and head for Ithilian," Wyatt said.

"Do you think this is a joke, Captain? You just lost half your men— dead."

Wyatt stepped close to her, forcing her to back away a little. "You needn't remind me what I've lost, Princess. I can name every single man who's died under my command … they were all good men, every one of them, and they were my friends. I've been fighting this war from the beginning, so I understand what's at stake better than most. If you have a plan that will improve our odds of success, then I would hear it."

Lacy held her ground even though she could feel her knees trembling. "That's just it, we don't have a plan. She'll charm you and your men the moment you get too close, and then what?"

"We just need to get close enough to put a few arrows into her," Wyatt said.

"That's assuming we can catch her off guard," Ayela said. "If she sees us coming, your arrows will be useless."

"She probably thinks we're all dead," Wren said. "That might give us a chance to surprise her."

"But not if we go into town as a group," Ayela said. "Regency guards don't take kindly to soldiers in strange uniforms."

"Fair enough," Wyatt said, dropping his pack and pulling out a worn leather cloak. "We'll go in with three teams of two, make our way to the docks and locate the witch. Everyone else will withdraw into the jungle and wait for us to return."

Lacy shook her head, "No. I'm coming with you."

"Are you any good with a bow? Can you fight?"

Her face fell. "Not really."

"Then you stay here," Wyatt said. "You'll be safer and we'll be able to do our job without worrying about you."

"But … the box is my responsibility," Lacy protested.

"You are a princess," Wyatt said. "As such, you'll have to become accustomed to sending others to fight for you. Now is as good a time as any to learn that lesson."

Lacy felt helpless, yet again. She knew Wyatt was right, yet desperately didn't want to accept it. Tears started to well up in her eyes even over her desperate desire to put on a brave face.

Wyatt smiled gently. "Deal in what is, not what if. That's one of Lord Reishi's favorite sayings, and there's wisdom in those words. The result is what matters and we stand a far better chance of getting that box back if you stay here."

"He's right, Lacy," Wren said. "If we go with him, he'll be too busy trying to protect us to focus on the job at hand."

Lacy swallowed the lump in her throat and nodded tightly. "Be safe, Captain."

"I'll do my best," Wyatt said, donning his cloak.

"I'll go with you," Ayela said. "I may have a thing or two in my bag that could prove useful."

"Very well," Wyatt said, selecting the rest of the detail. Once they were away, Lacy, Wren, and the remaining men withdrew into the jungle to wait.

The minutes seemed to drag on interminably until Lacy couldn't stand it any longer. It had only been half an hour, but it seemed like days.

"What's taking so long?" she asked no one in particular.

"They'll take their shot when they have it," a Ranger answered.

She wanted to say more, but thought better of it. An hour passed, then another. By this time, the Rangers were starting to look worried as well. A sound from the jungle brought a surge of relief. Lacy stood quickly, taking a few steps toward the sound just in time to see a man appear out of thin air, wisps of black smoke wreathing his form for just a moment. He smiled at her wickedly and then vanished again. A scream of pain was cut short by a gurgling noise somewhere behind her.

Another wraithkin appeared behind a Ranger, stabbing him through the heart, then vanishing. Pandemonium erupted among the Rangers as they scrambled to pair off, back to back, but their efforts were in vain. One by one, the wraithkin picked them off. Lacy watched in horror while the men around her died.

One Ranger got lucky and drove his sword into the mouth of one of the wraithkin, killing him almost instantly, but then died almost as quickly when another appeared behind him and cut his throat. The very one-sided battle seemed to last only seconds. The sudden quiet was filled with the soft noises of men breathing their last. Lacy and Wren stood in the center of a ring of carnage, bodies spilling their blood into the dirt—yet more names for Wyatt to remember.

Two wraithkin stood before them, smiling menacingly, fresh blood slowly dripping off the points of their long, black knives.

"Hello, Princess," one said.

"Hello, child," the other said.

"Prince Phane isn't finished with you."

"Yes, it was very rude of you to leave without saying goodbye."

They both laughed.

"You will come with us."

"There is no escaping."

Lacy pondered the totality of her defeat while she walked toward Stobi. A kind of detachment settled over her, keeping her despair at bay and giving her a few moments of clarity. The question her mind kept coming back to was: Why did Phane still want her alive? With the box on its way to Torin, she was of no use to him and yet she was still alive.

The wraithkin took them to the docks, where they met a platoon of soldiers led by Drogan. He was talking with the captain of the city guard. Lacy realized in that moment that Drogan had been Phane's chief agent of deception. He had guided her to this place and she'd trusted him because she'd needed his assistance so desperately. Another lesson learned the hard way—and much too late.

"We killed three Ruathan Rangers," the captain said, gesturing to three corpses lined up on the docks, "but we think a few more got away."

Lacy strained to see if one of the men was Wyatt, breathing a sigh of relief when she didn't see him, then feeling a pang of guilt a moment later. Three more lives gone.

"As long as the witch got through to her ship, Prince Phane will be happy," Drogan said.

"She did," the captain said, pointing out to sea. "Her vessel has almost reached the horizon."

"Very happy indeed," Drogan said, noticing Lacy for the first time. "Hello, Princess. It seems that we'll be traveling together again."

Lacy strode up to him and spit right in his face. He smiled humorlessly, very deliberately wiping away the spittle while a soldier grabbed her from behind and pulled her several steps backward. She struggled for a moment until the soldier wrenched her arm, eliciting a scream.

"Stop!" Drogan said. "The princess and the girl are not to be harmed."

Before Lacy could respond, the ocean lit up so brilliantly that everybody ducked instinctively, shielding their eyes. It was as if a second sun had materialized not a league out to sea. Moments later, a deafening crack washed over them, sending everybody to their knees, covering their ears as best they could. The light dimmed and the noise died away, leaving the world in awe and terror. Birds and animals fell silent—even the breeze through the trees seemed to still.

Everyone slowly stood, facing the water and searching for the ship that had been at the edge of the world, but it was gone, leaving nothing but a roiling ocean where it had been floating only moments before. Lacy had never seen such power, and from the looks of it, neither had any of the men surrounding her.

More importantly, she had no idea what had just happened, and not just to the witch and the ship, but to the box. Was it sinking to bottom of the ocean? If so, would that be enough to keep Phane from retrieving it? Somehow, she doubted that mere water would prove to be a sufficient barrier to his ambitions. But what if the box itself had been destroyed? And the keystone with it? Surely such a devastating release of energy could destroy it.

"Huh," Drogan said, shrugging to himself indifferently. "Secure the prisoners in the carriage. We'll be leaving at once."

Chapter 23

Alexander woke with a start, sitting up quickly, his all around sight coming into sharp focus almost instantly. The sudden movement made the pain in his head spike. He clenched his blind eyes shut and took a slow deep breath while surveying his surroundings.

He was locked in a bare cell, five feet on a side with a stone wall to the back and bars for the other three walls. There was a chill in the air and little light to see by. More curiously, there were a number of the same points of light floating around him that he'd seen in his bunkroom at Titus Grant's estate. He sat up with his back to the wall, pondering their significance, the slave collar chafing his neck with every movement.

The initial assessment of his situation wasn't encouraging, but he still hurt too much to worry about anything else at the moment, so he just kept breathing, tenderly feeling the lump on the back of his head where he'd been hit.

"Chloe?" he said in his mind.

"Oh, thank the Maker you're awake. I was so worried."

"How long have I been out?"

"Over a day, My Love. I thought I might have lost you … again."

"You'll never lose me, Little One. What happened to Anja?"

"She escaped into the sky. Last I saw she was flying west."

Alexander took a deep breath and let it out slowly. "At least that part of the plan worked."

"I can free you. I know the way out of the dungeons and there are only two guards on duty."

Alexander tried to get up, then quickly sat back down. "Maybe I'll just rest here for a few minutes. I don't think I'm in any shape to move right now, let alone fight."

A man two cells over sat up and looked at him—Titus Grant.

"Are you still alive, Pretender?"

Alexander started laughing softly in spite of the pain it caused.

"What's so funny?" Grant demanded.

"Just that your plan worked out about as well as mine did."

"It's not funny," Grant said. "They're going to sell my wife as a slave and execute me for treason unless we work together to get out of here."

Alexander started laughing again, each chuckle sending ripples of pain through his head. "Oh, it's kind of funny, especially the part about you being executed for treason."

"Maybe you don't realize how serious this is," Grant said. "Face it, I'm the only friend you've got right now."

This time Alexander tipped his head back and forced a mocking laugh, ignoring the pain.

"You'd rather die in here than help me?"

"Oh, they're not going to kill me," Alexander said, "at least not right away."

"Wouldn't you rather they didn't kill you at all?"

"You'd stab me in the back the moment you got the chance, and we both know it."

"That's just not true. I have nothing to gain by your death."

Alexander found himself wishing that he could see this man's colors, but even blind to Grant's aura, Alexander knew better than to trust him. Still, he might stand a better chance of escaping if he had some help.

"Perhaps killing me wouldn't do you any good, but alive I would be quite the bargaining chip. You might even get your charter back."

"Don't be foolish. The Babachenko knows my ambition now. He'll never let me live to challenge his authority."

"Maybe you're right on that count," Alexander mused, carefully lowering himself back to the floor.

"What are you doing?"

"I'm going to take a nap … my head hurts."

"Are you insane? We have to get out of here."

"Even if I trusted you, I'm in no shape to travel. I doubt I could even stand up right now without falling over."

"Unbelievable. You're supposed to be the great and powerful Lord Reishi, Sovereign of the Seven Isles, and you're just going to curl up and take a nap?"

"Seems like the thing to do," Alexander muttered.

But he didn't take a nap. Instead, he sent his mind to Chloe and spent the next half hour searching the warrens of the Andalian palace, mapping a way out of the dungeon and exploring the routes he might follow to reach the forges that lay even deeper still. Satisfied with his understanding of the layout, he sat up cautiously, testing the pain in his head. While it hadn't subsided as much as he would have liked, it had diminished to a manageable level … so he started making plans.

His objectives hadn't changed. The king was dead. Hopefully, that would put an end to the Lancers, but he wanted to be certain, and that meant destroying the forges and the Crown. After his reconnaissance, he was confident that he could reach the forges without too much difficulty, but he'd have a fight on his hands once he did. Twelve guards were stationed at the entrance when he and Chloe had floated past in the aether. Once he reached the forges, he faced the problem of destroying them. Each was an enormous magical construction fashioned from steel and stone. He would need more than his bare hands to undo them.

While he was considering his options, he heard an odd noise that sounded like it was coming from behind the wall he was leaning against. He stood quickly, pain surging in his head. Leaning up against the bars opposite the wall, he looked through with his all around sight and saw who was coming.

The Thinblade could destroy the forges.

Tyr stabbed through the wall at the back of the cell between Alexander and Grant, cutting a section away and letting it fall to the floor with a thump that reverberated down the dungeon hallway. He stepped through the hole into the cell, slowly looking this way and that, smiling with satisfaction at what he saw.

"Got you!" he said, cutting a hole through the bars of Alexander's cage with several haphazard strokes, sections of metal clattering to the floor.

"I have to say, I wasn't expecting you to ride to my rescue," Alexander said with a mocking smile.

Tyr leveled the Thinblade at Alexander, who just smiled as he gingerly tested the point with his finger, provoking Tyr even further.

"Don't test me, Pretender. This isn't a rescue. In the end, you'll end up at Phane's mercy. This way, I get paid and the Babachenko gets to suffer Phane's wrath."

"Well then, I guess we should be on our way," Alexander said.

"Cut me loose, Tyr," Grant said, his hands gripping the bars tightly. "I can help you. I have friends that can help you escape Andalia."

Tyr whirled on Grant. "So do I. But even if I didn't, I like the idea of you losing your head. Just wish I could be there to see it happen."

"I can pay you. I have silver."

"Again, so do I."

"Not this much," Grant said. "I'll pay you one million silver sovereigns if you help me escape Andalia."

"Do you really think I'm that stupid?"

Grant hesitated for just a moment too long. Tyr spat at him and turned back to Alexander who had stepped into the cell with him and was waiting patiently.

"What are you looking at," Tyr snapped, sheathing the Thinblade. "Get moving."

Alexander stepped into a dark and unused passage, the far wall completely unfinished, then went to his knees at Wizard Edric's feet, his collar constricting around his neck. He tried to turn around and step back into the dungeon, but Tyr shoved him to the ground. The slave collar closed off his airway and left him struggling for a breath that couldn't get through. He tried to regain his feet, but Tyr kicked him to the ground again, laughing at his predicament, letting the darkness of suffocation start to close in around him until he lost consciousness.

He woke with a gasp, the ruined collar lying next to him on the dusty floor.

"Get up," Tyr snapped.

Alexander raised himself to his hands and knees, but Tyr kicked him in the gut, sending him toppling to his side, gasping for breath.

"Lord Tyr, this is neither the time nor the place for this," Wizard Edric said. "The Babachenko will learn of this quickly. We have precious little time to escape the palace or we risk being apprehended."

Tyr squatted down so he could look Alexander in the face from just a few inches away, the smell of his acrid breath turning Alexander's stomach.

"When I'm finished with you, you'll beg me to give you over to Phane," he said, droplets of spittle spraying Alexander in the face.

Tyr roughly hauled him to his feet and shoved him down the passage. Alexander stumbled and only avoided falling by catching himself on the wall. He didn't look back, he didn't need to ... his all around sight told him that Tyr and Edric were right behind him.

"Tyr! Don't leave me here," Grant shouted just before Edric caused the ceiling to collapse, sealing the passage behind them.

"That should slow them down," Tyr said, shoving Alexander forward.

They followed a path rarely traveled in recent centuries, only the footprints of Tyr and his wizard visible in the layer of dust coating the floor. At every turn, Tyr commanded a direction and Alexander obeyed. If the temperamental, would-be king of Tyr had a plan to get him out of Mithel Dour, Alexander was happy to have him do the heavy lifting. It would be a simple matter to turn the tables on him once they were away, especially since Alexander was no longer constrained by the slave collar.

They delved deeper into the bowels of the ancient palace until it became apparent that they were approaching the level of the city itself. Alexander smiled to himself. Even if the passages they were traveling didn't lead to a door, the Thinblade would be able to open a passage for them without difficulty. Whatever else Tyr was, he seemed to have thought his escape plan through.

"I believe this is the place," Edric said.

"Stop," Tyr commanded, drawing the Thinblade and cutting a section of the wall away. It took several minutes to open a passage through the six feet of granite.

Alexander was surprised to see that they were still a hundred feet above the city.

"Cast your spell," Tyr said.

Edric nodded respectfully, muttering a few words before taking both Alexander and Tyr by the wrist. They all stepped out into the open air and fell gently to the streets below, where a carriage was waiting for them nearby, manned by two of Tyr's pirates.

Alexander went along for the ride; his moment hadn't arrived yet. The carriage traveled through the back streets, twisting and turning to avoid streets that were more frequently patrolled, until it came to a stop.

Tyr opened a shutter to the driver's seat. "Why did we stop?"

"The river has been diverted down the switchback road," the driver said. "There's no way out of the city."

"He knows," Edric said.

Tyr seemed to have an emotional meltdown right in front of Alexander without ever saying a word. His face contorted and changed colors while he struggled to master his distress. Alexander almost laughed, but thought better of it. Tyr was still his best bet for escape and testing his temper now would only result in rash and unproductive decisions.

"Take me to my estate!" Tyr finally snapped, slamming the shutter closed.

"Is that wise?" Edric asked, diplomatically. "If the Babachenko is aware of your involvement, your estate is the first place he'll look."

"Where then?"

"Perhaps the Grant estate would be vacant."

Tyr slammed the shutter open again. "Take us to Grant's estate instead."

As the carriage started moving again, Tyr sat glowering at Alexander, only growing more agitated when Alexander closed his eyes and rested his head on the back of his seat.

"Where's the Stone?" Tyr demanded.

Alexander ignored him.

Tyr slapped him across the face. "Where's the Stone?"

"Safe," Alexander said, fixing Tyr with his golden eyes and holding his stare until Tyr looked away, again trying to master his anger.

"I'm going to enjoy this, Pretender. I hope you hold out for as long as possible ... give me a reason to cut on you, take your life away from you a piece at a time."

"You need a reason to do that?" Alexander asked, closing his eyes again and leaning his head back.

"You think I'm bluffing?" Tyr snapped, barely controlled rage with a tinge of fear in his voice and colors.

"No, not at all," Alexander said without opening his eyes. "But no suffering within your power to inflict will ever cause me to give you the Sovereign Stone, and without me, it will be forever beyond your reach."

"I've heard bluster like that before, but they all break. Sooner or later, they all beg for mercy. You're no different."

Alexander sat forward quickly, boring into Tyr with his blind eyes. "I have endured such fear, pain, and despair ... the likes of which would crush your petty little soul into nothingness. Your limited mind can't even conceive of the trials that I've already survived, so save your threats, Tyr ... they're as impotent as you are."

Veins started to bulge from Tyr's temples, ripples of rage and fury coursed through his colors, but Alexander didn't back away. He held himself within reach, daring Tyr to lash out again ... and he wasn't disappointed. Tyr surged forward, grabbing Alexander by the throat and slamming him back into his seat, landing astraddle him and roaring into his face from only inches away with such force that his voice broke.

The edge of Alexander's mouth turned up just enough to mock the pirate king. Tyr flopped back into his seat, glaring at Alexander, once again struggling to master his temper.

While everything Alexander had said was true, he didn't relish the idea of being tortured, especially if that torment left him maimed as Tyr had promised. Fortunately, Tyr was keenly aware that he was little more than an errand boy charged with delivering Phane's prize, so Alexander had little fear that he would do anything too damaging to him. Phane would likely be quite unforgiving if Tyr delivered Alexander broken and without the Stone.

After a series of turns, the carriage stopped, wobbling when the drivers dismounted. Tyr opened the door and peered out.

"It looks abandoned," the lead driver said.

"Good, we'll do this in the stables," Tyr said, stepping out into the cool night air. "Stand guard."

Alexander obeyed Tyr's imperious gesture to exit the carriage and followed him into the stables without a word. Wizard Edric trailed them, but not too close. Alexander decided it would be best to kill the wizard first when he chose to make his move. Unfortunately, the wizard seemed to have enough sense to understand this and so kept his distance.

Tyr grabbed a chair from a small table beside the door and set it in the middle of the hay-strewn floor. Edric remained by the door. Alexander surveyed his surroundings, taking note of everything within reach that he might use as a weapon.

"Sit."

He nodded, approaching the chair, putting his hand on the back as if preparing to sit, then whipped the chair up and around in an arc, throwing it at the wizard. It caught him by surprise, slamming him into the wall and momentarily stunning him. The moment he released the chair, Alexander raced three steps to the nearest stall and snatched up the pitchfork leaning against it.

Tyr roared behind him. Alexander ignored him, taking a moment to set himself before throwing the pitchfork like a spear. It flew true and would have buried itself into Edric's chest had the wizard not flung his hands up and unleashed a force-push that sent the pitchfork flipping into the rafters and knocked Alexander to the ground at the same time.

Tyr kicked him savagely in the side, rolling him into the hay and knocking his wind out, leaving him curled in a ball on the floor, struggling to draw breath.

Tyr's pirates flung the door open a moment later. One said urgently, "The Lord Protector comes with a hundred men."

Shouts filtered through the night air into the stables. Sounds of hard boots on stone followed.

"We have to flee," Edric said. "The Babachenko will kill you for this."

Tyr bellowed in fury as if the sheer volume of his cracking voice could undo his precarious circumstances.

The door on the far end of the stables blew open, shattering into splinters. The Lord Protector stepped through a moment later, mace in hand, nearly insubstantial black plate armor covering him from head to toe.

Tyr seemed torn, looking at the Lord Protector for a moment as if sizing up his chances. In answer to his unasked question, the Lord Protector unleashed a blast of force that blew Tyr across the floor, leaving him dazed and sprawling near the door next to Edric.

"Now, Little One," Alexander thought.

Edric picked Tyr up, put one arm around his neck and nearly carried him out of the stables toward the cliff. Alexander smiled when he saw the Thinblade vanish, scabbard and all. Soldiers poured in past the Lord Protector, but they were too late to catch Tyr and Edric. They could only watch as the wizard hurled both of their bodies off the cliff. Alexander chuckled to himself as he was hauled to his feet and roughly turned to face the Lord Protector.

"There is no escape from Mithel Dour," the Lord Protector said, matter-of-factly.

"Looks like Tyr managed to escape," Alexander said.

"He was not our prisoner, though he may soon be."

"Just don't put him in the cell next to me … he's terrible company."

"Oh, you won't have to worry about that," the Lord Protector said, snapping a collar around Alexander's neck while two men held him from behind. "The Babachenko has decided to see to your interrogation personally."

Chapter 24

Alexander rode back to the Andalian palace escorted by a hundred royal guard and the Lord Protector. Given his circumstances, he found himself in surprisingly good spirits. While Tyr had failed to free him from the Andalians, Alexander had managed to take the Thinblade from him, a turn of events that Tyr was no doubt furious about. Even better, it was highly unlikely that Tyr would show his face in Mithel Dour anytime soon, especially without the power that the Thinblade gave him.

Alexander expected to be returned to the dungeon, but found the Lord Protector leading him into the warded part of the palace instead, while all but two of his guards returned to other duties.

"Stay close and stay hidden, Little One."

"I'm right here."

At the entrance to the central chambers of the palace, the Lord Protector touched a stone set into a panel in the wall, and the magical barrier warding the hallway before them vanished, reappearing once they were through and the Lord Protector touched a similar stone set into the wall a few feet past the ward.

The uniform of the guards changed within the inner sanctum of the Andalian ruling elite, becoming both more austere and more functional. Alexander could see in a glance that the guards' smocks were enchanted, though he couldn't determine the nature of the enchantment. He idly wondered if the smocks were produced by some form of magical device similar to the forges that was designed to churn out identically enchanted items in quantity.

The Lord Protector stopped at a set of ornate double doors, pulling the bell cord once. A rich peal rang out, reverberating throughout the nearby halls. A few moments later, a guard wearing an enchanted smock opened the door and bowed respectfully to the Lord Protector.

"Please, come in," he said. "The Babachenko is expecting you."

From the looks of the room, it was the entry hall of the Babachenko's personal quarters ... a curious turn of events. Alexander focused on memorizing the layout and looking for anything he might use as a weapon while he followed the guard into a more austere portion of the suite, finally arriving at a large bare stone room with a stout circular cage set into the middle of it from floor to ceiling.

The Lord Protector opened the cage door and looked at Alexander pointedly.

He stepped inside, noting that the bars were arranged within a magic circle cut into the floor. When the door closed, the cage shimmered with color, revealing that it too was imbued with some form of magic, a fact that might prove problematic in the near future.

"I can't get inside the cage, My Love."

He could hear the worry in her voice and tried to reassure her, even though he wasn't feeling terribly reassured himself.

After the Lord Protector and the guards left the room, Alexander sat down on the rickety little cot and considered his limited options. While Chloe could have easily moved the cell door of his previous prison into the aether, it was a near certainty that this cage was immune to her power. Coupled with the wards surrounding this part of the palace, escaping might prove to be very difficult without help.

Then there were the faint points of light floating all around the room, just like the ones in his other cell, just like the ones in his bunkroom in Grant's stables. He still wondered about their purpose.

While he thought through his options and goals, the Babachenko and Nero entered.

"You see, he is intact and well in hand," the Babachenko said, "and he will be quite unable to escape this cell."

"Provided he doesn't have help," Nero said.

"It would be very difficult for anyone to penetrate our defenses in this area of the palace," the Babachenko said.

"As difficult as assassinating your king?" Nero shot back.

"I have to admit, that was an unexpected turn of events. But, given our newfound understanding of his resourcefulness, we've taken additional precautions. You have my personal assurances that he will not leave this palace without your express consent, Lord Nero."

Alexander watched with great interest. The Babachenko's colors rippled with deceit and half-truth. Nero's demon-stained colors radiated contempt and a kind of hatred that would burn up a normal person's soul.

"I'm not comfortable with this," Nero said. "We should make him ready for transport to Karth immediately."

"You would deliver only half of Prince Phane's prize? I wonder if he would consider that a success or a failure?"

Nero glared at him, uncertainty dancing in his colors.

"Give me a chance to retrieve the Sovereign Stone," the Babachenko said. "My talents are uniquely suited to such a task, as you well know."

Nero didn't look convinced.

"Just imagine how much greater his gratitude will be when we deliver his most hated enemy along with the Sovereign Stone. Our actions will prove to be the turning point in this war, ensuring victory and earning a place of honor at Prince Phane's table."

"I'll give you two days," Nero said. "If you don't have progress to report by then, I'm taking him."

"As you wish, Lord Nero," the Babachenko said, and while his voice was placating and conciliatory, his colors flared with anger and indignation.

Nero vanished without even looking at Alexander.

The Babachenko smiled warmly, approaching the cage, but remaining out of arm's reach. "I trust the accommodations are adequate. While I regret such extreme measures, Lord Tyr's recent actions have given me little choice."

Alexander remained silent, scrutinizing his colors and waiting for the demands to begin.

The Babachenko forced a smile and pulled a chair over to the cage, sitting down and fastidiously adjusting his coat before returning his attention to Alexander.

"We have something in common, Alexander—may I call you Alexander?"

"It's my name."

"Straight to the point ... how refreshing," the Babachenko said, forcing another thin smile. "We both have better vision than most. In fact, I've been watching you carefully for the past year, and I must say, I'm impressed with what you've accomplished, especially given your limitations and disadvantages. Few could have stood against Phane for so long, but realistically, you had to know that it was going to end like this." He gestured to the cage.

"Between you and me," he said, leaning in conspiratorially, "I don't like the idea of submitting to Phane's rule any more than you do, but he's just too powerful to resist, so it only made sense to join him early on. While I've been watching you from afar, now that you're sitting here with me, I'm struck by how young you are."

Alexander schooled his expression while he watched deceit ripple through the Babachenko's colors.

"When I was your age, I was almost as idealistic as you are, but time and the pressures of responsibility have molded that idealism into pragmatism. I have countless people to think about—their well-being and security are my responsibility—so I chose the only honorable course that I could, the path that would cause my people the least harm.

"But I had something that you didn't ... I had the benefit of experience. I'm sure that if you knew then what you know now, you would have made different choices. And no one can rightfully fault you for that inexperience ... except, of course, Phane. He's become almost obsessed with you. I don't believe he'll stop looking for you until he's certain that you're dead."

The Babachenko shook his head sadly.

"It's such a shame to see one as talented as you, with such potential, lose everything for a few intemperate, youthful decisions."

"Where are you going with this?" Alexander asked.

"Ah, to the point, yes of course," the Babachenko said. "You see, I know what you really want—to live free. To live the simple life of a rancher without the cares and pressures of power, and I can help you get that. I can give you your life back. I can protect your family. You can have everything you've always wanted, Alexander, and Phane will never know. He'll think you're dead and he'll move on to other enemies."

"Let me guess ... you'll give me all of this for the Sovereign Stone," Alexander said.

"Nothing comes without a price," the Babachenko said with a helpless shrug. "I'm sure that if you think it through, you'll realize that Phane won't stop until he has the Stone. As long as it eludes him, he'll scour the Seven Isles for it, and you'll never be safe. But if he has the Stone, and he thinks you're dead, you'll finally be free."

"Do you really think you can deceive Phane?" Alexander asked, leaning in with interest.

"Well now, that part won't be easy, but I'm certain it can be done."

"So what would I have to do?" Alexander asked.

The Babachenko smiled warmly. "I would need the Sovereign Stone to placate Phane, but I also have a price of my own. There's a book within your Wizard's Den—a dark and dangerous work that Phane could use to become all but immortal. That can't be allowed to happen, so my price for helping you and your family is the delivery of the lich book along with the Stone."

"Is that all?"

"That's all I want from you," the Babachenko lied. "Deliver these two things and I will hand Phane a corpse that is indistinguishable from you. I will change your appearance, give you a house on a plot of good land, a herd and even provide you with protection. You'll finally be free of this war, safe, comfortable.

"I'm sure if you think about it, you'll realize I'm offering you a gift."

"And all for the price of handing the world over to Phane," Alexander said. "You make it sound like a bargain."

"But don't you see, Phane already has the world in his hand. You can't beat him. I can't beat him. He's already won and there's nothing anyone can do about it. Take my offer and save yourself."

Alexander started chuckling softly. "Did you really think this was going to work?"

The Babachenko sighed. "Not really, but I had hoped, and I still do. Perhaps with better information, you'll take my generous offer.

"You came here to kill our king, no doubt to disrupt the Lancers rampaging across Ruatha. I'm sure you, like most others, believe that the Andalian bloodline is failing and must be carefully concentrated through inbreeding to ensure that the Crown remains potent and the force lances continue to function. Of course, these are all lies. We don't inbreed our kings to make them viable, we inbreed them to make them manageable. There are, in fact, one hundred and seventeen people in this city capable of wearing the Crown.

"Within an hour of the king's death, the Crown was bound to another. Just long enough for your forces on Ruatha to mount an attack against our Lancers. Then, once your troops were out in the open, the power of the force lances returned. The result was nothing short of devastating. Your army is retreating in tatters."

Alexander schooled his emotions, his father's old lesson about good information in battle being necessary to victory playing out in the back of his mind. Because he'd believed something that wasn't true, and acted on that belief, good men were dead … or so said the Babachenko, anyway.

"Accept defeat graciously, Alexander. Take my bargain and be done with all of this death and pain."

"Here's my problem," Alexander said, "you're lying to me. There's something you want from me that you haven't revealed. And even setting that aside, I'm not going to hand Phane victory. He might win, but it won't be because I gave up."

"I feared as much," the Babachenko said, standing up and returning the chair to its place against the wall. "I had hoped that you would see reason. Perhaps pain will be more persuasive."

"Really? You've been through the trials ..." Alexander stopped short, examining the Babachenko's colors intently. "Now, that is interesting," he said, stepping up to the cage door. "You haven't been through the trials, have you?"

"Nonsense, of course I've been through the trials," he lied.

"How do you become a wizard, a mage no less, without surviving the mana fast?"

The Babachenko ignored his question, but his colors revealed distress. He went to the lone cabinet along the wall and removed a small glass jar, holding it up for Alexander to see. Floating within the water was a tiny blue jellyfish.

"This is a very special little creature found on the south coast of Andalia."

"You're threatening me with a jellyfish?"

The Babachenko chuckled. "I understand your skepticism, but it won't protect you. This creature possesses venom that causes almost a full day of intense agony, the kind of pain men kill themselves to escape. I've experimented with many forms of interrogation, but I've never discovered anything as effective as this. Even the most ruinous torture fails from time to time, particularly with stubbornly principled subjects such as yourself, but this has never failed me."

"There's always a first time."

"I want you to know that I take no pleasure in this. When we met in the slave yards, I was encouraged. And yes, I knew who you were the moment I laid eyes on you. I really thought I would be able to accomplish my goals without resorting to this kind of unpleasantness."

"If you knew who I was, why did you let me kill your king?"

"That, I wasn't expecting. I knew Grant was ambitious, but I never suspected he'd go against the very government that gave him his wealth and standing."

"So I guess your vision isn't that good after all."

"No one can see everything," the Babachenko said. "We're often blinded by our own hopes and expectations. Despite my talent in the art of divination, I can't see that which I don't think to look for."

"Huh ... that's the first thing you've said that actually makes sense."

The Babachenko held up the jar. "Will you cooperate and allow the jellyfish to sting you or shall I call for some guards to hold you down?"

"Better call your guards," Alexander said, stepping away from the cage door.

"I suspected as much," the Babachenko said, opening the chamber door and motioning to the men standing outside.

Alexander stood stock-still in the middle of the cage, eyes closed yet very alert, waiting for the guards to approach. The door opened; he held. The two men approached, each of them reaching out for one of his arms. Time slowed, the coming moments clear in his mind. Alexander slapped the back of the man's hand to his right, catching the guard's wrist with his left hand and yanking him off balance, snatching his dagger from his belt as he stepped past and behind him, then plunging the knife into his back. The guard fell forward with a wail of surprise and pain.

The second man's smock shimmered momentarily and then he was wearing the same wispy black plate armor that the Lord Protector wore. Alexander circled him, but he was really fixed on the Babachenko, who stood well away from the cage, but close enough.

Alexander raised his knife in challenge to the guard, then whirled, hurling the blade with all his strength, burying it in the Babachenko's left shoulder, just high and wide of his heart. He shrieked in pain, falling to one knee.

The second guard crashed into Alexander, slamming him into the cage bars and wrenching his arm around behind his back, then the collar began to choke him, cutting off his air and his consciousness.

Chapter 25

He woke on the floor, alone. The only evidence of the struggle were a few drops of blood and an angry welt on his forearm.

"This is going to be a long night," he said to himself, lying down on the cot and marshaling his will in anticipation of the coming onslaught.

At first, the area around the sting just felt warm, then the heat started to build, not hot like fire but hot like pepper, only this heat was spreading inside his arm with growing intensity. Within a few minutes, it felt like fire ants were eating his arm from the inside out, but it didn't stop there. Angry, prickly, burning pain spread through his entire body, filling him up until he felt panic at the edges of his awareness, clawing its way in, trying to steal his focus and undo his will to resist. He thought of the mana fast and the trial of pain. This didn't rise to that level of agony … at least not yet.

But it grew, expanding to envelop him in a cocoon of suffering so intense that he had to remember to breathe. Somewhere in the back of his mind he understood why men killed themselves to escape this pain, and it had only just begun.

He writhed on his cot while the pain intensified, at some point falling to the floor. Somehow it seemed worse if he tried to hold still, so he kept moving, straining and stretching his muscles until they cramped, contracting into knots of agony. It seemed like he struggled against the pain for a very long time before he felt himself slipping away into the firmament and blessed relief … until the collar started choking him and he slammed back into his pain-wracked body.

Renewed panic flooded into his mind. This kind of pain would drive his mind into the firmament, the only place it could find reprieve, and then the collar would choke him. As much as it hurt, he struggled to remain present in his own body, struggled to take one breath after another in spite of the clenched, suffocating constriction he felt around his chest and throat.

Time and again, his mind tried to slip free and he willed it back to face the torment, until he started to lose strength, started to become exhausted. Facing the very real possibility that this might be his end, he struggled against it with renewed strength, but it waned quickly, leaving him defenseless against the doom poised to consume him.

And then he was in the firmament again, scattered like so many times before, his mind and soul fractured. Instinctively, he fled into that place where the witness lived, where he could see the world dispassionately, without fear or despair, but it wasn't enough. Somehow this time was different. He reached out for the scraps of his identity left adrift in the ocean of creation while other parts of himself slipped away. The harder he tried to hold on to himself, the more of his essential self drained away, until there was nothing left but the witness, detached, uncaring, accepting.

He wasn't certain how long he simply watched the world form out of the formless, each moment created anew in a procession through time that had neither beginning nor end. In this place, he no longer cared about the outcome, wasn't concerned for his survival, felt no fear or pain or love. He simply was.

He was the watcher.

Thoughts of Siduri came to him unbidden and unexpected, followed by a great rushing sensation as if all of creation was passing through his consciousness at once. In the next moment, he was standing on a riverbank, whole and unharmed, yet somehow different, more like a memory than a man.

A family was playing in the water at the edge of the river not far from where he stood, three boys and their parents. Siduri looked up with a start when Alexander approached, his eyes going wide for a moment as if he suddenly remembered the truth of the world ... and his part in its plight.

"How did you get here?" he asked, standing to face Alexander, fear and guilt staining his complex colors.

"I'm not entirely sure. I think I might be dead."

Siduri slowly shook his head. "You wouldn't be here if you were dead. There's really only one way."

His wife and children vanished, followed a moment later by the little cabin set away from the river.

"What is this place?"

"This is where I live. It's my home. I created it from my memories."

"A construct," Alexander said.

"Yes."

"But it's not real."

Siduri poked him in the chest. "It's as real as anything else."

"No, it's not," Alexander said. "The real world is out there. Real people are suffering and dying in the real world and they don't have the luxury of such a well-crafted fantasy."

Siduri looked down at the mud along the riverbank.

"When I took the blood of the earth, you judged me," Alexander said. "And perhaps rightfully so. But now you're judging yourself. You can't even look at me."

"You don't belong here, Alexander," Siduri said without looking up. "Go back to your world; leave me to mine."

"This isn't the real world, it's make-believe. Come back with me," Alexander said.

"There's nothing for me there."

"Then why do you watch?"

Siduri looked down again.

"You watch because you know that what happens in the real world matters—it matters to countless families like the one you used to have. Help me."

"You know what happened the last time I interfered. I won't risk that again."

"Yes ... I know exactly what you did. You doomed the world, and only you can fix that."

"What do you mean?" Siduri asked, horror vying with hope in his colors.

"The Taker is a creature of bargains. He brought your children back from death, but you never paid his price. Until you do, the shades will torment the world every chance they get, and one day they *will* win."

"What are you saying?"

"I'm saying that your children will never be free of the Taker until you pay his price."

Siduri shook his head in denial. "You can't know that."

Alexander held him with his eyes, waiting for Siduri to work through the magnitude of what he was asking.

"No, you're wrong. My children are lost. Sacrificing myself won't bring them back."

"No, it won't, but it might set them free."

"No ... you have to leave, now!" Siduri said, his fear morphing into anger. "You have no right to intrude like this."

Alexander opened his hands helplessly. "I don't know how to leave."

Siduri grabbed him by the wrist and the façade of his past life vanished. They moved through the part of the firmament where Alexander had felt so detached and into the roiling, ever-changing surface where creation happened, and then Alexander was back in the cell, and the pain was back, except the collar was lying on the floor nearby, still closed.

Alexander crumpled to his knees, the agony overtaking him once again, then he rolled onto his side and moaned in renewed suffering.

"You're back," Chloe nearly shouted in his mind. "I thought you were dead, except you were just gone. Please don't leave me like that. I can't live without you. I almost went home." She broke down crying.

"I'm right here, Little One," he managed to think through the pain. "But I have to send my mind away again for a while, it'll help me survive the poison they gave me."

"You're coming back, right?"

"Yes," Alexander said, slipping into the firmament again, but only with his mind. The pain vanished like a cool breeze. He savored the relief of it while watching his body tremble, curled up in the fetal position on the floor. His transition into the firmament was easy, almost like second nature. He'd had so few opportunities to use his magic to its fullest since he'd arrived in Mithel Dour. It was as if resting his magic had strengthened it, like muscles given time to recover after a strenuous effort. Free of the collar, he decided to use the time to coordinate with his allies.

He thought of Isabel and the world rushed by in an instant before he found himself in an overly decorated room. Isabel was beaten and bruised, lying unconscious in bed. A severe-looking woman was sitting vigil beside her. Isabel's colors told an even more troubling story. She was weak, beaten nearly to death and just barely holding on to life. Emotions tumbled through Alexander: fear, sympathy, love, rage.

He materialized at the foot of the bed, fixing the startled woman with a murderous glare. "Who did this to her?"

She stood up, knocking her chair over, looking at him as if he were a ghost.

"Answer my question!"

"Prince Phane," she said, fear coursing through her colors.

"Will she survive?"

"Yes," the woman said, nodding tightly. "Prince Phane has commanded that she must survive."

Alexander vanished and reappeared just a step in front of her, causing her fear to spike even more. "See to it that she does, or you will answer to me as well."

He faded from sight and slipped into Isabel's mind, finding his way into her dreams. She was struggling against the Wraith Queen, fighting with all her strength, but losing the battle bit by bit, giving ground to avoid injury. Alexander imposed his will on the scene, but this was not a normal nightmare, it was induced by Azugorath, so he wasn't able to dispel her so easily. Realizing the true nature of the fight Isabel was locked in, he chose to attack the construct rather than the demon, casting away the deep, dark cavern where they fought and transforming it into a bright sunny day in the meadows of Glen Morillian.

Azugorath shrieked at the sunlight, vanishing with a roar of fury and hate.

"Hi," he said, appearing in front of Isabel.

"Is that really you?" she asked, hope and wariness in her voice.

"It's really me," he said, willing the scene to change, transforming the fields of Glen Morillian into the simple little altar where they were married in the Valley of the Fairy Queen.

She threw her arms around him, crying uncontrollably. He just held her, giving her as much love and strength as she could take in.

"I don't know how much longer I can fight her," she whispered.

"Just hold on," Alexander said. "I'm coming as soon as I can."

She nodded into his shoulder. "Lacy's here."

Alexander held her out at arm's length, new fear flooding into him. "Has she opened the box?"

Isabel shook her head. "I sent Wren to tell her the truth about everything and help her escape, but I don't know if they got out. The last thing I remember was Phane beating me senseless for breaking his magic mirror."

Alexander frowned questioningly.

"He used it to spy on us," Isabel said. "When he turned his back on me, I smashed it. He was so mad, I thought he was going to kill me."

"Fortunately, he doesn't want you dead. You're in bed right now, healing. Just focus on that."

She nodded, slipping into his embrace again. "I wish you could stay with me."

"Me too."

He held her for a long time, content to be in her soothing presence, even if it was just a dream.

"There's more," she whispered, as if she was afraid of breaking the spell by talking too loudly. "Hector's turned against us. He's helping Phane retrieve the Goiri bones."

"Why? Why would he do that?"

"Phane promised to bring his brother back from the dead."

"Oh, Dear Maker," Alexander said, looking up at the make-believe sky. "Hector better hope Phane doesn't make good on that promise. It'll be the worst thing that ever happened to him."

Isabel stepped back, looking up at him. "Are you safe? Are you well?"

"Let's just say I'm still alive and fighting," he said with a reassuring smile. "I wish I could tell you more."

"Me too, but I understand."

"I have to go now. I love you, Isabel."

"I love you too."

"Be strong. We're going to get through this. We're going to win. Hold on to that, no matter what."

"I will. Stay safe," she said, as he faded from her dream.

Alexander rose above the fortress city, considering his next move, and deciding, perhaps against his better judgment, to visit Phane. Floating through a window in one of the upper levels of the black tower, Alexander found him standing in a magic circle set into the stone just adjacent to another magic circle. He was chanting under his breath, dark magic roiling in his colors.

Alexander appeared nearby without drawing his attention.

"Hey!"

Phane snapped out of his spell, power draining from his colors.

"Do you have any idea how many hours I spent on that spell?"

"I hope it was a lot," Alexander said.

"I have nothing to say to you," Phane snapped, gesturing dismissively.

Alexander felt his psyche scatter into the firmament, but this time it was different. Always before, he'd felt fear at being scattered, fear that he would become lost, that the firmament would claim him, but this time he knew better. But more than that, after his recent experience, he seemed to have much greater control of how he experienced the firmament.

Not more than a second after Phane sent him away, he reappeared, smiling.

"You're losing your touch, Phane."

The Reishi Prince looked at Alexander's illusion with disbelief. For the first time Alexander saw something in Phane's colors that gave him hope—he saw a faint glimmer of fear.

"How?" Phane demanded.

"I think I'll just let you fret about that. I stopped by to let you know that I'll be watching you and there's nothing you can do about it."

"There's where you're wrong," Phane said. "As I understand it, you're sitting in a cage somewhere in Mithel Dour as we speak. It won't be long before Nero brings you to me and then I'll be able to do a great deal."

"Nero overestimates himself, and the Babachenko has his own agenda— one that doesn't seem to coincide with yours. I wouldn't count on my arrival anytime soon."

"I'm well aware of my servants' limitations," Phane said. "But I'm quite certain that both of them will do exactly as they've been instructed to do."

"And both will fail," Alexander said. "In fact, I put a knife into the Babachenko just a few hours ago. Tragically, I missed his heart by a couple of inches, but I did make him bleed. If I can kill their king and put a knife in the Andalian puppet master while I'm their prisoner, just imagine what I'm going to do to them once I escape."

"Now who's overestimating themselves? No, Dear Cousin, the Babachenko will hand you over to Nero and he will deliver you to me ... and then your wife will kill you for me."

"Speaking of Isabel, I see you've taken to beating women. I mean, I knew you were a coward and a thug, but really?"

"She behaved very badly, so I punished her. There's a lesson to be learned there, Alexander. The price for peace is obedience."

"So much for the Old Law," Alexander said.

"Your precious Old Law is a relic. Times have changed and the law must change with them."

"You miss the point of it entirely," Alexander said, "The principles defined by the Old Law are timeless precisely because they are derived from our very nature. Only those who wish to abuse the life, liberty, or property of others need fear it."

"It is you who fail to understand, *I* am the rightful sovereign, and as such, the lives, liberty, and property of every single person in the Seven Isles belong to me. You are the criminal. You stole the Stone from my father's corpse and took my birthright with it. I will not rest until I get it back. I will have justice, Alexander."

"You wouldn't know justice if it hit you in the head," Alexander said, fading into the firmament.

He thought of Lacy and found himself floating over a carriage escorted by at least a hundred of Phane's soldiers, but before he could look inside, he snapped back into his body, pain flooding into him like a tidal wave.

He was convulsing, spasming from the constantly clenched muscles which were constricting his chest and nearly suffocating him. He struggled to impose order on himself, casting back to his memories of the mana fast and the trial of pain for guidance. It was an ordeal like few he'd ever endured, but he finally regained control over his body, realizing after he did that he needed to be present to manage the torment wracking his body or it would overwhelm him again.

When the Babachenko returned many hours later, left arm in a sling, Alexander was sitting on the edge of his bed. Most of the burning pain he'd suffered over the past day had subsided, leaving a raw, hollow feeling in his arms and legs. He sat calmly meditating.

He watched the Babachenko closely as his colors flowed from smug certainty through confusion, doubt, disbelief, and finally, fear.

"How's the shoulder?" Alexander said, without opening his eyes or making any move to get up.

There was a long pause, the Babachenko scrutinizing Alexander as if he were trying to comprehend what had happened during the preceding hours, yet failing for lack of some crucial piece of information.

Alexander held up the collar, still clasped shut, and tossed it through the bars without opening his eyes. The Babachenko caught it, blinking with a mixture of disbelief and incredulity. Alexander was happy to see fresh fear ripple through his colors.

"How is this possible?"

Alexander ignored him, sitting quietly, legs crossed, eyes closed as if he was deep in meditation.

"The slave collars cannot be removed without the consent of the collar's master, unless you had help. Who did this?"

Alexander chuckled softly, opening his eyes but not bothering to get up.

"I've heard rumors that you are bound to a fairy," the Babachenko said, "but I never believed them." He started casting a spell. It seemed to take a long time, his colors undulating with power, before he completed the spell and looked straight at Chloe sitting atop the cabinet, hiding in the aether.

"He can see you, Little One. Hide!"

She darted through the ceiling and out of the room, taking refuge in the small spaces where no one could follow.

"So it is true, and yet ..." he paused, frowning to himself, shaking his head. "She couldn't have passed into the cage, even in the aether; the wards would have stopped her. So how then?"

He paced for nearly a minute.

"I have a traitor in my inner sanctum," he said to himself before facing Alexander again. "They gave you the antidote to the poison as well. That's it, isn't it? It's the only explanation that makes sense."

Alexander answered with a humorless smile.

"If you think your accomplice will be here to help you tonight, you're sadly mistaken. By helping you, they've revealed themselves to me. You see, I have a very special spell that I cast in areas I wish to monitor. It creates a perfect record of everything that happens in that space—a record that I can observe any time I wish."

"Huh, I wondered what those points of light were."

The Babachenko seemed startled. "You can see them?"

"I think you'd be surprised at what I can see."

His colors shifted abruptly to greed and power lust. Again, Alexander got the feeling that the Babachenko had plans for him beyond what he'd already revealed.

After a moment of internal struggle, the Babachenko set a stone on the floor and whispered a few words. The space over the stone shimmered briefly before a perfect, albeit somewhat translucent, image of Alexander appeared. It took only a moment to realize that it was a representation of what had transpired the day before, starting with the cage door opening and Alexander killing one guard and wounding the Babachenko.

With a word, the images sped up, moving through many minutes in just seconds. Alexander thought he was past being awed by magic, but this was truly impressive, and remarkably dangerous in the hands of someone like the Babachenko.

When Alexander simply vanished from within the cage, leaving the collar clattering to the floor, the Babachenko took a sharp breath and slowed the progression of the image through time, then reversed it so he could watch more closely.

Both he and Alexander stood stock-still when they saw Alexander's body vanish, holding their breath until he reappeared a few minutes later.

Alexander's mind raced, trying to make sense of this new development of his unpredictable power. Given that he had visited Siduri, the only explanation that made any sense was that he had transitioned bodily into the firmament just as the first adept had learned to do so long ago. The implications were staggering, but the challenge of mastering such profound power seemed somehow much more formidable than anything he'd faced thus far.

"How did you do that?" the Babachenko demanded, greed and lust shining brightly in his colors.

Alexander just shrugged.

"I will have that power," the Babachenko snapped, cutting off his words, realizing only a moment too late that he'd revealed too much.

"So the stories are true," Alexander said. "I was wondering what you weren't telling me."

"If you would just cooperate, I would give you back your life, just as I promised," the Babachenko said, ignoring Alexander's words. "If you keep resisting, I will have no choice but to resort to more extreme measures."

"Like what, torture? Why don't you watch the rest of my night. You'll see that I never got an antidote for your poison—I simply endured it. But then, if you'd actually survived the mana fast, you would've known that your jellyfish venom wouldn't work."

"Nonsense," the Babachenko sputtered.

"Where's the crystal chamber?"

His eyes widened slightly and his colors swirled with fear and deceit.

"That's your plan, isn't it?" Alexander pressed. "Take my link to the firmament so you can use the lich book to become immortal, then hand me and the Stone over to Phane like a good little servant. Aren't you worried he'll figure out what you're up to? I mean, I just did. And Phane can see pretty well himself."

"He can't see within Mithel Dour any better than he can see within Glen Morillian."

"So that is your plan, then."

"You're too clever by half, Alexander, but it won't help you."

"Knowledge of your enemy never hurts."

The Babachenko started pacing.

"What's the matter? Running out of time?" Alexander asked. "Phane's expecting me soon. Do you think he'll accept your stalling for long?"

The Babachenko ignored him, but his colors gave away his anxiety. He stopped abruptly. "If reason and pain won't persuade you, perhaps you'll respond to the suffering of your friends or family."

Alexander met his eyes, holding them until the Babachenko looked away. "You wouldn't be the first to try such a depraved tactic with me, and while I don't doubt your willingness to stoop so low, I don't think you have the time. My friends and family are all very far away from here."

"Are they? We'll see about that. I find it hard to believe that you would come here alone."

"I didn't. Remember the dragon? I came with her."

"Now that was quite a surprising turn of events, I must say. But no, there are others in Mithel Dour working with you, and I will find them. And when I do, you will give me what I want."

"Until then, I think I'll take a nap," Alexander said, lying down and closing his eyes, leaving the Babachenko staring at him, helplessness swirling in his colors.

Alexander slipped into the firmament quickly, flitting across the city, finding Jack in his little house. He appeared in front of him, startling the bard while he wrote a song mourning the demise of the Andalian king.

"Alexander, I've been so worried. What's happened?"

"I'm being held prisoner in the Babachenko's residence, behind the wards. Chloe is with me and Anja has fled, hopefully all the way back to the Spires. But that's not why I came. The Babachenko is going to be looking for any of my friends so he can use them against me. He's convinced that I have allies in the city and I suspect he'll be able to figure out who you are."

"Well now, that wouldn't be good," Jack said. "I've been contracted to sing at the king's funeral so I can't just vanish without raising suspicion."

"He's pressed for time, so he'll come for you the moment he figures out who you are." Alexander said. "Funeral or not, you need to flee the city."

"What about you?"

"I'm working on that," Alexander said. "Vasili Nero, turned wraithkin, is here to transport me to Karth. I figure my best chance to escape will come once I'm out of Mithel Dour ..."

Suddenly, he snapped back into his body, gasping for breath. A soldier was just closing the door to his cage, having replaced the collar around his neck. It released its grip on his throat the moment he returned from the firmament.

Satisfied, the Babachenko left without a word, after posted two guards in the room to watch Alexander.

Chapter 26

The Babachenko returned a few hours later, pulling a chair up to the cage once again. Alexander didn't bother to get up. He'd spent the time poring over every detail his memory contained about his completely unexpected experience in the firmament with Siduri. Unfortunately, he was under duress at the time, so his memory was suspect.

He'd tested the collar by slipping into the firmament, only to find that it worked as expected, constricting his throat until he returned of his own accord or his duress drew him back … which only led him to another question: Why did he project bodily into the firmament when he was being strangled by the collar when always before he was drawn back to his body by serious physical danger?

More importantly, how could he do it again?

He was pondering these questions when the Babachenko entered.

"I've been giving this situation a lot of thought. When I met you in the slave yard, I realized immediately who you were and understood just as quickly that you had hidden the Sovereign Stone. What I didn't suspect was just how far out of reach you had placed it. Now that I know your fairy is real, it all makes perfect sense.

"I've been using all of my powers, casting every divination spell I know in an effort to locate the Stone and I've failed each and every time. Now I understand why.

"That leaves me with a dilemma. In time, I may be able to devise a means of retrieving the Stone, provided I knew precisely where it was when your fairy moved it out of this world and into the aether. Unfortunately, Nero is becoming impatient."

"Why don't you kill him?" Alexander asked, still lying on his cot. "You said yourself, Phane can't see inside Mithel Dour and you could always blame it on me."

"That thought has crossed my mind, but Nero is a wraithkin. If I missed, things would go badly."

"So don't miss," Alexander said.

"You'd like that, wouldn't you? Watching your enemies kill each other? No, I have another idea," he said, motioning to the guard at the door.

A dozen men filed in, dark and angry colors all, but Alexander didn't need to see their colors to know the truth of these men. Each had the eyes of a hardened killer—eyes dead to empathy or remorse, windows into blackened souls.

"These men are assassins," the Babachenko said. "Each is quite capable in his own right, but together they are deadly beyond measure. Give me what I want and I will send them away. Refuse, and I will send them after those you love most, starting with your sister."

Alexander started laughing, just a chuckle at first but it turned into a deep belly laugh.

"You think this is funny?" one of the assassins asked. "You won't be laughing after I get done with your sister. I hear she's something to see."

Alexander sat up and looked at each of the twelve men intently, burning their images into his mind before he stood and faced them from behind the bars of his cage.

"You are all murderers. I can see that in your eyes. A few of you have magic … not much, but enough to make the difference some of the time. Mostly what I see in you is cowardice—abject fear that people will see you for what you really are, just as I see you, and the perfect knowledge that if they did, if they truly understood the evil within each of you, they would hunt you down and kill you without mercy, just like each of you has done to so many others.

"So here's your choice, walk away now or be marked for death."

A few of the men fidgeted; all of them showed a tinge of fear mixed with indignant anger in their colors.

"You're hardly in a position to make threats," one said.

"He's just blustering," another said.

"Don't be a fool, Alexander," the Babachenko said. "None of this needs to happen. Just give me the Stone and you will be free of this war."

"Did you really think this was going to work?" Alexander asked. "Do you have any idea what Phane has already sent against me and my family? These men are nothing compared to the creatures summoned from darkness that have hunted me for the past year. In fact, Nero could kill all of these assassins by himself. Your threats are empty."

The Babachenko shook his head sadly.

"You have your contracts," he said to his assassins. "Abigail Ruatha was last known to be on Fellenden in the central city. Bring me her head and you will have your silver."

The men started to file out, but hesitated when Alexander started chuckling, several of them looking back nervously as they left the chamber.

The Babachenko looked at Alexander intently, a frown slowly creeping across his face that morphed into an expression of new understanding. His colors began to shine with hope and unexpected optimism.

"You would let our own sister die," he said, pausing to look intently at Alexander before continuing. "I see now that I was mistaken about you. I thought you were a subject pretending to be a ruler, but now I understand the truth; you truly are a noble. Had I known that, I would have made you a far different offer."

"What are you talking about?" Alexander asked.

"Oh, come now, Alexander, you understand as well as I do; there are two kinds of people in the world: subjects and nobles. Subjects are encumbered by so many imaginary concepts like empathy, remorse, and honesty. Nobles, on the other hand, are free of such limitations."

Alexander stared at him as if he'd just transformed into some unspeakable creature from the darkness.

"It's all right, Alexander, you don't have to maintain your façade with me. You and I are cut from the same cloth; we're both nobles. I see that now. And I have to say, you've constructed such a masterful story of yourself as the everyman, champion of all those delusional values that subjects hold so dear, even I was taken in. But that was my failing and you have my sincere apologies for all of this unpleasantness. Had I known the truth of you, I would have invited you to my table with open arms."

Alexander wasn't quite sure what was happening, except that the Babachenko's colors revealed as much genuine sincerity as he was probably capable of feeling.

"We could have been allies … in fact, we still can be."

"What are you saying?" Alexander asked.

"I backed the wrong horse," the Babachenko said with a helpless shrug. "Phane would rule with fear and force. As you well know, every noble must be willing to strike fear into the hearts of his subjects from time to time. But you … you are the rarest of nobles. You've crafted so masterful a lie that your subjects actually love you and believe in you.

"That kind of power can't be matched by magic or steel."

Alexander schooled his expression and held his tongue.

"I don't blame you for being skeptical, I certainly would be, especially after how I've treated you, but I'm hoping we can get past all that."

"Why would I trust you?"

The Babachenko nodded self-deprecatingly. "An hour ago, I would have made a plea to your essential humanity, I would have tried to convince you to put your people first, I would have offered to place the Lancers at your disposal and implored you to consider the myriad advantages of forging an alliance with me.

"Now that we understand each other better, I will tell you to trust me only to pursue my own best interests, just as I will trust you to do the same. As long as our interests coincide, we're natural allies. What's more, Phane will never see it coming. Together we can play him against Zuhl until both are spent and then the Seven Isles will be ours."

"And what would you expect to get out of this?"

"We both know that you have far more to offer than Phane does."

"Wizard's Dust," Alexander whispered.

"Yes," the Babachenko said almost reverently. "As you've already guessed, Acuna wizards inherit their magic from the most elderly of our order. The first Babachenko constructed a crystal chamber deep under the palace capable of stripping one wizard of his link to the firmament and conferring it upon another. The process is arduous and dangerous, requiring substantial training and mental conditioning prior to the transference, but it has allowed the Acuna to retain power over the centuries, in spite of the fact that not a single cache of Wizard's Dust has been found on Andalia for over a millennium.

"While the crystal chamber has allowed our order to survive, our numbers have only diminished. In fact, my alliance with Phane has been quite costly in that regard. You see, most of the wizards he sent against you were from my order, so every time you killed one of them, you permanently reduced our number."

"And after Phane and Zuhl are defeated?" Alexander asked, filing the Babachenko's words away for further thought.

"In exchange for my allegiance, you would name me governor of Andalia, Karth, and Tyr, quite a reasonable price for undisputed mastery over all the Seven Isles."

"Your offer would seem far more sincere if it wasn't coming through the bars of a cage," Alexander said.

"Indeed, but men in our positions can't be too careful. After all, you did try to kill me yesterday."

"I suppose that's fair," Alexander said, pacing for a few moments, deep in thought. "If this alliance is going to work, I'll need a few things from you, starting with the recall of your assassins."

The Babachenko chuckled again almost wistfully. "Of course, of course … my mentor, the previous Babachenko, taught me many things, but the most important lesson of all was this: Any man will be reasonable and accommodating if you simply figure out what he really wants and find a way to give it to him."

"Words of wisdom," Alexander said.

"I think we finally understand each other, Alexander, or should I call you Lord Reishi?"

"Only in public," Alexander said.

"Of course," the Babachenko said, chuckling. "I've always found titles cumbersome. Consider the contract on your sister cancelled. Now, we should discuss tactics, since we still have Nero to deal with and it wouldn't do for him to learn of our alliance."

"Agreed," Alexander said. "In fact, it's probably best if I stay in this cage until we figure out how to manage him."

"You don't really trust him, do you, My Love?" Chloe asked in his mind.

"Not for a second, Little One, but his colors are sincere, so either his offer's genuine or he's figured out how to lie with his colors. Either way, this is an opportunity I can't afford to pass up."

The Babachenko continued, "I'm glad you suggested that. I feel it's necessary but was hesitant to bring it up."

"I could do without the collar though," Alexander said, tapping the thin metal ring around his neck.

The Babachenko smiled tightly, pausing just a moment too long before nodding, a faint ripple of uncertainty flickering through his colors. He touched his ring and the collar popped open with a click.

"Thank you," Alexander said, setting the collar on the bed and rubbing his neck. "Those things chafe."

"I imagine they do. Shall we discuss Nero?"

"We should kill him," Alexander said with an offhanded shrug. "Also, we should put an end to the fighting in Ruatha as quickly as possible; we're going to need those troops before this is over."

"I'll see to the Ruatha situation at once. As for Nero, while I understand the appeal of his demise, he is a dangerous enemy. A single misstep could be … ruinous."

"Give me a sword and call him in here."

The Babachenko slowly shook his head in near disbelief. "That would be suicide. He would kill us both."

"You don't have to be here when he arrives. You can leave as soon as you send for him; that way, if he kills me, you can claim ignorance."

"It's most gracious of you to think of my interests, but I would be remiss as an ally if I allowed you to take such an unnecessary risk. Surely, there must be another way."

"I'm open to suggestions," Alexander said with his hands held wide.

"Perhaps a ruse? We could tell him that you escaped. Send him to track you. When he returns empty-handed, we can always blame him for failing to apprehend you."

"Nero is a suspicious one," Alexander said, shaking his head. "He'll start his search right here and there's nowhere in this palace that he can't get to."

They both fell silent for a moment.

"We tell him that you're playing me to buy some time," Alexander said, schooling his expression.

"I don't understand."

"Tell Nero that you offered me an alliance to gain my trust and you need more time to get the Stone."

The Babachenko blinked, pausing for several moments. "He would certainly believe that," he said, swallowing involuntarily.

"It's what he wants to believe," Alexander said.

"He will expect swift action to recover the Sovereign Stone."

"We'll leave at dawn," Alexander said, nodding agreement.

"That ... that certainly is swift. Are you sure about this? Perhaps we should assemble a task force to accompany you. There are many stakeholders in Mithel Dour and they must be accommodated. Several factions will wish to send personal representatives on such an historic undertaking. Perhaps three days would make for a more prepared venture."

"If you insist, but I thought speed would be more desirable. The sooner we get the Stone, the sooner we can start building an army of wizards. I would much prefer a lightning fast ride that brings us back to the safety of Mithel Dour as quickly as possible. Your city is perfectly suited to our purposes since Phane can't see within. He won't know what we're doing until it's far too late for him to counter us.

"But all of that absolutely depends on secrecy, and you can't trust a large group of people with a secret ... ever."

"Your logic is irrefutable," the Babachenko said. "I will see to the arrangements." He started to get up, his colors steady and genuine.

"If we're going to make it look like I believe we're allies, I'm going to need nicer accommodations ... and a sword."

The Babachenko twitched ever so slightly.

***

Alexander wanted to laugh when the door closed behind him. The chambers were nothing short of palatial—guest quarters fit for a king with plenty of servants hovering around and guards at every entrance.

He had finally retired for the night, bolting the door behind himself and leaning his sword up against the nightstand. He drew a magic circle on the floor with a piece of charred wood from the hearth and sat down to meditate. The firmament came almost spontaneously.

He appeared in front of Jack, who was sitting at a table in an entirely different house than his public residence. He was writing by lamplight.

"Oh ... you startled me, again."

"Sorry ... weren't you supposed to be leaving town?"

"You suggested that; I was never convinced that leaving town without you was a good idea. Besides, I got word that we're expecting guests."

"Jataan?"

"Yes, but there's more. Anja is with them and she's back to being a girl again."

Alexander snorted, shaking his head. "She's persistent, I'll give her that. How far out are they?"

"A few days."

"Not soon enough," Alexander said. "I need you to get two fast horses and leave town right now. Get to Jataan as quickly as possible, then head for the Stone. I'll let him know you're coming."

"What's happened?"

"The Babachenko and I are tangled in a web of lies—we're both playing the other and we both know it."

"So, politics then," Jack said.

"Right up until one of us has the chance to strike, then it's back to war. We're leaving tomorrow morning to recover the Stone. I expect my escort will be highly dangerous."

"I'll leave at once," Jack said, gathering his notebook and quill.

"Chloe will find you when we get close," Alexander said, vanishing from his room and reappearing a moment later in the middle of the road leading from the western province to Mithel Dour. Jataan, Anja, and Lita reined in the giant Rhone steeds each was riding, stopping a few feet before him.

"Lord Reishi," Jataan said, nodding deferentially.

"I got help," Anja said.

"I see that," Alexander said. "I also see that you managed to become a girl again."

"I got help with that, too," she said with an impudent shrug. "You didn't really think I was going to leave you there, did you?"

"You'd be safer if you'd gone home."

"I know."

"Commander, Jack is coming to you and I won't be far behind him. Hold here until he arrives. He knows where you'll be going. Marshal what forces you can but stay out of sight until you hear from me."

"Understood, Lord Reishi."

"No, it's not," Anja said. "Why aren't we coming to get you?"

"Politics," Alexander said, fading out of sight and returning to his body. He slept like the dead, waking with a thousand questions swirling in his mind. A few moments after he woke, servants descended on him, sweeping him up and whisking him smoothly through a hasty morning routine that ultimately deposited him on the battlements of the palace with a small group of very dangerous men all standing behind the Babachenko.

"I'm afraid I have some troubling news to report," the Babachenko said. "Titus Grant has escaped our custody, along with his wife. The High Overseer is handling the matter himself, so I expect a quick resolution."

"I see," Alexander said, looking off the battlement into the distance for several moments. When the Babachenko started to fidget, Alexander nodded to himself.

"Perhaps this is an opportunity. Grant has his own agenda, to be sure, but he also has a well-funded organization. If we knew what he was planning, maybe we could mislead him into serving our interests."

"An excellent suggestion, Lord Reishi. I'll make the arrangements," the Babachenko said.

Alexander stepped up close. The Babachenko tensed almost imperceptibly, another faint shimmer of fear lighting up his colors.

"Making your enemy do your bidding is the sweetest part of power, don't you think?" he whispered, stepping past him to survey the men assembled as his escort.

"Perhaps introductions are in order," he said, casually.

"Of course, Lord Reishi," the Babachenko said, spinning quickly and stepping up on his right. "Your party is comprised of our very best: Lord Protector Kagosi, Royal Assassin Yasim, and Chief Overseers Bahar and Jago. A dozen Lancers will accompany you as well."

The Babachenko's colors may have been less than useful lately, but these men couldn't hide their essential nature. The Babachenko would describe them as nobles, but their colors were anything but.

"Excellent, I trust that you gentlemen understand what's at stake," Alexander said. "We must not fail and we must not delay. Lord Protector, take me to my steed."

The big battle-scarred Acuna mage nodded slowly. "By your command, Lord Reishi."

Alexander ignored the rest of the party as if they were beneath him, even though he knew that all four of these men were deadly in the extreme. The Lancers waiting for them at the base of the cliff had two rhone for each man and they'd also sent word ahead to Lancer outposts along the way to have fresh steeds ready. It wasn't long before they were out on the open road riding toward the western province with all possible haste.

Alexander would have preferred a horse, but no aspiring emperor of the world would choose an inferior steed, even if it would have been faster. While they rode, he mused about how cumbersome it was to live in a web of lies.

The rhone were powerful but lacked the endurance of horses, so the party had to stop to switch steeds frequently, arriving at a small Lancer outpost just before dark. It was little more than a stone wall surrounding a courtyard and a tower, but it housed a platoon of Lancers and plenty of spare rhone.

Alexander pretended to inspect the fortifications, the Lord Protector trailing behind him everywhere he went. He wound up on top of the tower with a very nervous watchman. Alexander looked out into the night, picking out the black, inky colors of Vasili Nero hiding in the shadows not far from camp. Farther out, just at the edge of his all around sight, were the telltale smudges of color that represented two groups of men camped at a good distance from each other, each following Alexander and his escort.

"Lord Protector Kagosi, I trust you're aware that we're being followed," Alexander said without turning.

He hesitated, uncertainty and guile swirling in his colors. "Yes, Lord Reishi. The Babachenko sent a reserve force to trail us."

"A wise precaution, but that doesn't account for the second party," Alexander said.

Kagosi seemed genuinely surprised. "I was not aware of a second party. Are you certain?" he asked, stepping up next to Alexander and peering into the night.

Alexander pointed in the direction of the enemy encampment. "Half a league."

"I'll send scouts at once," Kagosi said, turning on his heel and marching down the tower stairs. A few minutes later, two teams of three Lancers each thundered into the night.

"About as subtle as a battering ram," Alexander thought to Chloe.

"Who do you think the other group is?"

"Probably Tyr ... could be Grant; it's hard to say."

Kagosi returned to the tower, taking his place watching Alexander under the pretext of guarding him.

"Our following force has been ordered to engage the enemy and route them."

"Excellent," Alexander said, heading down the tower to his tent. He noted the four men standing guard, as well as Royal Assassin Yasim, who was sitting in a chair beside the entrance. Yasim stood, nodding almost imperceptibly. Alexander ignored them all and went to bed.

He woke in the night and slipped out of his tent, tapping Yasim on the shoulder, drawing his attention with a start. Alexander held a finger across his lips. Yasim nodded.

"Nero is just outside the camp," Alexander whispered. "I'm going to kill him, and I want you to come with me."

Yasim did an admirable job of schooling his expression, but his colors were another matter: fear, uncertainty, confused loyalties. After a brief internal struggle, he nodded once, then spoke with the guards, instructing them to hold their position as if Alexander was still in the tent.

Yasim motioned for silence as they approached the gate guard. After a whispered conversation, the guard slowly and quietly opened the gate just enough for Alexander and Yasim to slip out. A quarter moon, low in the sky, provided scant illumination. Alexander moved slowly toward Nero's position, while watching Yasim closely.

The Royal Assassin seemed distracted until Nero stepped out from behind a boulder thirty feet away.

"So now what, Pretender? You may have fooled these idiots, but I know better."

Alexander drew his sword.

"Oh, would that I could kill you now, but Master would be most displeased … him on the other hand …" Nero vanished, reappearing twenty feet closer, long black knife drawn.

"Back to back," Alexander shouted to Yasim. The assassin obeyed, dagger in hand.

Alexander stretched out with his mind into the coming seconds, spinning at the last possible moment, pushing Yasim aside and thrusting into Nero's head. His blade fell on Nero's helmet, glancing aside, knocking Nero back but doing little damage. The wraithkin vanished again.

Yasim seemed to disappear into the shadows even as Alexander heard him scramble to his feet. Alexander spun, slicing at neck height and catching Nero with just the last inch of steel across his throat the moment he materialized. His eyes went wide and he vanished again, this time twenty feet away. When he materialized again, he was running toward the west.

Yasim seemed to step out of the shadows. "You saved me," he said.

"Or I used you as bait," Alexander said, "it all depends on your perspective."

Yasim cocked his head, regarding Alexander intently, a smile slowly spreading across his face. "Your gambit nearly worked. A bold attempt."

Alexander wiped the blood from the slightly blunted tip of his sword and nodded to himself. "Nearly."

Sounds of rhone in the distance filtered through the night.

"The Lord Protector has become aware of your absence," Yasim said.

A few minutes later, they were quickly surrounded by Lancers.

The Lord Protector pushed into the circle and confronted Alexander. "Explain yourself!" he demanded.

Alexander regarded him coolly for several moments. "Lord Protector, I would be happy to brief you on the failings of your security, but not here. Give me a steed."

The Lord Protector took a deep breath and let it out slowly before snapping at the nearest Lancer to surrender his mount.

They returned to the keep where Alexander recounted the fight with Nero. After Yasim supported his account, Alexander left without a word and went back to his tent, wondering where Nero had gone and when he was going to show up again.

The next morning brought rain and a decidedly different kind of treatment from the Lancers and even the more elite members of his escort. Alexander surmised that an account of the fight with Nero had filtered through the barracks, because most of the junior Lancers wouldn't look him in the eye when he passed. They were afraid.

Once they were on the road again, the day passed without incident. Very few were foolish enough to attack a unit of Lancers out in the open.

The second night brought them to another fortification: ten-foot log walls with a well-spiked berm before it and a shallow moat filled with oil-soaked hay ten feet in front of that. Twenty-foot towers rose from each corner and the whole courtyard was a common space shared by livestock and people alike. It stunk.

Alexander took his meal to his tent, quietly drawing a magic circle after he'd finished eating. He slipped into the firmament moments later and appeared before Jataan, Lita, Anja, and Jack, who were all sitting around a small fire in the forest.

"Lord Reishi," Jataan said, standing.

"We're two days from the big meadow," Alexander said. "Here's my plan ..."

Chapter 27

The last leg of their journey across the plains brought them to the slaver camp at the edge of the western province where Alexander had been brought after he was captured in the forest. The place had been largely transformed into a well-fortified forward operating base for the Lancers working to put down the local resistance.

Despite their rhone steeds and force lances, or perhaps because of them, they were having very little success against the people who'd chosen to stay and fight for their homes. Alexander could see poor morale in the Lancers' colors everywhere he looked.

Commander Udane led Alexander and his escort across a muddy courtyard and into a wooden building, which had been hastily made from rough-cut lumber but looked sturdy enough. They went upstairs to the war room, a conference area with maps and rosters pinned to the walls and littering the large, central table.

Udane unrolled a map in the middle of the table, setting weights on each corner to keep it from rolling back up. He pointed at a mark and said, "We're here."

Alexander pointed to the big meadow and said, "We need to go here."

Kagosi and Yasim shared a quick glance.

"A day's travel through dangerous territory," Udane said. "I don't recommend it."

"Your recommendation isn't required, Commander," Alexander said, "but your assistance is. I will expect an escort capable of meeting any challenge we might find along the way. Have the men ready to leave in the morning. Where are my chambers?"

Udane looked to the Lord Protector before nodding curtly to Alexander. "If you'll follow me, Lord Reishi, I'll show you to your quarters."

Once there, Alexander dismissed Udane with a gesture and bolted the door, scanning the room for anything out of the ordinary. The closer they got to the Stone, the thinner the veil of lies wore. His escort team had never been able to hide their colors, but even their forced deference was beginning to erode. Alexander rubbed his neck where the collar had chafed him.

Moments after he lay down for the night, an alarm horn blew. When he opened his door, he found Yasim standing there.

"What's happening?"

"An unknown force approaches."

Alexander headed for the battlements, trailing Yasim behind him.

He found the Lord Protector on the northeastern tower. He was in the midst of casting a spell. Alexander looked out into the night, seeing a dozen men hiding in the shadows near the walls.

Shards of reddish force began appearing over the Lord Protector's head; each held its initial position for the count of a heartbeat before darting off into the night toward the men probing the camp's defenses. At first, a shard appeared every second or so, then two, then five, then ten at a time, all streaking toward the target area, ripping into anyone caught in the open. The barrage lasted for nearly a minute, sending hundreds of deadly magical blades at the enemy, tearing into the ground and stones, littering the area with mutilated corpses. Alexander saw two men flee into the night after the terrifying spell had run its course.

He'd wondered about the Lord Protector's calling. A force mage was formidable ... Alexander regarded him with renewed caution.

"Do we know who they were?"

"Not yet, Lord Reishi," Kagosi said. "Our men will investigate their remains and report."

"Well done," Alexander said, walking away before he had a chance to respond. He suspected either Tyr or Grant was behind the probing attack and decided that it didn't matter much, considering how forcefully the Lord Protector had repelled their advance. Another frontal assault was highly unlikely.

The warning horn blew again just before dawn. Again, Alexander found the Lord Protector on the northeastern tower.

"Report," Alexander said.

"We estimate a force of five hundred skirting our position and entering the forest on foot."

"Any idea who they are?"

"Brigands and bandits," Kagosi said. "The ones I killed last night were known associates of Nightshade."

"Interesting," Alexander said.

They set out at first light with the bulk of Udane's forces riding escort, two hundred Lancers, leaving a minimal guard force in the base camp. Kagosi and Yasim were becoming more anxious by the hour, but Alexander was getting calmer and more centered. The time for battle would arrive soon enough.

The Lancers seemed nervous as they wound through the forest on well-worn trails that, nevertheless, confined and constricted their ability to move and charge.

Alexander pulled up next to Udane. "Doesn't seem like the best terrain for Lancers to operate in," he said, off-handedly.

"It's not," Udane said. "If it were up to me, we'd burn the entire forest to the ground. See how well the resistance does against us out in the open."

"You could change your tactics," Alexander said.

"What do you mean?" Udane asked.

"Wear lighter armor, go in on foot, and learn to use a bow," Alexander said.

"We're Lancers," Udane said, spurring his rhone ahead.

They reached the meadow just after sundown, setting up camp in the rapidly encroaching darkness.

"We should discuss our plans for tomorrow," the Lord Protector said.

"It's simple enough," Alexander said. "We go search around the forest until I find the place where I hid the Sovereign Stone."

"Commander Udane has expressed serious security concerns," Kagosi said. "Perhaps it would be best to send Lancers to retrieve the Stone, so that your safety will not be compromised."

"I'll have a hard enough time finding the spot myself … there's no way your men would be able to find it without me. I have to go myself."

"As you wish, Lord Reishi," Kagosi said.

That evening, Alexander noticed that the security force around his tent had doubled. Now that they were getting close, the Andalians were getting nervous. Yasim nodded ever so slightly to Alexander when he entered his tent.

"Are you ready, Little One?"

"Yes, My Love."

"Jack should be waiting for you."

"I'll be back soon."

Alexander linked his mind with Chloe, watching through her eyes as she flitted through the aether, passing right through the trees of the forest. She flew with unerring precision, following a straight path between Alexander and the Sovereign Stone, and found Jack at the prearranged spot, covering a broken and rotting tree stump with his body and hidden by his magical cloak.

"Whoa!" Jack whispered when Chloe materialized inside the tree trunk, bringing the Sovereign Stone and Alexander's pouch with her in a dazzling flash of light. "You certainly know how to make an entrance, My Lady."

"Be careful, Jack," she said. "Everyone in the world is looking for this."

"Tell Alexander that everything's in place," Jack said, slipping the Sovereign Stone into the pouch and securing the pouch to a lanyard he wore under his armor.

"I will," Chloe said, flying up and kissing him on the cheek. "For luck," she said before vanishing in a ball of light. Jack adjusted his cloak and started moving through the forest.

Alexander gently disentangled his mind from Chloe's and lay back on his bed. Much would be decided in the coming hours, but for now all he could do was wait.

He woke with a start, not even remembering dozing off. The warning horn blew again. He reached out with his all around sight and took in the camp springing to life in preparation to meet an attack. He breathed a sigh of relief and pulled on his boots. Yasim was waiting for him at the door to his tent, as expected.

"Report."

"The force that entered the forest ahead of us is moving into position for a dawn attack from the north," Yasim said.

"They seem very determined for bandits," Alexander said. "How confident are the Lancers in the outcome of a battle?"

"Very … though I doubt it will come to that," Yasim said. "If everyone is smart, the Lancers will not go into the forest and the bandits will not come into the meadow."

"Stalemate … until I go looking for the Stone."

"Yes," Yasim said.

Shouts came from another direction, toward the little valley where Alexander had been ambushed and where the Stone had been hidden. He smiled when he saw Tyr leading a small band of men up to a Lancer guard post.

"He's certainly persistent," Alexander said.

"Perhaps too much so," Yasim said, looking to the Lord Protector for instruction. The look he got back said it all.

"I will return shortly," Yasim said. Alexander moved to get a better view, two over-armored guards trailing behind him.

As the Royal Assassin approached Tyr, the shadows around him began to coalesce into something more substantial, forming into two small flying creatures that looked almost like dragons, wing and claw and fang. Both darted out, closing the gap between him and Tyr with alarming speed, ripping into Tyr with soundless ferocity, yet falling on empty air. Tyr and Edric both vanished, their projections interrupted by the attack. Failing to draw blood on their first attempt, the two creatures turned to the four men escorting Tyr, tearing into them with such sudden viciousness that Alexander actually felt a little flutter of fear in his stomach. The four men died screaming. Their horses bolted, but not quickly enough to survive the onslaught.

The shadows vanished, and Yasim ordered Lancers to search for Tyr and his men, but before they were ready to leave, a flare of orange fire streaked into the sky from the west side of the big meadow and hundreds of men answered the signal at the top of their lungs.

"It seems that Tyr has assembled a substantial force as well," Yasim said, returning to Alexander.

"Nightshade to the north and Tyr to the west," Alexander said.

The Lord Protector stomped up. "I hope you know where you're going," he said to Alexander. "We can hold this position for as long as we want, but I can't guarantee your safety within the forest."

"It's close ... within an hour's walk due west," Alexander said.

"Tyr's men are dug in that way," Kagosi said.

"Well ... that's where we have to go," Alexander said.

The sky was just starting to lighten when Alexander saw Jack moving ever so cautiously through the camp. Alexander turned to conceal his cloak pocket from his guards.

"The Lancers are at a disadvantage in the forest," Kagosi said.

Jack got closer.

"That's where the Stone is," Alexander said with a shrug.

Jack slipped the pouch containing the Sovereign Stone into Alexander's pocket, then backed away slowly and quietly, fading into the morning shadows.

Alexander felt a little thrill of victory ... now for the escape.

"We're very close, Lord Protector Kagosi," he said. "Now is not the time to falter."

"We'll lose a lot of Lancers," Kagosi said.

"I believe you're right," Alexander said, without a hint of sympathy. He was discovering what a window it was into the minds of his enemies to pretend to be one of them. Trying to see things from their perspective was a challenge, but the insight it offered was invaluable … and frightening.

"By your order, Lord Reishi," Kagosi said, turning on his heel and stomping away.

As light broke over the treetops, a great battle cry went up from the north.

"Looks like the brigands have decided our course for us," Yasim said. "Come, you will be safer in the command tent."

Alexander followed, his eyes to the sky. Yasim led him to a large tent on the highest hill in the meadow, which was only five or six feet higher than the surrounding area.

A volley of arrows rained out of the trees, most bouncing harmlessly off the Lancers' armor and shields, but a few finding flesh. The Lancers withdrew out of bow range and the bandits fell back into the forest.

Soon the entire camp was up and mounted; some squads lined up on the perimeter while others positioned themselves to respond to any incursion with a charge. Whatever else they were, the Lancers were well-trained heavy cavalry.

One squad unleashed their force lances into the tall grass bordering the tree line, blasting three men who were trying to sneak into the camp. So far, the enemy to the north was just probing. Tyr's small army let out another battle cry. The jungle went very silent for a few moments, and then nine six-inch-diameter bubbles of liquid fire arched over the trees and splashed randomly into the camp, sowing seeds of panic and confusion.

When they were splashed with fire, several rhone raced off into the river, others fled into the trees. Tyr's forces attacked into that moment of confusion, racing into camp through the few perimeter guards still standing their post. One of the reaction forces blasted two men so hard they landed forty feet away in a jumble of broken bones. Tyr's men ignored the perimeter guards, slipping between them, turning the camp into a melee with most of the Lancers doing everything they could to remain mounted and stay in groups. When they could bring their lances to bear, the result was devastating, but that became harder and harder as Tyr's pirates moved into their midst, cutting at their legs, then dashing away to strike at other targets.

A horn blew, calling for the Lancers to fall back and consolidate forces. Over their heads, Kagosi launched a spinning ball of force shards three feet across. It hit in the middle of Tyr's advance force and exploded, sending magical blades in every direction, flaying flesh from everyone nearby and leaving a patch of blood and carnage where dozens of men had stood only moments before.

The bandits from the north attacked en masse, using the distraction of Tyr's probe to gain a few steps toward the guards before loosing their arrows. Two Lancers fell. The rest charged, blasting the row of archers back into the dirt. A second row of archers sprang up from their hiding places inside the tree line and loosed several volleys of arrows in rapid succession at the exposed guards, bringing them all down and wounding their rhone.

Men poured over the ridgeline, charging into the meadow through the gap they'd opened in the Lancers' line. The van met a force-lance charge that washed them away like smoke on a breeze, but the second wave was on the Lancers before their force lances could fire again, dragging them off their rhone and stabbing them to death.

The Lord Protector faced their front and began casting another spell, lobbing grapefruit-sized orbs of red force, one after the other, into the tree line. Each orb exploded on impact, sending the attacking bandits flying with each hit. It wasn't long before they withdrew, but not before they'd killed over a dozen Lancers.

"We're losing men," the Lord Protector said. "Tell me where the Stone is and I will send a platoon of Lancers to retrieve it."

"No, I have to go myself," Alexander said. "It's the only way."

"You'll get us all killed."

Alexander shrugged indifferently.

Kagosi worked through his emotions, his colors roiling.

"Udane, make ready to move into the forest," Kagosi snapped.

"Surely, you're not serious," Udane said.

"Follow my orders, Commander, or I'll find someone who will."

Udane shot Alexander a quick glare before throwing himself into command, shouting orders for the nearest Lancers to make ready to ride.

Tyr's forces had withdrawn into the trees, shouting taunts at the Lancers while consolidating their forces along the trail leading west. The Lancers fell back to a smaller defensive perimeter around the command tent and held their ground.

Alexander smiled to himself when he saw Nero appear on the south side of the meadow. When a Lancer shouted a warning of his presence, the wraithkin vanished, appearing twenty feet closer, disappearing again almost before he'd even materialized, then again, past the protective cordon of Lancers … blink … Alexander drew his sword … blink … Nero was standing among Alexander's escort atop the little hill, but still a good ten feet away from him.

"Aren't you early?" Alexander asked. "I thought you'd wait until after I retrieved the Stone."

"You're surrounded, Pretender," Nero said. "The ruse is over. Surrender your weapon."

"Come and get it."

"Lord Protector!" Udane shouted, pointing to the northern wood line and the hundreds of brigands charging toward the Lancer perimeter.

Not to be outdone, Tyr's forces gave a battle cry and charged into the meadow a few moments later. Alexander lunged toward Nero, but the wraithkin vanished, quickly extracting himself from the battlefield and vanishing into the forest to the south.

"Countercharge!" Udane shouted.

Two squads broke off from the defensive perimeter, charging to meet each attack. The strategy was a success against the first line, but the Lancers were vulnerable to arrows once they turned to regroup with the main force, several rhone returning without their riders.

A few moments of relative calm settled on the meadow while both forces closed the distance to the Lancers' final protective line. Alexander surveyed the battlefield and decided that everyone was fair game. Nightshade's brigands were thieves come to abduct him for ransom, Tyr was a thug, the Acuna was a crime syndicate, Nero was touched by darkness, and the Lancers served to prop up a government that had turned corruption into an art form.

Literally everyone on the battlefield was his enemy—and a few of them were definitely worth killing.

"Shield!" the Lord Protector shouted. The two chief overseers, quiet, yet ever-present, positioned themselves around the command tent to form a triangle with the Lord Protector. Several seconds of chanting by the three of them created a bubble of force over the entire Lancer contingent.

"Mount up," the Lord Protector snapped. "Form a column facing east."

Arrows began to pelt against the shield, causing ripples in the reddish-tinged magical shell.

"Don't you mean west?" Alexander said.

"This expedition is over," Kagosi snapped. "We'll be lucky to survive the day. We have to flee … now!"

Alexander shook his head in disgust, spitting at Kagosi's feet. "Coward."

Anger flared in Kagosi's colors. He stepped in close to Alexander. "Nero was right about one thing, the ruse is over, Pretender. Seize him!"

There was a second of hesitation, a moment while the nearest two Lancers struggled to make sense of the order. Standing face-to-face with the Lord Protector, Alexander brought his blade up along Kagosi's body, under his arm, slicing his armpit to the bone. The Lord Protector fell back in shock. The shield faltered, flickering for a moment before failing entirely. A barrage of arrows and stones suddenly began pelting them from two sides.

A dismounted Lancer attacked Alexander with his longsword, but the heavily armored man was slow and clumsy, bringing the blade down in a massive stroke. Alexander sidestepped, letting the blade hit the ground before kicking the man over and turning back to the Lord Protector, whose arm was nearly severed at the shoulder and bleeding profusely.

"Please don't kill me," he said weakly, struggling to remain on one knee.

"Too late," Alexander said, finishing him with a quick stab through the left eye socket, then spinning in response to a sense of moments to come, blocking the Royal Assassin's dagger an instant before it would have plunged into his back. He counterthrust, but his blade turned aside, a flicker of color registering on impact with Yasim's magical defenses. The Royal Assassin backed away, commanding two nearby Lancers to attack from behind. Alexander took in Yasim's dagger, dark and dangerous, powerfully enchanted. He took in the two soldiers moving to flank him. And he took in the crush of enemy about to engulf the Lancers from two sides … and he waited.

He waited for his enemy to act, to commit. In that moment, he had power like no other. Chief Overseer Bahar launched a spell into the coming throng, an arc of red-hot lightning hit the nearest bandit in the chest, coring him out in a ball of molten flame, then leaping to the next two closest men, doubling again and then again, killing thirteen people with startling quickness.

The brigands faltered for only a moment, taking force-lance blasts and getting back up, until they were close enough to pull the Lancers from their steeds.

One of the soldiers behind Alexander attacked, thrusting toward his leg, but he slipped sideways just enough for the blade to go wide and plunge into the dirt, then he swept his blade up, taking the soldier's head, quickly catching the man's body with his left hand while slipping to the side and pushing the corpse into another soldier coming for him.

"There's still time to run away, Yasim."

"If there's time to run away, then there's time to kill you," the Royal Assassin said, leveling his hand at Alexander. Cold, numbing weakness gripped him, bringing him to his knees. He dropped his sword from lack of strength. Yasim smiled, seeming to absorb the strength that Alexander was losing.

Alexander saw it coming well before any of his enemies did, but only because he was looking for it, hoping that it would come soon. He heard a shout, half warning, half fear ... then another, followed by several more. Yasim's spell faltered when he saw it. Alexander's strength returned quickly and he staggered to his feet.

The wyvern landed lightly with one foot on the ground, carefully gripping Alexander with the other and launching into the sky amid shouts of sudden confusion and anger from the Lancers and the Acuna, followed by a renewed battle frenzy with all sides fighting savagely for survival.

While certainly not comfortable, the ride wasn't entirely unpleasant, lasting only a few minutes before the wyvern landed gently and set Alexander on the ground in a clearing filled with seven other wyverns, as well as his friends.

"Lord Reishi," Jataan said.

"Well done," Alexander said.

Jataan nodded deferentially. Alexander gave him an affectionate pat on the shoulder, then smiled at the Sky Knight.

"I'm Kiera, witch, Sky Knight, and now a member of your elite guard," she said proudly, after sliding to the ground. She was tall and lanky, thin but wiry, with fiery red hair and sharp features.

"Thank you for the rescue," Alexander said. "I'm glad you were able to pull it off without taking a hit."

"You're welcome," she said, patting her wyvern's knee. "I never had any doubt."

"Outstanding," Alexander said, turning back to Jataan. "Are we ready?"

"Yes, Lord Reishi."

Alexander dumped the Sovereign Stone out of the little pouch into his hand. It pulsed with a soft red light. He put it around his neck, then opened the door to his Wizard's Den, his friends following him inside.

"You'll be needing this," Jack said, holding up the dragon-scale shirt.

"Thanks for looking after it for me." Alexander said, taking it with a smile.

"Truth be told, it probably took better care of me than I did of it."

"I know what you mean," Alexander said, taking off his tunic and donning his armor. He started to strap his throwing knife to his belt when Jataan deliberately cleared his throat.

"Mage Gamaliel sends gifts," he said, presenting a staff in one hand and a dagger in the other.

"Luminessence," Jataan said, holding up the staff, "was fashioned from the vitalwood and is imbued with powerful light-focused magic.

"Demonrend," he said, holding up the dagger, "was fashioned from the steel of a fallen star and enchanted to banish any demon with a single hit. The Guild Mage bids you use them well."

Alexander took Demonrend, feeling its weight and admiring its perfect balance. It was an ideal blade for a close knife fight, but it was also balanced to be thrown. He strapped it to his belt along the small of his back.

Luminessence felt warm to the touch, seeming to come to life in his hands, beginning to glow a few moments after he grasped it. The more he poured his will into it, the brighter it got, filling the Wizard's Den with brilliance, then more, yet without ever blinding any of them. Alexander felt a connection to the staff begin to form. He willed the light brighter still, staring straight at it without harm or even discomfort, drinking in the light as if it were nourishment, then willing the light to subside.

"That was impressive," Jack said.

Jataan nodded, frowning slightly. "I should have been blinded by such light, and yet I could see more clearly than ever."

Anja and Lita nodded silently.

The staff was stout, just over an inch in diameter, six feet long, shod in four inches of silver on each end. The entire surface was carved with elaborately combined magical symbols. Its colors screamed of power and light. When Alexander willed it to produce dim light, the top shod began to glow softly, then winked out with a thought. It was as if the staff had become an extension of his body, sensing his will and obeying his thoughts as quickly as one's hand moves by command of one's mind.

"For the moment, I think I'll leave Luminessence right here," Alexander said, leaning it against the doorframe and stepping out into the night.

"Be ready," he said, facing his friends in the Wizard's Den. "There's no telling what will be waiting for you when I open this door."

"We'll be ready," Jataan said.

Alexander nodded. "Is everything else in place?"

"Yes, by morning the forward operating base will be burned to the ground and what remains of the Lancer contingent will take heavy casualties from our militia ambushes."

"Excellent," he said, closing the door and mounting up behind Kiera. After she helped him lace in, she prodded her wyvern into a roar, signaling the launch command. Eight Sky Knights took to wing, gaining altitude slowly as they floated east toward Mithel Dour.

Chapter 28

Isabel drifted into awareness shrouded in a cocoon of distant pain, recoiling into the sanctuary of oblivion again and again before gaining enough sense of herself to hang on to consciousness. She was in a bed. Other people were in the room, but she couldn't see them. A moment of panic seized her, flooding into every part of her body.

Was she blind?

Her hands came up involuntarily, sending a wave of pain through her body, but revealing that her eyes were bandaged.

"Ah, she lives," Phane said.

It all came back to her at once. She was free of the constant nightmare induced by Azugorath while she'd been unconscious, but she was still Phane's prisoner ... and ... she had managed to resist the Wraith Queen—no small thing. Phane had beaten her for breaking his mirror. She tried to smile but could only manage a wince.

"Take off her bandage," Phane said.

Gentle hands began unwrapping the bandage around her head. She let them work. The light was painful, but she could see, at least as much as the swelling around her eyes would permit. Her face felt bruised and battered.

Dierdra looked at Isabel's face and eyes, examining her injuries before nodding to herself with a sigh of relief.

"She'll mend, Prince Phane," she said, bowing out of the way.

Phane sat down on the edge of the bed, smiling at Isabel as if he were genuinely relieved that she was recovering from the beating he'd given her.

"I knew you'd pull through," he said. "Never doubted it."

"Glad to hear it," Isabel said, thickly.

"You just rest now. Your friends will be along in a few days; we'll talk again then," Phane said, patting her on the leg with a cold smile before strolling out of the room, leaving her in Dierdra's care.

Isabel mostly slept for the next two days, waking only long enough to eat or drink before going back to bed, and then never fully waking. She tried to focus her mind on the light within, working to penetrate the veil of darkness cast across it by Azugorath, but she failed with every attempt. The harder she pushed, the more the Wraith Queen resisted her efforts.

She woke groggy, but with renewed strength, carefully easing out of bed and gently stretching her stiff muscles.

"You shouldn't be out of bed, My Lady," Dierdra said, hurrying through the service entrance.

"I'm hungry ... something with substance," Isabel said, easing back onto the bed.

"Yes, My Lady."

Dierdra returned a few minutes later with a tray of food: stew, bread, cheese, and vegetables.

Isabel started easy with a few spoonfuls of the stew's gravy to wake her belly, but before long, she'd nearly cleaned the platter and felt much better for it. After eating, she went to the balcony, sitting heavily on one of the lounge chairs and closing her eyes for a nap.

By the following morning, she felt almost whole again, except for a halo of pain that seemed to float around her head at all times. It wasn't intense but it was constant, a reminder of just how far she could push Phane. Still, breaking that mirror, taking that capability out of his arsenal, that was worth a beating.

Dierdra returned an hour after clearing lunch, white as a sheet. "Prince Phane will be dining with us tonight. He said to expect guests."

"Thank you, Dierdra."

Since she'd awakened, Isabel had been worrying about Wren and Lacy, reasoning that Phane had recaptured them, but hoping otherwise. That hope was dwindling quickly. Given her condition, it wasn't time to act; all she could do was wait.

Phane arrived well before dinner with flowers and a bright, joyous smile.

"You've come so far so fast," he said, carefully placing the vase of flowers in the exact center of the table. "I didn't even expect you to be on your feet by now, let alone up to entertaining guests."

"Your concern is touching," Isabel said.

"Isn't it though? Let's not forget, you brought all this unpleasantness on yourself." He shook his finger at her. "You had no right. That mirror was irreplaceable."

She didn't respond.

"I thought as much. Come with me." He led her down to a large supply room; a few guards were stationed inside. Phane gestured to the only chair in the room. If she'd had more strength, she would have stayed on her feet.

"Bring them in," Phane said.

A guard opened the door. Five people, all strangers to Isabel, filed in and stood a few feet in front of the wall. The door closed, all five of them jumping at the sound.

"Pick one," Phane said.

"What? What for?"

"Not important, just pick one."

"Tell me why or I'm not playing your game."

"I see," Phane said, turning casually to the five frightened people. With a gesture, he smashed all five of them into the wall so hard that their heads and torsos were crushed—literally popped—leaving crimson splatter marks on the walls where they hit.

"You bastard!" Isabel shouted, surging to her feet and lunging at him. He caught her with his magic and lifted her off the ground, gently depositing her back in her chair.

"Stay," he said, giving her a stern look before gesturing to the soldier at the door. Another five people filed into the room, fear palpable in their expressions as soon as they saw the five fresh corpses.

"Pick one."

"I hate you."

"I can do this all day," Phane said. "Shall we call in the next group?"

"No, I'll pick," she said, scanning the five souls whose lives were in her hands and landing on the oldest man in the bunch. He had kind eyes and a weathered look about him and he nodded sadly when she settled on him, stepping forward.

"Take me, My Lady. My life is mostly behind me."

"Well said, old man," Phane said, snapping his fingers at a guard. "Remove him and let him go unharmed."

"Pick another one," Phane said.

A wife, a husband, a brother, a daughter.

Isabel couldn't speak past the lump in her throat so she just pointed at the middle-aged man.

"Free the rest of them unharmed," Phane said, lifting the man Isabel had selected off the ground with his magic, then slowly drawing him through the air, turning him to face him and holding him a foot off the ground.

"He's afraid," Phane said.

"I'm sorry," Isabel said, hanging her head.

"Oh, now, now, Isabel ... you don't even know his fate ... but you're going to find out, right now."

Phane cast a spell, still holding the condemned man off the ground with his magic. A set of four small rings of reddish energy materialized in midair. Phane moved the man to the four magical rings, aligning two with his ankles and two with his wrists. Then each ring snapped into place, suspending the man a foot off the ground, completely helpless.

With a few words, Phane burned a magic circle into the stone floor, bright red symbols fading quickly through orange, then to black.

"Please don't do this," the man begged. "I've never done anything to you."

Phane laughed in his face, forced and deliberate, devoid of humor.

"Let him go," Isabel said.

"Or what? That's the real question, isn't it? It's the only real question. What can you do? What will you do?" He held her eyes but pointed to the helpless man. "I'm going to have my way with this man and there's nothing he can do to stop me. He's powerless; I'm powerful. That's the only reality that matters—certainly the only reality that matters to him right now."

"Please don't do this ..." the man begged, crying.

"What do you want, Phane?" Isabel asked.

"I want to show you the consequences of your actions," he said, gesturing toward her, lifting her off her feet, putting her back in her chair and binding her there with a spell.

"Don't do this, Phane."

"It's already done," he said, facing the condemned man squarely. "It was done the moment you broke my mirror." With a gesture, the man slid through the air until he was floating in the center of the magic circle.

"Ready?" Phane asked with a smile, but then his visage transformed into a mask of unbridled rage and he began chanting in a guttural and angry language. Wisps of darkness started to swirl around the floor beneath the man. His fear spiked into panic. Phane cast about on the floor until he found a pebble the size of a ripe pea … grasping it with his magic, he brought it up floating in front of him and then propelled it through the man's heart, stabbing through him cleanly like a pike.

The man gasped and sputtered, his life's blood spilling forth, pooling inside the magic circle. But then the blood started moving, flowing toward the circle, into the symbols. The air grew heavy in the room, then suddenly cold. Isabel felt a dark and unnatural presence arrive. It felt unclean, as if the air itself had been spoiled.

"I have paid your price," Phane said. "Will you show me?"

The corpse hanging by Phane's magical shackles began to convulse, wracking violently as if it were struggling to get free of the bindings. Then the struggling stopped as abruptly as it had begun, the body hanging limp and lifeless for several moments before the head snapped back and craned out as far as it could reach toward Phane, its face seeming to spasm and contort unnaturally.

"Yes," said a voice that was decidedly not human.

A chill of dread raced up Isabel's spine.

"How has my plan unfolded?"

The area inside the magic circle became translucent, like moonlight with shadowy substance, then abruptly started showing images: Druja boarding a ship, followed by Rankosi disguised as a deckhand; the box exploding once the ship was a league out to sea; Lacy and Wren's capture and secure transport back to the fortress city. The last image faded away and the darkness lifted, leaving a half-desiccated corpse floating in the middle of the room.

With a wave of Phane's hand, the spell ended and the corpse crashed to the ground.

"This is what I must resort to since you broke my mirror," Phane said. "You will choose my sacrifices from now on … as punishment."

"You have the real box," Isabel said, ignoring his very terrifying threat. She felt sick to her stomach, but pushed it aside and imposed control on her emotions as only a witch could.

"Of course I have the box," Phane said. "I replaced it with a weapon inspired by your own Mage Gamaliel scarcely five minutes after Lacy Fellenden fell asleep the night she arrived." He looked at her, shaking his head. "Did you imagine that it could be otherwise? My prize walks right through the front door and you think I would leave it in another's care?

"I have all three keystones, my dear Isabel … it's just that I can't get to one of them right now."

"That is a problem, isn't it? But why the fake box?"

"Isn't it obvious? My enemies want the box as much as I do, so I put a powerfully enchanted fake into play. It was a simple matter to ensure that it fell into one of my many enemies' hands. After that, I could take their life with a single command. I had originally intended to end the Sin'Rath once they'd gathered on Ithilian, but I couldn't resist when I saw the shade board the ship with Druja."

"Aedan is dead?"

"If that was the dragon's name, then yes," Phane said. "I suspect the shade is especially unhappy with me, but it was well worth it. He's dangerous enough as it is, but intolerably so in possession of a dragon. As for the witch, well … I've always hated the Sin'Rath."

"I mourn Aedan," Isabel said, "but I can do without Druja, and I'm happy to hear that the shade is preoccupied with you. More importantly, you still can't open the box."

"Not yet, but more paths to victory become available to me every day."

"What are you talking about?"

"Hector, Trajan, Lacy, Torin … all of them represent a way to open the box. One of them will deliver, sooner or later. But even if they don't, I can still win. Your beloved is a prisoner on Andalia. Once they persuade him to hand over the Stone, he will be delivered to me."

"So your people don't have the Stone now, then?" Isabel said.

"It's only a matter of time."

"If you say so."

"As I understand it, Alexander is entangled in a web of lies with the Babachenko. He believes that he and the Andalians are working together in their efforts to recover the Sovereign Stone."

Isabel tried to maintain her composure, but she couldn't help herself. She broke down laughing, then slowly sat down to mitigate the pain her convulsions caused in her still-healing body.

"The Babachenko assures me that he's created a spell capable of thwarting your beloved's ability to see a person's aura."

"What about everyone else?" Isabel asked. "All of the other people who have to be around him if you're going to make sure he doesn't escape. Do you really think you managed to lie to him?" She started laughing again.

"It won't matter," Phane said. "Nero is there with ample forces. If the ruse doesn't work, we'll simply take Alexander without the Stone."

"I bet that wouldn't feel like much of a victory."

"No, but it may be necessary. Besides, I'd wager that you would make for high-value leverage against Alexander. He might do just about anything to protect you."

"He'd better not," she said.

Phane frowned at her, shaking his head. "I'm not sure I will ever understand you," he said, finally.

"I'm certain you won't."

"It doesn't have to be this way, Isabel," Phane said. "I'll give you anything you want."

"You don't have anything I want."

"Don't you understand?" he snapped. "I'm offering you the world. You can rule over the entire Seven Isles in my name. I'll let you run things any way you like."

"I understand exactly what you're offering and I reject it," Isabel said.

"You know, it doesn't have to be you, Isabel. I'm sure that any woman I chose in all the Seven Isles would be flattered by my attention."

"Until she got to know you."

"You try my patience."

"What? Are you going to beat me again?"

"I just might, but later," Phane said, motioning to the guard at the door the moment he heard the knock.

It opened wide and Lacy and Wren were herded into the room, followed by a stout man and a half dozen female guards.

"Well done, Drogan," Phane said. "Report for duty tomorrow and don't ever return to this house. Men are not allowed here, except in unusual circumstances."

"I was sent to retrieve them," Drogan said. "Job isn't done until you deliver the goods to the boss."

"Indeed, and a job well done at that," Phane said. "You are dismissed."

Drogan nodded awkwardly and excused himself, followed closely by two of Phane's female guards.

Isabel searched Wren's eyes for any sign of encouragement but found none, and her initial appraisal of Lacy found the princess wanting, or at least out of her depth. Things were going from bad to worse.

"Ladies, do come in," Phane said. "I've taken the liberty of preparing a dinner for us all."

Isabel nodded to Wren, almost imperceptibly. She came to Isabel's side and took the chair to her right without ever seeming to look up.

"What is the meaning of this, Prince Phane?" Lacy demanded.

"The meaning is quite simple, Princess. You are my prisoner. You can either sit at my table on your own, or one of those very large men over there will pick you up and put you in your chair."

Lacy started to say something else but thought better of it, clenching her jaw shut before she took the seat next to Wren.

"Excellent, I believe we're beginning to understand each other," Phane said, opening his Wizard's Den with a gesture. He slipped inside, then quickly stepped back out, closing it behind himself with a word. He held up the box containing the third keystone and set it on the table in front of his chair.

"Lacy … I want you to open this box."

"Don't do it," Isabel said.

"I won't," Lacy said.

Phane sat down, motioning for the nervous servant to fill his wine flagon, then taking a long drink before returning his attention to the table.

"Can't say I expected you to cooperate, but I think I'll hang on to you just the same," Phane said, tossing two collars onto the table in front of her and Wren.

"Put them on," he said.

"What do they do?" Lacy asked, picking up the collar and looking at it suspiciously.

"They're called Andalian slave collars … you'll both understand how they work much better after you put them on."

Wren put her hands flat on the table and stared forward.

"I won't put it on," Lacy said. "I'm not a slave."

"That's where you're mistaken," Phane said, holding her in her chair with his magic, the collar floating off the table and roughly snapping into place around her neck.

Wren sat with her hands on the table, ignoring his order. The other collar floated up, closing around her neck with a click.

"If you try to leave the city, your collars will choke you," Phane said. "Otherwise, you're free to pass through any door that will open for you. Now, enjoy a meal with me," he said, smiling brightly.

Servants entered with a wide variety of dishes. Isabel ate freely, building strength for the coming days. She ignored Phane's attempts to engage her in small talk, focusing on her food until he gave up and shifted his interest to Lacy.

"So … tell me, Princess, how does it feel to hold the fate of the world in your hands?"

Lacy looked at him without responding.

Good, Isabel thought, continuing to eat.

"Surely, you of all people understand that Zuhl is unstoppable," Phane said.

Lacy seemed ready to speak but held her tongue at the last moment.

Isabel picked up a roasted bird leg and took a big bite.

"His army is beyond us all," Phane said. "But you could defeat him … right now … and it wouldn't cost you a thing. In fact, I would defend Fellenden with all of my power and name your family Protectors of the Realm. You cannot hope to do better."

Isabel stopped eating, looking pointedly at Lacy.

She gritted her teeth, leaning toward Isabel. "I know," she said, then turned back to Phane.

"I'm not going to open that box. Not later today, not tomorrow, not ever."

Isabel nodded to herself, taking another bite from her roasted bird leg.

"We'll see," Phane said. "You are of secondary importance right now. Watch and learn who I am and what I have to offer … then make your decision."

"Do I really have a choice?" Lacy asked.

"No," Phane said, "not really."

"Then out with it," Lacy said. "What do you want?"

"I want my birthright, just as I imagine you want yours," Phane said. "You are a princess, noble by blood, and that deserves respect—respect that I'm willing to pay … provided that you recognize me as the rightful Reishi Sovereign. Only together can we stand against Zuhl."

Lacy sat stone-still, almost charmed by Phane's words until Wren started giggling under her breath, dispelling his carefully woven lie with simple

incredulity, sending him stomping away from the table with the box and leaving
the three of them laughing under their breath.

Isabel knew that their little victory would come at a cost, but she relished
it just the same. "We won't have much time," she said. "I hope you're serious
about that box. If you open it, the world will die."

"I know—I'll never open that box," Lacy said, "but Phane has other ways
of getting inside it."

"Indeed I do," he said, sauntering back into the room from his Wizard's
Den without any hint of ire. He sat back down and refilled his flagon with wine.

"Let's talk about power, shall we?" he said, holding up the slaver's ring
on his finger and tapping it gently. Lacy and Wren both began to choke, struggling
to breathe while Phane watched them like bugs in a jar.

"Stop it!" Isabel said.

Phane tapped the ring again and the collars relaxed, leaving Lacy and
Wren gasping and coughing. Phane smiled at their discomfort, waiting patiently
for them to regain their composure.

"I own you … both of you belong to me now. I have all of the power and
you have none. Obey or suffer. Those are the new terms of your lives. Do you
understand?"

They both nodded timidly.

"Excellent," Phane said. "Now, I'm going to explain the state of the
world in the hopes that you, Princess Lacy, will come to see that you've picked the
wrong side." He raised his hand to forestall her protest. "Listen before you answer.
I rule Karth outright. Andalia is openly loyal to me. Most of the islands of Tyr are
under my control. The Ruathan Army is fighting the Lancers to a stalemate and
they're about to be blindsided by Elred Rake from the north—he'll deliver a
crushing blow, I assure you. The tide will turn against Ruatha after that, forcing
those loyal to my dear cousin to retreat into Glen Morillian where they will
remain."

Isabel listened to Phane, hoping beyond hope that Alexander was
watching, yet knowing that he probably wasn't.

"Ithilian has been taken by the Sin'Rath, as has your brother," Phane
continued. "You will receive no more support from Abel, and Torin is quite
beyond your reach. Zuhl has put his ships to sea with great success, never
wavering from his objective of capturing the Iron Oak Forest and Fellenden with
it. Your people are battered and broken, most are refugees, scattered and displaced.
However this war turns out, they will be impoverished by it.

"I'm going to win, Lacy. I'm going to rule over all of the Seven Isles.
Isabel's faith in her husband is admirable, but what she fails to accept is that
Alexander is wearing one of those slave collars around his neck right now as we
speak. He's already lost. It's too late for him, but it's not too late for you, or for
Fellenden."

Lacy shook her head.

"I'm offering you salvation, Lacy. You can be the Queen of Fellenden;
you can rule as you see fit. You can protect your people from the famine and
suffering that will befall them without my help."

"I'm not going to help you," Lacy said. "Not ever."

"Just remember that I offered you every chance," Phane said, turning away from her as if she no longer existed.

"Wizard Enu's death was a setback," he said to Isabel. "His spell to separate you from your will was brilliant. With him gone, I'm left with few options. I could try to create a potion or charm, but the simplest plan would probably be to re-create Enu's spell."

"Take your time," Isabel said.

"Even after all this," he said, gesturing to the bruising that discolored her entire face and left her eyes puffy, "you insist on being flippant. When are you going to learn to respect me?"

"When you do something worthy of respect," Isabel said, holding his eyes with hers until he walked away from the table, shaking his head.

"I suppose I could always send an assassin to kill the fairy," he mused.

"What makes you think you'll get anywhere near Chloe without Alexander seeing you coming?" Isabel said.

"Not Chloe ... what's her name? The child fairy."

"Sara?"

"That's the one."

"Why? What's she got to do with any of this?"

Phane laughed at her, shaking his head in disgust as he sat back down and took a long pull from his wine flagon.

"I'm fighting children! None of you have even a basic knowledge of magic ... and I even told you how it works."

"How what works?"

"Your link to the realm of light flows through Sara," Phane said. "If I kill her, your link goes away and Azugorath will have her way with you."

"You wouldn't dare," Isabel said, knowing full well that he certainly would dare if he thought he could get away with it. "Ilona would stop you."

"Unfortunately, I believe you're right on that second count," Phane said. "That leaves Enu's spell—two, maybe three days lost to re-create it. I was hoping to avoid that."

Isabel held her tongue while her mind spun. Pieces were starting to fall into place. If killing Sara would close her link to the realm of light, then banishing Rankosi should close her link to the netherworld. She could be free of the darkness ... permanently.

There was a way. Not an easy way to be sure, but there was a way.

"This cursed isle is almost totally devoid of wizards," Phane said. "I had the Andalians send me Enu, and now he's dead, like most of the others they sent. Understandably, they're not happy about the situation, but I think I have a solution that will please them."

"Aren't you afraid of the shade?" Isabel asked, ignoring his musings.

He frowned for a moment, then smiled. "Not really. He'll try to take me but he'll fail. Then he'll try to kill me, and he'll fail again. Then, he'll get frustrated and make a mistake. When he does, I'll press him into service."

"How? He's already in the world. What can you possibly offer him?"

"The shades have unseemly appetites that can be leveraged ... but enough about them. I'm trying to explain how thoroughly you've already lost this war and how futile your resistance really is.

"I'm going to capture your wizards one by one and strip them of their magic, bestowing their power upon candidates from within my forces who demonstrate exceptional aptitude and loyalty. Your Wizards Guild will be diminished while mine is increased—yet another path to victory.

"Speaking of which, I just got a report from Hector's expedition. They've reached the swamp. It shouldn't be long now."

"That swamp might just eat them alive."

"Face it, Isabel, you've lost ... on every front. You're just prolonging the inevitable. I've cultivated so many paths to victory that I can't help but win. For example, I have a company of my best trackers hunting Trajan. He's fled to the northern jungles."

"Good luck tracking him in there," Isabel said.

"Admittedly a challenge, but well worth the resources I've committed." Phane shook his head incredulously. "Don't you see, I have a plan to win, many plans, in fact ... and you don't. You've never had a chance against me. I set my plans into motion within days of waking from my long sleep. I have vast resources working toward my objectives ... whole island kingdoms waging war by my command. You are a prisoner. Your husband is a prisoner. All is lost. Surrender. I will be merciful."

Isabel couldn't help but laugh, looking Phane right in the face past her swollen eyelids and bruised cheeks. "You mean like this?"

Lacy and Wren looked down at the table.

"You deserved that and you know it," Phane said, pointing his finger at her face. "Anyone else who did what you did would be dead or dying very badly right now. A beating was lenient. In fact, you may well suffer additional punishment at my whim."

"You call that mercy?"

"In your case, yes," Phane said, standing abruptly. "The three of you will remain on these estate grounds until I return in a few days. We'll continue this conversation once I've mastered Enu's spell."

He left them without another word.

"What happens then?" Lacy asked.

"According to Phane's plan, I'll kill Wren, then feel so guilty about it that I'll embrace the netherworld and help Phane kill my husband."

"That's insane," Lacy said.

"I know, but given the circumstances, it's not entirely implausible," Isabel said, continuing to explain her situation with Azugorath in as much detail as she could. Lacy listened with intent horror, shaking her head from time to time while Isabel detailed her entanglement with the Wraith Queen.

"So, if this demon gains control, she'll make you kill Wren," Lacy said.

"That's Phane's plan," Isabel said. Then she looked at Wren. "That's why I sent you away earlier than planned. Wizard Enu succeeded in casting his spell, but fortunately, you were out when Azugorath took control of me."

"So what do we do now?" Lacy asked.

"I'm not entirely sure," Isabel said. "Those collars complicate things."

They spent the better part of the next two days talking, first about Phane and his strategies and his lies, but then about more mundane things, like their childhoods, their friends and family, their hopes for the future.

Despite Isabel's first impression, she came to like Lacy, but that didn't change her assessment of her—the princess was in over her head. But then, Isabel had to remind herself how inexperienced she'd been the day she left Glen Morillian with Alexander not so very long ago.

Lacy had come far, especially considering her burden, but she couldn't hold her own in a fight and that would be a problem. What's more, Lacy knew it, confessing that she wished she could go back in time and learn how to fight.

Isabel tried to remain upbeat with her two friends but inwardly she was facing a kind of doom marching inexorably toward her with every passing moment. Phane would cast the spell and Azugorath would assert her will.

Wren would die.

Isabel didn't know if her soul could withstand what would come next.

After the first two days, after they'd said all they had to say and fell silent, the tension began to build. Every passing moment ratcheted up Isabel's anxiety, fear gripping her in a way she'd never felt before, not during the mana fast, nor while she carried the Goiri bone, not ever.

She was going to kill Wren.

A glimpse of the kind of guilt such a thought evoked was enough to send a thrill of panic coursing through her.

She jumped when the door opened. Phane stood in the doorway, savoring their fear ... that was all it took for Isabel to regain control. In a moment, she remembered her training at the fortress island and detached herself emotionally so she could face her enemy with a clear head.

He seemed more smug than usual—not a good sign.

"It's time," he said, closing the door loudly, causing all three of them to jump again. "I've learned Enu's spell."

The moment closed in around Isabel. She was out of options. Wren was forfeit. She summoned her anger, building it quickly before muttering the words she'd remembered by rote to help her mind focus on seeing the results she desired. Light, bright and hot, streaked from her hand and hit Phane's shield right in front of his chest, dissipating in a scintillating display of color.

"Run!" Isabel shouted.

"Not so fast," Phane said, touching his slave-master's ring and dropping both Lacy and Wren to their knees, gasping for air. He released them after watching them struggle for several seconds. They gasped for air, each breaking into a fit of coughing.

"I really like these," he said. "I'll have to have the Babachenko send more."

Isabel started to get up, but he pushed her back into her chair with his magic, holding her in place while he cast a spell. She tried to brace for it, tried to resist, but it came over her like a wave, separating her body from her free will, leaving her totally vulnerable. Azugorath seized the opportunity, flooding into Isabel's psyche with all of her hate and bile.

"Finally," the Wraith Queen said, standing triumphantly in full possession of Isabel, looking down on Wren without pity. "Is this the pittance you want killed?"

"Yes," Phane said.

Lacy staggered to her feet and bolted forward, launching herself headlong into Isabel's midsection and crashing to the ground on top of her, then she rolled to the side a moment later, struggling to breathe past the slave collar's constriction.

"Don't try my patience, Princess. You are not nearly as valuable to me as Isabel is." He left her writhing on the floor, strangling.

"Please. Kill her quickly," Phane said.

Azugorath approached Wren. Isabel could hear the words of her light-lance spell begin to form in her mind. She saw her hand raise toward Wren, heard her lips breathe life into the words of the spell, but then Wren did something that surprised everyone … she started singing.

Not the timid, under-her-breath singing that always made Isabel smile, but loud, full-throated, unabashed song shouted to the sky with passion and pure joy. The kind of song that calls forth thunderous applause. Her voice rose and fell, holding every note without rush, as if in that moment, her greatest purpose was to fill the room with music.

Isabel watched through stolen eyes and was in awe.

Wren had chosen her favorite song and was delivering a masterful performance, so much so that Phane and even Azugorath both seemed stunned by it, neither seemingly able to put what they were seeing and hearing into a context that they could comprehend.

Isabel understood perfectly. She reached for the veil shrouding the light and met it with love for Wren, love for her music, love for Alexander, and love for life itself. She didn't struggle with it, or fight it, or rail against it, or confront the veil in any way. Instead, she simply held all of the love she could muster up to it, and the realm of light responded. At first, just a glimmer shined through, but moments later, life-giving light flooded into her psyche … and then it was gone. Azugorath had pulled back again, choosing to defend the veil blocking Isabel's connection to the realm of light over maintaining control.

"I know how to fight you now, Phane," Isabel said, turning to face him.

"One battle does not win the war," he said, motioning to Lacy and releasing her collar. "Next time, I'll gag your little friend before I hand you over to Azugorath."

He left the room, whistling a tune.

Chapter 29

Alexander smiled when he saw the ruins of the Lancers' forward operating base, still burning and spewing soot into the air. Plans in the west of Andalia were going well. The people remaining in the western province had taken to the Old Law with enthusiasm, then taken to the battlefield to defend it. Lancer fortifications were on fire all along the boundary between the western forest and the plains. Talia had leveraged two hundred Rangers and eight Sky Knights into an insurgent army of well over three thousand militiamen.

That small army had launched its first major offensive during the night, attacking every significant Lancer position along the border with fire, then withdrawing and regrouping, moving north to prepare for the primary objective.

Over the coming days the militia would move along the north coast, taking one seaport after another, but never attacking the shipwrights, instead offering them jobs farther west, then burning the docks, the shipyards and the port buildings before moving on.

Alexander set aside all of the other battles taking place around the world and focused on the coming minutes. He could see Mithel Dour looming in the distance, its thousand-foot semi-circular cliff cutting an unnatural face into the mountain range at the heart of the Andalian Isle. The palace cliff looming up behind it completed the other half of the circle, together defining the city's boundaries.

The wyverns floated in well above the city, silent on the wind and invisible against the grey night sky. Alexander tapped Kiera on the thigh, pointing to Grant's balcony. She nodded, leaning into her wyvern, tipping into a dive, and quickly losing several hundred feet of altitude before pulling into a shallow descent. The remaining seven Sky Knights held course for the palace.

Alexander saw the men positioned around the balcony and the yard, all of them hidden, but not to his sight. Easily fifty men, overseers, armed with clubs and armored in scale mail, hidden around the otherwise vacant Grant estate ... all of them waiting.

The Babachenko knew he was coming.

It made perfect sense. He was a divination mage. Acquiring knowledge with magic was his stock in trade.

"Enemy," Alexander shouted into Kiera's ear. "Drop me quickly, then fall away and come back around."

She nodded, smiling into the wind and guiding her wyvern with a combination of leg pressure and delicate tugging on the reins, bringing the beast into a flaring landing on the balcony, terrifying two men who were trying to hide behind the balcony railing, sending them scrambling for the stables.

The wyvern leaned forward, her snapping jaws just outside the stable doors, her bladed tail hovering over the side path leading toward the house along the balcony. Alexander pulled his lacing free and slid to the ground, linking his mind with Chloe before he hit. Several overseers seemed to appear out of the shadows. He ignored them, calculating the distance to his target. Chloe came into existence, spinning into view in a ball of light, bringing the Thinblade with her into the world of time and substance just moments before he reached it. His sword in hand, he assessed the situation and chose to flee.

But before he could, a club hit him in the back, knocking him to one knee, pain radiating from the point of impact. Men rushed in from all sides. He set the pain aside, drew the Thinblade and focused on the moment. Three men were closing in on him, all of them raising clubs that could put him out with a hit.

He slipped to the right, sweeping up with the Thinblade, taking one of the overseer's hands, moving past him, putting the screaming man between himself and the other two overseers, giving him just enough time to sheathe the Thinblade and swing up behind Kiera.

"Hang on!" she shouted.

He was glad he obeyed. The wyvern bounded backward to avoid an all-out assault by ten men rushing toward them, then tipped sideways, falling into a steep dive with the cliff face at her belly before leveling out and gaining altitude, turning gradually back toward Mithel Dour. As they floated over the city streets, Alexander pointed out his target. Kiera nodded, taking the reins of her wyvern and guiding her into a gentle landing on the roof of the mining barracks.

"Thank you, Kiera," Alexander said.

"I can still come with you."

"I know, but I suspect that Talia is depending on you to help him carry out his plans against the shipyards."

"Perhaps."

"If I have need, I will call," Alexander said, letting himself slide to the edge of the roof and then drop to the ground, orienting himself briefly before heading across the courtyard and into an office, listening for the wing beats of Kiera's wyvern as he ran.

He was grateful that the place was vacant. Grant's betrayal had caused an interruption in the mining business, but it wouldn't last. The Babachenko probably already had people working on the problem.

Alexander opened the door to his Wizard's Den and stepped inside, leaving it open and gesturing for everyone waiting inside to sit at the table. He went to his magic circle and sat down, meditating for several minutes while he scouted the way ahead. His reconnaissance complete, he closed the door to his Wizard's Den and took his seat at the table.

"We have an opportunity. One that could turn the tide of this entire war ..." he paused, looking down at the table.

"But ..." Jack said.

"I have to keep certain details from you," Alexander said.

"If that's necessary, then so be it," Jataan said.

"No ... not so be it," Anja said. "I want to know what's going on."

"I can't tell you. I know it's not fair, but it is necessary. I need you to trust me."

"I don't like this," Anja said. "I'm willing to fight right beside you, but I want to know what I'm fighting for."

"You're fighting for the Old Law."

"Not good enough," Anja said.

"It's the only thing that is good enough to fight for," Alexander said. Anja harrumphed.

"What *can* you tell us, Alexander?" Jack asked.

"I can tell you that the beings that built this city are still here ... they're dormant, and I know how to wake them up."

"Beings? What beings?" Anja asked.

"They're called Linkershim," Alexander said. "And I think they can help us with the Andalians."

"So it's how you plan to revive them that you can't tell us then," Jack said.

"Stop guessing, Jack. I can't tell you and you can't write about it. If the wrong people discovered this, they could destroy everything ... literally. The sovereigns were very insistent."

Jack nodded, grudgingly accepting Alexander's explanation. Anja's frown deepened.

"I expect heavy fighting in the coming hours," Alexander said. "We'll be descending into a mine owned by Titus Grant, who just recently escaped from palace custody. He has a number of men in the tunnels we'll be traveling through, and it's possible that he's taken refuge in the mines himself.

"Once we're through the mines, we'll enter a vast underground city that was built many millennia ago. The path will be treacherous and there's no telling what lives down there.

"The Babachenko is aware of our presence in the city, so he'll be sending soldiers. Our enemies are dangerous. We should avoid them if we can or kill them quickly if we can't ... our objective really has nothing to do with them, except that they're in our way."

Alexander strapped on the Thinblade, checked Demonrend, and picked up Luminessence before opening the door of the Wizard's Den. After everyone filed out into the cramped little office, he closed the door, willing his staff to produce a dim light, just faintly illuminating the room.

"There's a hidden door on that wall," Alexander said.

Jack had it open within a minute. "It's been used recently."

"Grant," Alexander said. "He's the only man I've ever met who doesn't have colors and he can make you not see him."

"What does that mean?" Anja asked.

"He has the ability to make one or two people at a time just not see him. They don't even know he's there, even if he's standing right in front of them."

"How's that possible?"

"You're a dragon that looks like a girl ... you tell me."

Anja frowned.

"My point is, don't try to engage him. I can beat him with Chloe's help, but he can kill any of you and you won't even know he's there until you're dying."

Jataan frowned.

"He can't make me not see him if he doesn't know I'm there," Jack said.

"Let's just try to avoid him," Alexander said. "We don't need anything from him."

"Fair enough," Jack said.

Alexander led the way down the narrow corridor. Not only had it been used recently, but it had been used by a lot of people, and judging from the irregularity of the boot prints, not soldiers. The door at the end of the corridor was closed. Alexander approached it cautiously, extinguishing his light and looking into the adjacent room with his magic. It still didn't have the range of his normal vision, but indoors, his all around sight could look far enough ahead to let him explore an area with his mind very quickly.

Two men stood guard, one next to the door, the other near a bell set up next to the mineshaft. Alexander opened his Wizard's Den, ushered everyone inside, closed the door and explained the situation. It took them all of two minutes to decide on a plan and step back out into the corridor.

Alexander verified that the men were still bored and unaware before he threw the door open, stepping forth and raising Luminessence. It erupted brilliantly, filling the cavern with light as bright as the sun, blinding the two men, yet leaving Alexander and his friends able to see clearly.

Jataan raced across the room, moving impossibly fast, closing the distance to the man near the bell in a fraction of a second and hitting him with the palm of his hand in the center of the torso, then tipping the man over onto this back and maneuvering him into a choke hold.

Anja stepped in next, leveling a vicious right-handed punch at the man next to the door, knocking him senseless, his head snapping back and forth before he hit the floor.

Alexander dimmed the light. Lita seemed a little taken aback by the sudden violence, unleashed so overwhelmingly, but she held her tongue. Jataan and Anja tied and gagged their captives.

Alexander knew better. The men guarding this shaft worked for Grant and he was a criminal of the highest order. His henchmen deserved little in the way of sympathy or mercy. There was also the issue of their colors. They were both brigands—probably cutthroats. If anything, Alexander felt like he might be shirking his responsibility by not killing them.

"Watch your step," he said. "These stairs are old."

"I'll say," Jack said, looking down the mineshaft at the wooden staircase winding into the darkness. "Are you sure they're going to hold?"

"I've been down them once before. They're mostly solid," Alexander said, leading the way down the shaft. Aside from the few broken or missing boards, the stairs were rock-solid, no doubt because the bad boards had all been broken when Grant's men passed this way. He was thankful that the room at the base of the stairs wasn't guarded or his light would have given them away for sure.

He raised his staff, bringing up the light, illuminating five passages leading from this one hidden shaft. The new boot prints led into a tunnel opposite the one Alexander wanted. He dimmed his staff again, the top shod glowing just enough to light their way and entered the tunnel leading to the central mineshaft. He was relieved to find virtually no evidence of recent passage.

It took half an hour before they saw a flicker of light in the distance. Alexander doused his light and they walked on in total darkness, using the wall for guidance as they approached the opening into the central mineshaft room, which was really a series of equipment and supply rooms surrounding the main-shaft elevator. Several working tunnels ran away from this level in different directions. Ten overseers were guarding the tunnel that Alexander was interested in.

"Overseers" Alexander whispered. "They're armored and carry weighted clubs that they can throw very well. They like to fight in groups, overwhelming an opponent with superior numbers and they're absolutely the enemy."

"Understood," Jataan said, drawing a dagger.

"We'll hit them hard and fast—hopefully prevent them from raising an alarm," Alexander said. "There'll be more down the tunnel and still more up the mineshaft."

They crept out of the tunnel, using supply crates and ore bins for concealment until they got as close as they were going to get—about twenty feet to the side of the tunnel entrance, behind a row of rail carts. Alexander put Luminessence into his Wizard's Den and drew the Thinblade. Jataan and Anja both nodded their readiness.

Alexander stretched his mind out into the coming moments and sprang from cover—racing silently without a battle cry or shout of warning, reaching the first completely surprised overseer within seconds, cleaving him in half with a stroke, following through into the next man, taking most of his head simply by allowing the Thinblade to follow its arc.

Jataan threw his knife into an overseer's heart from about six feet, then grabbed the knife, pulling it free before the man fell, moving on to the next closest enemy with his customary efficiency, leaving a path of dead men, veins ruinously opened to the world with terrifying speed and precision.

Anja swept into the battle with her broadsword, swinging it in great swaths through one flank of the overseers, leaving them hacked and dying on the ground.

The entire battle took only seconds. The overseers didn't have a chance. Surprise coupled with overwhelming force made for a decisive combination.

The tunnel that Alexander had helped dig not so long ago was lit every fifty feet by oil lamps, just enough light to keep people from wandering into the walls, but certainly not enough to see by. He kept up the pace, moving as quickly as he dared through the shadows, not wanting to shed any light of his own for fear of being detected by those guarding the other end of the tunnel. During his clairvoyant reconnaissance, he'd counted ten more overseers.

When they got close, a bell tolled, raising the alarm. The overseers sprang into action, breaking into two groups of five, one group pointing at Alexander with their clubs, the other group pointing at Jataan. They didn't advance, instead holding position before the entrance to the underdark while an eleventh man took up a position on the stone slab at the center of the three overlapping magical circles and started casting a spell.

Alexander was easily a hundred feet away, not close enough to reach him in time and not far enough away to avoid his spell. He broke into a run, charging toward the overseers, but he slowed to a walk when the wizard called forth a shield wall that blocked the tunnel twenty feet in front of his men.

With a triumphant smile, the overseer went to the alarm bell and muttered the words of a spell. Then he struck the bell firmly with his club. Aided by magic, its peal reverberated throughout the entire city.

"More overseers will be coming … soon," Alexander said, trying to penetrate the shield wall with the Thinblade. When he pushed the magic sword through the red, glowing barrier, the scar it left closed almost instantly.

He cut into the wall beside the shield, removing large chunks with a few swipes.

"We have company," Jack said.

"Anja, watch my back. Jataan, hold this ground," Alexander said as he pulled a chunk of dirt out of the hole he was cutting to circumvent the shield.

"Understood," Jataan said.

"The overseers can see what you're doing," Anja said. "They're moving troops close to the wall."

"I count ten men approaching," Jataan said. "Not overseers, though … maybe Grant's people."

Alexander came out of the hole and sent his sight down the tunnel. Grant wasn't among the approaching men, and none of them had magic. He breathed a sigh of relief, estimating how long it would take to break through beyond the shield and frowning at the work he'd done already before turning toward the approaching people.

"Hello," Alexander said, his voice echoing down the tunnel.

"Who are you? Why are you trespassing?" their leader asked, approaching cautiously, eyeing the overseers beyond the shield. He turned to a much younger man behind him and said, "Run, tell Lord Grant." The young man nodded and raced off into the dimly lit tunnel.

"My name is Alexander and I have no interest in your mines."

"No, just the real valuables beyond the overseer's shield."

"Who do you represent?" Alexander asked.

"Lord Titus Grant."

"Grant is a fugitive. He's been stripped of his title, his charter, and his accounts. In fact, I'd be surprised if he could even pay you."

"Oh, don't you worry about that. Lord Grant pays us on time and he pays us well. Now, these are his mines and you don't have his leave to be down here, so surrender your weapons and come with us. Wouldn't want things to get messy. Two men, a woman, and a girl … against the ten of us. Odds aren't exactly in your favor."

"You heard the bell, right?" Alexander asked.

The lead man nodded.

"So did the Babachenko. More overseers are on their way right now. If you're quick about it, you might escape the tunnel before they close it off."

The man looked back quickly, then inspected the shield wall again, counting the number of overseers lined up beyond. "This isn't over," he said. "Lord Grant will decide how to deal with you." He and his people withdrew quickly.

"Huh," Alexander said, turning back to the hole he was digging. When he got in deeper, Anja helped him clear chunks of dirt and rock from the rough passage he was cutting. The overseers behind the shield seemed to be getting nervous, moving the entire unit to face the spot in the wall where Alexander was most likely going to come through.

Muffled echoes of fighting reverberated down the length of the tunnel— Grant's men probably hadn't gotten out in time to avoid the overseers. Alexander kept digging, cutting away a pyramid-shaped chunk of stone and opening a small hole into the section of tunnel beyond the shield.

An overseer jabbed his club through the hole. Alexander cut it in half with a flick of the Thinblade.

He turned to Jataan and Anja and said, "Be ready." He drove the Thinblade into the wall and cut a doorframe in the stone, ensuring that each cut was slightly angled so the stone slab would fall outward. He saved the top cut for last.

"Line up behind me," he said.

He cut the top section of the stone, then put his foot in the middle of it and pushed, stepping out onto it as it fell. While the overseers scrambled to get out of the way, Alexander launched off of the stone slab into their midst before it hit the ground and shattered into hundreds of pieces.

Jataan and Anja were through moments later, each moving left and right to attack the overseers on their flanks.

Flicking the Thinblade out backhanded, Alexander snapped the tip of the blade through the nearest overseer's throat, then stepped back in the other direction and brought the blade across in a broad sweep, killing two more.

From several feet away, an overseer threw a club at him, scoring a direct hit on the back of his left shoulder. While his armor blunted the damage, the hit was still numbingly painful and knocked him to one knee, staining his trousers with the blood of the men he'd just killed. Another overseer started to bring his club down on Alexander's head, but was blown off his feet by Lita's force-push spell.

Jataan worked his way through the overseers quickly but methodically, cutting here, stabbing there, killing each man he engaged with seemingly causal ease.

Anja howled like a banshee, wading into the startled men with her broadsword, cutting three down before the rest could respond.

Alexander regained his feet and immediately took five shards of magical force right in the center of his chest, each hitting with sufficient energy to knock him backward a foot or two, delivering punishing blows but not penetrating his dragon-scale armor. The wizard looked at him incredulously when Alexander stumbled backward and fell, badly battered and bruised but still alive.

Jataan threw his bloody knife at the wizard but it bounced off his shield. The battle mage darted across the room, quickly recovering his knife before moving around behind the wizard.

As he raised his dagger, it abruptly transformed into a war hammer. He set himself, got a firm grip, and smashed the shield with as much force as he could bring to bear. His strike rebounded, knocking him off the pedestal, but the wizard's shield failed with a pop.

The Acuna wizard looked around in a panic before throwing a black pellet to the ground. A ball of grey smoke quickly engulfed him, obscuring his position for a moment before fading away and revealing that he'd vanished. A small ember trailing black smoke floated through the passage that Alexander had cut around the shield and down the tunnel.

Chapter 30

"Everyone all right?" Alexander asked, wincing in pain as he got to his feet.

"You, least of all," Lita said. "Let me take a look at your wounds."

"I'll be fine," Alexander said.

"Nonsense," she said, putting her hand lightly on his chest and muttering the words of a spell under her breath. She smiled serenely, her eyes closed while she nodded to herself as if she were receiving instructions.

"You're badly bruised, but nothing is broken or bleeding," she said. "You'll heal, but it will be painful. When we stop, I can accelerate the process but not until you have time to sleep for the night."

"Perhaps we should be on our way," Jack said, looking through the red-tinged shield at the tunnel filled with approaching overseers. They were still a few hundred feet away, but there were a lot of them.

"Let's go," Alexander said, sheathing the Thinblade and hobbling toward the giant entry hall to the underdark. He hurt all over. The force shards had hit harder than he would have imagined—easily hard enough to cut straight through a man wearing normal plate armor.

"I see Mage Gamaliel made you a weapon," Alexander said to Jataan.

The General Commander of the Reishi Protectorate actually smiled. "Yes, Lord Reishi. The Guild Mage presented me with a most wonderful gift. He calls it a Weaponere's Stone." Jataan held up a smooth lump of dull grey metal that looked more like a piece of slag than a weapon … until it transformed into a dagger. "With only a thought, I can make it into any weapon I wish. That by itself is potent, but it was also crafted to magnify the magic that is naturally imbued upon weapons that I wield, making it ideally suited to my needs."

"Sometimes I think Mage Gamaliel has contributed more to this war effort than any other person," Alexander said, climbing up into the entry hall, marveling again at the giant stone fir trees that served as pillars holding up the ceiling hundreds of feet overhead.

Jack stopped a few steps inside the hall, looking around and whistling to himself. "I could take notes on this place for an hour."

"Probably not the best day for that," Alexander said.

"Right … pity, though."

They hurried across the enormous hall to the corridor entrance on the opposite wall. Alexander opened his Wizard's Den midstride, snatching Luminessence from just inside the door, and lighting their way with his staff, illuminating the artistry of the corridor—a forest road covered over by branches of trees grown together, yet done completely in stone. He raised the light considerably once they reached the balcony overlooking the great chasm at the heart of the underdark.

Although most of the bridges across the chasm appeared to be broken, a few in the distance still looked intact, and the remnants were enough to demonstrate great power at work. A variety of stone buildings and balconies were set into the walls above and below stretching out as far as Alexander's light could reach.

"And I thought the entryway was impressive," Jack whispered. "Please tell me I can write about this place."

"Most of it," Alexander said.

McGinty seemed to ooze up out of the floor right in front of Alexander and take form: a three-foot-tall humanoid made out of mud, yet with reasonably lifelike features.

Jataan started to move, but Alexander stopped him with a gesture.

"You brought other fleshlings," McGinty said.

"Yes, these are my friends."

He seemed confused for a moment. Then he asked, "What is their purpose?"

"To help me navigate the underdark," Alexander said.

Jack leaned forward a bit, giving him a sidelong look.

McGinty paused again.

"I take it you two have met before," Jack said.

"In a manner of speaking," Alexander said.

"I sensed the memory, but only briefly," McGinty said.

"Yes."

"Bring it quickly. Come to the well alone," McGinty said, oozing back into the stone floor, completely vanishing into the cracks.

"The memory?" Jack said.

Alexander shook his head very deliberately.

Jack nodded reluctantly.

"We're going to the other end of the chasm," Alexander said. "The cliff walls on each side are riddled with passages and chambers; some are passable, while others are caved in. Also, there are things living down there."

"What kind of things?" Anja asked, grimacing.

"Let's just do our best to avoid them," Alexander said. "Now, that staircase looks like the most promising way in."

There were several staircases leading up and down along the walls on each side of the balcony, as well as a number of bridges arcing away, then ending abruptly, broken a few dozen feet over the black of the chasm.

Most of the stairways were also crumbling, but the one Alexander chose was solid, though worn by time. It led down a hundred feet along the right side of the underdark, then transformed into a corridor with a four-foot railing made of stone but fashioned to look like a row of cornstalks separating the pathway from the dark of the chasm. Pillars that looked like tree trunks interrupted the railing every hundred feet or so, joining the outside edge of the corridor floor with the overhanging ceiling ten feet above.

Jack stopped to inspect the railing, smiling in wonder. "This is really remarkable. I've never seen such intricate work. The buildings in the city have the same grace but nowhere near the detail."

The voices of overseers shouting from the balcony above filtered down to them.

"Right ... best be going," Jack said.

Alexander dimmed his light and led the way, passing a number of doorways, ignoring them all. Most of the doors were closed and secure, made from stone and perfectly set into their frames. From the footprints on the floor, it was apparent that others, probably agents of the Babachenko, had recently been down here, no doubt looking for more Linkershim to power the forges.

A few footprints turned through a door that had been broken in half. Alexander peered inside the room, but saw no signs of life so he pressed on, sticking to the path cut into the chasm wall. As far as he was concerned, the less time he needed to spend wandering around the myriad passages riddling the massive underground cliffs that defined the chasm, the quicker he could finish his work here and go get Isabel.

The downside to traveling along the chasm wall was that they were exposed and visible, even at a great distance since they needed light to travel by, and light in the underdark could be seen for a very long way.

The overseers were well behind them when one of the wizards launched a bright white flare out into the chasm. It seemed to move slowly, traveling in a straight line until it hit just below the cornstalk railing a few dozen feet ahead of Alexander, sticking to the wall and continuing to shine brightly. It didn't do any damage, but it did mark their location. The overseers quickly began filing down the staircase from the balcony.

Alexander stopped, leaning against the wall for a moment while closing his eyes and reaching out with his all around sight. Unfortunately, it was so dark that he couldn't see enough to be useful. If he wanted to have a good look around, he would need to use his clairvoyance along with some illusionary light, and there just wasn't time for that right now.

He pressed on, choosing the quick and easy path toward his objective, even though that made him far easier to track. The underdark was vast, so the more distance he could cover toward the well of memory, the better.

His chest hurt from his wounds. Every step, every breath, every movement brought a new jab of pain. He tried to focus on it and master it as he had so many times in the past, but his mind wouldn't cooperate, so he just endured it, step-by-step.

They came to the first bridge arcing away from the corridor ... it was broken just a few feet from the railing. It looked like it was made of stone, but had no supports and was only an inch or so thick. It was railed on both sides with a perfect replica of a grapevine, down to the last detail, yet done in white marble. They passed more bridges that arced away from the path, but none were intact.

At each locked door, the footsteps marring the ancient dust moved on, while each open door appeared to have been investigated. If the overseers were careful observers, they would be able to track Alexander no matter where he went, given the layer of dust caked onto the floor.

"I can see their lights behind us," Jack said.

Alexander pressed on for over an hour, staying well ahead of the overseers, and maybe even gaining a little ground on them. Then the pathway simply ended, falling off into a fissure in the cliff face that had ripped a five-floor section wide open. It was three floors down to a level where they could traverse the fissure. He noted that the footprints stopped here and turned around.

"We either go down a few levels on ropes or back to the nearest door and into the underdark," Alexander said.

"Perhaps both are in order," Jack said.

"You want to split up?" Alexander asked.

"No. But opening that last door we passed might send the overseers off in the wrong direction while we disappear below."

"Not a bad idea," Alexander said. "You get the ropes set."

The door was about a hundred feet from the fissure. The overseers were close enough that Alexander could see them with his all around sight. He trotted up to the door and slashed through the locking mechanism and frame. It lurched slightly, then swung wide open. An insect of some sort tumbled out. It was three feet long with spiked chitin in five sections along its back and nine-inch pincers on either side of its maw. Two more insects tumbled out on top of the first, which was struggling to right itself.

As Alexander backed away, he saw five more coming out into the corridor. They must have built a nest right next to the door, he thought, chiding himself for not looking before opening it. Those thoughts vanished when the first three insects got on their feet and started coming his way.

"Bugs!" Alexander shouted. "Go quickly, all of you."

The giant insects were fast. The first three reached him at about the same time. He swept the Thinblade across their bodies, cutting them in half, but not before the third in line managed to lock on to his leg with its pincers, cutting into both sides of his calf and dropping him to one knee.

He looked up, estimating how long he had before another six were on him while swiping the Thinblade through the pincers still attached to his leg and pulling them loose, wincing in pain, fresh blood beginning to flow.

Jataan darted past him, his Weaponere's stone becoming a ten-foot pike that he used expertly to keep the insects from advancing, killing three in a second. One went over the cornstalk railing and started crawling along the outside toward them.

Alexander regained his feet and yelled, "Fall back!"

His leg hurt. It almost couldn't support his full weight, but he managed to work his way backward while Jataan killed bugs with surprising efficiency, modifying his weapon into a spear when they got closer, then into a sword. They kept coming, filling the passage and crawling along the outside of the cornstalk railing, advancing as fast as Alexander and Jataan could retreat.

"Go!" Alexander shouted to Jack over his shoulder, swiping through a bug crawling over the railing into the corridor. Jack slid down the rope into the fissure.

"Go, Lord Reishi, I will hold them," Jataan said.

The battle mage was fighting an epic battle, spinning, stabbing, slashing, killing dozens of insects, but they kept coming, spilling over their dead in waves, large numbers going over the railing and onto the wall of the chasm.

"Be quick," Alexander said, then slid down the rope, descending into a pitched battle three levels below. Anja was close to the edge of the chasm, hacking every bug that came around the wall. A dozen lay dead at her feet. Jack was close behind her and less than visible while Lita stood farther back, shield in place, casting a spell.

A bug fell near Alexander. He flicked the Thinblade through its head. Jataan was sliding down the rope. Another three bugs fell around Alexander while dozens more crawled over the edge above and started picking their way down.

Alexander killed two bugs before a third locked its pincers around his leg a few inches below where the first one had bitten him. He cut its face off with a swipe of the Thinblade and pulled the pincers off his leg. His trouser cuff and boot were soaked with blood and he was starting to feel light-headed.

A force-push from Lita blasted five or six bugs out into the chasm—Anja looked back at her with a frown when they passed over her head.

When Jataan hit the ground, Alexander opened the Wizard's Den.

"Inside, quickly!" he shouted.

Jack slipped inside without taking his hood down, kicking a bug along the way, sending it skittering across the floor.

Lita was in next.

A wave of bugs fell off the path above, six landing all around them, then four more.

"Anja!" Alexander shouted.

Anja ran for the door, slashing a bug along the way and sending it flying away in two pieces. Another landed right next to her and locked on to her leg. She stabbed it through the head, driving the tip of her broadsword into the dirt, then tore the body off with her free hand and threw it at the nearest bug before darting inside the Wizard's Den, followed quickly by Alexander and Jataan.

The door closed behind them and the sound of skittering stopped.

Chapter 31

Alexander sat down on the nearest bed, tenderly probing the four gashes on his lower leg. "Everyone all right?"

"You seem to make a habit of getting beaten up the most," Lita said, pulling a chair up next to him. "Let me have a look." She laid her hand on his leg and closed her eyes, muttering under her breath.

"Well, the good news is, they're not poisonous," she said. "The bad news is, those are some pretty nasty wounds. Lie back, let me clean them and spell them to speed the healing."

Alexander eased himself onto the bed and let Lita go to work. She cut away part of his trouser leg, then gently cleaned and bandaged his wounds. Only after she'd done all of the more mundane work of a healer did she cast her healing spell. Isabel had told him once how rare healers were among the Reishi Coven. While Lita couldn't channel the realm of light like Isabel could, she was a very capable healer.

Alexander felt warmth and soothing detachment fill his leg, then spread into the rest of his body, lulling him into a deep, restorative sleep. He woke with a dull throbbing in his leg. Peeling away the bandages, he was surprised just how well it had healed, even though the wounds had yet to fully close.

Lita came bustling over when she saw that he was awake.

"Let me see," she said, peering at the four crosswise gashes on his lower leg, shaking her head. "These haven't healed as well as I would have liked. Let me make a poultice and put on a clean bandage." She didn't wait for Alexander to respond before hurrying away.

Jack pulled up a chair and sat down. "I'm sorry."

"What for?"

"Suggesting you open that door," he said. "Wasn't such a great idea after all."

"You couldn't have known … but I could have, if I'd just looked. If anyone's to blame, it's me."

"Do you think they're still out there?"

"I'm hoping the overseers attracted their attention."

"That would certainly make sense," Jack said. "My money's on the bugs."

"There did seem to be a lot of them. Let's hope we don't run into another nest."

"All right then," Lita said, sitting on the edge of the bed. "This might hurt a bit." She carefully spread a green paste into his wounds, then wrapped his leg with fresh bandages.

"You should eat something before I spell you again," she said. "Have to keep up your strength."

Just then Anja woke in the bed next to his, sitting up and stretching with a giant yawn. She seemed to come to her senses a few moments later and frowned, looking down at her leg. Her wounds weren't as bad as Alexander's, but even with Lita's healing spell, her injury still hadn't fully healed either.

"I didn't like those bugs at all," she said.

"Me neither," Alexander said. "Hopefully, we can avoid them from now on."

After breakfast, Alexander eased himself back into bed.

"Are we ready?" Lita asked.

"Not quite yet. I need some counsel before I go back to sleep."

He smiled at her quizzical frown, then touched the Sovereign Stone, his awareness abruptly transferring from the world of time and substance to the Reishi Sovereign Council.

He sat down at the table and detailed everything that had transpired, starting with his voyage from the Spires right up to the present moment. He dredged his memory for everything of significance or importance that he could offer them: Anja, the Goiri, Luminessence, Demonrend, the Tyr Thinblade, the keystone box and Lacy, progress with his magic, and finally culminating with an exhaustive recounting of his experiences with McGinty and Siduri.

"The news about Anja is disturbing," Balthazar said. "Protect her well; your life may depend upon it."

"I know," Alexander said. "Bragador seemed willing to accept her daughter's decision for now, but I doubt she would forgive me if Anja got hurt."

"Your magic seems to be progressing rapidly," Constantine said, "especially given your experience with Siduri."

"I agree. My ability to see coming threats has proven to be reliable and it's dramatically improved my abilities in a fight. My all around sight continues to gain in range, though I still can't see as far as my eyes could. My illusion magic is becoming easier and more versatile, though I still have to be meditating to use it.

"My most important questions center around Siduri."

"Understandably so," Balthazar said. "Are you certain that you transitioned physically into the firmament?"

All of the sovereigns leaned in with interest.

"Yes, absolutely. I was on the ground choking to death and then I found myself in the firmament. When I returned, I was standing in the cage and the slave collar was lying on the floor. Later, the Babachenko revealed that he has magic capable of showing all that has transpired in a given space over previous hours or days. His spell showed me locked in my cage, lying on the floor one moment, then simply gone the next, only to reappear standing up several minutes later."

"Remarkable," Dominic said.

"Indeed," Balthazar said. "While in the firmament, what was your sense of it? How was it different than your usual experience?"

"Usually, I feel like I'm floating on an ocean, at the surface. I can focus my attention on any point in the world or I can spread out across the entire surface and listen to the music of creation, but this time, it felt like I was drowning in the ocean, like my consciousness was scattered and I couldn't get it back. I've been scattered before by Phane and by the wards around the fortress islands, but I was always able to reassemble my consciousness. This time, it felt like I was slipping away—dying. Then I thought of Siduri and I was there with him in a constructed world of his making."

The sovereigns shared looks across the table.

"Lies," Malachi said, sitting back with a scowl. "None of that's possible."

Alexander ignored him.

"There is great risk in what I'm about to suggest," Balthazar said, "but I see no other way to pursue this capability."

Alexander nodded.

"I suggest that you project your mind into the firmament and then deliberately cause it to be scattered, but don't reassemble it immediately. Allow yourself to reach that place where you feel like you're fading away, and then think of Siduri.

"If you can place your mind into the same state as it was in while you were physically within the firmament, then you may be able to reach out to the first adept at will."

Alexander felt a little thrill of fear. He had always felt panic and desperation when he'd been scattered into the firmament. Every time, it had been a mad struggle to reassemble his consciousness. Letting himself go—letting himself cease to be—allowing his unique identity to melt into the firmament was a daunting prospect.

"What if it doesn't work?"

"You may die," Balthazar said.

"I see. Are there any other suggestions for how I can pursue this new capability?"

"You could always kill yourself," Malachi said with a malicious smile. "After all, that's what it took to make it happen the first time."

Alexander glared at him.

"Perhaps that's not an entirely meritless suggestion," Darius said.

"Yes, my son may have inadvertently offered something of value," Demetrius said.

"How do you mean?"

"Your life was being threatened very slowly when you transitioned into the firmament," Demetrius said. "If you were able to re-create such an experience in a controlled environment, you may replicate the event, though I would be concerned about exiting the firmament given that you required Siduri's assistance the first time."

"That seems a bit extreme."

Malachi snorted derisively. "That's why you'll lose."

"I would recommend that you pursue the first avenue and seek out Siduri's assistance in the matter," Balthazar said. "He may be the only one who can help you learn to control this ability."

"He seemed reluctant to help me."

"Then you must be persuasive," Balthazar said. "From your account, this Siduri has a conscience. He feels guilt and remorse for the damage that he's caused the world. He wants his children to be redeemed. Use these desires to help him see his only true path to redemption."

"He's afraid, and I don't blame him. I'm not sure that anything can overcome that."

Balthazar shrugged helplessly.

"Perhaps this constructed world of his deserves some attention," Darius said.

"How so?" Balthazar asked.

"I would be interested to know how real this construct actually is," Darius said.

"It felt as real as the world of time and substance."

"More to the point, how detailed is his re-creation? How faithfully has he rebuilt the world?"

"Ahh ..." Balthazar said, realization lighting up his face. "A proxy world."

"If it's actually a creation rather than an illusion, the implications are staggering," Darius said.

"I don't understand," Alexander said.

"Of course you don't," Malachi scoffed.

"It may be that Siduri has in fact created another world," Darius said, "a world where he can do and be as he wills because it is entirely his creation."

"That may explain how he was able to travel into the netherworld in the first place," Balthazar said. "Theoretically, in a world that was his creation, he could simply step into the aether and then open a portal to the netherworld, provided the assumption is correct, that he has omnipotence within his creation."

"Did you see any limitations to the environment while you were there?" Darius asked.

"Not that I recall," Alexander said, "but I had other things on my mind at the time."

"Understandable," Darius said. "I suspect that you would find a less than complete world if you did some exploring within his construct."

Alexander nodded to himself, thinking about his magic. He'd reached a point where further advancement required him to take real risks, yet the potential gains could easily prove to be the decisive factor in the entire war. He had no choice but to make the attempt, even though the idea of becoming lost in the firmament was terrifying.

"Thank you," he said as he stood up. "You've given me a lot to think about."

"One other thing," Balthazar said. "Luminessence may have the power to destroy the Nether Gate, though I believe it would destroy the staff in the process."

Alexander sat back down.

"If the staff were thrust into the portal while it was open, I believe that both items would be destroyed. Light and dark cannot coexist in the same place at the same time ... the rules of reality won't allow it."

"Huh ... that is good news."

He walked away from the table and opened his eyes to find Lita sitting nearby, waiting for him to return. She cast her healing spell on his leg again, putting him into a deep sleep for another six hours. When he woke, he felt good enough to get out of bed, provided he had his cane. He frowned when he realized how familiar it felt in his hand. He'd spent much of his time on the dragon isle leaning on his cane; now he needed it again, though he suspected his leg would be much better by the following morning. Lita's healing magic wasn't fast, but it did work.

He went to his magic circle and sat down with some effort, crossing his legs gingerly and grimacing at the pain.

Jack frowned questioningly. "I thought the door had to be open for you to go anywhere."

Alexander paused, weighing how much he wanted to tell his friends, knowing that they would object if they had any idea what he was considering, but deciding that they deserved to know.

"I had a new magical experience when I was a prisoner. The Babachenko poisoned me with a venom that caused extreme pain, so much pain that I began to lose my grip on reality and started involuntarily slipping into the firmament. But when I did, the collar would start choking me, bringing me back, only to slip away again, until I thought I was dying. Then something unexpected happened. I found myself in the firmament—physically."

Jataan's eyes went a little wide. Lita gasped. Chloe spun into existence, then disappeared again.

"The Babachenko confirmed it for me with one of his divination spells. I actually vanished from the world of time and substance for several minutes, leaving my slave collar behind, and then reappeared back in my cell.

"The sovereigns have suggested some exercises to help me better understand what happened and learn to control it … but they're dangerous."

"How so, Lord Reishi?" Jataan asked.

"The first involves me deliberately scattering my mind into the firmament."

"You'll die," Lita said.

"That is my understanding as well, Lord Reishi," Jataan said. "I urge you to reconsider."

"Just out of curiosity," Jack said, "what happened while you were in the firmament?"

Everyone looked at the bard.

He shrugged. "Alexander wouldn't be considering this unless he had good reason, and I suspect that his experience in the firmament has something to do with that."

Alexander nodded, quietly grateful to Jack for giving him an opportunity to introduce Siduri and explain his part in the history of the world without revealing the existence of the blood of the earth. He felt a nagging sense of guilt about misleading his friends and a squirming sort of frustration in his belly at having to remember the lies he'd told so far just so he could keep them straight.

How deceivers went through life telling one lie after the next without their guts constantly being tied in a knot was a mystery to him.

"I met someone there."

"In the firmament?" Jack asked.

"Yes," Alexander said.

He spent nearly an hour explaining everything he could about Siduri, his history and the nature of his power, while carefully omitting any reference to the blood of the earth. His friends sat silently, listening with rapt attention to his account. Even Jack was at a loss for words when he finished.

"I need Siduri's help to master this new talent and the only way I know to reach him is to get lost in the firmament."

"What if you can't get back?" Jack asked.

Alexander shrugged.

"You'll die, that's what," Anja said. "And with us trapped in here."

"You do have a point there," Alexander said. "Honestly, I wouldn't know how to scatter my mind into the firmament anyway. I think I'll need the help of the fortress island wards to do that and I can't get there with the door closed."

"So what's your plan then?" Jack asked.

"Actually, I'm not quite sure. My relationship with the firmament seems to be changing and I want to explore that a bit."

He closed his eyes and quieted his mind. He could see the worry on his friends faces and in their colors before he slipped into the firmament. Rather than try to go anywhere or see anything, he chose to delve into the depths of the firmament itself. It was a struggle at first, his mind resisting, hints of panic dancing on the edge of his awareness, yet he pressed on, willing himself deeper into the ocean of creation, beneath the surface where reality happened.

The deeper he went, the quieter it got, the song of creation fading away and leaving only stillness and solitude. As he pushed further, he began to slough off many of his worldly concerns, his cares and worries becoming trivial and ephemeral in the face of such vast, untapped creative potential. Piece by piece, Alexander lost himself in the firmament, until there was nothing left but the witness, detached and unconcerned, aloof, yet fully aware.

There he found a kind of duality. A sense of immense isolation permeated his being, offering sensations of peace and belonging so fulfilling that he couldn't imagine ever letting them go, while at the same time he felt a profound connection to all life everywhere, a kinship like nothing he'd ever felt before, a oneness that subtly shifted his understanding of reality.

In that place of deep quiet, Alexander was content to rest, floating serenely. Time and substance were no longer his concern. They'd become abstract concepts in the face of the void, the quiet emptiness from which all things of substance were born and to which all things of substance would return. In that place, seeing reality as a whole, his worldly concerns seemed like distant dreams, fleeting and illusory.

He had found peace.

But then the peace was interrupted by a faint cry for help. Distant, yet insistent, a voice that should have been familiar called out for his help. Like remembrance of a dream, the source of the voice came to him: it was Chloe. As if a scrap of his personality snapped into place, he remembered who she was and what she meant to him.

He heard her again, farther away, an edge of panic and despair in her tiny voice. She was in trouble. Another fragment of his psyche returned to him. She needed his help.

With an act of will, he reassembled his essential being, transforming from the detached witness back into himself in an instant, willing himself toward the surface of the firmament, casting his awareness across the whole of creation and finding Chloe in a construct of her own making, oblivious to the plight of the world, lost in a fantasy that looked exactly like the Valley of the Fairy Queen.

"Short people aren't supposed to be here," she said chidingly, when Alexander appeared before her.

"Chloe, it's me, Alexander."

"That's a good name, but you're still not supposed to be here. The way out is that way." She spun into a ball of light and vanished, giggling.

Realization of what was happening slammed into him and he snapped back to his own body, severing his connection with the firmament immediately, and by extension, cutting Chloe off from it as well.

He opened his eyes and found himself slumped over in his circle, pillows propping him up so he wouldn't fall off the low table that the circle was set into. Jack and Anja were pacing, Lita was sitting nearby, and Jataan stood against the wall with his hands clasped behind his back, worry etched into his swarthy face. Chloe lay unconscious just inside the circle on a little pillow.

Alexander was suddenly overwhelmed with a sensation of thirst followed by hunger. When he stirred, everyone in the room came rushing to his side. Chloe woke a moment later, buzzing into the air, spinning into a ball of light, buzzing higher and higher with each spin until she was at the ceiling.

"He's back!" she shouted.

Alexander tried to speak, but his throat was so dry he started coughing, a rough, dry, sharp cough that felt like he'd swallowed broken glass. Lita gently brought a cup of water to his lips. He seized it, gulping it down as quickly as he could, spitting most of it right back up in a spasm of coughing and wheezing.

Jack handed Lita another cup of water.

"Slowly," she said, holding it up to him.

Alexander had to make an effort to sip the water. Every part of his body cried out for it like he was dying of thirst, but he took just enough to wet his mouth and throat, swallowing with effort, before taking another sip, then another, until he was able to drink freely. Then he drank until his belly felt full, but still he wanted more.

"That's enough for now," Lita said. "Any more and you'll get sick. Let's get you back to bed."

He tried to walk but his legs wouldn't do as he wished, so Jack and Jataan nearly carried him, easing him down carefully. His muscles were cramped and stiff, sore and disobedient. Once in bed, he relaxed a bit, but the pain mixed with his dehydration and hunger made the thought of sleep seem impossible until Lita started casting her healing spell. A few moments later he was out.

He woke hungry and thirsty. Fortunately, Lita and Jack were ready, offering him a cup of water and a meal as soon as he opened his eyes.

"How long was I gone?" he asked between a drink and a mouthful.

"Almost three days," Jack said.

Alexander felt a little thrill of fear race up his spine. He'd become lost in the firmament.

Chloe buzzed into existence, floating over his plate in front of him. "We thought we'd lost you, My Love. I was so worried."

"I'm sorry, Little One. Thank you for coming to get me."

"I didn't even know if I could do that, but we didn't have any other choice. No matter what we did, you wouldn't wake up." She started to cry.

"Hush, it's all right, you saved me, Little One."

She floated down and landed on his knee, struggling to stifle her tears.

"How did you find me?" he asked.

"I didn't … you found me," Chloe said. "When we couldn't wake you, I sent my mind into yours and immediately found myself in the firmament. I vaguely remember the first few seconds being disorienting and confusing. I called out for help, but then I was back in the Valley of the Fairy Queen with my family, living as we have for thousands of years. It felt so natural, so real, that I didn't even realize it wasn't. I would have stayed there if you hadn't broken your link with the firmament and forced me to return."

"What happened, Alexander?" Jack asked.

"I got lost in the firmament," Alexander said. "It's hard to explain. I was in a place of such profound peace that I didn't want to leave. Time had no meaning … I was simply content to be. Even now, I feel a longing to go back there, like I'm being called home."

"Well, don't," Anja said. "You almost died, just like I said you would."

"I know," Alexander said quietly.

"Any contact with Siduri?" Jack asked.

"No. In fact, once I got to this place of peace, I forgot all about him."

"Maybe you ought to give it some time and some thought before you try that again," Jack said.

"You're not going to try that again, are you?" Anja asked.

"I have to," Alexander said. "Siduri is too important to ignore. He can help me master my magic and he may be the key to destroying the shades once and for all."

"But it almost killed you," Anja said.

"I'll be more careful next time and I have some experience to build on, but Jack's right, I need to think about it for a while before I try again."

Chapter 32

Several bandage changes, followed by further healing spells, followed by sleep, brought Alexander to the moment he'd been silently dreading. He was on his feet, his leg strong enough, though still a bit tender, his weapons and armor in place, Luminessence in hand. Jataan and Anja flanked him on either side with Lita and Jack well behind them.

Alexander looked to Jataan and Anja in turn; both nodded. He willed the door open, dimming the light in the room to almost nothing in the same moment. Silence and darkness. Alexander breathed a sigh of relief, bringing the light up a bit. Jataan peered outside, listening for any hint of a threat.

"I believe they've gone," he said.

"Good," Alexander and Anja said in unison.

"Keep an eye on the door while I have a look around," Alexander said, going to his magic circle.

His leg gave him a few jabs of pain when he sat down to meditate, but once he'd cleared his mind, he slipped into the firmament easily, bringing his awareness into being above his head. He floated out the door and up three levels to the open-sided corridor they'd followed into the underdark, then to the door he'd opened, using only his aura vision to see. A steady stream of insects was moving into and out of the room, but the ones coming out were all going toward the main entrance, away from Alexander and his friends.

He floated toward the way they'd come in. The corridor was littered with the well-picked-over corpses of dozens of overseers, some insects stopping to search for a last scrap but most crawling over the stripped bones without pausing. At the next open door, about half of the insects turned into the underdark, while the rest continued on toward the entry hall.

He floated to the balcony and found a garrison of soldiers setting up behind a shield wall that warded the threshold between them and the entry corridor. The bugs had reached the shield and a few seemed to be stationed on the balcony, but the rest fanned out like search parties taking every viable pathway into the underdark.

Alexander drifted through the shield and into the enemy forces assembling beyond and found them wanting. While several of the ranking overseers were Acuna wizards, most were little more than organized thugs. Palace guards or even Lancers would have been better suited to the task, but the overseers had jurisdiction over the city proper and they weren't about to give that up, even if it meant losing many of their own men.

Alexander could see the fear in them. They whispered stories of how the first group of overseers to venture into the underdark had never returned. Officers talked of plans, but the men looked nervously through the shield wall at the enemy, as inhuman and impersonal as it could get, flowing by like a river, ignorant of strategy, impossible to negotiate with, driven only by hunger and instinct.

He snapped back to the fissure and began exploring in the direction of the well of memory. The main pathways along the chasm wall were collapsed, broken in multiple places for several thousand feet. He floated through the dark as a ball of light, inspecting the open-sided corridors cut into the chasm wall but found none leading away from the fissure that were intact for any significant distance.

That left the underdark. He returned to the fissure and searched the area, looking for passages out. Finding three, he followed each for a distance. One wrapped back around in the wrong direction. Another ended in a cave-in. The third eventually led up a flight of stairs and connected to a hallway that seemed to be the underdark's version of a road, long and straight and well-supported. More importantly, it looked intact for quite a ways in both directions. Alexander returned to his body and opened his eyes, closing the door to the Wizard's Den, just to be safe.

"There were a lot more bugs than we thought. Fortunately, they've branched out in the other direction."

"That might complicate getting out," Jack said.

"Not nearly as much as the regiment of overseers camped at the entrance."

"I take it the bugs did win," Jack said.

"Very much so. Most of the overseers are terrified. Fortunately, all of that is happening back there. I think I've found a way through. Try to be as quiet as possible. I'll keep our light to a minimum; I don't want to draw the bugs' attention."

They slipped out of the Wizard's Den under a very dim light from Luminessence. Everyone followed closely behind Alexander, taking great care to make as little noise as possible.

The fissure had opened a crack in a nearby wall. Alexander slipped through it and into a large room that might have once been a public bath. Bringing his light up to examine the art on the walls, he revealed a continuous fresco of fair-haired, frail-looking creatures tending to the lands and forests around them. They were depicted as wielding great magic for the betterment of the world they'd chosen to act as stewards for.

"The ancient history in this room alone could inspire a hundred songs," Jack said.

"I know what you mean," Alexander said. "I wish we had more time."

The only door out of the room led into a tiled room filled with several benches situated between floor-to-ceiling armoires. Through that room and into the next hall, they found a straight corridor with stone doors every fifty feet or so on either side. Alexander ignored them, stretching out with his all around sight, looking for any hint of a threat in the distance, but finding only cold, empty passages and long-abandoned rooms.

Around a corner, they found a mound of dirt and stones with a crystal shard about a foot long poking out of the top.

"Hey, look at this," Anja said, picking up the shard and holding it close to Alexander's light.

"Be very careful with that," Alexander said. "It's alive."

Jack inhaled sharply, his eyes going wide as he angled for a closer look. "This crystal is a sentient being?"

"Yes."

"And these built all this," Jack said.

"Yes."

Anja gently set it down atop its pile of dirt and rocks.

"How interesting," Lita whispered.

Alexander waited for the question he knew Jack wanted to ask next, but Jack just winked at him with a smile. They continued into the underdark, winding through what looked like a residential community. Alexander found it hard to understand why anyone would choose to live underground. It was dark and the air was stale. He already missed the sun.

Before long, he found the staircase leading up to the long hall. The hallway was twenty feet wide and just as high, running straight in both directions. Alexander suspected it had once been an underground thoroughfare for this side of the underdark. Now, he just hoped it was unused.

It certainly sounded that way, as quiet as a tomb with air just as still. Every noise felt like a trespass. He brought up the light and waited for a moment, listening for a response from some denizen of the underdark, but heard nothing.

With a shrug, he set out, his friends trailing behind him. Not five minutes later, they came to an intersection with another passage half the size of the one they were traveling. Left led toward the chasm, right went deeper into the underdark. Alexander continued going straight.

At regular intervals, they encountered similar intersections with smaller passages, occasional staircases appearing more sporadically. Alexander found himself relying on his hearing as much as his vision, stopping at each intersection to listen for any hint of a threat, but it was dead quiet for several hours.

"This place is huge," Jack whispered.

"As big as a city," Alexander said.

"Must've been a sight to behold at its height," Lita said.

"Indeed," Jataan whispered.

A few minutes later, Alexander thought he heard something so he doused his light, plunging the passage into total blackness. Everyone froze, stopping in their tracks and holding their breath. Faint sounds of people talking filtered through the underdark.

Alexander sent his all around sight down the corridor, but he reached the limit of his range before he found the source of the voices. He opened the door to his Wizard's Den, lowering the light to almost total dark at the same time. Once inside the protection of his magic circle, he slipped into the firmament and sent his awareness down the hallway. Almost a league of corridor brought him to a large room that served as the intersection of two large corridors along with several sets of stairs going both up and down.

A dozen overseers stood in a circle around the Acuna wizard who'd tried earlier to stop Alexander from entering the underdark. Several of the overseers were shouting at the wizard all at the same time.

"You got us into this ... how're you going to get us out?"

"He's lost."

"That wouldn't be so bad if he hadn't collapsed the tunnel we came in through."

"He's been nothing but trouble; we should leave him."

"His magic might be useful."

"You mean like when he collapsed the tunnel?"

"Had I not collapsed the tunnel," the wizard said, "you would all be dead. Now, I suggest you lower your voices. She may know of another way into this chamber." He gestured toward the multiple staircases and passages.

"Do you really think that thing might come back?" an overseer whispered.

"Perhaps," the wizard said quietly.

"We've got to get out of here."

"I agree. We should go that way," the wizard said, pointing toward the passage that Alexander and his friends were traveling.

"No!" several said hotly.

"That's deeper in."

"Are you sure?"

"You want to go the wrong way."

"The exit's that way," another said, pointing in the opposite direction.

"I assure you, that is the passage we want to take," the wizard said.

"You said those exact same words earlier today."

"Yeah."

"Look where that got us."

"Earlier today, we were running for our lives," the wizard said. "The path I chose was necessary at the time. This path is necessary now."

"You know full well the only reason we got away was because the bugs stopped to eat our fallen."

"And because we entered the underdark through a door that I was able to secure behind us," the wizard said. "Had we stayed in the open-sided corridor, we would have been overtaken. You would all be dead."

"You think you would have survived?"

"Most assuredly," he said, his shield flaring just enough to make it briefly visible.

"Why do you need to be using your magic right now?"

"Yeah, don't you trust us?"

"Not especially," the wizard said, "but I do have an obligation to apprehend the fugitive and your help would be invaluable."

"You want us to do our jobs? Down here? This place is trying to kill us. We need to get out of here."

"He's right."

"I told you, we should leave him."

"Maybe you're right."

"What was that?"

"What was what?"

"I thought I heard something."

"You're imagining things."

"No, he's right."

Everyone fell silent.

Click … click … click. Chitin on stone.

"Quickly, follow me," the wizard said, racing through the cordon of overseers surrounding him and heading toward the underground road. Several overseers followed him without hesitation, while a group of five stayed where they were, listening to the darkness.

Click … click … click.

Alexander saw it emerge from a stairwell, crawling up onto the wall and then to the ceiling where it coiled around a pillar, eyeing the five remaining men.

A centipede. Twenty-five feet long and two feet wide, with barbed black chitin covering the entire length of its segmented body, two-foot serrated mandibles surrounding its mouth, two multi-jointed legs ending with oversized pincers jutting from its body a few feet behind its head, a foot-long stinger on its tail.

"The wizard can make light," one of the overseers said, holding up his lamp so he could see how much oil he had left.

"I hadn't thought of that."

"Maybe we should stick together."

They all nodded to each other before starting toward the passage.

The centipede launched from the top of the pillar, uncoiling quickly yet silently. It hit one of the men in the middle of the back, slicing him clean in half with its mandibles, crashing into the ground with a clatter and using the momentum to carry it into the remaining four men, taking two men's heads with a pincer each in lightning-quick strikes. The last two men got the worst of it. The centipede coiled around them both, raking them with its razor-sharp barbs, stripping flesh away in chunks and filling the underdark with screams that died out in gurgling gasps.

Glistening with blood, the centipede froze in place, its antennae flicking this way and that. After a moment, it began to eat.

Alexander opened his eyes and closed the door to his Wizard's Den, bringing up the light and gesturing toward the table. He spent a few minutes explaining what lay ahead, both the overseers and the centipede. He had never liked bugs, but this one really made his skin crawl. He did his best to describe it in complete detail.

"That sounds quite beyond me," Jack said.

"I suspect that it's beyond me as well," Lita said.

"I'll kill it," Anja said.

"No, you won't," Alexander said. "It's fast, and every part of it is deadly. We're going to avoid it."

"What if we can't?" Anja asked.

"Then Jataan and I will kill it."

"I'm going to help too," Anja said.

"No, not with this thing. It's too fast. Besides, we're going to avoid it," he said pointedly.

She frowned.

"It seems like this road is heading in the right direction," Jack said. "Are we going to take a detour to avoid that chamber?"

"No, we'll wait," Alexander said. "I want to give the overseers time to get well past us. Hopefully, the bug will finish eating and go take a nap."

Chapter 33

Alexander crept along the wall, the fingers of his left hand lightly brushing the stone. One by one, his companions followed behind him through the dark. He held Luminessence, but kept its light extinguished, fearing that any illumination might alert the centipede to their presence.

Even in total black, Alexander could still see the colors of things, so he was confident that he would see the predator insect in time to take refuge in the Wizard's Den. He had wondered why this underground road seemed so desolate. Now he suspected it was because it was part of the centipede's hunting grounds.

They walked for a long time in complete darkness. Alexander had to remind himself to relax his muscles; he kept finding himself so tense it was giving him a headache. He was starting to think that his plan had worked, that the centipede had moved along, but then he saw a slight glimmer of color on the floor ahead.

He stopped, listening for a moment before lighting the hall with Luminessence. Five overseers were torn apart, their blood still sticky, parts of them scattered haphazardly down the passage. The centipede had eaten only part of one, leaving the rest to feed some other denizen of the underdark ... or to rot.

Alexander noted the unusual trail of blood leading back toward the intersection chamber, two wavering patterns of tiny streaks of red running generally parallel. As they gained distance from the grisly scene, the blood trail diminished, then vanished altogether. Alexander extinguished his light again, relying on the wall and his magic for guidance. They crept forward slowly and quietly.

Click ... click ... click.

He froze, listening intently and looking ahead with his all around sight. They were only a few hundred feet from the intersection room. The centipede had returned to the top of one of the support pillars where it was lying in wait, clicking its pincers every so often.

Alexander opened the door to his Wizard's Den.

"Let's see if we can draw it out," he whispered. "I'd rather fight it in this corridor than in the intersection room. If things go badly, we'll retreat into the Wizard's Den."

When everyone had made what preparations they could, Alexander lit the corridor with Luminessence, filling the passageway with light for hundreds of feet in both directions.

Click ... click ... click.

The creature started toward them, tentatively inching down the underground road, but then turning and scurrying away when it reached the edge of the light.

"I guess it doesn't like light."

"Good to know," Jack said, checking his vial of night-wisp dust.

They approached the intersection room cautiously, stopping at the threshold to look and listen before venturing inside. The centipede was nowhere to be seen, but the remains of overseers were scattered across the floor … a grisly reminder that it was still out there.

"I see light," Jack said.

In the distance, down the corridor leading toward the chasm, flickered several faint points of lantern light.

"Overseers," Alexander said. "They've seen us for sure. Let's keep moving."

He led them out of the intersection room along the same road they'd been traveling, farther into the underdark, no longer attempting to conceal their location by keeping the light low, but instead letting Luminessence fill the passage with bright and clear illumination. While it would give away their position, he hoped it would also keep some of the more unpleasant denizens of the deep from bothering them.

They began to notice bits of bone and splotchy stains on the floor. When they came to a doorway without a door, Alexander drew the Thinblade before angling for a look inside. The room was twenty feet on each side. Remnants of past meals were scattered around a large pile of eggs mounded up in one corner.

"I don't like the looks of that," Jack said.

"No. Let's be somewhere else when mama comes home."

"The overseers have reached the intersection room," Jataan said.

"Yeah, and it looks like a lot of them, too," Anja said.

"Right, let's go," Alexander said, setting a faster pace than before.

Echoes of unintelligible shouts from behind them filtered down the corridor, but the only thing Alexander could make out was anger. He didn't relish fighting the overseers, but they seemed like a far more manageable foe than the centipede.

Their angry shouts abruptly transformed into shrieks of fear and barking commands, followed by screaming and the flash of a spell.

"Well, that worked out," Alexander said without slowing his pace.

Another hour brought them face-to-face with a stone statue of a man in plate armor—a sentinel. It stood in the middle of the corridor, still and silent. A few dozen feet behind it, the corridor was partially blocked by an enormous stone door. The door looked to have been built to completely block the corridor, yet it had been blasted asunder, cracked down the middle by some magic beyond Alexander's understanding. This door could have repelled any army, stopped an onrushing flood, protected against any siege, yet magic had undone it, fracturing it right down the middle, opening a crack wide enough for a man to pass through.

When Alexander came within a dozen feet of the sentinel, its eyes began to glow a soft red and it brought its spear and shield up into a defensive stance.

"You shall not pass," a distant voice said.

"We've come to revive the Linkershim," Alexander said. "We are not enemies."

"You shall not pass."

"Who commands you?"

"You shall not pass."

"Not a terribly responsive fellow," Jack said.

"How about some light, Jack?" Alexander said, opening the door to his Wizard's Den and setting Luminessence just inside. Jack held up his night-wisp dust, replacing the soft, warm, life-affirming light of Alexander's staff with a harsher, more glaring light.

"Perhaps you should allow me," Jataan said.

"No, I don't think so, Jataan," Alexander said. "I've fought one of these before, and my sword didn't even put a mark on it. But I suspect this will do the trick nicely." He drew the Thinblade.

"As you wish, Lord Reishi."

Alexander advanced slowly, stretching out into the coming moments with his mind. The sentinel moved quickly, thrusting hard with its spear over the top of its large round shield. Alexander turned sideways, letting the tip go past him before bringing the Thinblade up through the haft. Three feet of the sentinel's spear fell away, turning to ash and leaving little more than a line of grey powder where it hit the floor.

The sentinel didn't hesitate, dropping its damaged spear and drawing its sword before pressing the attack, raising its shield high and thrusting low, targeting the inside of Alexander's leg. He slipped aside, cut the blade of the sentinel's sword, then swept up through its shield and forearm. The sentinel froze for a fraction of a moment, then turned to ash and fell to the floor in a grey cloud.

There was a moment of silence before the whole world seemed to vibrate. The enormous door started to grind and move.

"Run!" Alexander shouted. "We have to make it through!"

He darted ahead, racing through the narrow passage while the block of stone creaked and complained, coming to life for the first time in centuries. He wasn't sure what had happened, but he was certain that he didn't want to be on the wrong side of the door when it closed. They reached the other side, racing into a room so big that Alexander couldn't see the far wall with his all around sight. A forest filled the room, created in perfect detail down to the texture of the bark and the haphazard ground cover, all made entirely of stone and metal.

The world seemed to rumble as some ancient mechanism struggled to move the broken door, then there was a jolt and the fissure in the enormous door slammed shut with a deafening crack that echoed throughout the forest room.

"I guess we won't be going back that way," Jack said.

"Probably not," Alexander agreed, retrieving Luminessence from his Wizard's Den and filling the immediate area with light.

The detail was breathtaking. Leaves made of copper adorned stone replicas of a wide variety of deciduous trees, while giant firs reached up to the ceiling several hundred feet overhead, acting as support pillars for the cavernous chamber.

"How big do you think this room is?" Anja asked.

"Huge," Alexander said. "I can't see the far wall."

Jack whistled, shaking his head in wonder.

"I never imagined a place like this even existed," Lita whispered.

"I know what you mean," Alexander said.

A noise filtered through the stone forest—voices in the distance.

"Sounds like overseers," Jack said.

"They certainly had time to get ahead of us while I healed," Alexander said. "They're probably crawling all over the underdark by now."

"So where to now?" Anja asked.

"Let's see if we can find another passage that runs along the chasm wall."

They stayed near the wall of the forest room on their way toward the chasm. As much as Alexander wanted to explore, there was nothing to be gained. And since the room was so big, they could easily get turned around within the maze of stone trees and lose valuable time. The wall offered a point of reference that Alexander hoped would lead them straight to the chasm.

And it did, opening onto a balcony running for a full league along the chasm wall, the entire length of the forest room. Stone trees stood at the edge of the balcony, holding up the ceiling three hundred feet overhead.

"Looks like you're right," Jack said, pointing out into the darkness.

They could see clusters of light in the distance, both back toward the entrance and across the chasm, but the thing that caught Alexander's attention was the giant pillar in the middle of the chasm that was encrusted with glowing crystals.

"Did any of you see that when we first entered the underdark?"

"No," they said in unison.

"In this darkness, it should have been visible ... provided it was glowing when we came in."

"What are you thinking?" Jack asked.

"When I killed the sentinel, the underdark seemed to take notice. I'm just wondering if I triggered something."

"You think you woke up some ancient security apparatus?" Jack asked.

"Possibly," Alexander said. "That sentinel wouldn't have been there, and that enormous stone door wouldn't have been there, if someone or something didn't want to secure this part of the underdark." He pointed to the edge of the balcony. "There's no corridor running along the chasm wall that joins the previous part of the underdark with this one. Seems we've entered a more secure part of the city."

"Maybe that means we won't run into any more bugs," Anja said.

"We can hope," Jack said.

They set out along the balcony, keeping a close eye on the artificial forest filling the cavernous space to their right. A bridge arced away from the balcony to the glowing pillar in the middle of the chasm. It was wide, easily broad enough to drive a horse-drawn cart across, and the railings on each side looked like perfect rows of oversized tulips, three feet high. A few were broken, but most were intact and flawless.

"Should we try the bridge?" Jack asked.

"Let's see if there's a corridor along the chasm wall leading from the other side of the balcony first," Alexander said. "A lot of those bridges don't look entirely stable, so I'd rather avoid them if we can."

Muffled voices filtered out of the stone forest. Alexander reached out with his all around sight, sweeping through the artificial trees until he found the platoon of men. Most were Lancers, but without their force lances. They were led by an Acuna wizard who'd brought along a few overseers for good measure.

"Seems they ran out of overseers and started sending in Lancers."

"This entire place is probably crawling with them by now," Jack said.

"Let's keep moving," Alexander said, continuing along the balcony, staying close to the railing. The sheer size of the forest room was impressive but it only served to underscore the vastness of the underdark—as big as any city in the world and bigger than most. He couldn't help wondering anew about those who had lived here so long ago.

Several more bridges arced gracefully away from the balcony into the darkness. All looked intact, but Alexander ignored them, hoping the balcony would join with a corridor running along the wall of the chasm, but his hopes were in vain. The balcony ended without a way off save the bridges or whatever passages might lead out of the forest room.

Not a minute after they turned back to try one of the bridges, men started filing out of the forest several hundred feet ahead of them, fanning out across the balcony and drawing weapons, the overseers shouting orders to the soldiers, forming them into two ranks stretching across the balcony, blocking escape by any route except the forest.

"Run or fight?" Jataan asked.

Before Alexander could answer, a blue sphere the size of an apple shot forth from the wizard's hand, crossing the distance with alarming speed. Time seemed to slow. Alexander saw the coming moments, and they were devastating. He moved quickly, pulling Anja away from the balcony, nearly throwing her toward the forest just a moment before the force sphere detonated. His friends were all blown toward the forest, scattering them across the stone floor, dazing them all. He was blown from his feet toward the chasm, over the railing and into the deep dark.

He'd known what was going to happen to him the moment the Acuna wizard cast his spell, but it was far preferable to losing Anja to the dark. He saw the balcony railing pass beneath him, then nothing but endless darkness. Gravity started to claim him.

He opened the door to his Wizard's Den and tumbled inside, the portal suspended in space over the void a dozen feet from the railing. He hit hard, landing poorly, Luminessence clattering across the floor. Willing himself to his knees and then to his feet, he looked out the door but couldn't see past the railing. He heard shouting and boots running on stone.

Stepping up on a chair, he could just see over the railing. Jataan was up. Anja was racing toward the railing with a look of wild panic that melted into relief the moment she saw him standing in the doorway of his Wizard's Den. Soldiers were advancing on Jataan. He strode calmly toward them, no hint of a weapon in his hands.

"Don't scare me like that," Anja said.

Alexander tossed her a coil of rope, tying one end around his waist.

"Got it?" he shouted.

Anja wrapped the rope around her waist and nodded. Alexander stepped off the edge into the darkness and fell in an arc defined by the length of the rope, his feet landing hard against the wall below the balcony. Anja started pulling, drawing him up and over the railing just in time to avoid a sword stroke.

He hit and tumbled, rolling to his feet, the Thinblade coming free … and then he was lost in the moment, the battle joined, men coming from several directions at once as the enemy ranks closed in around them. Alexander didn't think or plan or choose his moves, he simply let them happen, taking life and limb with each stroke, seeing the coming moments as if time had slowed just for him, allowing him to act with perfect knowledge. He was always right where he needed to be to avoid the next attack and deliver his next strike. Death piled up around him.

Jataan had engaged and was fighting a swarm of enemy soldiers, several already dead or dying. Jack was still down from the force sphere. Lita was hovering over him, extending her shield around him while she tended his injuries, ignoring the overseer standing over them both, beating on her shield with his weighted club.

Anja gave a battle cry that sounded more like the roar of a dragon and threw herself into the fight, cleaving the nearest man in half with a stroke of her broadsword, striking fear into the other men facing her.

The soldiers fell quickly, blood pooling around their corpses, but the wizard stood off a good distance casting another spell … and he'd been at it for far too long for the outcome to be good. An amber sphere of light leapt from his outstretched hand and shot toward the melee. Alexander saw it coming, but there was nothing he could do. It stopped not ten feet from him and expanded to a diameter of fifty feet in a blink. When the amber passed through each of them, it left them encased in magical energy, completely frozen in place—paralyzed and helpless, except for Jack and Lita. Her shield had protected them.

Fortunately, the remaining few soldiers still standing nearby were also frozen by the spell. Alexander willed the door to his Wizard's Den closed, then he reopened it right next to Lita. She didn't even hesitate, grabbing Jack by his arms and dragging him inside. Alexander willed the door closed, then focused on struggling to break free of the spell holding him in place.

"Well, as messy as that was," the wizard said, looking at the carnage all around him, "we have our prize. The Babachenko will be pleased."

"Do you think he'll let me keep this one?" one of the overseers asked, savagely hitting Anja in the belly with his club. She fell backward like a rag doll, crumpling helplessly to the ground. The big man stood over her, leering at her with a purposeful smile.

"Do you think he'll mind if I kill this one?" the other overseer asked, standing in front of Jataan. "I mean, look at this." He gestured to the dead soldiers all around the battle mage.

As hard as he struggled, Alexander couldn't break free of the spell. The wizard stopped ten feet before him and smiled, holding up a slave collar.

"Do as you will with them," the wizard said to the overseers. "The Babachenko only wants this one."

Alexander tried to vanish into the firmament, but nothing happened.

"Honestly, where did you plan to go down here?" the wizard asked, shaking his head.

"Ever been stabbed in the gut?" one overseer asked Jataan amiably. "It takes a long time to die." He hooked his club to his belt and slowly drew his curved knife, holding it up so Jataan could see it.

"I see you're fighting with a straight dagger," he said, angling to get a better look at Jataan's blade as if they were friends comparing weapons.

"I prefer ..." he started to say, but never finished. Jataan's dagger abruptly transformed into a spear, the point driving into the overseer's eye and out the back of his head.

Alexander opened the door to his Wizard's Den a few feet behind the Acuna wizard.

"This should make you more manageable," the wizard said as he slowly approached with the slave collar.

Lita stabbed him in the back, the tip of her dagger coming out of his chest. Shock, dismay and disbelief played across his face just before he slumped to his knees and died—the effect of his spell vanishing with his life.

Free of the amber light, Jataan and Alexander swept back into battle against the remaining few soldiers, quickly dispatching those that didn't flee.

While they fought, Anja regained her feet and dropped her sword, snarling at the overseer who'd hit her. She was clearly in pain, hunched over, protecting her midsection even as she advanced on the man. There was a moment of wariness in his colors, but it faded quickly. He seemed to decide that she was just a girl—no real threat.

"You want to play?" he asked with a menacing smile, raising his club.

Anja didn't raise her guard or respond to his jibe, instead shuffling toward him resolutely. When he drew back to hit her, she sprang, closing the remaining distance before he could bring his club down, hitting him in the groin with the palm of her hand hard enough to lift him a foot into the air, then grabbing him by the crotch and throat, spinning half a turn and throwing him over the balcony railing out into the chasm. His scream seemed to last a long time before it faded into the dark.

She slumped to her knees and Alexander raced to her side.

"Easy," he said, catching her and carefully picking her up, carrying her into his Wizard's Den and laying her gently on a bed.

"How's Jack?" he asked Lita.

"He hit his head. I couldn't wake him, so I put him to bed and spelled him. We'll know more in a few hours."

Jataan was the last one in after retrieving Anja's sword.

Chapter 34

"She'll be fine," Lita said quietly. "Just some cracked ribs. I'm more worried about Jack—he hit his head pretty hard."

Alexander nodded helplessly.

Lita put a reassuring hand on his shoulder. He forced a smile. Being injured himself was far easier than this; seeing his friends hurt made his stomach squirm. He felt so helpless. For all his magic, he had no power to help them.

"Jataan, watch the door," Alexander said as he headed to his magic circle.

Jataan took up his post, stepping out onto the balcony and sweeping the area for any sign of threat. "The enemy has retreated."

"Good, I'm going to have a look around."

Alexander slipped into the firmament and then coalesced his awareness above his head, gliding into the underdark and flitting to the entrance with a thought. The balcony and entry hall were now a staging area for Andalian soldiers moving into the underdark. They were already collecting Linkershim and loading them into a wagon for transport to the forges, while platoon-sized forces were systematically expanding their area of control.

The nest of bugs had been killed, though from the stains on the floor, it looked like it had been a costly battle. The Royal Assassin and the High Overseer stood with the Babachenko on the balcony, looking out into the underdark.

"He has nowhere to run," the High Overseer said.

"Perhaps, but I underestimated him once before," the Babachenko said. "I don't intend to do so again."

"We have reports of a bright light along the right-hand wall near the other end of the chasm," the High Overseer said. "Unfortunately, there's no direct route to that area since many of the corridors, bridges, and stairways are impassable."

"None of that answers the most nagging question," the Babachenko said. "Why did he come back? He was free of us. His Sky Knights could have flown him anywhere he wished to go, yet he returned here—why?"

The two men flanking him fell silent.

Alexander projected laughter behind the Babachenko, causing him to spin around, looking for its source. Satisfied with the fear and uncertainty in the Babachenko's now easily readable colors, Alexander left them, floating down the middle of the chasm, noting the units of soldiers searching both sides of the underdark.

He reached the giant pillar connected to the forest balcony and saw that it was linked with many bridges arcing off in different directions, connecting both sides of the underdark as well as a number of other large pillars rising from the darkness below and disappearing into the darkness above.

He moved to the end of the chasm and found that it closed down on both left and right as well as top and bottom, all of its walls culminating in a large room, which was open on either end, one side facing the chasm and the other facing an enormous cavern beyond. The floor was a hundred feet square and the ceiling was thirty feet high. The floor, ceiling, and walls were made of smooth granite. Several large doors opened in each side wall. It appeared that all passages and bridges in this end of the underdark funneled into this place, creating a choke point.

Standing in the exact center of the room was a ten-foot-tall creature that reminded Alexander of the stone giant conjured by Mage Dax in the battle for Ruatha's Gate. This creature was made from a collection of stones that seemed to be held together, not by crackling blue magic, but by red-hot fire. It stood stock-still.

Alexander circled it, then moved past it to the edge of the room. A single bridge abutment marked the center of the opening, but there was no bridge. In fact, Alexander saw no other way into the cavernous chamber beyond, except through the guardian chamber. Unlike the rest of the underdark, this place had no balconies or structures built into the walls. He moved forward and found what he was looking for—the well of memory.

The shrine was built atop an enormous stalagmite rising out of the deep dark.

McGinty materialized out of the stone, his imperfectly formed face struggling to convey dismay. "Why have you brought so many fleshlings into the underdark?"

"I didn't … they're hunting me."

"They are taking the Linkershim. You must stop them."

"I can't … there are too many. But I can wake the Linkershim, provided I can get here."

"I can sense the memory. It is closer, but the guardian has been awakened. Your path will be more difficult now."

"You mean that giant sentinel back there?"

"Yes, the guardian will not allow you to pass."

"It looked like it was made out of stones," Alexander said. "I can cut it into pieces."

McGinty cocked his head. "You do not understand its true nature."

"Regardless, I still have to get from there to here. How am I supposed to do that? I can't fly."

McGinty looked like he was trying to frown. "The fleshling who stole the memory could fly."

"Well, I can't."

"But you're a fleshling."

"We're not the same. Fleshlings are all different."

"You all look the same."

"Be that as it may, I still can't fly."

McGinty struggled to frown again.

"I will bridge the gap for you when you arrive, but the guardian will follow. You must be quick or you will die."

"Fair enough," Alexander said. "Can you help me find my way to the guardian?"

"Find your way?"

"I don't know how to get there."

McGinty seemed to be consulting with some source of information, his incompletely formed head cocked at an odd angle for a few moments.

"There is a path across the bridges that is still passable."

"Good. Can you show it to me?"

"Show?"

"It's so dark down here that I can't even see the bridges you're talking about."

"You require light."

"Yes."

McGinty cocked his head again and the underdark came alive. Hundreds of floating points of light began to glow, each suspended in midair, fixed in place and distributed throughout the chasm in seemingly random fashion. The soft glow illuminated the entire length of the chasm, filling the underdark with light and revealing its true majesty. It was a creation of such beauty and intricate detail that Alexander could scarcely help thinking of the Linkershim with a sense of reverence. Any race that could create such a place deserved to thrive.

Alexander intended to see that they did.

"Thank you, McGinty. I'll get to the guardian as quickly as I can."

McGinty melted back into the stones and Alexander floated back the way he'd come, taking another quick look at the guardian, then stopping to marvel at the gossamer web of bridges filling the chasm at this end of the underdark. Giant pillars served as anchor points for each span, buildings and platforms encrusting many of the pillars. Stalagmites and stalactites also played a role in the bridge network, with yet more structures built into and on them.

Unfortunately, the sudden light made it far easier for the Andalians to move about. A platoon of soldiers on the opposite side of the chasm was picking its way across a damaged part of the underdark toward one of the bridges that would eventually lead them to the forest-room balcony.

Alexander opened his eyes. Jataan and Lita were standing just inside the door, looking out at the myriad points of light.

"It's beautiful," Lita whispered, taking Jataan's hand.

Alexander smiled to himself. In the midst of war and hardship, love could still blossom, even in the most unlikely of places.

"Yes, but it also negates one of our tactical advantages," Jataan said.

"Oh, you're always so serious. Just enjoy it for a moment."

"That's good advice, Jataan," Alexander said.

Jataan turned, letting go of Lita's hand. "Lord Reishi, what has transpired?"

"I spoke with McGinty. He lit the place up for us, but that means we have to move. Lita, I'd like you to remain in the Wizard's Den to look after Jack and Anja."

"Of course, Lord Reishi."

She laid a hand on Jataan's shoulder. "Be careful."

He nodded, stepping out into the underdark and scanning the vicinity for any sign of threat. Alexander followed, leaving Luminessence leaning against the wall just inside the door.

The illumination of the underdark made it more difficult for him to see the enemy moving around in the distance, but Alexander knew they were closing in. He walked briskly toward the bridge leading to the pillar in the center of the underdark, keeping a close eye on the forest. It too had been illuminated, revealing the true majesty of its artistry. Silver and gold had been woven into many of the trees and artificial foliage, giving the forest a glittering quality that would have captivated the heart of any treasure hunter. Aside from briefly marveling at the craftsmanship, Alexander ignored it in favor of scanning for danger.

Steps before they reached the bridge abutment, he froze in place.

Click ... click ... click.

He put his finger across his lips. Jataan nodded, a sword seeming to materialize in his hand. They crept toward the bridge, keeping a close eye on the forest, but they were both looking too low. The stone trees reached three hundred feet overhead. It was only in the moment that the centipede launched itself from a tree that Alexander's magic warned him of the threat.

"Bug!" he shouted, drawing the Thinblade.

The centipede fell in a graceful arc that would have brought it down on top of Alexander, but Jataan intervened, pushing him aside, his sword morphing into a pike that he braced against his instep, angling the point to catch the centipede in the mouth. And he succeeded, piercing the tiny brain of the deadly creature, killing it instantly. Gravity sent its lifeless body tumbling toward Jataan. He tried to avoid it, but it was too big, and it fell too haphazardly, crashing down on top of him, the razor-sharp barbs bristling from its chitin segments cutting into him.

Jataan didn't cry out or even complain, but it was plain to Alexander that his life hung in the balance. With a thought, the door opened, and Alexander dragged Jataan into his Wizard's Den.

Lita's face went white. "What happened?" she cried.

"The centipede," Alexander said.

Lita fell to her knees at Jataan's side. She was distraught, tears welling up as she took his hand. "Oh, Dear Maker, you can't die."

"Lita!" Alexander snapped. "Put your feelings aside and save him."

She looked up, dashing her tears away, leaving a streak of fresh blood across her cheek. Then she nodded firmly before turning back to Jataan, casting her spell to assess his injuries. "Bring me my bag, quickly," she said, a tremor of fear running through her voice.

Alexander set the bag open next to her. "What can I do?"

She handed him two clean towels. "Apply pressure here and here."

Alexander did as he was told, holding back the blood spilling from Jataan's wounds as best he could, watching Lita go to work with a kind of detachment that most people simply couldn't muster. She worked for almost an hour, sewing, cauterizing, closing off the bleeding before his life spilled out onto the floor. By the time she'd finished bandaging his wounds, Jataan's normally swarthy face was a white mask, pale and deathly. He lay in bed next to Jack and Anja, both still unconscious from Lita's healing spell.

Alexander swallowed hard at the sight of Jataan's faltering colors. He'd been hurt badly, more seriously than Alexander would have thought possible. Surely, no swordsman could have ever done such harm to the battle mage.

"Will he make it?" Alexander asked quietly. He wasn't sure if he wanted to hear the answer. Jataan had just rejoined him. In spite of their history, Alexander felt safer with him by his side than any other. The battle mage had proven his loyalty and his prowess time and again … and now he lay on the cusp of death for his unflinching willingness to put himself between Alexander and danger.

"I don't know," Lita whispered with a renewed tremor in her voice.

Alexander took a deep breath and let it out slowly, looking at his injured friends, all placed in harm's way because they chose to accompany him into danger. It took an act of will to set aside his feelings and focus on the task at hand. As much as he wanted to sit with them, to be there when they awoke, he had work to do and the enemy was closing in.

He opened the door, taking Luminessence with him when he stepped back out into the underdark.

"Wait, what are you doing?" Lita asked.

"What I came here to do."

"You can't go by yourself. It's too dangerous." She stood, collecting her bag.

"No, Lita. They need you more than I do right now."

"Jataan would be very upset with me if he knew I let you go out there alone."

"Not half as upset as you'll be with yourself if he dies and you're not by his side doing everything in your power to save him. Stay here. Look after them. I'll be fine."

He didn't wait for her answer as he closed the door and headed for the bridge. It felt solid underfoot, even though the stone was only an inch thick.

A shout from across the chasm caught his attention. A platoon of soldiers had spotted him and they were moving toward another bridge that would bring them to the giant pillar that was the hub for this part of the bridge network.

Alexander started running, the heels of his boots striking the stone rhythmically. Another party emerged on a balcony jutting from the other side of the chasm but several levels higher than the bridge he was crossing. His all around sight told him it was Titus Grant with twenty of his men.

The underdark was getting crowded.

A flash of warning exploded in his mind with such urgency that he threw himself to the ground a fraction of a moment before a light-lance burned through the space he'd just been occupying. Yet another Acuna wizard. He was starting to suspect that the Acuna had deployed every one of their members to pursue him.

Alexander was up and running again, his breathing heavy, sweat starting to bead on his brow. A string of force shards, red and deadly, leapt from the wizard's outstretched hand. Alexander ducked again, the shards smashing into the railing of stone tulips, shattering them into gravel that pelted him painfully, but without injury.

The soldiers had reached the bridge abutment and were running as quickly as their heavy armor would allow, while the wizard, flanked by two overseers, held at the balcony, casting spells at Alexander.

Grant pointed at him, then he and his people vanished into the underdark.

Alexander reached the pillar. It was ringed with a series of platforms, each joined to those above and below by stairs that wrapped around the pillar, and each anchoring several bridges that arced away in different directions.

Alexander traced his route across the bridges, using the pillar for cover against the Acuna wizard's spells. His route firmly in mind, he started up the stairs to the level above, rounding the corner cautiously. As the wizard started casting another spell, Alexander ran, reaching the platform above and turning onto a bridge railed with stone rose bushes, thorns and all.

He listened to his mind while he ran, waiting for the next assault to come, and he wasn't disappointed. A force sphere streaked toward him. Without breaking stride, he opened the door to his Wizard's Den right in front of himself and raced inside, closing the door just a moment before the spell detonated. It could have easily blown him off the bridge into the dark.

The Acuna seemed to have lost interest in capturing him alive.

Chapter 35

"What's happening?" Lita asked.

"Battle," Alexander said, opening the door and racing out into the underdark again.

The wizard had left his perch on the other side of the chasm and was now following his men, a happy fact that gave Alexander time to reach another platform wrapped around the last ten feet of a giant stalactite. Two bridges leapt away on the opposite side, one going higher, the other lower. Alexander took the high road.

Grant and his people emerged ahead of him along the far wall of the chasm and started tying off ropes so they could lower themselves to a balcony below. A bridge arced gracefully from that balcony to the next pillar in Alexander's path. He picked up the pace, his breathing becoming labored from exertion.

The soldiers had reached the central pillar behind him and were ascending the stairs to reach the bridge he'd taken. Ahead of him, the chasm was narrowing and the network of bridges was beginning to converge on a single platform perched atop a giant stalagmite. Several bridges joined to this platform, but only one spanned the distance from it to the guardian chamber.

He would have to face some of Grant's men before he could reach the last platform. Several were racing across the bridge to intercept him at the next pillar, while still more slid down ropes from the level above to join the fight. Grant watched.

Alexander slowed as he approached the next pillar. Three of Grant's men were there, spread out across the bridge abutment, weapons at the ready. The first fired a crossbow bolt. Alexander turned sideways, allowing the bolt to pass within inches of his chest. The other two loosed crossbow bolts as well. He spun right, avoiding them with relative ease. All three drew shortswords and advanced.

Another crossbow bolt sailed past him from a quickly approaching cluster of five more men, racing toward the pillar from Grant's position. Alexander ignored it. His danger sense hadn't alerted him to it, so it wasn't a threat. The first three men waited for him at the abutment, twenty feet … ten feet.

Alexander lit up Luminessence like the sun. The light felt warm and soothing, not too bright, no glare, just clean pure light. But the men facing him dropped their weapons, covering their eyes as if they'd been gouged out with hot pokers, shrieking in pain from the sudden onslaught. Two of the group running to join the fight recoiled so violently from the sudden brilliance that they threw themselves over the railing and into the void.

Alexander strode through the men cowering on their knees and holding their hands over their eyes. Once past the immediate threat, he dimmed the light since it took an effort of will to maintain such intensity, and continued toward his objective.

Seconds later, he saw the Andalians reach the platform where Grant's men were recovering from temporary blindness. The three men who'd faced Alexander were quickly overpowered and thrown from the balcony, while the remaining brigands in Grant's employ held back, launching a volley of crossbow bolts at the soldiers. A few Andalians fell, but most defended against the attack with their heavy shields.

Alexander left them to it, noting that Grant and a number of his people hadn't descended down the ropes and were now moving back into the warrens of the underdark, leaving those who had moved to intercept Alexander to fend for themselves against the platoon of soldiers. The fight was a stalemate until the Acuna wizard arrived and killed five of Grant's men with a series of red-hot force shards. The remaining brigands broke and ran. The soldiers and wizard laughed at them, mocking their cowardice, but didn't pursue.

Alexander reached the final pillar standing between him and the last platform before the guardian chamber. A sentinel stood in his path, eyes glowing, spear and shield at the ready. He marched toward it, assessing the field of battle with each step. This platform was different than the rest in that there were no railings, just a thirty-foot-diameter circle of stone with three bridges joining it on one side and a single span without railings arcing away on the other. A guardian before the guardian.

He stepped onto the platform, stopping to face the sentinel.

"You shall not pass," a distant voice said. "This way is forbidden."

Alexander stretched out with his all around sight. Soldiers and brigands were converging on his position from a number of directions. The Acuna wizard was nearly in position to throw a spell. Then a man went flying off the near edge of the guardian chamber, screaming into the dark.

Soldiers had reached the guardian ahead of him.

He strode toward the sentinel, reaching into the moments to come with his mind, seeing the thrust a moment before it became reality, spinning around it and past the sentinel, then breaking into a dead run, leaving the inanimate sentry behind as he sprinted across the bridge that would deliver him to the guardian chamber.

Danger flared in his mind an instant before a blow hit him square in the middle of the back, hard as a hammer. It knocked his wind out and sent him sprawling on his face, Luminessence clattering across the floor, coming to rest on the edge of the bridge, three feet of the enchanted staff hanging out over the void.

Alexander scrambled forward, all other thoughts pushed aside as he dove toward the edge of the bridge, catching the staff just before it slipped over, rolling onto his back and holding Luminessence to his chest with both hands. He lay there for a moment, schooling his breathing and calming his heart.

A man's scream was cut short by a loud thump, then another man went over the edge of the open-ended chamber that Alexander was struggling to reach. He staggered to his feet just in time to see soldiers lumbering toward him, struggling to move quickly under the weight of their armor. Then the Acuna wizard began casting a spell.

He unleashed Luminessence again, filling the chamber with a flash of light so bright that everyone nearby had to look away or cover their eyes. The wizard's spell went wide, a bubble of liquid fire whizzing past him into the guardian chamber and splashing against the ceiling, dripping orange-hot fire into the room below. A solider screamed.

Alexander was up and running again, pain in his back jolting him with every step, but he pressed on, reaching the guardian chamber just as Grant and a dozen of his brigands stopped at the threshold of an oversized door on one side of the room. A dozen soldiers were already dead, their bodies broken and burned. A dozen more were surrounding the guardian, trying to bring it down while trying harder to avoid its stone fists.

Alexander skirted to the right of the guardian, putting it between him and Grant's men. It lunged, striking at a nearby soldier with both fists in unison, catching him in the chest and blowing him backward scores of feet, his still, dead corpse coming to rest against the wall. Another soldier stabbed the guardian in the knee, his sword sinking into the red-hot magic joining the stones and melting in a shower of sparks. A backhanded swat by the guardian sent the man flying silently off the far edge of the open-ended chamber.

When Alexander reached the midline of the room, the guardian spun toward him, hurling a lava-red stone the size of a man's head. He turned to avoid it, but it grazed him across the chest, burning his tunic and heating his dragon-scale chain to the point of searing. He cried out, pulling the chain away from his skin, then emptying his waterskin on it, turning his face away from the sudden cloud of steam.

The Acuna wizard and his men reached the chamber's edge, stopping to assess the situation before the soldiers began to advance toward Alexander. He flipped Luminessence to his left hand and drew the Thinblade.

"McGinty!" he shouted.

He inched toward the far edge of the chamber, drawing the guardian's attention again. It threw a stone at him, the rock heating to orange-hot in an instant. Alexander dodged, feeling a wave of heat as it zipped past his head and hit the wall behind him, shattering into scores of glowing pebbles.

The guardian started lumbering toward Alexander.

At least it isn't fast, he thought to himself, watching it sweep aside two Andalian soldiers with a single backhanded swipe of its misshapen hand. They fell still and smoldering. With each step, it gained speed, a juggernaut bearing down on him.

Alexander held his ground, reaching into the coming moments, waiting for the right time to move. The guardian seemed intent on simply running him over, building speed with each step until it was in a headlong dash that it couldn't stop if it wanted to.

Alexander could feel the heat of the unnatural creature, see the magic holding the stones together, feel the thump, thump, thump of its footfalls … and still he waited, watching the advancing soldiers as well as the guardian. The soldiers hesitated, waiting to see if the guardian would do their work for them.

He calmed his mind and closed his blind eyes, waiting until the last moment. The smell of singed hair filled his nose, heat washed over his skin—he spun left, Luminessence filling the chamber with brilliance, blinding everyone except Alexander and the guardian, the Thinblade whipping around and catching the guardian across the back of its legs, cleaving them cleanly in two and toppling the creature into a clattering jumble of stones skittering across the floor. Alexander stopped, facing the jumbled mess of glowing stones spread out before him, letting Luminessence dim to a gentle glow. Everyone else stopped as well, all of them watching Alexander … until the glowing stones started to move, coming together, reassembling themselves.

Its movement dispelled the moment of stillness and the battle resumed, a crossbow bolt fired by one of Grant's men shattering against Alexander's back, his dragon-scale chain shirt preserving his life yet again. The six soldiers nearest him charged as one, a line of shields and swords moving in unison.

Alexander ran for the far side of the chamber.

"McGinty!" he shouted again.

The strange little creature rose up out of the floor, looking at the scene of battle with as much dismay as his incomplete features could convey.

"Bridge the gap!" Alexander shouted, ducking to avoid another crossbow bolt.

"Look out," Chloe said, buzzing into view.

Alexander took a hit in the middle of his back that knocked him to his knees. He hadn't seen it coming and his magic hadn't warned him, but the strike was very real, a dagger point brought down full force. Chloe virtually ripped his mind away from his body and showed him the enemy he faced—Titus Grant. Grant raised his dagger again, this time aiming for the back of Alexander's head.

He rolled to the side, avoiding the strike but leaving himself flat on his back looking up and seeing nothing, yet seeing Grant through Chloe's eyes. Rather than fight, he blinded the brigand with his staff, flooding the chamber with light again, stunning his enemies with blindness, but noticing that the brilliance produced by Luminessence was less than before and it seemed to require more will and effort.

The guardian was nearly fully reassembled, yet still on its knees, stones skittering across the floor toward it, adding to its bulk and size as they became incorporated into its enormous body.

Alexander let the light lapse when he saw the bridge materialize behind him. He'd seen this magic before—Blackstone Keep. He spun and ran with every bit of speed he could muster. The bridge arced gracefully, spanning five hundred feet to the shrine where the well of memory resided.

Grant cursed, backing away from the bridge abutment even as he ordered his three closest men to give chase. Shards of red-tinged magical force whizzed past Alexander, narrowly missing his head. He ignored them, focusing on speed. A dozen soldiers followed on the heels of Grant's men while the wizard and the remaining soldiers engaged the brigands.

A crossbow bolt grazed Alexander's shoulder, drawing a thin line of blood. He took a sharp breath, trying to ignore the pain, his breathing heavy, his lungs and legs on fire. Nearly to the platform, exhausted from running, a volley of crossbow bolts arced through the air toward him. He dodged, turning to avoid a hit, but he wasn't fast enough. A bolt hit him in the side of the left thigh, its point protruding from the inside of his leg just above the knee.

He stumbled and fell a dozen feet from the end of the bridge, crying out in pain and surprise, Luminessence clattering onto the platform and coming to rest not far from the well of memory. He looked back. Grant's three men were bearing down on him, not thirty feet away, and a dozen soldiers were another hundred feet behind them, but behind them all was the guardian, building speed with every step, closing the distance with frightening quickness.

Staggering to his feet, then falling again when he tried to put weight on his wounded leg, Alexander revised his assessment of the guardian's speed. He crawled the last few feet, bruised and battered, bloody and in pain, coming to his knees once he reached the platform, ignoring the sharp stab of agony as he swept the Thinblade through the bridge a foot away from the edge of the platform, starting at the nearest side and allowing himself to fall forward so he could reach the far side of the bridge with a single stroke.

Rolling onto his back, struggling to catch his breath, Alexander watched the guardian crash into the soldiers, trampling several and sending the rest flying off the sides of the bridge. Past the onrushing guardian and the rapidly closing brigands, Alexander saw Grant casually kill the Acuna wizard, stabbing him in the back.

Alexander was spent. All he could do was watch the three brigands and the guardian close the gap, but then a loud crack reverberated through the underdark and the bridge broke. The nearest of the brigands leapt for the platform, catching the edge, then slipping over until he was holding on for dear life.

"Pull me up," he shouted.

With a derisive snort, Alexander reached out and brought the pommel of the Thinblade down on his hand and the man slipped free, falling into the darkness with a fading scream.

Alexander lay still for several moments, regaining his composure and his breath. Across the gap, Grant stood at the edge of the guardian chamber with what remained of his men, watching Alexander … but he was too far away to do more than watch.

Alexander sat up and carefully cut the shaft protruding from his leg, then gritted his teeth and pulled the bolt through from the barbed end, stifling a whimper. Blackness threatened to envelop him, but he brought himself back with a sheer effort of will, forcing his pain into the background and focusing on the task at hand.

McGinty rose up before him.

"Did you bring the memory?" The strange little creature almost sounded excited.

"Yes," Alexander said, willing the door to his Wizard's Den open.

McGinty seemed alarmed when he saw the people within.

"No others may be here."

"They're not here, they're in there," Alexander said. "Lita, bring me that strongbox, please."

She obeyed dutifully, remaining within the Wizard's Den. "You're hurt," she said. "Let me tend to that."

"Later," Alexander said, unlocking the strongbox and removing the vial containing the blood of the earth. "I won't be long."

He closed the door.

McGinty tried to frown. "Where did they go?"

"Like I said, they were never here; they were in there. Can you bring me my staff?" he asked, pointing to Luminessence.

McGinty seemed momentarily confused until Alexander waggled his finger at it, then he shuffled over and lifted it from the stone floor.

"This is vitalwood," he said with as much surprise as he could seem to muster.

"Yes."

"But the vitalwood died out, and the fay with them."

"There's one left," Alexander said. "I found the branch that this staff is made from nearby it."

McGinty held it out as if it were sacred, offering it to Alexander. He took it with a smile and leveraged himself to his feet, using the staff as a crutch.

"If the vitalwood yet live, then the fay may return."

Alexander shrugged, pain and exhaustion rippling through his body. "Maybe … I don't know."

He hobbled over to the altar, leaning heavily on Luminessence, running his finger along the edge of the crystal bowl and sighing to himself before he started cleaning the debris from the well of memory.

"Forgive me, Isabel," he whispered, pulling the stopper from the vial with his teeth and dropping it to the floor. He hesitated for just a moment, swallowing hard before tipping the vial and allowing the single drop of blood of the earth to spill forth into the well of memory. It splashed against the side of the bowl, scores of tiny beads rolling to the lowest point and collecting into a single drop.

The air became very still, as if the world itself was expecting something. The hair on his head stood up and then the four little mounds of dirt piled nearby started to stir, each coalescing into a creature of different form and shape. One took on a humanoid appearance while the remaining three seemed to vanish into the stone, molding it back into perfect form after they'd passed.

"They're awake!" McGinty said, his voice filled with as much joy as Alexander could have imagined.

The sole Linkershim who remained on the platform seemed to regard Alexander carefully before refining its appearance to become a perfect imitation of him, except he was made entirely of stone and dirt.

"Thank you," he said awkwardly, as if spoken language was foreign.

"You're welcome."

Alexander noticed movement in the distance, across the gap in the guardian chamber. He could see Grant and his men backing away while the opening on this end of the guardian chamber was being walled off. Two

Linkershim, each formed a bit differently, drew stones from the floor and ceiling to build the wall, completely sealing off the chamber containing the well of memory from the rest of the world.

"We will remove the fleshlings from the underdark and unbuild Mithel Dour," the Linkershim said. "But we will not harm them, as McGinty agreed."

"Within the palace, there are two forges ..."

"Those devices will be unmade as well," the Linkershim said, a hint of anger in his inhuman voice.

"Good," Alexander said.

"You will be welcome in the underdark, though not soon."

"I'm honored. I look forward to seeing what you build next."

"Other fleshlings will not be welcome. We shared our building with fleshlings before and they repaid us with death."

"I understand your distrust," Alexander said, "but please understand, not all fleshlings wish you harm. Most would admire your work."

"You will not be disappointed. When the Linkershim build for joy, the result is worthy. And we have much joy now."

"If you'll show me the way out, I'll leave you to your building."

"As you wish," the Linkershim said, transforming into a stone chair.

"Sit and you will be transported to safety under the sky," McGinty said.

Alexander nodded, gently easing himself into the chair.

"It was nice meeting you, McGinty. Take care of the Linkershim."

"You are an honorable fleshling, Alexander Reishi," McGinty said, attempting to bow.

The chair and the surrounding stone floor sank into the platform, taking Alexander with it until he was completely encapsulated in stone. He lit the little space with Luminessence, watching the ground move around him, forming and reforming according to the will of the Linkershim. He felt the sensation of movement, but couldn't determine which direction he was going. Minutes passed. He started to feel a bit uncertain about his situation, the air grew thin and he felt a bit lightheaded.

Then, quite suddenly, he was under the sky. The capsule melted around him and he found himself atop a mountain in an ancient temple overlooking Mithel Dour from across the lake behind the palace. The sun was setting, orange and red, behind hazy clouds on the horizon, framed by an ancient stone arch, worn and broken. A stone bowl occupied the center of the temple altar, while ancient statues of men and women stood nearby.

With the help of Luminessence, Alexander got to his feet, and the Linkershim transformed from a chair into a likeness of him again.

"Behold, the unmaking of Mithel Dour," it said.

Alexander limped to the railing for a better view of the city. It looked like the palace was imploding, stones being drawn toward some central mass within, walls and ceilings collapsing in on themselves, yet not scattering as gravity and inertia would dictate, but instead coalescing into a form, a form that rose slowly, accumulating stones, adding them to its mass until it was a giant of epic proportions, standing easily a hundred feet tall where the palace had once stood.

"How can it be so big?" Alexander asked.

"That is many Linkershim working together as one."

The giant smashed the back wall, allowing the lake to pour forth into the city in a great torrent, water splashing into the streets, flooding a foot deep—more than enough to send the inhabitants of Mithel Dour into a panic. It took only minutes for the entire contents of the mountain lake to wash into the city, driving the people toward the cliff wall.

Then the giant focused on the palace, dismantling it a stone at a time, but leaving one elevator intact to ferry those trying to escape to the city below. Buildings, so beautifully made so long ago, started crumbling when other Linkershim began arriving in the city to help unbuild it.

The people were in a panic until they reached the cliff wall and found that the river had been redirected over the waterfall and the exit tunnel was open. Water flowed gently from the streets into the tunnel, soaking everyone trying to escape the dying city.

Another Linkershim rose up out of the temple floor, forming into the shape of a pedestal. Resting atop it was the Andalian Crown.

"This must be unmade as well, but it is beyond our power to do so," the Linkershim said.

Alexander smiled, slicing the Andalian Crown in half with the Thinblade. A shimmer of magic expanded away from it, dissipating into the evening sky.

"Goodbye, Alexander Reishi, and thank you," the Linkershim said. Then it melted into the floor, leaving the stone exactly as it had been moments before.

"You're welcome," Alexander whispered, before opening the door to his Wizard's Den.

"Didn't expect sunlight," Jack said from his bed.

"Glad to see you're feeling better," Alexander said. "If you can manage it, you might want to see this."

Jack eased himself out of bed and came to Alexander's side, blinking a few times at the scene unfolding below. Anja and Lita joined them as well.

"How's Jataan?" Alexander asked.

"He'll mend," Lita said with a relieved smile.

"In that case, today turned out to be a pretty good day."

Jack chuckled. "When you said you were going to destroy this place, I wasn't expecting anything quite so thorough."

Hundreds of Linkershim were moving through the city. Buildings were simply melting into the ground as they passed, leaving a clean, level stone platform where once a great city had been. The citizens of Mithel Dour, now refugees, were streaming out of the city to the plains below.

"As usual, I had help," Alexander said.

"Looks like you hurt yourself again," Lita said. "Go on, sit down, let me take a look at that leg."

Here Ends Linkershim
Sovereign of the Seven Isles: Book Six

www.SovereignOfTheSevenIsles.com

The Story Continues...

Made in the USA
Middletown, DE
24 August 2020